GENEROUS LIES

ROBIN PATCHEN

Dear Jeanette,
may the Lord bless
you & yours. I hope you
enjoy the book.
In Christ
~ Robin Patchen

JDO PUBLISHING

For Nicholas.
Your adventure is only beginning,
and I couldn't be prouder of you.

ALSO BY ROBIN PATCHEN

Chasing Amanda

Finding Amanda

A Package Deal (part of the Matched Online anthology)

Hidden Truth series

Convenient Lies

Twisted Lies

Generous Lies

Innocent Lies

ACKNOWLEDGMENTS

There are so many people involved in writing and publishing a book. Without these people in my life, this story and all my stories would be nothing more than files on my laptop.

Thank you, Quid Pro Quills—Kara Hunt, Jericha Kingston, Candice Sue Patterson, and Pegg Thomas. Also, thanks to Normandie Fischer, Sharon Srock, and Terri Weldon. Your critiques make me a better writer, and I'm proud to call each of you friend.

Thank you, Ray Rhamey, for your insightful edits.

Thank you, Lacy Williams, for your marketing brilliance.

Thank you, Chuck Robinson, Marvin Stoll, and Lance Lang, for guiding us through the most challenging time of our lives.

Thank you to my family, who puts up with me and all my imaginary friends.

And, of course, thank you, my Lord and Savior, Jesus Christ, for the grace that makes living possible.

ONE

Of all the strange things Matty O'Brien had seen his father do, this was the strangest.

It started with Dad's phone call asking Matty for a ride. That was odd, but not as odd as what came next.

Matty got to the airport, hoping he'd make it back home in time for the biggest party of the summer, and then he parked curbside, waiting where Dad had told him to. Security police were up ahead, urging cars along, and they'd get to him soon.

He drummed the steering wheel. "Come on, Dad. Where are you?"

He shouldn't complain. Any opportunity to see his dad needed to be taken. Maybe Dad just wanted to spend time with him.

Right. Matty was no A-student, but he wasn't stupid enough to believe that. At least he'd get some money. He could always count on Dad to pay him for his time, if nothing else. Assuming Dad ever got here.

A minute later, Dad stepped out. Good ol' Frank O'Brien He was wearing a charcoal gray suit with a bright blue tie that made him look every bit the businessman he was. Like Matty, his dad had light brown hair, only his was graying at the temples.

And those fancy shoes had to cost as much as Matty's car. To be fair, to call his car a beater would be an insult to the other beaters on the road.

Dad looked him right in the eyes for a quick second, then his gaze moved on. He glanced to his right, his left, and behind him, but not at Matty again. What was he looking for? Matty considered getting out and waving, but he thought better of it. Maybe something was wrong. Dad always had a reason for what he did.

This was getting a little scary.

People entered and exited through the door on the far end of the terminal. Seemed like that was where most of the action was happening. A family came outside, then a couple of businessmen pulling small bags followed by a huge dude with blacker skin than Matty'd ever seen. Maybe he'd come in on the same flight as Dad, from somewhere in Africa. Matty hadn't asked which country.

The black man looked around before he stepped to the far side of the bank of doors, out of Matty's line of sight.

Dad finally approached Matty's car. He yanked open the passenger door, pulled a small package from inside his suit coat, and shoved it in the glove box. He handed a piece of paper to Matty. An address was written on it.

He leaned into the car. "Deliver it to that address on Sunday at noon."

"Don't you need—?"

"No matter what you do"—he looked at something behind the car Matty couldn't see, then scanned the area before focusing on Matty again—"don't let that package out of your sight, and don't let anybody else see it. We could get in a lot of trouble."

"What is it?"

Dad didn't seem to register the question. His face was pinched, his gaze darting everywhere. Matty'd never seen his dad nervous, and the sight had him scanning the surroundings too. Was Dad looking for cops? Something worse?

Dad said, "I'll call you later," before he backed out of the car, slammed the door, and disappeared inside the terminal.

Seriously weird.

Matty's hands shook as he pulled away from the curb and into the airport traffic. Surely his father wouldn't get him involved in anything dangerous. Dad was always talking about mitigating risk, protecting what was important. Matty was important to his father, so obviously he wouldn't pull him into anything that bad.

Right?

As he inched forward in traffic, he noted the black man's gaze reflected in the rearview mirror. Matty felt the little hairs on the back of his neck stand up.

He took a deep breath. Whatever was in the package, Matty would get it delivered on time. Maybe then he'd get to have a real conversation with his father.

He was back in Hempstead, New York, within thirty minutes and only few blocks from home when his car coughed, spluttered, and died. He managed to pull it over on the side of the road before the wheels stopped turning.

Great. No conversation with Dad, no car, and a package that needed to be delivered on Sunday. He stepped out of the car, slammed the door, and called his mother.

"Ma, the car died again."

She sighed, a sound he'd heard too often lately. The last thing she needed was more trouble. Hard enough raising two kids alone, working full-time, and trying to make ends meet without having to worry about her almost grown-up son's car.

"Don't worry," Matty said. "I'll take care of it. I just wanted you to know why I wasn't home."

"Where have you been?"

Nope. Not dumb enough to tell her the truth. She'd kill him if she knew he'd been to meet his father. "I'm close enough to walk. I'll just leave it here for now."

He ended the call and grabbed the package from the glove

box. It was a little bigger than a deck of cards but weighed much less, wrapped in brown paper and sealed with packaging tape. It wasn't drugs—dogs would've picked up on that. And why would anybody transport such a small amount of drugs? He shook it, felt a slight shift inside that told him nothing.

It was obviously something valuable.

Matty imagined what it might be. A flash drive with secret information, maybe enough to take down some totalitarian government? Maybe his father was only pretending to be a criminal. Maybe he was working with the authorities.

Right. Then why wouldn't Dad have handed the package off to a cop?

Matty looked at the address. Dad had written it on the back of one of those paper luggage tags you get when you check in for a flight. Just a street address and a town—Oceanside—but no name.

Maybe this was the cop Dad had to get the information to. Maybe he was really a hero, a federal agent, or a spy! The idea fizzled before it could take hold. Matty knew better.

He shoved the package and the address in his pocket and started walking. He was used to carrying contraband and looking innocent. He'd done it often enough with drugs. Walked right by cops all the time with pills or weed in his pocket—stuff he intended to sell—so the package didn't bother him a bit as he turned the corner toward home.

Like father, like son.

He paused in front of the two-story house that belonged to one of the guys in his class. This was where the party was taking place.

Laughter rang through the air, and the steady beat of music drew his gaze. He checked the package in his pocket—safe and sound—and peered into the windows. Inside, a couple of guys he went to school with were chugging beer from red plastic cups.

And the girls. From what he could see, the girls had gone all-out with the makeup and hair and clothes.

He took two steps toward the door and froze.

He'd be an idiot to go in there.

On the other hand, his mom was always telling him to branch out, find some new people to hang out with. There were new people in there, and the ones he wanted to get to know looked primed for fun in their short shorts and tight shirts and glassy eyes.

Aiden must be there. He never missed an opportunity to party. Sure enough, Matty saw Aiden's father's car. Matty's car might be a piece of junk, but at least he had his own. Not that he would fault Mr. Kopp for not buying Aiden a car. Aiden's dad was just about perfect, taking Aiden and Matty to their baseball games, getting them ice cream, going with them to the arcade. So maybe he'd been strict about the car, but at least he was there. At least he cared. Aiden had no idea how good he had it.

There were other cars he recognized from school. Cars of friends. And there was his ex-girlfriend's little Miata. If Priscilla was here, then the rest of her crew was, too. Hot girls galore.

He stared at the door. The package seemed to warm in his pocket. Dad had trusted him, and he wouldn't let him down.

He'd turned to leave when the front door banged open.

"Hey, Matty."

The voice floated over the music. He turned in time to see Priscilla pull the front door closed and stagger down the three steps to the sidewalk. She slipped, righted herself with the help of the rail, and moved toward him. "I saw you through the window. You aren't leaving, are you?" Her voice was soft and slushy. His ex-girlfriend's mood shifted faster than the Long Island wind in a hurricane. Last time he'd seen her, she'd dumped him.

Seemed the wind had shifted again.

"I gotta get home." But even as the words left his mouth, he knew he wouldn't be going anywhere, not with the way she was looking at him.

She pressed against him, wrapped her arms around his neck. "You got something for me?"

He could think of a few things.

"I can pay you tomorrow."

He pushed her away. "Not right now."

"Can you get me something, though? A couple oxies?"

"Don't they have some inside? I sold—"

"Ran out. They're smoking, but you know I hate that. I need you."

He thought of the package in his pocket. It was safe there. He also had a small bag of pills. Always liked to have a couple in case he ran into a customer. "Okay, I got something for you. But maybe I'll just give them to you." He pulled her between the two houses. It was dark back here. He didn't mind sharing if it meant he might get a little action. Priscilla was always more fun when she wanted something.

They were just getting started when he heard a screech of tires. He pushed her off him so fast she tumbled into the dirt. He felt his pocket—the package was still there—then held out his hand for Priscilla. Once she was upright, he crept along the edge of the house as another car stopped, this one with blue lights spinning.

He swore under his breath. Idiot. He should have kept walking.

He turned and headed for the backyard, but as he rounded the corner, he saw flashlights along the fence line. More cops. The place was surrounded.

And Matty was carrying...what?

He opened his wallet and dumped the pills in the grass, then ground them into the dirt with his feet.

"What'd you do that for?"

He turned back to find Priscilla had followed him and was staring wide-eyed at the place he'd dumped the pills.

"You want to go to jail?"

"But I would've—"

"You don't need to be any higher than you already are. You can thank me later. Go inside."

"But I'll get caught! What if they make us take drug tests?"

He heard banging, deep voices, a door slamming open, kids screaming.

He focused on Priscilla. "There're a lot of kids here. They can't test everyone. You'll be safer inside." And he needed her out of the way.

"What should I say?"

"You were sick. You went outside. Alone."

"But—"

"I'll be right behind you." He yanked her to the bottom of the stairs that led to the back door. "Go."

She glared but climbed the steps. He waited until the screen door slammed behind her, leaving him in the semi-darkness.

There were flashlights everywhere. He was surrounded by cops.

As much as he'd like to believe the package in his pocket was a flash drive, his father a spy, he wasn't that stupid. Whatever it was, Dad wouldn't want it shoved in some evidence locker. Even if it wasn't illegal, Matty couldn't let it get confiscated. Dad would never forgive him.

The thought his stomach flipping over. Not that. Anything but that.

Keeping low, he inched toward the sidewalk, glimpsed the back bumper of Aiden's dad's car. If it got searched... Well, Aiden didn't have any priors. And his dad was a fed. Aiden would probably be fine. And if Matty was right and the package didn't contain drugs, why would anybody search it? Not like drug dogs would sniff out packaging tape.

He gazed at the houses across the street. A few neighbors were peeking around their curtains, watching the action, but they would be drawn to the light, not the shadows.

Did Matty dare? He looked at the front door. Cops had gone inside. There were radio cars on either end of the street, positioned to stop kids from escaping. They'd search everyone who tried to walk away, search every car that approached. Fine. Matty would have to tell Aiden to leave his car until morning. It's not like it looked like a kid's car. The cops would leave it alone.

Now he had to get there.

He crept forward, careful to stay away from the streetlights and the glow from the house. He managed to cross the short lawn quickly, then crawled along the sidewalk to the back door of Aiden's car. Gently, he opened the door—Aiden always forgot to lock it—and slid inside. The dome light lit up, so he pulled the car door closed as fast as he could, careful not to slam it. The noises from the house drowned out the little sound the door made.

The car was nearly immaculate. The only thing in the backseat was an empty shoebox—Air Jordans. Aiden had been showing them off all over town.

Matty pulled down the backseat to give him access to the trunk and climbed into the tiny space. It was full of stuff—a blanket, a box of granola bars, a couple bottles of water, a first aid kit, a flashlight. Mr. Kopp was prepared for every emergency. It took some finagling, but Matty managed to push the stuff to one side and open the compartment where the jack was kept. Then he shoved the tiny box into that space and put the cover back on.

The package would be safe there. Aiden would be ticked, but whatever. Matty would throw him a couple of hundreds—or a few oxies—and his friend would get over it.

Matty had just climbed out of the trunk and righted the seat when he heard the wail of a siren. He hit the floorboard, banged his knee, and stifled a yelp. The siren neared, then cut off. Shouts, feet thumping right outside the car. He peeked. An ambulance. Paramedics running into the house.

Someone was hurt, maybe worse. Maybe the drugs he'd supplied...

No time to worry about that now.

He sat on his knees, looked both ways. The cops down the

street were focused on the road. The ones on the sidewalk were focused on the ambulance, the front door, and the kids coming out.

Silently, he slid from the car, closed the door, and crept back toward the house. He stayed low, pretended to be tying his shoe, then stood and joined the throng of kids now standing on the sidewalk, all staring at the door.

He kept his head down and waited. When he was questioned, he'd say he was just walking by and stopped to see what going on. He hadn't been drinking, never did drugs. And he could direct the police to his car, broken down just a few blocks away. He could walk away from this scot-free. Pick up the package from Aiden tomorrow. No problem.

The screen banged open, and a paramedic backed out with a gurney. Matty strained with the rest of the crowd to see the person lying on the gurney as the paramedics came down the three steps and approached the ambulance. The face was obscured, but the dark hair was on the long side, just enough to annoy a really buttoned-up dad. Feet stuck out the end. Air Jordans.

TWO

Garrison Kopp had never won Father of the Year. No chance he was in the running this year, either.

He glanced at the clock—ten-thirty. Aiden had another half hour before he'd be late, but Garrison couldn't relax. He stood and muted the baseball game. The Pirates were losing anyway.

Now the house was too quiet. He longed for the days when he and Aiden would watch a ballgame together or, better yet, throw the football in the backyard. Of course this tiny rental house hardly had a yard. Besides, these days, Aiden wanted nothing to do with his old man.

Garrison wandered into the kitchen and put his dishes into the dishwasher. Aiden hadn't eaten at home—again. Always someplace better to be, someone better to hang out with.

"He'll come back," Garrison's mother had said. Maybe Mom was right, but then Garrison and his sisters hadn't made the same stupid choices Aiden was making. And it was a different world now. With cell phones and computers and constant access to all the junk the media had to offer, not to mention the easy access to porn and girls and drugs.

Drugs.

Just the word made Garrison's insides clench. It would be

easier if he didn't know so much, hadn't seen so much, seen people with every advantage in the world utterly ruin themselves for just one more hit. Seen his own wife throw away everything they had for a lifetime of quick highs and lingering numbness. The futile search for euphoria in an ever-increasing pile of empty bottles.

For all the temptations out there, drugs scared Garrison the most. Because they enticed Aiden the most.

Tonight, when Aiden got home, Garrison would make him pee in a cup, see if there were any drugs in his system. Maybe that made him a crappy father. Well, who cared if it did? He wasn't going to lose his son to addiction. Not the way he'd lost his marriage to it.

After wiping down the kitchen counters, Garrison headed upstairs to grab a drug test kit from the box he'd ordered off Amazon. The thing better work.

He was pocketing the little package when his cell phone rang downstairs. Probably Aiden saying he'd be late. Again. At least he'd called this time. That was a step in the right direction.

Garrison ran down the stairs, snatched the phone, and looked at the number.

Didn't recognize it.

"Garrison Kopp."

"Mr. Kopp." The man's words were clipped, unfriendly. "This is Officer Finnegan. You have a teenage son, Aiden?"

He stifled a swear word. "What happened?"

"Not sure exactly. We got him in an ambulance."

A thousand images flicked through his mind like a slideshow. No time for that now.

Garrison reached for his keys, but they weren't there. Aiden has his car.

Fine. He'd Uber. "Where they taking him?"

The police officer told him the name of the hospital.

"On my way."

GARRISON SAT by his son's bedside. At least Aiden had calmed down. He was sleeping restlessly, his wrists still restrained and connected to the bed rails. They hadn't feared escape—he wasn't under arrest, thank God. But the drugs had kept Aiden hallucinating all night, screaming for relief. The nurse had insisted on the restraints when Aiden grabbed her arm so tightly, he'd left a mark.

She was a kind woman, though. Slight and pale and young but much stronger than she looked. Garrison had managed to pry his son's fingers from her forearm, and then she'd shaken it off. "Drugs make monsters out of the nicest kids."

That's when Garrison's eyes had first tingled.

Aiden had once been a nice kid. He'd never hurt a woman. He'd been raised better than that. But the drugs, they were stealing him, chipping away at his very Aiden-ness, making him a monster Garrison feared he soon wouldn't recognize.

When Aiden finally relaxed, Garrison sat back in the chair in the tiny room and waited for his son to wake up, to realize what he'd done.

Garrison was dozing when someone knocked on the door.

He looked up to see the doctor he'd met earlier step inside. "Still sleeping, I see."

Garrison sat up and wiped his tired eyes. "He's been out for a couple hours."

"Not surprised." The man checked the computer, then walked around the bed beside Garrison and leaned against the wall. "Tox screen showed LSD, opiates, alcohol, and marijuana in his system."

The words bounced around Garrison's brain, but he couldn't make sense of them. Surely his son hadn't done all those things, not in one night.

"We're assuming," the doctor continued, "that the LSD

caused the issues that brought him here. A bad trip. Happens a lot."

Bad trip, bad drugs. He'd love to believe Aiden had been slipped the acid. But he hadn't been slipped alcohol or pot. And opiates, as in Oxycodone. Charlene's drug of choice, and one of the most addictive things out there. Had Aiden gotten the pills from his own mother?

"Thing is, there's a lot of oxy in his system," the doctor said. "A lot, which leads me to believe he's built up a tolerance to it. Like he takes it often." He paused, let the words sink in. "I know this is a lot to process. I ordered a psych consult to talk with you about rehab."

Rehab.

A good idea, though the thought had him wanting to argue, to fight.

How could his own son need rehab? How had they ended up here?

"We would recommend you take him straight to a facility. There are some decent state-funded—"

"No." Garrison swallowed. Shook his head. "Rehab's a good idea, but if he's going to do it..." He trailed off, knowing how hit-or-miss it could be to get someone into one of the better facilities. And there were fewer beds for juveniles.

"I'll figure something out."

The doctor's smile was sad. "This is not something you want to put off, Mr. Kopp. The sooner you intervene, the better it'll be."

"I know. Unfortunately, I know."

The doctor left. A few minutes later, the psychiatrist came in, talked with Garrison, and gave him a handful of pamphlets on drug addiction and their options. He thanked her but tossed the paperwork in the trash as soon as she walked out.

Rather than rush into a decision, Garrison needed to get Aiden away from here, isolate him. He grabbed his phone and searched for a place to stay.

Within minutes, his eyes were crossing. He couldn't make sense of the vacation rental websites—probably going a night without sleep wasn't helping. He could find a hotel, but anywhere worth visiting was already booked. He and Aiden might kill each other if they had to share a crappy little motel room.

Besides, he didn't want to go just anywhere. He wanted to go to Nutfield, New Hampshire. He wanted to see Samantha.

Maybe he should feel guilty for that. But it wasn't just that he missed her. He could use her level head right now. And he needed an ally. Besides, if anybody could scare up a good rental house for him, Sam could. And if that rental happened to be close to her...all the better. He'd planned all summer to make it back to Nutfield, to explore a more personal relationship with the beautiful brunette who'd so intrigued him earlier in the year.

He checked his watch. Almost seven. She was probably awake, and anyway, he didn't want to wait another minute to make a plan.

Her number rang three times before she answered.

"Garrison?" Samantha's voice sounded tired, and he would've kicked himself if he'd had the energy.

"I'm sorry. I forgot it's Saturday."

She cleared her throat. "No problem. You didn't wake me."

"Right. The phone did."

Her laugh was short. "What's wrong?"

"Aiden..." His throat closed, and he squeezed his eyes shut, thankful she couldn't see him. It took a moment before he could speak without emotion.

Samantha waited silently.

"Aiden apparently dropped some acid last night and had a bad trip. We spent the night in the ER."

"Oh, no. I'm so sorry. Is he OK?"

Garrison looked at his son's pale face, the dark circles ringing his eyes. "Yeah. He will be, but this is the wakeup call. I need to get him in rehab. I think maybe I knew, but I was... I'm so stupid."

"You're just like the rest of us, figuring life out as you go along."

A wise answer, and one of the reasons he liked Sam so much.

"I don't know exactly what we're going to do," Garrison said. "But I do know I've got to get him out of here, away from his friends and the drugs and..." And his mother, but Garrison didn't say that. No need to bring the ex into this conversation. "I could take him to my folks' house in Florida, but my dad... He'll just make things worse. I know you're plugged into the rental market. Maybe you know a place I could rent."

"Oh. That's a great idea. Let me think..."

Garrison closed his eyes and let himself hope. If Sam didn't have an idea for him, he'd find something. A cabin in the mountains, far from the lakes and summer fun. He'd seen and discounted a few of those. Not much to do on the slopes in the summertime, and he could use Sam's support right now.

"I have a two-bedroom place that's empty," she said. "I needed to replace the roof, but they finished up this week. I just haven't had time to put it on the website yet. It'll be perfect for the two of you."

"We'll take it. How much—?"

"Don't worry about it."

"Sam, you can't—"

"I'm not going to argue with you."

Bad enough he'd asked for her help, now he was taking something from her. He didn't like that. He'd figure out a way to pay her eventually, but he didn't have the energy to press the point right now. He still had so much to do, like locate his car and bring it to the hospital. Maneuver Aiden into it, which might be difficult, considering the kid's current state. Go home and pack and hit the road.

He'd focus on that—getting on the road. Once they were headed to New Hampshire, everything would look clearer.

Samantha said, "When will you be here?"

"We'll leave sometime this morning."

"Call me when you know, and I'll make sure the place is ready for you."

He took a deep breath, probably the first since he'd gotten the call the night before. It wasn't a complete plan, but it was a start. It helped to know the next step. "Thank you. You can't know how much this helps."

THREE

Samantha Messenger climbed into her Isuzu Trooper, pulled out of her condo complex, and hoped like crazy the cabin really was ready. Her contractors were very reliable, but she hadn't checked on the place since they'd called a couple days before and said the roof was finished.

June, July, and August found her cabins at nearly full capacity, booked months in advance. If not for the unexpected roof leakage, this one would have been, too.

Thank heaven for the leaky roof.

She drove toward the lake and tried to focus on all she had to do to get ready for Garrison. Trying not to think about the man proved futile.

For the hundredth time that morning, she told herself it was wrong, so wrong, to be happy Garrison was coming. The circumstances were tragic and heartbreaking. But the fact that he'd called her, wanted her help, wanted to see her...

But his call hadn't been about the two of them, nor had it been about the romance that never quite was. It had been about Aiden. Garrison obviously hadn't been thinking of her except as a friend who owned rental properties. She had to be careful not to read too much into it, or it would hurt so much more when he left.

And of course he would leave. A man like Garrison Kopp would be bored to tears in her tiny little New Hampshire town, living her tiny little New Hampshire life, and Aiden? The teenage boy would want nothing to do with this place, not after growing up in the chaos and busyness of New York.

Sure, Nutfield was a wonderful place—safe and secluded. But Garrison didn't long for safety like Sam did.

Garrison wasn't a hider. He'd never stay in Nutfield.

And she'd never be able to leave.

Which was why she was alone and always would be. And wasn't that a perfectly reasonable explanation for spending her life in solitude?

She needed to shake off silly thoughts would take her nowhere good. She wasn't alone. She was surrounded by friends and family who loved her. It should be enough. It was enough.

The narrow road that ringed this edge of Clearwater Lake was protected by a canopy created by trees along both sides. Cabins were nestled on small lots all around—wood-sided, painted, aluminum-sided, and log, they were all different shapes and sizes, most built decades before by families searching for an escape from their busy city lives. Those families had mostly held onto their lakeside cabins, enjoyed them with kids and grandkids and friends, passed them down to the next generation.

Investors had come along when the market dipped and the value of vacation homes plummeted. Samantha had bought her first when she was only twenty-four years old. Not even a decade later, she owned sixteen cabins out here, and she was hoping to buy another one or two in the off-season. Late spring, summer, and fall were the high seasons for renters. Most folks would wait until after foliage season to put their houses on the market so they could get one more good weekend out of the place before they had to say goodbye forever.

She hated to capitalize on other people's hardships, and she'd even tried to help a couple of families hold onto their homes. But repairs and routine maintenance were tough when you didn't live nearby. Frankly, it seemed most people felt free when they finally sold the cabins, which had turned from places of refuge to burdens of debt. Now, when a lake home came on the market, Sam looked at it as an opportunity to make a deal that benefitted both parties.

She turned into the driveway of the two-bedroom cabin, which sat a good half mile from the main road. This cabin was tiny, yes, but it was very secluded, with thick trees on three sides and the lake on the fourth. It would be a good place for Aiden to recover and for Garrison to try to reach his son. Maybe here, they could reconnect. If not here, then Sam didn't know where they could.

She parked her SUV and peered up at the roof. It looked perfect, as she'd known it would. This was one of the few cabins she hadn't updated yet. After purchasing it the winter before, she'd hoped to make a little money off it before she poured cash into it. Fortunately—aside from the roof—the place had been structurally sound.

The sight inside the front door brought a smile. She hadn't been here in a while, and she'd forgotten all the brown. The walls were covered in knotty pine paneling. The kitchen cabinets matched. The furniture had come with the house, and, with the wood tones, practically blended into the space. Even the floors were hardwood. The fireplace...that was a different story. It was spectacular. Flanked by tall windows, the stacked gray stone went all the way to the tip of the cathedral ceiling along the back wall. What would have been just rustic and woodsy was chic because of that fireplace. This winter, she'd make the rest of the little place match that one grand feature.

Every surface was covered with dust. After ensuring the electricity and plumbing were working properly—no reason they wouldn't be, but it never hurt to check after a big project like a new roof—she headed back to the car for her cleaning supplies.

The place would be ready before Garrison and Aiden arrived, and with luck, she'd have time to make a run to the grocery store for them.

That wouldn't be too forward, would it? Buying them some supplies?

No, it was the right thing to do. She'd do it for Reagan or Brady, Nate or Marisa. Garrison was a friend, just like all the rest, and she'd support him however she could while he was in Nutfield. She knew what it meant to need a friend, so that's what she'd be. And she'd be satisfied with that.

FOUR

Garrison shifted in the fake leather chair by his son's bed. Aiden was still sound asleep and didn't look to be waking up any time soon. There was no time to sit here and watch his kid sleep.

He needed to locate his car. Fortunately, the keys and Aiden's phone had been in his pocket when he'd been brought in the night before. Garrison had taken both. Now he just had to figure out where the party had been.

He took his phone into the hallway and dialed the local police department. After explaining what he wanted three times, he finally managed to get an address.

He checked on Aiden—still sleeping—and summoned Uber for a ride to his car. The Camry seemed fine, so that was something, especially since Aiden had left it unlocked again. The least of Garrison's worries. He swung through the Dunkin' Donuts drive-through on his way back to the hospital and picked up a large coffee, a breakfast sandwich, and a dozen donuts.

By the time he returned to the hospital, Aiden was awake.

"Hey, kiddo. How you feeling?"

Aiden turned his face away from his father's, but not fast enough to hide the moisture in his eyes.

Garrison clasped his son's shoulder. "You gave me a scare."

"Sorry about that."

He squeezed the shoulder gently. "We'll talk about it later. Right now, I'm just glad you're okay."

Behind him, a woman with the raspy voice of a chain-smoker said, "We looked for you."

Garrison turned as a new nurse, not the gentle one from the night before, walked in and gave him a hard stare.

"Went to get the car, so I could take him straight home."

"You shouldn't leave your son in the ER alone. He's a minor."

She was right, of course. On the other hand... "Seemed safer to leave him alone here than to leave him alone later while I searched for my car. And he was sleeping. And he's seventeen years old."

"Mmm-hmm." She didn't say another word while she checked Aiden's blood pressure and temperature. Finally, she turned to leave.

"Any idea when we can go home?"

"Be patient, sir." It had to be some kind of skill to put so much disrespect in three words. "He's not our only patient." She left the room and slammed the door.

"Geez, Dad, what'd you do to piss her off?"

He turned back to Aiden. "Just being my normal charming self."

"That explains it."

Garrison chuckled as he sat beside the bed. The laugh died quickly, and the room filled with tension as thick as peanut butter.

He had food on the brain. "Are you hungry? I have donuts in the car."

"No."

"Okay."

Aiden closed his eyes.

What should Garrison do? For all her faults—and they were myriad—Charlene would know how to handle this. What to say, what to do. Later, she'd salve her pain with a couple pills, but in the moment, she'd be top notch. Garrison—he didn't have a clue. He wanted to touch his son again, to hold him like he had when he'd caught Aiden and Matty on the roof throwing rocks at passing cars. They'd been, what, nine years old? Ten?

Garrison had sent Matty home after a call to his mother, then reamed Aiden out for the utter stupidity, the selfishness, the danger.

He could still remember the boy's wide, teary eyes, that trembling lip, the uttered, "I'm sorry, sir. It won't happen again."

When Garrison was sure Aiden had gotten the message, he'd pulled his boy into his arms and held him like a toddler, patted his back, reminded him how much he loved him.

Now, Garrison longed to gather this man-child in his arms. But would Aiden push him away like he'd been doing ever since Garrison and Charlene had split?

He'd only tried to protect Aiden, yet here they were. And they'd been lucky. All those drugs...

The thought of what could have happened had Garrison's eyes stinging again. He took Aiden's hand and waited for the boy to yank it away.

But Aiden didn't.

He met his son's eyes. "We're going to get you help."

Aiden looked away, but the hand stayed put.

"I love you more than you'll ever know," Garrison said.

Aiden nodded but kept quiet.

What else was there to say? They sat in silence until the nurse returned and said they could go.

GARRISON GLANCED AT AIDEN, who was asleep in the passenger seat. At least the kid hadn't protested when Garrison told him the plan. All he'd said was, "Why New Hampshire?"

"I have a friend there, and she has an empty cabin she can loan us."

He'd waited for the boy to question him further, especially about the *she* part of his statement, but apparently Aiden hadn't had it in him. Garrison had packed a bag for each of them and taken them to the trunk of the car. For some reason, his emergency supplies were all shoved to one side. Who knew what Aiden had been up to? He threw the suitcases in.

They'd been driving more than four hours when Garrison pulled off the interstate toward Nutfield.

Aiden didn't stir. Garrison was so tired he could hardly keep his eyes open. He could have used some conversation. Even silent tension would've worked. It was one thing to stay up all night, but all the emotions had taken their toll, too. His eyes felt like sandpaper, his arms like dead weights. He sipped his third cup of coffee and focused on the fact that they were almost there.

He glanced at his phone's screen, at the map to the address Sam had texted to him.

He turned off the main road and got his first glimpse of Clearwater Lake since March. Back then, he'd come here to help rescue a four-year-old girl from the greedy dirtbag who'd kidnapped her. Last he'd heard, Marisa and little Ana were doing well, living right here in Nutfield. Maybe Garrison would get to see them and Nate while he was here.

But unlike last March, he was the one who needed help this time. He didn't much appreciate the new role his son had given him—pathetic, clueless father. He hated being the needy one, but no one knew better than he what a farce his heroics had been —the powerful former FBI agent, here to protect the world. What a joke. Maybe it was good to be honest with Sam, to be vulnerable. Maybe it would be okay for her, for all his friends in Nutfield, to see him like a normal person, not an agent, not a hero.

He glanced at his sleeping son, thought again of all the drugs that had been in the boy's system.

Yes, Garrison needed help to figure this out, and he'd take it wherever he could get it. If that meant ruining his chances with

Sam, then so be it. Aiden came first, and getting him clean trumped everything else.

Ten minutes later, he turned the car onto what looked like a path in the forest. The narrow dirt drive led to a little wood-sided cabin.

A white Isuzu was parked out front.

His heartbeat raced. It had been nearly five months since he'd laid eyes on Sam. How would she see him now?

He wished circumstances were different so he could make a different impression on the woman who'd so captivated him. He'd probably planted himself forever in the just-friends garden.

He parked beside Sam's car and nudged Aiden. "We're here."

Aiden sat up, stretched, and looked around. "Geez, Dad, could you have found anyplace more secluded?"

Garrison lightly punched him. "Keep it up, we'll be headed to Canada."

Aiden opened his car door. He was about to step out when Samantha exited the cabin.

Aiden froze, turned to him, eyebrows raised. "A friend?"

"We met last spring. Remember I told you about the case I helped solve—"

"She's the one with the kid?"

"No. She was just helping them out."

"Right," Aiden said. "A friend."

"Just—"

"Whatever."

Garrison stepped out of the car and walked to the bottom of the front porch steps.

Sam had on a Plymouth State T-shirt and blue jeans, and both had splotches where she'd splashed something on them. Her long brown hair was pulled back in a ponytail, and she wore no makeup.

She was so beautiful, his heart nearly stopped.

She hiked her purse over her shoulder, walked down the steps, and stood a foot from him. He'd forgotten how tiny she was, slender with curves in all the right places. The top of her head reached almost to his shoulder. He longed to hug her, to touch her, but with Aiden behind him, he didn't dare.

"Hey," she said.

"Thanks for all this."

"It's my pleasure." Her gaze darted to Aiden's door. The kid still hadn't stepped out. "I hope it's not a problem I'm here. I thought I'd be finished before you got here. You made really good time."

"I'm glad you're here."

She smiled, and a little pink tinged her cheeks. Wow, he was in trouble.

The car door slammed, and Garrison snapped out of it.

Sam blinked twice. "I was just finishing up. The place is clean, the linens are washed."

"You didn't have to do all that."

Aiden stopped beside Garrison.

"This is my son. Aiden, this is Samantha Messenger."

Aiden stood there, half awake, and stared.

Garrison nudged him, and the kid remembered his manners. He reached forward and shook her hand. "Nice to meet you."

At least in that way, Garrison had trained his son well. Shake hands, make eye contact, speak clearly.

"It's a pleasure to meet you, too. Your father's told me a lot about you."

"Right. I'd hate to hear what he said."

"All good stuff. He's very proud of you."

Aiden frowned, gave his dad a side look.

Garrison clasped the boy on the shoulder. "I am, of course." He turned to Sam.

She held his gaze a moment, then dug in her purse and pulled out her car keys. "I grabbed a few groceries, just enough to get you through breakfast tomorrow."

"You didn't need to do that."

A shadow crossed her features. A moment passed, then, "That's what friends are for."

Friends. Of course.

"The cabin key is on the kitchen table. Let me know if you need anything."

"Will do." He wanted to follow her to the SUV, talk with her privately, thank her again for all she'd done. Instead, he watched as she backed out and drove away.

"Right," Aiden said. "Just a friend."

Garrison ignored him and climbed the steps.

FIVE

Matty tossed his cell on the bed, then snatched it back up. Why wasn't Aiden answering?

Matty had scoured the web to make sure there wasn't some article about a kid dying of an overdose the night before. There had been a write-up on the bust—*Teen Rushed to ER after Police Break Up House Party*—but all they'd said about Aiden was that there was no more information available.

So he'd thrown on his jeans and walked the couple of blocks to the house where the party'd taken place the night before. No Camry.

Matty dialed again, got voicemail again, and paced the tiny room he shared with his little brother. Jimmy was already gone to his soccer game. He'd asked Matty to come, but Matty would go nuts if he had to watch a bunch of ten-year-olds falling all over the stupid field. Sometimes he liked to go and support his little brother. He knew well enough what it was like to score on the field and then realize nobody you loved cared enough to be there. Mom tried to make the Saturday games, but when Matty'd been a kid, she'd hardly ever made his. So he tried to be there for Jimmy. God knew their father wouldn't bother.

He should have gone back to get the package out of Aiden's

car last night. But he'd been scared there'd still be cops around. He'd planned to wait a while, sneak out of the house around four, and get the package then. But he'd fallen asleep.

And what kind of friend was he that he cared more about the package than about Aiden? His friend hadn't looked good when they'd put him in the ambulance the night before, but from what he'd heard from the other guys at the party, Aiden had dropped a couple hits of acid. Probably just a bad trip. The acid would have worn off by now. He'd be fine.

At least Matty hadn't supplied the acid. Then he'd really feel like a jerk, sending his best friend to the ER.

Aiden's dad had probably flipped his lid, grounded him for the rest of his life, but whatever. Aiden would be eighteen in a few months, and then he could do whatever he wanted.

Matty, on the other hand... If he didn't get that package delivered the next day, what would happen? To him? To his dad? He'd thought about calling his father, but he'd decided against it. No sense telling Dad he'd lost the package. Not ever. He'd get it back, and everything would be fine. His father would be proud of him.

Matty tried to imagine what that would look like, but he couldn't conjure the image. He'd never seen pride on his dad's face.

But what if he didn't recover the package and get it delivered? What would his father say? That image, the anger, the disappointment—that was easy to imagine.

He couldn't sit here any longer.

He stuffed his phone in his pocket, grabbed his backpack, and left the house. When Aiden's parents divorced, Mr. Kopp had rented a house nearby so Aiden could stay near his friends. His dad's place was a little further than his mom's, but Matty could walk it in fifteen minutes. He'd just have to ask to see Aiden, get the keys to the car somehow, and get the package.

Little house after little house after little house. To a stranger, the streets probably all looked the same, but not to Matty. You could blindfold him, stick him on just about any street within a mile of his house, and he'd know where he was right away. He'd walked and biked and skateboarded every road since he was old enough to leave the house, and he knew Hempstead like he knew the route to his bathroom.

The streets were busier than he'd have thought, but then, when was the last time he'd been out and on foot this early on a Saturday morning? Who leaves the house voluntarily before eleven on the weekend? Stupid people or poor saps who have to work. Matty preferred to do his work at night, a deal here, a deal there, a couple hundred in his pocket.

He walked faster and finally turned down Aiden's street. Houses were smaller here than where Aiden's mom lived, even smaller than Matty's house. Matty figured Mr. Kopp had made good money with the FBI and now as a forensic accountant. Forensics sounded cool, but add *accountant* and suddenly it sounded like the most boring job ever. Why would somebody quit the FBI to do something like that? Maybe Mr. Kopp was sorry he'd done it now.

Matty slowed as he neared the house. There was a one-car garage, but it was full of sports equipment, old bicycles, and boxes they'd never unpacked. Which meant the car should have been parked in the driveway.

It wasn't.

Matty swore under his breath and ran to the front door. Maybe Mr. Kopp had just gone to the grocery store.

He rang the bell, waited, then rang it again. He pounded on the door.

No answer.

He sat on the stoop and pulled out his phone. He couldn't stand it any longer. If Aiden wouldn't answer the phone, maybe Mr. Kopp would.

He dialed, and a moment later, Aiden's father answered. "Hello?" The single word sounded weary, broken.

"Hey, Mr. K. I heard about what happened last night. I was

wondering how Aiden is." There. Sounded concerned, a perfectly normal reaction for a best friend.

"He's doing all right."

Matty waited, but the man said nothing else.

"Anything I can do for you guys?" Matty asked.

"No, thank you. We're good."

Matty swallowed, closed his eyes. "I just wondered if I could come over and see Aiden later, maybe."

"We're not at home."

"Oh." He crossed his fingers. "When will you be back?"

"Not sure right now, kiddo. I'll tell Aiden you called."

And just like that, Mr. Kopp hung up.

That had been about as helpful as a paper cut.

Matty's phone rang. Maybe it was Mr. Kopp calling back. He looked at the screen, and his hope crashed like dead bird.

Dad.

SIX

After Sam left Garrison and Aiden, she drove around the lake and surveyed her cabins, which were all full this weekend. The lake buzzed with the sounds of speedboat motors, rang with the laughter of skiers and spotters and swimmers. It was late afternoon, and somebody'd fired up a charcoal grill. The scent of hamburgers and hot dogs filtered through her open window and made her mouth water.

She drove to the small beach, grabbed her bag, and found an empty picnic table beneath the trees. The vacationers had congregated near the water and in the sun, so they were far enough away to be background noise. The table was rough but relatively clean. She set up her laptop and connected to the Wi-Fi in her nearest cabin. She'd bought a Wi-Fi booster for that cabin specifically so she could sit out here and work, a perk of ownership.

She'd been thinking about this ever since Garrison's call that morning. She didn't know much about addiction recovery, but she knew there were a lot of options—many of them bad. Maybe she could help narrow Garrison's choices.

She opened her browser, started to type, and stopped.

Was she overstepping? She and Garrison were friends,

nothing else, and although she was always willing to help friends with research, with whatever they needed, her friends would ask. Garrison hadn't asked, but he had to be overwhelmed. And hadn't he confided in her, wanted her help to find a place to stay? Would he think her too forward if she dug into rehab places? Would he suspect her motives?

What were her motives?

She pushed the laptop away and stood. She didn't want to ask herself that question because she knew, deep down, what the answer was. She had feelings for Garrison that went beyond friendship. Ridiculous as it was, she was falling for the guy and had been since the first time she'd seen him, back when she still feared he'd throw Marisa, her new friend and a woman whose daughter had been kidnapped, in jail. But wow, how he'd come through for them, helped Marisa and Nate get to the bottom of the mystery that had had Marisa running for her life. If not for Garrison, would Marisa have ever gotten her daughter back?

Sweet little Ana. Who knew what would have become of her if not for Garrison?

He'd swooped in like a hero, then disappeared abruptly, and she'd feared she'd never hear from him again. It wasn't as if they'd even had time to develop a friendship in the one day they'd spent together. Then out of the blue, he'd called a few weeks later. He'd dropped out of the investigation looking for Marisa's daughter because his son had been getting in trouble more and more, sneaking out, taking off. Sam had little experience with teenage boys, but she knew how to listen.

Their friendship had developed over the next months during those phone calls. They'd laughed together, shared secrets, even worried together as Garrison had told her his fears for his son. But until this morning, they hadn't seen each other again. Garrison was too afraid to leave Long Island, even when Aiden was at his mother's house, because of her addiction issues and Aiden's drug use. He'd invited Sam to visit, but she couldn't do that.

Thank heavens she'd had a good excuse. Summer was her busy season, and she needed to be close by. It was true—mostly. Sure, her management company could handle just about everything, but the cabins were her responsibility, the guests her guests, and she felt she needed to be close, just in case.

Nothing had happened, of course, except for the leaky roof that had proved to be advantageous for her and Garrison, and the management company could have handled that. But even if she'd known the summer would go smoothly, she wouldn't have driven to Long Island. How could she have?

She wouldn't have made it as far Manchester.

As soon as Garrison figured out her issues, he'd shake her off like an insect.

Fine, there was no future for them. They were just friends, they'd always be just friends, and friends did stuff for each other. And if it bothered him that she'd started investigating rehab centers without his blessing, so be it. The sooner their friendship ended, the sooner that little flame of hope would be snuffed out, and she could go back to her life the way she'd planned it.

She stared at the families in the water and on the beach. Two beautiful little children sat on the shore and splashed in the gentle lap of the waves. The little girl was maybe three, the boy still crawling. Their parents watched from a few feet away.

Sam sat alone in front of her computer and opened her search engine.

SEVEN

The next morning, Garrison grabbed his laptop and a cup of coffee and eased into a chair at the table on the back porch. The sun shone brightly through the tall pines, and the air was already warm, but the roof over the patio kept its harsh rays off him. Did nothing for the humidity, but it was too early for that to matter much.

The lake had teemed with activity yesterday, and people were already out this morning, even though it was barely nine o'clock on a Sunday. Seemed folks wanted to get a few hours of play in before heading back to their homes and lives.

Down to earth, homey. A great place to vacation, and so different from Long Island. Not that he didn't like his home, but this life was more his speed. He'd done the big city thing. When he'd been with the FBI, he'd been required to work in one of the larger cities for at least a short time, and since Charlene had grown up in New York, the choice to move there had been a no-brainer. He'd spent eleven years at the NYC office before retiring and taking a job as a forensic accountant, and he would have stayed longer—he'd loved being an agent with the FBI—but his family needed him. Not that being around more had helped anyone. Apparently Garrison was such a great husband and father that his ex-wife and his son both needed drugs to survive living with him.

He stood and leaned against the railing, gazing at the lake beyond. The temptation to blame himself for their drug use was strong. He'd done enough self-evaluation after Charlene left him to know the root of that. If he believed he'd caused Charlene's addiction, then he could make himself responsible for fixing it. Believing he could fix Charlene had only made things worse, though. He'd eventually come to realize that though their marriage hadn't been perfect, Charlene's turning to drugs hadn't been his fault. She could have tried to save their marriage instead of popping pills and downing liquor to make herself feel better.

He hadn't been the cause of her addiction, and he wasn't the cause of Aiden's, either.

Maybe if he kept saying it, he'd convince himself it was true.

At least he and Aiden had a peaceful place to figure out the next step. But figuring out anything would require a lot more sleep than he'd allowed himself. Sure, the king-sized bed in the master had been very comfortable, but he hadn't been able to shake the worry that Aiden would wake up and take off. Finally around two a.m., Garrison had given up, propped himself on the sofa in the living room, and watched TV, dozing here and there. Aiden had hardly moved since he'd fallen into bed at dusk. Amazing, considering how much the boy had slept the day before.

There'd been no talking to Aiden on Saturday. Too many drugs in his bloodstream. Maybe today, he'd be normal again.

Garrison returned to his seat and opened his laptop, closed it again. He couldn't think about work, couldn't figure out what their next step should be, couldn't seem to make himself do anything he needed to do.

Fine. There was one thing he could do, call Charlene.

He braced himself and dialed. She picked up on the second ring.

"Why are you calling me so early?" she said. "It's practically dawn."

"You have time to talk?"

"I'd rather sleep."

"It's about Aiden."

A pause. He heard rustling, then, "What happened?"

Much as Charlene had blown it as a mother, she still loved their son in her own halfhearted way. Maybe the two of them could repair some of the hurt between them and work through this together. "Friday night, he was taken to the ER. He'd been at a party and using drugs. The doctor thought—"

"Wait a minute. Did you say Friday night? Friday, as in two days ago?"

"Yeah. They called me, and—"

"Why are you just calling me now? I can't believe you didn't call me yesterday. How could you—?"

"That's why."

"What's why? What are you talking about? How dare you...?"

He moved the phone away from his ear and waited until the shrieking stopped. "I didn't call you first, because your first thought is always for yourself. He's fine, by the way."

"Well, I mean... Obviously he's fine, right? Of course he's fine."

Garrison took a deep breath. "He took LSD, and the doctor thinks he had a bad trip. They did a blood test to see what drugs were in his system."

"Why? You said it was LSD."

"And alcohol, marijuana, and opiates."

Silence.

"Like the painkillers you take."

"You think he got them from me?"

"Do you have any pills missing?"

"I wasn't born yesterday, Garrison. My medications are locked in a box and hidden."

"Could you check, just in case?"

She sighed. "Hold on." A minute later, "He didn't take my pills."

"He's getting them somewhere. Whether it's from you or not doesn't matter. He had enough in his system that the doctor thought he's probably built up a tolerance, which means he's been taking them often, and for a while."

"This isn't my fault. I know you think it is, but it's not. I take those pills because my back hurts. I have to take them."

"Again, this isn't about you."

"I know you blame me. You think that if I'd quit and live my whole friggin' life in pain, we wouldn't be having these problems. But how did you expect me to do that, huh? How was I supposed to live without them?"

Having a mother who was an addict had obviously influenced Aiden. But having a barely-there father for so many years of his life hadn't helped. "Charlene, this isn't about you, and it isn't about me. We've both made mistakes. Right now, we just have to figure out what to do next."

"Bring him over this afternoon."

Garrison looked at the lake. Charlene would lose it when he told her he'd left the state without telling her. Not that he needed her permission.

Charlene continued, "We'll sit down and talk to him."

"I've talked until I'm out of words. This is beyond talking."

"What does that mean? You going to write him off like you wrote me off?"

"I didn't..." He ran his hand over his hair. The woman was utterly irrational. He was tempted to remind her one more time that this situation wasn't about her.

"So what is your brilliant plan?" she asked. "You gonna ground him, take his phone?"

Garrison still had Aiden's phone and intended to keep it for the time being. That was nothing compared with what he planned to do. "We need to consider rehab—"

"No. No flippin' way you're sending my son to one of those... those prisons. You have no idea what those places are like."

"And you do? You never went."

"I looked into it, to appease you. No way are you doing that to our boy."

"What's your bright idea?"

"You need to keep a better eye on him. You work from home most of the time. How is he getting away with all of this with you there, anyway? You need to watch him better."

You, you, you. She wasn't about to take him back in her house —not that Garrison would let his son live there again.

"It's not that simple, which you would know if..." He stopped when he heard a noise. He turned to see Aiden pushing the door open. "I have to go."

"We're not done talking about this, Garrison."

"We are for now." He hung up in the middle of her angry tirade, set the phone down, and smiled at Aiden. "You need some coffee?"

He shrugged and sat at the table. He stared at the lake. "Nice place."

"It is." He followed his son's gaze. A pontoon boat puttered by pulling a couple of kids on a tube. A man drove the boat, a woman and a younger child watched the tubers from the back. He couldn't see their faces, but he imagined they were all smiling.

He glanced at Aiden. The expression on the boy's face— longing and sadness—had Garrison rubbing a tingling sensation from his eyes. Grown men weren't supposed to cry, especially not multiple times in the same weekend.

"You ever been tubing?"

Aiden looked at him, looked back at the lake. "Nope."

"I thought, maybe with a friend or something." Garrison studied Aiden's profile, the dark circles under the boy's eyes, the faded skin tone. His too-long hair was messy and greasy. He still wore the clothes he'd had on Friday night.

How had his son drifted so far? He thought of the boats out there on the water. The good thing about drifting was what drifted away could be brought back. One way or another, he would bring his son back home. "How about water skiing? Ever done that?"

"Nope."

"It's not easy, but you're strong and coordinated. I wonder if we can rent a boat on this lake. What do you think? You want to give it a try?"

The tiniest flinch, maybe even an almost-smile. And his eyes had brightened for a moment before they dimmed again. "Whatever."

"I'll take that as an enthusiastic yes."

Aiden turned to face him, opened his mouth, closed it, and stood. "I think I will get some coffee."

"Help yourself. Then come back outside. We need to talk."

While Aiden went inside, Garrison stared at the water and wondered if Charlene was right. Were rehab centers like prisons? Could they help his son? He'd tried to do some research the day before, but there were so many places, so many different options. Outpatient or inpatient. Thirty days, sixty, ninety. Close to home, far away, luxury or state-funded. Twelve-step or not. There were rehab centers for teens only, some for boys in their late teens and early twenties. Some all male, some co-ed. When he'd tried to get Charlene to go to rehab, the research hadn't been so hard. Maybe because she was a grown woman and not a child, his child. And maybe because, deep down, he'd known she wouldn't go.

Garrison needed to talk to somebody who knew about this kind of thing, but who? He couldn't think of a soul he'd trust with this. Not anybody who knew about addiction, anyway.

Way back when Charlene had started using, someone had suggested he go to those Al-Anon meetings. Maybe if he'd done that he'd know how to handle things now. At least he'd have some connections. As it was, he had nothing. No idea what to do. No support whatsoever.

Aiden returned, sat beside his father, and stared at the lake. "Can I have my phone back?"

"Not right now."

"Dad, there are people who must be wondering if I'm okay. My friends will be worried."

"Matty called me yesterday to ask how you were doing." The kid had sounded off, even after Garrison had told him Aiden was fine. But Garrison couldn't worry about Matty, too. "I told him we're going to be out of town for a while."

"But... What do you mean? How long?"

No idea how to answer that. Garrison said nothing.

"I have work," Aiden said.

"I called them yesterday. They're not expecting you."

"I don't go, they're going to fire me."

"It's not like there aren't other fast food joints on Long Island."

"I like that job."

"I guess you should have thought of that—"

"Here it comes." Aiden crossed his arms and focused on the water. "This is where I get the lecture."

Garrison could do without the attitude. "I was thinking this might be where I got an apology."

Aiden shrugged. "Sorry."

He studied his son's profile. "You'd make a lousy politician."

Aiden turned to give his father a smirk.

"Politicians sound sincere even when they're full of crap. It's a skill you should work on if you ever decide to run for office."

"You're so not funny." Aiden turned back to the lake.

They watched a speedboat pulling a skier. The skier wiped out, and the driver turned to pick him up. When the engine slowed, the people's laughter rang across the water.

He glanced at his son. No smile there, but the anger had faded.

"You okay?"

Aiden shrugged. "I just wanted to try it."

"Was it the first time you'd done acid?"

"Of course."

Sounded like a lie. Garrison had enough experience interrogating criminals that he could pick up lies like desperate guys could pick up ugly girls at last call. At least with most people. It wasn't so easy with Aiden.

"What about the other drugs in your system? First time you did those, too?"

Aiden turned now. His face paled a little. "What other drugs?"

"They did a blood test."

A pause, then, "Oh."

Garrison waited.

"I was just having a bad day. I wanted to—"

"Have you ever considered telling me the truth?"

"I don't want...I don't want you to worry about me."

"So you're lying for my sake. How very generous of you."

"It was the first time—"

"Let's try this. Why don't you quit lying? I already know more than you think I do. Remember, I am an investigator." He hadn't investigated anything yet, but it wouldn't hurt to let Aiden believe he was way ahead of him.

Aiden turned his gaze back to the lake. The skin around his mouth was tight. His hands were clenched into fists. Garrison could practically see the gears spinning in the kid's head, could imagine the thoughts in there. *What does Dad know? What can I say to get out of this?*

Aiden's hands relaxed, and his mouth softened. He'd come up with a plan. Aiden turned to face him. Took a deep breath.

His eyes filled with tears.

"I've been smoking pot for a while. Like on the weekends and after work."

"Never at work?"

"Not that it would matter. A monkey could make tacos, but, no, I don't usually go to work high."

Not usually. Which meant not always, but probably often enough. Garrison waited, hoped his son would admit to the rest.

Aiden sipped his coffee. His hands were shaking. Good. He should be nervous. It meant something that he still cared what his dad thought.

"I drink a little at parties, but I don't really like alcohol. Makes you feel like crap the next day."

Only if you over-consume, which Aiden obviously had.

"Okay." Garrison waited.

Aiden looked down, took a breath, looked back up. "I've taken some oxy, too. Sometimes."

"Define 'sometimes.'"

He shrugged.

"Every day?"

He shrugged again. So yes, every day, at least once a day, probably more.

The truth of it hit him. He'd feared it, but to have Aiden confirm it, it all seemed that much more real.

Garrison should ask how Aiden had paid for the drugs and where he'd gotten them. He could wear his son down, get the information. Interrogations hadn't been his specialty at the FBI, but he could do them. He'd honed his powers of observation. But Aiden wasn't a suspect, and the details weren't that important right now.

Garrison took a deep breath. When he blew it out, he forced away all the questions, the need-to-knows his mind was demanding. This wasn't about catching the kid in his lies or proving a case in court. It was about getting him help.

"Thank you for being honest with me."

Aiden nodded, ducked his head.

Garrison reached out, grasped the boy's shoulder, and squeezed. "Nothing you said, and nothing you've done, changes how I feel about you. You're my son, and I love you. I'll always love you."

Aiden's shoulders slumped.

Garrison crouched beside his son and reached for the boy's shoulders, drawing him close. He barely noticed the rank odor of unwashed hair as Aiden's tears fell on his T-shirt. His fingers brushed the sharp outline of bones on a frame that had lost muscle mass in the last weeks.

How had that happened? How had he not noticed?

The feeling of his son in his arms felt so right, so pure, and so terrifying. The boy was here, but his heart was still elsewhere. His heart was focused on the drugs that would eventually destroy him, if he didn't get help.

Garrison wanted his son back.

Not until Aiden pulled away did Garrison take his seat again. He turned his chair to face Aiden's. "The thing is, I think it's time for us to get some help."

Aiden sniffed. "What do you mean? Like a counselor or whatever?"

A counselor might have been a good idea six months or a year before. Aiden had seen one when Garrison and Charlene split, but not for long. He'd been fine. He'd said he was fine. But nothing about this was fine. "I think we're beyond that."

Aiden narrowed his eyes.

"We need to consider rehab."

Aiden pushed back his chair. "No way."

"I know it's not what you want. It's not what I want, either. But we need help."

"It's not that bad. I can quit on my own."

"Last month when I caught you smoking pot, you told me you would quit. Yet here we are."

"I'll really do it this time."

"I hope you do. And I'm going to get you help."

"I'm not going to rehab. Mom won't make me go. I'll go live with her."

The threat hung in the air between them. Garrison wasn't about to tell Aiden his mother wouldn't take him back. The last thing the kid needed was to learn his mother's love didn't extend quite that far. Charlene did love Aiden. She just loved her drugs and her freedom more. A lot more. "You're not going back to live with your mother."

"You can't stop me."

"I can, actually. You are my responsibility."

"She has rights, too. She'll fight for me."

No, she wouldn't. And Garrison had full custody, not that it would make much difference in another six months when Aiden turned eighteen. All the more reason to get the boy in rehab now when he had no choice in the matter.

"Here's the deal, son. You're a minor, and you're an addict."

"I am not an addict."

"And we're going to get you help. You can be a part of the process of choosing a place, or you can sulk and stay out of it. Either way, you're going."

EIGHT

After church, Samantha went home to change her clothes and then headed toward the lake. She was turning off the main road when it occurred to her that she should have called. Of course she should have called. Any idiot would know that. She was so accustomed to dropping in on her friends unannounced. Rae and Brady, her oldest friends, were used to it, and their son Johnny squealed in delight when she showed up. He was almost one now and crawling all over the house.

When she stopped by Marisa's new place, her friend always acted as if Sam were a long-lost sister. Marisa, her fiancé, Nate, and her daughter, Ana, had only moved to Nutfield a few months before, but they'd become dear to her already.

Even Eric, one of the cops in town—a single guy a few years younger than she was—would hardly lift an eyebrow if she stopped by his house unannounced.

But Garrison... She should have called first. Even though she felt closer to him than to any of the others, he wasn't a drop-by-whenever kind of friend—not that he lived close enough to find out. Besides, Aiden was there, and Sam figured the teen would want her around about as much as he'd want a zit on his nose.

Fine, she'd call.

She pulled over on the narrow road that circled the lake and dialed Garrison's number. It was nearly noon. Surely he was awake.

Just when she thought it would go to voicemail, he picked up.

"Hey," he said, "I'm glad you called."

"How was your night? Did you sleep okay?"

A pause. "The bed was very comfortable."

"That wasn't the question." She waited a beat, then said, "Worried?"

She imagined him running his fingers through his cropped hair. "Yeah."

"I just got out of church," she said. "I added you and Aiden to the prayer list. I hope you don't mind. I didn't use your names of course."

"Yeah, okay. That's fine." His tone sounded dismissive.

"You don't believe in prayer?"

"I don't know. I never really tried it. You do?"

"Of course." This conversation wasn't going the way Sam had imagined it in her head. "You know I'm a Christian, right?"

"Yeah, I know. Prayer just feels... I don't know. Weird."

Sam considered and rejected a lot of responses to that. She settled for, "Not to me. What are you up to?"

"Aiden's resting, or maybe sulking, in his bedroom, and I'm trying to research rehab facilities. Do you know how many there are? And they're all different. It's maddening. I just want some grown-up to tell me what to do."

"Some people might consider you a grown-up."

"Only people who don't know me."

She laughed, and her tension drained. "I might be able to help you with that. In fact, I hope you don't mind, but I get a little compulsive about things like this and did some research yesterday. I made some calls, looked up reviews, stuff like that. I have a list for you and a phone number, a guy who has some experience. It's a place to start."

She waited, but Garrison didn't say a word. Great. He was insulted.

"I'm sorry." She couldn't keep the sadness from her voice. She'd thought...well, what did it matter what she'd thought? "I should have checked with you—"

"No, it's fine. You just caught me off guard." He seemed surprised, maybe pleased. "It's good to have a place to start. Thank you."

Phew. "You're welcome. As it happens, I'm at the lake. I thought I'd stop in." Fear filled her as if she were taking on some dragon instead of talking to a man. Well, a dragon she might be able to handle. Just research *how to kill a dragon*. But men? Google would be no help, and she was utterly out of her element. "I even brought lunch, if you guys are interested."

"Samantha, you have officially moved to the top of my *favorite hot chicks in New Hampshire* list."

"It's good to know there's a list."

"Oh, a long one. A long, long list, and you're on top."

"Gee, what an honor."

His chuckle was smooth and sweet, like warm syrup over pancakes.

She'd blame her growling stomach for that thought.

"When will you be here?" Garrison asked.

Her cheeks warmed. At least he couldn't see her. "I'm about two houses down. I didn't want to stop in without calling."

"Come on over."

She hung up and parked in the driveway thirty seconds later. With a sack in one hand and her bag in the other, she climbed the porch steps. The door opened before she could knock, and Garrison stood in the opening.

Holy smoke, he was handsome. He seemed slightly less exhausted today. He was a foot taller than her five-four frame and had the broad chest and jawline of some kind of German superhero. His eyes, though. Blue as an autumn sky and just as clear. Garrison's smile had her residual anxiety melting away. "Hey."

"Hey yourself." She slipped in the door, dropped her bag on the sofa, and took the food to the small table in the eat-in kitchen.

Garrison grabbed some plates. "Smells delicious. What'd you bring?"

"I got a couple of Reubens and fries. I remember you ordered that at McNeal's the first time you were there."

"You remember that? I'm impressed."

Here came her flaming cheeks again. She focused on pulling food out of the sack. "I also brought a cheeseburger, which I hoped Aiden would like. I remember you saying you guys grill out a lot."

She set the sandwiches and her salad on the small table.

"That for you?"

"Yeah. But I might steal a french fry."

He looked at the mountain of fries on the table. "I think we have enough. Not sure about Aiden, though." Garrison's gaze traveled to the doorway that led to the living room and the hallway where the bedrooms were.

"Is he okay?"

Garrison shrugged. "Can I get you something to drink?"

"Water's fine," she said.

He filled two glasses and sat at the table beside her. His forehead creased. "He hasn't eaten since Friday. Not a bite. He looks really sick. I made him take a shower, thought that would help. After he got out, he went back to bed."

"You're worried."

"Just... I don't know much about oxycodone withdrawal."

"Hmm." Her gaze took in the empty counters. "Did I leave my bag in the living room?"

Garrison walked out, returned with her bag, and handed it to her.

She pulled out her Mac. "Go ahead and eat."

"What are you doing?"

"Looking up oxycodone withdrawal symptoms to see if you have anything to worry about." She found a website, perused it quickly. "Looks like it's very rare for oxy withdrawal to be dangerous. Nausea, sweating, chills, anxiety... Those are the more common symptoms. That's probably—" Sam cut herself off. As if she knew anything about what Aiden was going through. She closed the laptop and set it on the kitchen counter. "But if you think it's something more serious—"

"No, no. I bet that's it. I'm just not thinking. I should have looked that up myself."

She reached across the table and laid her hand on Garrison's. "You haven't slept since Thursday night, right? And you're in a situation you never thought you'd face."

He flipped his hand and laced his fingers with hers. "I'm so glad you're here. I can't imagine doing this by myself."

Her hand felt so right in his. For a moment, she allowed herself to believe there could be more between them than friendship. The thought had her heart racing.

The sound of a clearing throat had them both jumping.

"I, like, smelled the food and..." Aiden stood in the doorway, shook his head, and gave his father the meanest look she'd ever seen.

Garrison stood. "Come on in. Sam brought you a burger."

"Forget it."

"Come in." Garrison's tone left no room for arguing. "You're being rude."

He jutted his chin toward them. "Looks like you're being friendly enough for both of us."

Garrison started to respond, but Sam beat him to it. "Aiden, please join us." Sam forced a bright smile. "I didn't know what you'd like on your burger, so I just had them put the cheese on it. Everything else is on the side. McNeals makes the best fries you'll ever eat."

"Want a glass of water?" Garrison asked.

"I'd rather have a Pepsi."

"'There's no soda," Garrison said, "but there's still some of that lemonade Sam brought us yesterday."

He looked at his dad, looked at the food, and shrugged. "Whatever."

He sat beside Sam but didn't make eye contact.

Well, great. Fantastic start. Nothing like alienating the son right out of the gate.

This was a race she definitely wasn't prepared for.

Garrison poured him a glass of lemonade and took his seat again. As they ate in silence, Sam chanced a couple of glances at Aiden. He looked a little better today. His shoulder-length brown hair had been washed and combed, and his skin seemed to have more color than it had the day before. His brown eyes weren't as glassy as they'd been. Where the day before he'd been slouching, almost as if he'd felt ill—which he probably had—right now, his back was javelin-straight. He wasn't as tall as his father yet, but he was easily six feet and likely still growing.

"Sam," Garrison said, "Aiden and I were thinking of trying out water skiing. Is there a place on the lake where we can rent a boat?"

"There's a marina on the other side, but you can use my boat."

Garrison paused, sandwich halfway to his mouth. "You have a boat? You never told me that."

"I haven't taken it out much this summer. I've been so busy." And who was she supposed to go with? Most of her friends were couples with kids. The few single friends she had at church were so focused on their careers they hardly had time to socialize. "I took Nate, Marisa, and Ana out once, and they use it a lot. Just let me know. The thing is, if you want to ski, you need a third person as a spotter."

"Right," Garrison said. "Good point. Do you have time to join us this week?"

Sam glanced at Aiden, caught the scowl. "Maybe you could ask Nate. His schedule is pretty flexible."

Garrison's gaze flicked to his son. "Okay, I'll give him a call. Thanks."

"Let me know when, and I'll bring over the equipment. I keep most of it in my storage unit."

The three ate quietly, the silence oppressive. Sam should have dropped off the food and left. Obviously Aiden didn't want her here, and she could have told Garrison about the rehab places she'd found over the phone. But she was here now, and it would be rude to leave in the middle of lunch. Not that Aiden would complain, but it would make Garrison feel bad, and that was the last thing she wanted to do.

"So, Aiden," she said, "you like water skiing?"

He didn't look up from his burger. "Never done it."

"Have you tubed?"

"Never been on a speedboat."

She glanced at Garrison, who shrugged. "We didn't get away much in the summers. Aiden had baseball, and I had work. And his mother..."

Whatever he'd been about to say died. She didn't look to see Aiden's reaction, but she could picture it.

"His mother," Garrison continued, "is what we call 'indoorsy.' Her idea of recreation is the mall." He smiled at Aiden. "Right, kiddo?"

"Whatever."

Garrison blew out a breath.

Aiden pushed back from the table.

"You barely ate," Garrison said.

"I'm not hungry." He was halfway to the door when he paused and turned. For a moment it looked like he was going to say something rude.

Samantha braced herself.

Then his expression softened the tiniest bit when he faced her. "Thank you for lunch. The fries were really good."

She smiled. "My pleasure."

Aiden headed toward the bedroom, and Sam met Garrison's gaze and smiled. "So, I can't tell. Does he hate me?"

Garrison's smile was slight. "I think he hates me, but that has nothing to do with you."

"I'm sure it's not that bad."

"It is. And if he knew you were helping me find rehab facilities, he'd hate you, too."

"Ah. I take it he's not excited about the prospect?"

"That's one way to put it. He's hardly spoken to me since I mentioned it."

After they finished their meals, Sam grabbed her laptop and positioned it so Garrison could see. She opened the spreadsheet she'd created. "The thing is," she said, "there are so many choices. I talked to a guy who runs some sober living houses around here, and he had some ideas he thought you might consider."

"How do you know him?"

"One of the couples at my church has a son who's an addict. I called the mother yesterday, and she put me in touch with this guy. I have his number for you so you can talk to him yourself. I told him where you guys live and asked him about rehabs near there. He had a few suggestions, but he also thought you might consider getting Aiden into a place further from home. He said he's seen situations where kids do better when they know they don't have any options. They can't just call a buddy to come pick them up when things get rough."

"Hmm. I hadn't thought about that."

"Of course, that means you're not as close to him, either. It limits the time you can spend with him."

"But I can work from anywhere. I have an office, but I hardly ever go in. As long as I could find an apartment nearby, I could be there."

"What about his mother, though?"

Garrison's smirk told her what he thought of the question. "If he's far from home"—he lowered his voice and glanced at the door—"she'll have the perfect excuse not to visit. If he were nearby, she still wouldn't visit, and that would break his heart. He'd find a way to blame me."

Samantha couldn't imagine having such a mother. Her own lived to be a homemaker. When Sam walked into her childhood home, her mouth watered just from the memories of all her delicious meals. And most of the time something was bubbling on the stove.

She wanted to reach out, to take Garrison's hand again. She glanced at the empty doorway, remembered Aiden's expression, and kept her hands on her laptop. "So you'd be open to looking at places outside of New York?"

"Sure. Or upstate would be fine. Or..." He paused, almost smiled. "Near here."

Near here. Near her. She swallowed the smile and nodded. "That family I told you about—their son was in an inpatient facility in Dover. That's not far from here. Now he lives in a sober living house, and I think he's doing pretty well."

Garrison sat back and shook his head. "I can't tell you what it means to me that you've done so much work."

"I'm good at research."

"Looks to me like you're good at a lot of things." He scanned the room, then returned his gaze to her. "Real estate mogul—"

"I'm hardly a mogul."

"How many places do you own?"

She shrugged. "Enough to let me quit my day job, so that was nice."

"And you're enjoying a little more freedom?"

"Yeah." She was, wasn't she? She kept busy with the houses and the renters, and of course with her friends. But she missed the camaraderie she'd had with her coworkers in the Nutfield town offices and with the cops in the department that shared the building. She spent a lot of time alone these days, and conversations with her contractor didn't exactly fill her companionship void.

Garrison's frown told her he must've seen something on her face—the man was too observant.

"It's different than I thought it would be," she said.

"I get that." He glanced at the doorway where Aiden disappeared. "When I retired, I thought Aiden and I would spend so much time together." He shrugged as though it didn't matter. "I had all these plans, things he and I could do. But...it was too late. I'd blown whatever chance we had to be close because I'd worked so much when he was younger. And his mother and I fought all the time. I started to avoid being at home. Which was stupid and totally my fault, and it only hurt Aiden. And it seems..." He shook his head, forced a smile. "Anyway, it's lonely working by yourself all the time."

Of course he'd understand. "Lonely," she agreed. "And quiet."

Their gazes met, and those sparks she'd noticed the first time she met him started flying. Neither spoke. Neither had to.

No. She hadn't imagined it. He felt it, too. The question was, what could either of them do about it?

And the answer was—absolutely nothing.

NINE

Aiden was going to puke. And it wasn't just the thought of rehab.

He'd been sick ever since he'd woken up in the hospital the day before, but he'd been smart enough not to eat.

He should have skipped the stupid cheeseburger. His stomach had been growling, and he'd smelled the food. Like an idiot, he'd gone to investigate, then gotten sucked into lunch with Dad and *her*.

Sam.

Stupid name for a girl. And so what if the food had been good? She'd probably poisoned it.

He hated her. Dad had dragged him up here because he wanted to see his girlfriend. This spontaneous trip had nothing to do with Aiden. It was all about Sam. Dad didn't care about Aiden at all.

Ugh, he was being ridiculous. He slammed his hand into his pillow, which only made his hand hurt. And his head.

Because the shakes and nausea weren't bad enough.

He shivered, wiped sweat off his forehead.

This totally sucked.

If he ever felt normal again, he swore, he swore on...on some dead person's grave...that he'd never take another drug in his life.

Crap. He needed one. Just one, to take the edge off.

He swallowed the nausea down, stared at the ceiling, waited for it to pass.

Images of rehab filled his mind. What would it be like? Prison, probably. With guards and locks and crap. No way.

He pushed those thoughts away, and thought about the party. No, that was no good. He hated to think what he'd looked like, what he'd said and done, that had landed him in the ER. Had he totally embarrassed himself? He was probably lucky he hadn't crapped himself or taken off all his clothes or something.

The last thing he remembered was laughing like a hyena. Everyone had been laughing, right? Or maybe not. Maybe they'd been laughing at him.

Idiot, idiot, idiot.

If only he could make some calls, find out what had happened. Except Dad had taken his phone. Aiden would probably be lucky if he ever got it back.

He had to do something. Anything to take his mind off this, all of it. He couldn't sit in this room by himself anymore.

He sat up. And waited.

Okay, his stomach was better. Not perfect, but not about to hurl lunch all over the bed, either. He stood, didn't move, just in case. His legs ached. Everything ached. He had to work to stand up straight. To look normal.

He opened the door and peeked into the hallway, listening.

He'd heard a car leave a little while ago. Maybe an hour. Maybe ten minutes. He had no idea. Did that mean Sam was gone?

He crept out to the living room. Empty.

In the kitchen, he saw Dad through the back door. He was on the phone on the porch. His forehead was propped on his hand, his fingers messing up his stupid crew cut. His shoulders were hunched.

That wasn't how Dad was supposed to look. Where was the

confidence? Where was his I-know-more-than-you-so-get-in-line attitude?

Aiden had always wanted to smack that attitude away. Looked like he'd finally done it.

Funny how that didn't make him feel better.

He was on his way back to the bedroom when he heard a car door slam.

He obviously wasn't thinking straight, because he opened the front door. And who else could it be but Sam? Back again.

She was leaning in the backseat of her SUV. She turned, spotted him.

Crap. Now he'd have to be nice.

He stepped outside. "Need some help?"

Her jaw dropped as if it had never occurred to her he could be polite. She managed to force out, "If you wouldn't mind."

He joined her at the car. She grabbed two grocery bags and backed up to let him get the rest. He leaned in, saw what she'd bought. "Pepsi. Thanks." Fine. So she wasn't a total witch. Unless she'd just bought it to get on his good side. Not a friggin' chance.

He pulled out the two twelve-packs and the remaining bag.

"Does your dad like Pepsi, too?" she asked. "I didn't think to ask him."

Was she serious? "You don't already know?"

She stepped back, and Aiden closed the door with his hip and started toward the front door.

"I've only met your father once in person," she said. "It was last spring when he helped out some friends of mine."

Aiden maneuvered all the groceries into one hand, opened the front door, and stepped back to let her go first. Showing off his manners, since she obviously thought he was a complete screw-up. "I figured, since you let us use this place..."

"We're friends." She headed to the kitchen. "We talk on the phone sometimes."

Aiden dumped the groceries and soda on the counter as

something occurred to him. He turned to face her. "You're the person he has those long conversations with."

She shrugged, busied herself unpacking the grocery bags. "Like I said, we're friends."

Friends who hold hands. Which was more than friends. "Looked like more than that earlier."

She put away two boxes of cereal. "This is hard for him, Aiden. You must know that."

No kidding. He opened one of the cases of soda and started stowing the cans in the fridge. "I'm not an idiot. I know this is hard for him." He slammed the fridge shut. "It's hard for me, too."

She tilted her head to the side, and her eyes filled with...what was that? Pity? She stepped forward and rested her hand on his arm. "Of course it is. I can't imagine what you're going through. Your pain—it's breaking your dad's heart. I know that's hard to understand. He loves you so much."

He stared at her hand.

She let him go and stepped back. "Sorry."

He opened the fridge again and grabbed a Pepsi. Opened it. Took a sip. It was warm. What was he supposed to say now? Could he just walk away?

He turned, focused on making eye contact and not hunching over. Both were hard.

She sat at the kitchen table and nodded to the seat beside her.

Right. Like he wanted to chat.

"And I tend to be like that," she said. "Touchy-feely, my brother called it. He used to get so mad when we were little because I always wanted to be right beside him. I was trying to comfort your dad. That's what you saw."

Whatever. But she seemed to be waiting for him to say something. "It's not like him and Mom are ever going to get back together."

"Do you want them to?"

Aiden looked beyond her, out the back door to where Dad

was still on the phone. He was looking at his laptop screen now. Aiden thought of his mother, of how different they were. "They can't stand each other. And my mom..." He wasn't going to talk to the witch about his mother. "They hate each other. They're so totally different."

"Funny how you can love them both, right? Even though they're so different?"

"They're my parents, so I kind of don't have a choice."

"Love is always a choice."

He shrugged, sipped his Pepsi. It churned in his stomach, and he hunched over despite himself. He'd needed company, but now he wanted to be alone. He knew in an hour, maybe less, he'd yearn for company again, for a distraction. There was no distraction from this... this pain. "I'm gonna go lie down."

"Let me know if you need anything."

He reached his bedroom and stepped inside and set the soda can on the nightstand. Dad was busy, and Sam was here to distract him.

Maybe Aiden could find his cell phone.

Dad had hidden it somewhere. Probably in his room. Aiden went back to the door, listened for noise. Sounded like Sam was in the kitchen.

Aiden stepped into the hall and closed the door behind him, then crept to Dad's room.

And searched. The bureau, the closet, Dad's suitcase.

No cell phone.

The master bathroom, all the drawers, even inside Dad's shaving kit. No luck.

Where had Dad hidden it?

Crap. He had to find it. Had to call Matty and find out what was going on at home. See if he could figure out what had happened Friday night. Had Matty been at the party? Aiden tried to remember.

Couldn't, but Matty had to have been there. He'd said he would be.

The phone wasn't here. Aiden stepped out of Dad's room and froze.

Sam was in the hallway, looking right at him.

They stared at each other a moment too long before she said, "Are you okay?"

"I was just... Yeah, I'm fine."

"I was going to the bathroom."

He brushed past her and entered his room. "It's empty." He slammed the door behind him and collapsed on his bed. He'd failed to find his phone. Everything hurt. He wanted to curl up in a ball and die.

Had Sam thought it was odd he'd been in his dad's room? Would she question him? What were the chances she'd just go away?

With this chick, slim to none.

Sure enough, a minute later, there was a knock.

"What!"

She opened the door a crack. "You were looking for something?" she asked.

Now that he was lying down, he wasn't sure he could move, so he didn't bother. "Are you a cop, too?"

"I wasn't spying," she said. "I just needed the bathroom."

"Don't you have anything better to do than lurk around here?"

There was a pause. He waited to hear his door close, but no such luck.

"What were you looking for?" she asked.

He sat up, furious. He turned to face her, to scream at her, to tell her to get the heck out of his business. But she looked so friggin' sweet, all sympathy and friggin' kindness. And Dad would be ticked if he yelled at his girlfriend.

So fine. Whatever. "I was looking for my phone."

"Oh," she said. "Have you asked for it back?"

Duh. "He said maybe later."

"Any particular reason you need it?"

For the thousandth time, he stifled the urge to tell her to mind her own friggin' business. But maybe...maybe she could help him. Dad obviously liked her and listened to her. It couldn't hurt to suck up a little. "Like, all of my friends saw me get taken to the hospital the other night. I need to check in, tell everybody I'm okay."

"Oh." She nodded like she got it. "That makes sense. I guess all you can do is ask again."

"Maybe you could—?"

"Nope." She smiled, like that would make it better. "I'm not dumb enough to jump in that battle. You can figure this out without me."

Aiden lay back down and faced the wall. "We can do all of this without you."

He waited for her to leave, but she still didn't.

"Have you apologized," she said, "acknowledged the"—a pause, like she was searching for a word—"the fear you caused him?"

Apologized? Yeah, he'd done that, hadn't he? Like, maybe he hadn't done what she said exactly, but he'd said he was sorry. Right?

"I'm just saying," she continued, "maybe if you start there, your father would be more willing to let you use your phone." She backed out of the doorway. "Sorry to intrude."

TEN

Matty was so totally screwed.

He rode his bike around the block at Aiden's father's house for about the twentieth time, convinced the Camry would pull in any minute now. Every time he passed, he saw the same empty house, empty yard, empty driveway. But he couldn't give up. He wouldn't until they got home. Whenever that would be.

He'd finally broken down and called Aiden's father on Saturday afternoon, but Mr. Kopp wouldn't put Aiden on the phone. Said he was sleeping. Jonesing for some oxy, more like. Aiden had been using it every day. Too much, and Matty'd told him that. That's why he didn't use the stuff himself. He had no desire to get addicted. There was nothing impressive about a person who couldn't survive without his next fix.

When Dad had called, Matty explained what happened, explained that the cops had searched him and that if he hadn't stowed the package, it would have been confiscated.

"Really?" Dad's voice had sounded...tolerant. Barely. "You couldn't have told them it was a gift for someone? And why would you have been searched? Did they search everybody?"

"They did." Most everybody. Matty'd gotten a quick pat-down. "Didn't seem smart to take the chance."

"I see."

The pause that followed had Matty's stomach churning. "I was trying to be smart, to stow the package where nobody would find it."

"So where is it now?"

"I don't know exactly. Aiden isn't answering his phone, and Mr. Kopp—"

"This is your friend's father? The fed?"

Right. He'd told Dad about Mr. Kopp.

"Not anymore. Now he's a forensic accountant. He quit—"

"I know who he is and what he does. I keep tabs on what you're doing, who you're spending time with."

Matty felt a little surge of joy at the words. His father did care.

"So how do you intend to get the package back before tomorrow?"

"They have to come home soon."

"No. In fact, they don't *have* to do anything."

"There's no way I could've known—"

"I understand. Do your best to get the package back right away. I'll call you in the morning."

Then the phone had gone dead.

As promised, his father had called that morning, but Matty hadn't answered. Aiden was gone, Mr. Kopp wasn't saying when they'd be back, and Matty had no idea what to do.

His phone rang. Dad. Again. He rejected the call and texted. *Working on it.*

Dad's reply had been short. *No more excuses.*

Matty'd been calling Aiden's cell phone. It went straight to voicemail every time. Mr. Kopp had only told him they were out of town. Totally vague.

He read Dad's text again. Dad was right—no excuses. All he needed was a hint of where Aiden was, and he'd get there. His car was still stranded, but he'd borrow his mother's. She wouldn't give him permission, but she wouldn't report the car stolen, either. She didn't have the money to bail him out of jail. He'd find Aiden, get the package, and get back.

A hot, humid breeze blasted him in the face as he rounded the corner and passed the Kopps' house again. Still empty.

He was so totally screwed.

And hungry.

Stomach growling, he turned his bike toward home. He'd grab lunch and then come back and wait.

He was nearly home, lost in thought, wondering if his father would cut him out of his life completely after this. That's why he didn't notice the man until he stepped right in front of Matty's bike.

Matty yanked his handlebar to the left and squeezed the brakes. His tire slid on the street, and he tried to plant his foot, but his ankle twisted. He and the bike wiped out. Pain shot up his leg.

The pain was nothing compared to his anger. Hands fisted, he twisted, his butt scraping on the gravely street, and turned to confront the jerk.

The black man Matty had seen at the airport reached out to help Matty stand. "Forgive me. I did not mean to frighten you."

Matty's anger turned to fear, and for one stupid moment, he thought about running. But the ache in his ankle and the fact that he was on his butt squelched that thought. And anyway, where would he go? This guy obviously knew where he lived. They were two doors down from his house.

The man stood with his hand outstretched, silent. No smile.

Matty took the hand and stood, then backed away, nearly tripping over his bicycle. "Uh, it's—"

"I would like to speak with you." His voice was deep, and he spoke with an accent. Sounded French. The tone was polite when he added, "Please, get in the car." The man opened the back door of a smallish silver SUV and waited. His skin was as dark as night, his eyes bright. A scar cut across his neck from just below his ear almost to his Adam's apple. He was well over six feet and slender, like a basketball player. But too old for that, maybe forties. His skin was pockmarked. He wore a white shirt buttoned up to the top and black slacks.

No way was Matty getting in that car. He knew how this stuff worked. He'd get in, and nobody'd ever hear from him again.

The man reached into his pocket, and Matty stepped back on his sore ankle, hit the bike, and stumbled over it. He nearly fell, righted himself, and was about to bolt when the man held a cell phone out so he could see the screen.

"This is your father, no?"

Matty took in the image. The picture had been taken from a distance. Dad wore the business suit and blue tie Matty had seen Friday night. He was standing beside a baggage carousel.

Should he deny it? Should he run?

"Please," the man said. "I do not want to hurt you. And I'd rather not have to meet your mother." He turned his phone back to himself, swiped across it, and showed the image to Matty.

He could make out his mother's face in the front seat of her car. Jimmy sat beside her eating a taco. Taco Bell—their after-church ritual. Matty used to go to church with them, before...all this. The picture had to have been taken that morning.

"That is your mother, yes? Allison O'Brien?"

He gazed at her face, at Jimmy's. What had he done? What had his father done to put them all in this situation? "Yes."

"I will not hurt you. I would only like to talk."

Whether the man would hurt him or not didn't matter. He wouldn't pull his mother or his brother into this mess. With trembling hands, Matty moved his bicycle to the sidewalk and climbed into the backseat of the SUV.

Another man, also black, but not as dark, sat in the driver's seat. He didn't turn to look as Matty slid to the far side.

The man sat beside him. He put his phone in his pocket and shifted to face Matty. "I am Robert. I work for my government in the Democratic Republic of Congo. You have heard of it, no?"

"Uh...it's in Africa, right?"

The man's lips twitched, his dark eyes twinkled. "That's a very good guess. What gave it away?"

"Your accent."

Robert smiled, and his white teeth seemed to shine against the black of his skin. "You're funny, Matthew. Yes, the DRC is in Africa. It is the largest nation on the continent, about three times larger than your Texas. It is a nation rich in resources, and it's my job to make sure those resources work for my people and are not stolen away."

Matty thought of the tiny package his father had given him. What had Dad taken, a couple grains of corn or something?

"Your father gave you a package Friday at the airport."

"No." Matty scrambled for a story. "He didn't. He just decided to get a different ride home. Because there was this party I wanted to go to and if I'd taken him home, I wouldn't have gotten back in time. So he said he'd take an Uber."

"Uber. The car service, yes?" Robert tapped his temple as if he was considering that. "Except he didn't get in a car. He boarded a flight."

No. All this time, Matty had assumed his dad was back in the city.

"He flew to the Bahamas Friday night."

"Oh." He swallowed, scrambled again. "Well, then, that explains why he didn't need a ride home."

"I am surprised," Robert said.

"Well, that's what happened."

"No," the man said. "Not at your story, which is rubbish, we both know. I'm surprised that you're not a more skillful liar. I thought you would be more like your father."

"Don't talk about my—" He pinched off his words before he could finish. What did he know about his father, anyway? Obviously not nearly enough. But whatever he was, the man was still his father. And Matty had to keep his promise to him.

"If we can't talk about your father, then let's talk about the package. Do you know what's inside it?"

"No." He caught himself too late. "What package? I told you—"

"Have you delivered it yet?"

Matty kept his mouth shut this time.

"You are not talking now. I understand that. Your father has put you in quite a position, hasn't he? You can either keep your word, or you can do the right thing. Doing the right thing, that is to betray your father. But doing the wrong thing—that is always to betray yourself."

Betray himself? That didn't even make sense. "For all I know, you're like some sort of warlord or terrorist or something. How do I know you are who you say you are? And anyway, this has nothing to do with me."

"I am neither a warlord nor a terrorist, and unfortunately, young Matthew, this has everything to do with you. All the power is in your hands. If you deliver the package to your father's friend, you will cause many people great trouble."

"How? My father wouldn't hurt anybody."

"Not directly, perhaps. But hurt them he will."

"What people?"

"Besides yourself and your family?"

A threat, a direct threat. Against himself, Mom, and Jimmy. "My family has nothing to do with this."

"Your father—"

"He has nothing to do with us. With my mother and my brother. He barely has anything to do with me. You need to leave my family out of this."

"Nobody will be in any danger if you just give me the package."

"I don't have it."

"Ah. You have delivered it already. That is unfortunate. Very bad for you, but perhaps, if you tell me where you took it, we can recover it, and then you and Allison and Jimmy will be safe."

No mention of his father being safe, but Matty could only do so much. His mind churned. He could tell this guy the address his father had given him. That might solve his first problem. Maybe Robert, or whatever his real name was, would let him go. But then what? Robert would find out Matty had never delivered the package and be right back at his doorstep. And Matty's father would find out Matty had betrayed him.

He had to talk to his father, find out what to do. So, all he could do was stall.

"I haven't delivered it yet, but I don't have it, either. I have to get it. When I do, then I'll give it to you."

The man's eyebrows rose. "Will you?"

"I..." He swallowed. Would he deliver it to this guy? Protect his mother, but betray his father? There was no way out of this, no way to keep all the people he loved safe. But this was his father's doing. Right now, Matty just had to get out of the SUV. Then he'd figure out what to do. Dad would figure a way out. "Yes. I'll deliver it to you, as soon as I get it."

"And where is it now?"

"That's a long story. I'm not exactly sure."

"You have *lost* it?"

"No. Not exactly. It's just...I know where it is, so—"

"Tell me where it is, and this will all be over."

Over. He'd take that—if only he could. "I can't."

Robert sighed, looked at the man in the front seat, who continued to stare straight ahead. Finally, Robert turned back to him. "I am frustrated that you will not tell me where it is. You say you'll hand it over, but yet you stall. Why?"

"I'm telling you the truth. As soon as I get it, I'll hand it over." Unless Dad had a better idea for him.

"And what assurances can you give me?"

"You know who I am. You know where I live. It's not like I'm going to make my family relocate to...to Canada or whatever."

"Ah, yes. I would find you in Canada."

Matty swallowed. "Well anyway, I'm like, seventeen. So I don't have that kind of power over my mom."

"In my country, you would be a man, and you would have the power."

"I am..." He let the words trail off. He didn't feel like a man. He felt like a little boy, and all he wanted was to crawl into his mother's lap. Except she wouldn't have a solution to this, either.

"I'll get you the package as soon as I have it."

"Give me your phone."

Matty considered refusing, but in the end, he unlocked it and handed it over. Maybe this guy wouldn't hurt him. Maybe he would. Matty didn't feel like finding out.

The man pressed the screen. Matty couldn't see what he was doing, but it took a minute, maybe two. "Ah, yes..." he said. "Your phone is different from mine. Here we are." Another phone rang, and Robert pulled it out and silenced it. When he handed it back, he said, "I have saved my number as Robert Jones. If I call you, I expect you to answer me. I will need updates. You understand?"

Great. One more person riding him. "Yes."

"If you need assistance in retrieving the package, you would be wise to call me. Do not contact your father's friends. They are unsavory people. Can you agree to that?"

He didn't even know those people, didn't have a phone number or a name. Seemed a no-brainer. "Yes."

"Do not contact the authorities. That will only complicate matters for all of us, and I'm sure you don't want your father to go to prison because of his activities."

Prison. Matty didn't want to think about it.

"Contact me and me only as soon as you have the package. And do it quickly. We need to have it by tomorrow at noon."

Matty swallowed. Tomorrow was Monday. Surely Aiden and his father would be home by then. "Okay. Robert Jones. Is that your real name?"

The man smiled, showing those white teeth again. "It is not."

He climbed out of the SUV and held the door open. "Have a nice day, Matthew."

Matty stepped out, grabbed his bike, and pushed it toward his driveway, wondering why Robert hadn't told him not to contact his father. For some reason, the thought brought no comfort.

ELEVEN

Garrison ended the call and sat at the patio table. He hadn't been offered a solution, hadn't been given any guarantees, but the guy he'd spoken to, Reed, understood what Aiden was facing. He'd walked the path before and knew the steps Garrison needed to take.

He felt a little guilty for his first reaction when Sam had told him she'd done research for him—that flash of irritation he'd had to hide because he hated it when people thought he needed help, that he couldn't manage all by himself. But could he, really? He never would have found Reed's number. He'd still be surfing the internet aimlessly.

The guy had given him answers, a lifesaver in the middle of a stormy sea. The waves were still roiling, the thunder still booming, but now he had something to hang onto.

Sam knocked twice on the door. He motioned for her to join him on the patio, and she pushed the door open and sat beside him at the table.

"I saw you were off the phone."

He took her hand and squeezed. "Thank you. You have no idea what a relief it is to talk to someone who can tell me what to do."

"So that guy—?"

"He was addicted to painkillers, like Aiden. But much worse. Like twenty or more pills a day for years. And then he got arrested, lost his family, lost everything. Totally hit bottom. And you know what he said about hitting bottom? He said, 'It's good to hit bottom. That's where the solid ground is.' Can you imagine?"

She nodded. The blue skies and bright trees reflected in her eyes. "That's a great way to look at it."

"He told me about a few rehab centers in New England. We talked about where Aiden would do better, near here or closer to home, and he agrees that Aiden might be better off farther from home. That knowing there's no way a friend is going to come pick him up can help him mentally be where he is and do what he needs to do."

"That makes sense. It looks like he gave you some hope."

Garrison started to agree, then tempered his words. "He also told me the relapse rate is really high. When I asked for a percentage, he wouldn't give me one. Said it would only depress me. I did enough research..." He paused and thought about whether he should just say it. Then he sighed and continued. "When I was hoping to get his mother help, I learned enough. I know most relapse eventually."

"Your son isn't a statistic, he's a person, and if he wants to be sober, if he does what he's supposed to do, then he'll be sober, and the numbers won't matter at all."

Garrison stared out at the lake, which was buzzing with activity. Happy families. Or maybe they just looked that way from afar. Maybe they all had their problems, too, and they'd put them away for one day to enjoy each other.

Sam was right. Aiden wasn't a statistic. If he got clean, it would be his choice. Garrison could force him into rehab now, but he'd be eighteen in January. Then he'd be able to make his own decisions. He could choose to clean up, to finish school and go to college, or he could choose to be an addict.

The thought of it made Garrison sick to his stomach. His son, his only child, lost to drugs. Maybe lost forever.

Not if he could help it.

"So did he have some recommendations for you?"

Garrison dragged his gaze away from the water. After a moment, her question registered. "He gave me the names of ten places he thought I should research."

"It's good to have a starting point. Maybe I can help."

He was about to refuse, but he remembered her ability to find stuff online. She'd found him, hadn't she, despite his unlisted number? And thank God she had. He'd helped Marisa and Nate search for her missing daughter. Not that he was taking credit for finding her—they'd done that all their own. But if Sam hadn't found his number, he'd never have met her. "If you have nothing better to do. Maybe if we find a few places today, Aiden and I can go see one tomorrow..."

The back door opened, and Aiden stepped out. He and Sam shared a look he couldn't read. Something between the two of them. Interesting.

Aiden turned his attention to his father. "Um, can I talk to you?"

"Have a seat."

Sam stood. "I should probably..."

"You don't have to leave," Aiden said.

Garrison turned to his son, shocked the words had come from him.

"I mean, I don't care if you stay. I'm just gonna talk to Dad for a minute, and then I'm going back to bed. I feel like sh...uh, crap."

"I'll just wait inside, then."

"It's okay. Really."

She sat back down, though Garrison could tell she wanted to go in. Well, he didn't blame her. Who would choose to get involved in this mess?

Aiden looked at her again, then back at Garrison. There was definitely something going on there. So, had Aiden asked her to stay because he thought she'd be an ally, or had he hoped to ingratiate himself with his father? And no, Garrison didn't believe for a second Aiden had done it out of the goodness of his heart.

Reed's words from the conversation just moments before came back to him. *Addicts are all liars and manipulators. He's gotten away with this so far because he's good at it. If you love him, if you want the best for him, you won't trust anything he tells you.*

Garrison hated the suspicion, but he'd need to hang onto it if he was going to help his son. And that meant not taking anything at face value.

"Go ahead, son."

"So... I just wanted to tell you how sorry I am. I like...I get how hard it must have been for you when you got the phone call on Friday. That I'd been taken to the hospital and... I get that it scared you. And it's probably, like, even more embarrassing for you than for somebody else, 'cause you're like an FBI agent, so you fight crime, and now your son's a total loser."

Garrison grasped Aiden's arm. "You are not a loser. Don't talk about my son that way."

Aiden's eyes filled with tears. So maybe he was sincere, at least a little. Still... Aiden must want something.

"And you are not an embarrassment to me," Garrison continued. "You're my son, and I love you, and I'm proud of you. A few bad choices do not a life make."

Aiden swallowed, sniffed, and nodded. "Anyway, I just wanted you to know that I get it, and I'm sorry. And like... I love you."

Garrison wrapped Aiden in a hug. Maybe the kid hadn't started sincere, but those words sure sounded like he meant them.

He took his seat again. Aiden remained standing.

Sam wiped her eyes.

The suspicion seeped back in. Why had Aiden asked her to

stay? Not that he was complaining—he wanted her there, too. But why did Aiden?

"I feel like I'm gonna be sick," Aiden said. "I'm going back to bed."

He turned, nodded to Sam, and went inside.

When the door closed, Garrison looked at Sam and lifted his eyebrows.

"I might have suggested he apologize to you."

"You two talked?"

"He helped me with the groceries." She blinked twice, looked beyond him, and went very still. "Then I bumped into him in the hall."

He considered what he'd just seen. There were downsides to being a trained interrogator. He thought about some of his techniques. He could get her talking about something else, see if the nonverbals went back to normal, and then return to the subject of Aiden and see if those clues returned. He could keep questioning her, wear her down. She wouldn't last three minutes in a real interrogation. Too honest. That was her problem. She had no experience with withholding the truth.

Of course, even if she'd been a trained liar, he'd have picked up on it.

Not that he had with his son. Apparently Garrison had a blind spot there.

"Here's the problem," he said. "Something about what you just told me wasn't the truth."

Her shoulders slumped. "I didn't lie. I just didn't tell you everything."

"Why?"

"I don't want to. So I'd prefer you didn't ask."

He opened his mouth, closed it again.

"Look, ask him, okay?" she said. "I'm happy to be here, but I'm not getting between you two."

He made eye contact, held her gaze. She didn't flinch.

He blew out a breath. "Should I be worried?"

"If I told you not to, would it help?"

"Good point."

He didn't like it, but he wouldn't push it.

"So," she said, "shall we get our laptops and start researching?"

He wiped the back of his hand across his sweating forehead. "Inside."

"Agreed."

They sat at the kitchen table and each took half the list of rehab centers. They read, talked, and compared until Garrison's stomach growled a couple hours later.

"Did you say you went to the grocery store?" he asked.

She shrugged. "I picked up a couple of things. Thought you wouldn't want to go out today."

He stood, kissed the top of her head, and walked to the fridge.

He was halfway there before he realized what he'd done. He'd kissed her for the first time. Okay, not on the lips, though he was thinking about it now.

He wouldn't turn to see her reaction. Nope, he'd act like it was the most natural thing in the world that he'd just kissed her.

He looked in the fridge, saw steak and ground beef. His mouth watered. "Remember that list of hot chicks in New Hampshire?"

"I remember I was on top."

"You've just blown the list away." He turned, smiled. "Really, I can't tell you how much I appreciate it. How much do I owe you?"

She waved him off. "Don't worry about it."

"You need to let me pay for the groceries." And the house, but he wouldn't bring that up again just yet.

"Fine." She pulled a receipt out of her pocket and slapped it on the table.

"You're mad?"

"I like doing things for people," she said. "I don't like it when people don't let me."

"Like you haven't done enough already."

She nodded to the fridge, which was still standing open. "It's a little early for dinner."

He grabbed a hunk of cheddar and a knife, snatched the crackers, and returned to the table. "This'll hold me over."

She chuckled. "Men. Bottomless pits."

"And proud of it." He sliced a hunk of cheese and offered it to her. After she rejected it, he popped it in his mouth. Good stuff. "I like this place I've been looking at. It's in Vermont, though. Kind of far. How about you?"

"This one looks good, too. It's the place my friends sent their son, the place I told you about earlier. It's not far from here, maybe forty-five minutes." She told him what she'd learned, and he agreed—it did sound good.

"We can check it out tomorrow," Garrison said.

"Good idea. You should call, tell them you're coming."

His knife paused mid-slice. He met her eyes. It's not like he needed her, but having her around seemed to help him stay sane, stay focused. She was good at asking the right questions. And she'd been with him to this point. So no, he didn't need her help, but he'd sure like to have it. "I'd love it if you'd come with us."

The question had seemed so innocent. So why did the color drain from her face? At least he wasn't surprised by her response. "I'm sorry. I can't."

TWELVE

Sam tried not to meet Garrison's eyes. The man was far too observant, but it wasn't as though she'd lied.

She couldn't go to the rehab center with them. Their visit was about Aiden, not about her. She'd only be a burden. The problem was, how could she convince him of that without telling him the truth?

She chanced a glance in his direction, saw that he was studying her, and focused on her computer screen. "There's another place here, if you don't like that one. It looks good."

When he didn't say anything, she looked at him again, saw his lips closed in a tight line.

"Not that it's my business," he said, "but do you have other plans?"

She could lie, except he'd know. Considering how long she'd kept this secret, she'd never outright lied, and she wouldn't lie to protect herself now, either.

"Not exactly."

"You don't want to tell me."

He'd phrased it as a statement, not a question. He could tell something was wrong. What should she do? Pretend she wasn't going with them because she didn't want to? But that would be a lie, too. Even with all the tension in this house, she wanted to be here. And not just as support—though there was that. No, she wanted to be here because she cared about this man, and she cared about his son. There was nowhere she'd rather be.

Well, except maybe not as the subject of Garrison's scrutiny.

She sighed and faced him. "I have stuff to do." His steady gaze made her squirm. "Work stuff. You know."

He nodded once, slowly. "Okay. That's fine. It's not like it'll be a fun trip."

"I wish...I do want to go."

He lifted those expressive eyebrows again.

She didn't want to tell him the truth. They'd been getting so close, and what would he think of her? Probably that she needed medication. Therapy. She should go to some inpatient facility, too. And wouldn't that be fun for him, to have both Aiden and her in an institution? Except he'd support Aiden. Why would he bother with her? Why would anybody?

She closed her eyes. Her faith had convinced her she was worthy of love and, most of the time, she believed that. She was valuable and precious, a child of God. Even if she felt like someone's idiot cousin.

Garrison hadn't treated her that way, though. He'd liked her, from the start, and he still liked her enough to invite her into his tragedy, to share his darkest moments with her.

And here she was, holding back.

She swallowed, prayed for help, for words, and opened her eyes.

He was watching her. Of course he was. His expression looked...guarded. And maybe a little hurt.

"I have this problem." Her hands shook. Her stomach churned. She crossed her arms. "I have some anxiety issues."

He waited for her to continue, but she was scrambling to find the right words, a way to say this without sounding like the nutcase she obviously was.

He ran his hands over his short hair. "So, going with us will cause you anxiety?"

"Not being with you. That's fine. It's the...going."

"What do you mean?"

"It's better than it used to be. I'm working through it. For a while, I didn't like to leave my house. And now I can go all over Nutfield. And there are even some places in Epping..."

She let her voice trail off. She could see by the way his eyes widened that he was shocked enough. What would he say if he heard the rest of it?

"What do they call that? Agoraphobia?"

She nodded. For some reason, the label bothered her. Stupid, she knew. She and her counselor had beaten that horse to death, but Sam knew what her problem with the label was—pride. Who wanted to be labeled with anything? Wasn't she more than just an agoraphobic? She was a real estate investor and landlord and decorator and home remodeler. She was a Christian, a daughter, a sister, a friend. She didn't want to be defined by her mental illness.

And what was the solution? Overcome it.

She was trying. She'd made strides. Years before, she hadn't wanted to leave her house. But she'd forced herself to get help. And now, look at all she could do.

Garrison took her hand. "I'm sorry. All those times I tried to talk you into coming to Long Island to see me."

"You didn't know. I should have been honest with you."

He squeezed her hand. "I just thought you didn't like me as much as I liked you."

"Oh." Heat rose to her cheeks. "I did. Do. But..." Her words were all jumbled. He had liked her, but did he still? Did he, now that he knew she was crazy?

She could hear Marlene's voice in her head. Her counselor would say, *You're not crazy. You're just imperfect, like the rest of us.*

Easy for Marlene to say. She'd never freaked out and thought she was having a heart attack during a trip to the mall. She'd never been rushed to the hospital thinking she was dying only to be told she had an anxiety disorder.

After that episode, Sam had vowed she'd never put herself in that position again. She'd kept that promise, and she'd managed to hide her fears. Most people had no idea she had a problem. The mask she'd worn looked so normal, so healthy.

And now Garrison knew the truth.

"You seem confident," Garrison said. "And you're obviously able to go a lot of places, or else how would you be able to do all you do?"

She kept her gaze on the computer screen in front of her. "I've been working on it. I've gotten to where I can go anyplace in Nutfield. And to the Walmart in Epping, as long as I go when it's not crowded. And there's a Lowe's there. There are some furniture stores not too far. When I need something I can't buy nearby, I just order it online."

"So... It's not that bad, really. If you *have* to go somewhere—"

"My contractor went with me to a lot of those places the first few times. I told him the truth from the start, and he's been very helpful."

Garrison frowned and let go of her hand. "So glad to hear you have someone you can rely on."

His tone sounded anything but glad. She realized with a little jolt that he was jealous. She couldn't help the smile. "My contractor's in his seventies. He reminds me of my grandfather."

Garrison blew out a breath. "Oh, good. I was picturing one of those guys from HGTV."

"Older than Bob Villa with a beer gut like a beach ball."

Garrison's laugh filled the room. "That helps. Thanks."

She laughed with him, and relief filled her. She'd told him the truth, and he hadn't run. That was something.

Garrison sliced a piece of cheese, paired it with a cracker, and popped it in his mouth. He watched her while he chewed. When he'd swallowed and sipped his water, he asked, "So how come you trust your contractor to take you places, but you don't trust me?"

"It's not that. What if I have an anxiety attack? You and Aiden don't want to deal with that. You need to focus on him, not worry about me."

"Does it happen often, these anxiety attacks?"

She knew what he would say if she told him. "They can happen at any time."

"That's not what I asked."

"I have no control over them. They just come on like...like a hurricane. Except you can see those coming. More like an earthquake."

"And when was the last time you experienced one of those earthquakes?"

She sighed. "It's been a while."

"Define *a while*."

"Years. It's been years, but that's because I'm careful."

"When you went to Epping with your contractor?"

She shook her head. "It was fine. But I felt safe because he was with me."

"I see."

She grabbed his hand. "Not that I wouldn't feel safe with you. That's not at all what I meant."

"Right."

"But it's not worth the risk."

His nod was slow, like he was just figuring something out. He shifted away from her, focused on the screen again. "I understand."

She thought back, realized how her words must have sounded. "Not worth it for *you* to take the risk that I might freak out in front of Aiden and ruin your time together. I would take the risk." She touched the back of his hand. "I would take the risk for you. But—"

"You're saying you would come, but you don't want to embarrass us. Is that it?"

"Exactly."

"Then it's settled. You'll come."

No. No, she couldn't. She'd lose it and embarrass herself and Garrison and Aiden. This would be hard enough for them. She didn't need to add to the awkwardness by having a panic attack. What would Garrison think when he saw it? What would Aiden think?

Aiden was the answer.

"Okay." She pushed back in her chair, too antsy to sit. "Okay, I'll go with you, but only after we ask Aiden and explain my condition to him. If he's on board with taking a crazy person along, then I'll go."

THIRTEEN

Garrison studied Aiden as he came into the kitchen late Sunday afternoon. He seemed better. After sleeping all day, again, the color had come back to his cheeks. Maybe the detox process was ending.

"How you feeling?"

Aiden shrugged, looked at their laptops on the kitchen table, and smiled. "You guys playing *World of Warcraft* or something?"

Garrison glanced at Sam, who looked perplexed. His chuckle felt good. "It's a computer game."

"Oh," she said. "I've heard of it. But I didn't know..."

Aiden shook his head, nearly smiled.

Garrison stretched. They'd been sitting too long. "Let's get out of here." He turned to Sam. "Isn't there a beach nearby?"

"It's about a five-minute walk."

"I don't remember packing my swim trunks," Aiden said.

Garrison had packed for him, but he doubted Aiden remembered any of that. "I got them. If we had a Frisbee—"

"I think there's one here." Sam brushed past Aiden and disappeared into the other room.

Aiden opened the fridge, grabbed a Pepsi, and stared at the shelves.

Garrison said, "You hungry?"

"Yeah, actually."

"That's good." He wanted to say it was a good sign, a sign his son was recovering from the drugs, a sign they could move on. But he kept his mouth shut.

"Steaks look good," Aiden said. "She got T-bones."

"Our favorite."

"How did she know?" Aiden turned and regarded his father.

Garrison wondered what information his son was searching for there. "Good guess, maybe."

"Hmm."

Like he didn't believe him.

"You know, she and I are just friends."

"That's what she said." Aiden opened the can and poured the soda into his mouth.

No need to argue the point. Either Aiden would believe him or not. He and Sam knew the truth. Just friends. Friends who wanted to be more. But between Aiden's addiction and Sam's issues, maybe *more* wasn't meant to be.

Maybe not right now. But maybe someday. He wouldn't give up.

Maybe she wouldn't either.

Aiden sat, and Garrison took his place at the fridge. Steaks, salad, ranch dressing. He looked in the cupboard where she'd stored food earlier and found two big baking potatoes. Apparently she'd not planned to stay. Well, they could share.

He turned on the oven, washed the potatoes, and wrapped them in foil he found in a drawer. He was popping them in the oven when Sam returned.

"Found it." She held up a faded red Frisbee. "I remembered some old beach stuff in the closet in the hall."

"Excellent." Garrison turned to Aiden. "Get changed. We're going to the beach."

The kid sighed, but his lips twitched like he wanted to smile. Garrison would take it.

He turned, regarded Sam's pretty sandals. "Those won't get ruined, will they?"

"Oh. I thought I'd just head home."

"No. You have to join us. We have a good hour and a half before the potatoes will be ready. We'll hang out down there, then come back here and grill."

Her gaze flicked to Aiden, back to him, then to the floor. "I don't want to intrude."

"It's fine," Aiden said. "We want you to join us."

Sam looked up, surprise in her eyes. "You're sure?"

Aiden shrugged. "You bought 'em. You ought to eat 'em."

Whatever Aiden's motivation, he was being awfully cooperative. More than he'd been in a long time.

Garrison probably should have sent Sam home. He needed to spend time alone with his son, but Sam's presence was calming, and with her there, Garrison and Aiden got along better than they had in a long time. Maybe it was the circumstances. But maybe it was Sam herself.

They changed, locked up the cabin, and walked along the road side by side, only moving to single file when a car drove by. Very little traffic at this hour on a Sunday. Most of the folks who were heading back to their homes had probably left already, and the rest were likely settled for the afternoon and evening. Tree limbs hung over the road, and sunlight filtered through and danced on the gravel as a breeze rustled the leaves. The cabins on their left were near the lake, like the one he and Aiden were staying in, so they were hardly visible through the trees.

"These are the oldest cabins on Clearwater Lake," Sam said. "A couple were built in the fifties, but most were built in the late sixties, early seventies."

"Have some been updated?" Garrison tried to imagine fifties-era cabins and what they would look like. He could almost hear the slamming of screen doors, see the huge ovens and vintage Frigidaires.

"Some have," she said. "Not yours, obviously. It's still vintage sixties. But I'll fix that this winter."

Aiden looked across his father to Sam. "What are you going to do to it?"

She smiled at him. "I'm not sure yet. You have any ideas?"

He looked forward, narrowed his eyes. "I think the wall between the kitchen and the living room should come down. And you should put an island there with barstools so it's all one big room."

Garrison looked for Sam's reaction and wasn't disappointed by her wide smile. "That's exactly what I was thinking."

His son's eyes lit. "Yeah?"

"But I'm trying to figure out what to do with the back wall. Those little windows don't cut it—"

"Not with that awesome view."

Garrison shifted so they could walk beside each other, and so he could watch them both without acting like a spectator at a tennis match.

Sam said, "Maybe a bay window in front of the kitchen table, sliding glass doors."

"Could you just make the whole wall windows?" Aiden looked forward, thought for a moment. "Obviously the fireplace is the focal point, but on either side, what if it were all windows? Or maybe doors on both sides, then windows going to the ceiling."

She laughed. "That's a great idea. Might be out of my budget, but if I were going to live in it—"

"You should. It could be an awesome house."

"I agree. Great bones. Sort of small, though, with only two bedrooms."

By the time they reached the beach, Aiden and Sam had mentally remodeled the entire cabin, and Garrison had gained a new appreciation for his son. He'd known Aiden was good at art, but he'd had no idea about his interest in remodeling. Maybe Aiden hadn't realized it, either.

It struck him, amazed him, really, how purely unique Aiden was from himself and Charlene. Somehow they'd created this beautiful, talented human being who looked a little like him and a little like her but was utterly himself, utterly different and apart from them. Aiden had gifts they didn't have, talents neither of them could comprehend. He was so... separate. And yet, still that same child Charlene had carried, the one Garrison had held and rocked and taught to throw a ball.

Aiden walked to the water, took off his flip-flops, and waded in. He turned and yelled, "Cold." He ran back to where they stood on the sandy beach. "Not like the ocean, though. We can handle it."

"I need to get good and hot first," Garrison readied the Frisbee. "Go long."

Aiden jogged to the far side of the beach, and Garrison let the Frisbee sail. Aiden dove to catch it, rolled, and stood. "Your aim's off," he called.

"You're just slow." Garrison ran to catch the Frisbee. It sailed past him. When he grabbed it, he looked for Sam, saw her sitting at the picnic table.

"You're not playing?"

"I catch as well as I throw. Which is to say, not well."

"Your loss." He sailed the Frisbee to his son, hyper-aware of Sam watching. Whenever he glanced over, he'd see her smiling as if she were having the best time in the world.

The beach was empty, but the sun was still hot, and soon Garrison dripped with sweat. He caught the Frisbee, bent at the waist, and tried to catch his breath.

"You done, old man?"

He stood to find his son just a few yards away. "Old man? I'll give you old man."

He dropped the Frisbee and launched himself toward Aiden, but of course the teen was quicker. They raced to the water, where Aiden slowed, probably thinking Garrison had given up the chase. Not a chance.

He tackled his son, sent them both sailing into the cold lake. They came up laughing. Aiden splashed him, and he splashed back, until they were both howling with laughter. They raced to a floating dock, then climbed up and jumped off a few times before racing back to the beach.

This was what it was supposed to be like. Laughter and games and play. Not drugs and hospitals and rehab.

The thought killed his fun.

He checked his watch. "You hungry?"

Aiden splashed him one last time for good measure. "Starving."

When they turned to the beach, Garrison realized Sam had left. His heart sank, but he didn't let on to Aiden. "We forgot towels."

"Brilliant, Dad."

"Hey, you forgot them, too."

"Whatever."

And just like that, they were back to their familiar pattern.

A breeze kicked up, felt cold on his wet skin. "By the time we reach the cabin, we'll be dry. Grab your shoes."

They'd almost made it to the road when Sam returned, towels under her arms as she rushed down the road. "Sorry. I didn't want to interrupt."

They took the towels and dried off. "Thanks," Garrison said.

"Yeah," Aiden added. "It's cold in the shade."

"Especially if you're wet," Garrison said, hoping to get back some of the camaraderie he and his son had shared.

Aiden ignored him and headed back to the cabin.

GARRISON WAS quiet as he prepared the steaks for dinner. Sam glanced at him with raised brows, but at least she didn't ask what was wrong. What would he say? Their trip to the lake had been ruined because he'd forgotten towels? It sounded so stupid. It was stupid. How was this his life?

Life with a teenager. An angry teenager. An addicted teenager.

He stepped outside to start the grill. He'd hoped to do this with Aiden by his side, but the kid had disappeared into his bedroom as soon as they'd gotten home. Fine. Garrison would make dinner, and Aiden could do the dishes after. Time the kid started helping out. He'd learned to pull his weight at home, and he could darn well do the same here.

He got the grill to the right temperature and set the T-bones on it. He closed the lid, decided he'd set the table. When he opened the door, he found Aiden had already laid out placemats and dishes and was gathering silverware.

He must've looked dumbfounded because Sam said, "Aiden offered to help."

"Oh. That's... thanks, son."

Aiden shrugged and started laying the utensils on the table.

Garrison met Sam's eyes, and she smiled.

Well, something had happened. He wouldn't complain. He stepped back outside to check the steaks and give them more time together. Sam was definitely a good influence on Aiden.

By the time the steaks were finished, Aiden's dark mood had lifted. He spent the meal recounting funny tales from his childhood for Sam, who was laughing so hard by the end that tears ran down her cheeks.

"Sounds like you were a holy terror."

"Nah," Aiden said. "Just a normal kid."

"Normal?" she asked. "My brother was nuts, but he never climbed on the roof in a costume to scare little children on Halloween."

"It was hilarious when that one kid peed his pants."

Garrison shook his head. "Hilarious for you. I spent ten minutes apologizing to the kid's mother."

Aiden's laughter faded, slightly. "Yeah, I guess it wasn't funny for the kid."

Sam wiped her cheeks. "Makes a good story, though."

The boy's smile was wider than Garrison had seen it in years. "Oh, we're full of stories. Dad, tell her about the time you decided to bake me a birthday cake."

Garrison remembered the lopsided cake, the batter he'd somehow managed to get on the ceiling. "Let's save some stories for another time."

Aiden agreed, started clearing the table without being asked.

Wow. Garrison looked at his son, looked at Sam's smiling face. This fresh attitude his son was wearing—that was Sam's doing. And he thought Aiden knew it, too.

"So, kiddo," Garrison said.

Aiden set the plates in the sink and started the water. "Yeah."

"Why don't you leave the dishes for a minute? I'd like to talk to you."

Sam pushed back in her chair. "It's time for me to go."

Garrison grabbed her hand, needed her presence. She was like the soft center of a Nutter Butter, keeping the cookies from crushing each other. "Please stay."

She looked at Aiden, who said, "I don't mind," as he returned to his seat.

She seemed uncertain.

Aiden said, "It's not like you don't know everything, anyway, right?"

"Um." She looked at Garrison for help.

"It's fine. Dad's allowed to have friends."

Wow. Every once in a while, the kid surprised him. He focused on Aiden. "We need to talk about rehab."

The boy sat back, crossed his arms.

Sam started to leave again. "Really, I should—"

"You don't have to," Aiden said. "It seems... It's better when you're here."

Yup, Aiden saw it, too.

"Okay." She pulled her chair toward the table again, folded her hands.

"What do you think?" Garrison asked him.

"Does it matter?"

"It matters what you want, of course," Garrison said. "Not that you'll be able to make the final decision by yourself. But together, I think we can do this."

"Mom wouldn't make me go to rehab."

"It's not your mom's decision, Aiden."

"She has rights, too."

Garrison thought about his response, felt like every word might be weighed on some big scale someday—words that helped versus words that harmed. If there were more of the second, would his son be lost forever?

Nope. Wouldn't think about that. "I'd prefer you go voluntarily."

Aiden slumped in his chair, the posture of defeat. Maybe defeat was good. Maybe defeat was the first step—because his son had been defeated, not by Garrison, but by drugs.

When Aiden said nothing, Garrison tried a new tactic. "Would you say you've felt good these last two days?"

"I don't know. I guess not."

"You've been sick. And you know why?"

Aiden didn't answer, but of course he knew.

Garrison said it anyway. "You've been sick because your body is detoxing from painkillers. Right?"

"I guess."

"Which means you've been taking a lot of them. Enough to cause you to need them, right?"

No answer.

"Have you been craving them?"

Another shrug.

"Has it been hard?"

"What do you want me to say?"

Garrison resisted the urge to sigh. "If we take all that information—the fact that you've been in withdrawal, the fact that you're craving drugs, the fact that you've used enough to cause you to feel sick—we have to come to the conclusion that you have a problem. Do you agree?"

"I just... I can quit on my own. I don't want to go to rehab. Like, how would that even work? School starts in a month. Would I be done in time?"

Garrison met Sam's eyes. Based on everything they'd read that day, Aiden wouldn't be home in time for the first day of his senior year. But getting him healthy was more important than getting him through school. First things first.

"We'll have to see what the experts recommend," Garrison said.

"Isn't that what you two were doing all day?"

"Only so much we can find out online. Tomorrow, we're going to see one of the places we found. We'll go early, maybe be back in time to hit the lake in the afternoon." He looked at Sam. "If that's okay with you."

"You're welcome to the boat whenever you want it."

He looked at his son. "What do you say? We can do it together."

Aiden looked at his father, then at Sam. "Are you coming?"

"Um..."

"If you want her to," Garrison said.

"But you should know..." Sam's voice shook. She was obviously uncomfortable sharing her secret, and here she was telling a second person in one day. "I have an anxiety disorder so sometimes I get these panic attacks."

Aiden sat up straighter. "What do you mean?"

"The first time, I thought I was having a heart attack. I tend to stay close to home, to avoid certain situations, to keep from having them."

"Weird. It happens a lot?"

"It's been a while."

Aiden said, "So do you want to come with us?"

"Only if you think I can help."

He looked at Garrison. "Okay, fine. I'll go. Sam can come. But on one condition."

Here it came, the reason for Aiden's good attitude, for his kindness toward Sam, for his willingness to go. Garrison braced himself.

"Can I please have my phone back?"

He blew out a breath. Thought a minute. Nodded. "Tomorrow, when we're in the car, you can use your phone for a little while. But I'll be reading your texts and listening to your phone calls. I don't think you need to have unfettered access to your friends."

"So like, I can't have any privacy?"

"You've had enough to get yourself into serious trouble. I've given you a lot of freedom, and you've used it poorly. Now, we have to back off, start fresh. I know it doesn't seem fair."

"It's not fair."

"Life isn't fair, kiddo. Get used to it."

Aiden looked like he might argue, then glanced at Sam, who held his gaze. He looked back at Garrison. "Okay, fine. Deal."

FOURTEEN

Monday morning about three seconds after his mother left for work, Matty hopped on his bike and headed for Aiden's house. It was really humid but cool, so his skin felt chilly in the breeze.

Maybe Aiden and his dad had come home late the night before. Mr. Kopp had to work. Aiden had to work. It wasn't like they'd had a vacation planned or anything, and they hadn't been getting along lately. Obviously, they'd get sick of each other and want to come home.

As he rode, Matty kept telling himself all the reasons why it made sense that Aiden and his dad would be there. He'd talked himself into it, so that when he turned the corner on their street, he totally expected to see the Camry parked in the driveway.

But the driveway was empty.

For good measure, Matty knocked on the door—not that he hadn't done that a thousand times in the last two days. He rang the doorbell and even peeked in the windows. The house looked deserted.

Matty was screwed.

He sat on the front porch steps and considered his options. They all sucked.

He'd called his father about a thousand times since Robert

had left him at the curb the day before, but Dad wasn't answering. Something was wrong. Dad should have been calling him, texting him, nagging him to get the package delivered. Instead, he'd gone dark.

Gone dark. Like he was Jason friggin' Bourne.

Matty didn't want to think about what it might mean. That Robert's people had gotten to his father. They knew where he'd flown the other night, so it wouldn't have been that difficult. They'd figured out who Matty was—probably ran his license plates after the scene at the airport. They must have had some connections. Would those connections have told him where in the Bahamas Dad was staying? Were these the types of people who killed their enemies? Robert had said he worked for the government, but that didn't mean he was a good guy, right?

Matty had done just enough research on the Democratic Republic of the Congo to know their government wasn't all that stable. There'd been some civil war a few years back, and lots of refugees had gone there from other wars in Africa, and there was unrest all over the country. Even if Robert was a government agent or whatever, who knew what kind of guy he was.

But if Matty didn't hear from his father, he'd have to turn the package over to Robert. He wasn't going to risk Mom and Jimmy's safety to protect Dad.

All that was assuming he ever got the package back.

Another thought occurred to him. He could just tell Robert where the package was. The man could probably figure out Mr. Kopp's location somehow, or maybe get his government to contact the U.S. government, and have them call. Maybe it could all be, like, official or whatever. Assuming Robert was who he said he was.

Except Robert had said not to contact the authorities. That meant he wouldn't, either.

Who was to say Robert wouldn't just find Aiden and Mr. Kopp, kill them both, and take what he wanted?

No way Matty would drag two more people he cared about into this mess. He'd have to get the package back himself.

Matty was nearly home when his phone rang. Probably his brother wondering where he was. He pulled it from his pocket, looked at the number, and nearly crashed his bike. He managed to stop and connected the call. "Where have you been?"

"We left town for a few days." Aiden's voice sounded stronger than it had in a long time. "My dad took my phone. What's up with you? It looks like you called me a bunch—"

"When are you going to be home?"

"I don't know, man. A few days probably. It's like... There's stuff going on. Dad wants me to consider some rehab places."

Rehab? Was it that bad? Matty felt a sharp pang of guilt. He was the one who'd introduced Aiden to drugs in the first place. Matty'd tried them, never cared for the feeling of being out of control. But Aiden had loved them from the very start. And now...rehab.

"That sucks," he said because he didn't know what else to say. And right now, he couldn't think about his friend's problems, not with his neck on the line. "Where are you?"

Matty heard Mr. Kopp's voice in the background. "I'd rather you not tell him where we are."

So, wait. Mr. Kopp could hear Matty through the phone? That wasn't good.

Aiden said, "My dad doesn't want me to tell you."

Matty lowered his voice. "Dude, I'm in trouble. Can your dad hear me?"

A pause, then, "I don't think so, not right now."

"I need you to come home. Or tell me where you are so I can come to you."

"No can do. We're not even in New York."

Matty swore loudly, and Mr. Kopp said, "Nice language."

Crap, crap, crap.

"Look." He kept his voice at barely a whisper. "A hint. Something. I gotta know where you are."

"Uh, so like we're staying on this lake—"

"Son..." Mr. Kopp's warning tone was clear.

"Geez, Dad. We could be in, like, Wisconsin, the land of a thousand lakes."

"It's Minnesota," Mr. Kopp said. "And it's ten thousand."

"See," Aiden said. "Like he's gonna check every lake in freakin' America."

They were arguing about lakes while Matty's whole stupid existence was in danger. And Aiden was right—knowing they were on a lake was about as helpful as knowing they were in a place with trees. He was so screwed. "I'm in trouble. I need you to come home."

"I like... I went to the hospital Friday night. They had to keep me all night, and now..." His voice trailed off.

Frustration had him pounding on his bicycle handle. He finally had his friend on the phone, and he still couldn't get to the package. "I know about that. You're okay now, though, right?"

"Yeah. Now."

"Listen. I need you to talk your dad into coming home, like, today. Like, ASAP."

There was a pause. "Are you hurt?"

He was afraid Mr. Kopp would hear something. He whispered, "I'm in trouble."

Mr. Kopp said, "Is something wrong?"

"His girlfriend and him got into a fight," Aiden said. "He doesn't exactly want you to hear all about it. Can *he* at least have some privacy?"

Matty could hear Mr. Kopp's sigh.

Aiden said, "So, what'd she do?"

Aiden was playing along, but Matty still needed to be cautious. If Mr. Kopp got any indication what was going on, he'd turn the package over to the authorities, like, yesterday. "It's a long story, but I'm just saying, I need you home. Right away. Or I'm in big trouble."

Aiden said, "She can be such a bi—"

"Watch your mouth," Mr. Kopp said.

"Sorry." To Matty he said, "I don't know how I can help."

"I'll tell you when you get here. Just talk your dad into it. Tell him... Tell him you have a school function or something you can't miss."

"I don't think that'll work."

Matty wanted to scream. He couldn't raise his voice above a whisper. "Then send me a pin where you are."

"Yeah, we're like, driving right now, on our way to this rehab place in—"

"I mean it, son," Mr. Kopp said. He raised his voice and said, "No offense, Matty."

Sure, man. None taken. He'd only known them for like a decade, but whatever. "It's serious. Like life-and-death serious. When you get where you're staying, send me a pin, and I'll come there."

"Sounds like your girlfriend's really lost her mind this time. You should dump her for good."

Aiden was assuming the problem was related to Matty's drug dealing. He'd been telling Matty to quit dealing drugs for months, despite the fact that he was Matty's best customer. Too dangerous. Aiden had said it so many times. And Matty had thought it was dangerous. Apparently it was nothing compared to working for his father.

No reason to set Aiden straight right now. If Aiden thought it was related to his dealing, that was fine with Matty. He didn't feel like telling his friend with the great dad how crappy his own was.

"I just have to figure this thing out, and I need your help to do that. Then I'll get out." Matty realized as the words came out that he meant it. This stress, the worry about getting caught, the fear of the people he had to work with—they weren't worth it. And working with his father wasn't, either. The closeness he'd longed for had never materialized. And look what his dad had gotten him into. He'd find another way to make the money he wanted, and if that meant Dad didn't contact him anymore, so be it. "I need your help. Please."

"I hear you, man. I gotta go."

Just like that, Aiden was gone. Matty was no closer to the package than he'd been before, but maybe Aiden would get his dad to come home. Maybe he'd send his location, and Matty could get to them. The trouble was, none of that was going to happen by noon today.

FIFTEEN

Sam couldn't concentrate on Aiden's end of the conversation with his friend, and after he returned the phone to his father, she couldn't concentrate on Garrison and Aiden's words.

She could feel the band that tethered her to Nutfield stretching, trying to pull her back. Any second it would snap, and then what?

She visualized the paddle balls she and her brother used to play with when they were little, the way the little rubber ball would always come back and bounce off the paddle, until it didn't. Until the rubber band broke, and the ball sailed wildly through the air to smash into whatever was unlucky enough to be in its path.

When her band broke, what would she hit? Who would she damage?

She'd lost her mind, agreeing to this, going to a strange place with two people she hardly knew.

She forced a deep breath, blew it out slowly, counted to ten. Did it again.

Think truth, she told herself. What was true?

She knew Garrison and trusted him. Garrison wouldn't let any harm come to her.

But Aiden was just a kid. It wasn't right that she'd put them in this position, not when they were so stressed already. What a terrible idea this was, her joining them. Why had she let Garrison talk her into it?

Looking between the front seats and out the windshield was a mistake. They were headed over a rickety bridge. She squeezed her eyes closed, imagined the icy waters beneath. The current. The cold. The beautiful numbness at the bottom.

No. She needed to remember the truth. It was summer, so the water wouldn't be icy. And they weren't going into it. She was safe.

The car reached the far side of the bridge, and Sam blew out her breath.

Garrison and Aiden didn't need this. They probably didn't even want her here anymore, and they certainly wouldn't if she freaked out. And what if she did? Then what would happen? Garrison would be horrified, and Aiden? He'd be disgusted.

That's what she was. She was disgusting. Ridiculous. She was like a cartoon character of a crazy person, a person trying hard to pretend to be normal when she was so far from normal.

She could feel her blood pressure rising with each mile.

Truth. She had to focus on truth.

"How you doing back there?" Garrison asked. "You're awfully quiet."

I've lost my mind, thank you. I think it fell out about ten miles back. "I'm okay."

"You're doing great. You want me to pull over for a minute, give you a chance to breathe?"

Such a kind offer. Garrison was kind. He'd protect her, and he'd forgive her if she had an anxiety attack. She'd survive this.

Truth.

She'd debated all the way to the cabin that morning about whether or not she should coach him on how to handle it if she freaked out. It seemed so stupid, but if she did have a panic attack, he needed to be prepared. When she'd arrived and Aiden had run to get his shoes, she'd started to. "If I should happen to, you know, lose my mind—"

"I looked it up last night. What a panic attack looks like, how to handle it. Do you take any medications for it?"

She'd been prescribed some. She pulled an orange bottle from her pocket. "One of these."

"Great. Do they work?"

She hadn't taken one in so long, she couldn't really remember. But she nodded just the same. "I'll take one if I start to panic."

"I'll remind you, if you need me to." Garrison had gone to the trouble to research her condition. That was sweet and sad at the same time. She hated to be so needy, especially now that he needed her.

"So...?" he asked from the front seat.

He'd asked her a question. Right. Did she want to stop? "We're almost there."

He glanced at her in the rearview mirror. "You're a little pale."

"I'm okay." And she was. Sure, her heart rate had picked up, but she wasn't sweating. She wasn't feeling sick. She could do this. It didn't hurt that they weren't going far from home, only to Dover, a town she'd been to many times in her life. Even if it had been years, Dover was familiar.

So far, so good. How she would feel in an unfamiliar environment, she didn't know.

They arrived at the facility and pulled up to the guard station. Garrison explained who they were, and a moment later, the gate opened.

"It's like a prison," Aiden said.

Sam looked at the manicured grounds, the pretty flower beds, the athletic fields across the way. The buildings were mostly one- and two-story, aluminum-sided in different colors, scattered across the place. It looked like a college campus.

Apparently all Aiden saw were the guard and gate.

They pulled in front of the building marked for visitors and parked. This one was longer and two-story. There were a couple of entrances. Beyond the one for visitors was one marked *Infirmary*. She remembered from her research that this place had medical personnel on staff.

Like a hospital. Or maybe like a mental institution. This was the kind of place they'd send her to if she couldn't keep her mind under control. Except mental hospitals probably weren't nearly this nice. She imagined true mental hospitals. Bars on the windows. Angry women manning electronically locked doors. Burly orderlies with syringes of sedatives for the truly crazy ones.

Patients talking to nothing.

Screaming. Padded walls. Shackled wrists.

Her hands shook. Her heart raced. She had to get out.

Garrison opened her door, crouched down to look at her. His eyes narrowed. "You okay?"

She forced in a deep breath and looked around again. A college campus. A small college campus, like a liberal arts school. Nothing scary here. She could do this. She forced another deep breath, blew it out, and nodded.

She took Garrison's hand, let its warmth calm her, and stepped out of the car. A slight breeze caught her hair, lifted it before setting it gently on her shoulders. She picked up a floral scent she couldn't place, the sound of laughter coming from inside one of the buildings, of birds singing in the trees, of the rustle of leaves. Her heart rate was returning to normal. For Garrison, she would do this.

Garrison rested his hand on the small of her back and looked at his son. "Ready, kiddo?"

The boy walked forward, all confidence and swagger. They entered the building and stopped to speak with a receptionist, who asked them to have a seat.

It felt like a hospital waiting room. Smaller, but there were magazines on the tables, a small TV mounted in the corner tuned to a morning show.

Aiden sat on the far side. She'd expected him to cross his arms, maybe slouch a little, but she'd been very wrong about his behavior. He sat up straight, stretched out his legs, and acted like he owned the place. Sam and Garrison had hardly settled when the far door opened and a young man stepped out. He approached Aiden.

"Hey, man. I'm Luke."

Aiden stood and shook his hand. "Aiden."

Oh, my. The boy was behaving like an adult.

Aiden turned to them as they stood. "This is my father, Garrison Kopp, and our friend, Samantha."

Our friend. That sounded nice.

She guessed Luke to be in his mid-twenties. He had light brown curly hair and a slender but fit build.

"You guys follow me. I'm going to give you a tour and answer your questions."

A tour. Her hands started to shake. No. She was okay. This was a drug rehab facility for teen boys, so even if she was crazy, they wouldn't keep her here. She could do this.

If she couldn't do this, well, that'd probably be the end of this...whatever it was with Garrison. Then she could go back to her life as she'd designed it. Considering it was her own design, though, returning to it felt as attractive as a stint in a place like this.

SIXTEEN

Garrison followed Aiden and Sam out of the building and onto the grounds, where Luke pointed out the various buildings. Houses where the young men lived, a building for meetings and classes, another that held a workout room. They peeked through the windows, saw the equipment. Aiden seemed impressed with that.

There was an outdoor area covered with a roof but open on all sides. An empty fireplace sat on the far side, but a few logs lay beside it, as if the summer might turn chilly any minute. And in New Hampshire, it just might. A handful of guys were perched on lawn chairs and at the picnic table smoking cigarettes. Someone said something, and they all laughed.

"They're allowed to smoke?" Garrison asked.

"The adults are, not the kids. If they get caught smoking, they're disciplined. But they manage to do it anyway. Most addicts are addicted to nicotine." Luke stopped at the corner of the next building and turned to face him. "A lot of them vape, but we don't allow vapes on campus. It's impossible to police the vape juice."

Sam must've looked confused, because Luke addressed her. "Vapor cigarettes, like e-cigarettes," he explained.

"Oh," she said.

"They give up one addiction for another?" Garrison asked.

Luke's smile was kind. "The thing is, both will kill you, but nicotine takes a lot longer. And people won't come if they can't smoke."

Garrison wanted to argue, but what did he know about this? What did he know about any of it?

He turned to Aiden, whose gaze was on the guys in the smoking pit. "Do you smoke?"

Aiden turned. "No. I mean, I've tried it, but I don't like it."

"Don't start."

"Don't worry. I won't."

Sure. Why would he worry? The kid had apparently tried everything else, but Garrison was supposed to believe he'd draw the line at cigarettes. He was tempted to look for a mirror, see if he had *idiot* stamped across his forehead.

He glanced at Sam. The smile she offered was tight. He shouldn't have asked her to come. This was no kindness to her. Yet, she seemed to be handling it. If they accomplished nothing else today, maybe the trip would give her the confidence to take the next steps in fighting her personal demons. He wanted to hold her hand, but maybe Aiden's generosity wouldn't go quite that far.

Luke led the way to another of the larger buildings and stopped at the doors. This time, he pushed the door open and gestured them inside.

It was an oversize living room. Three long couches were arranged in a U and faced a giant flat screen TV. Bookshelves filled with books, magazines, and DVDs covered two walls. Chairs had been pushed along the back wall. A game table was surrounded by four chairs, and a deck of cards, a pad of paper, and a pen lay on top.

"This is the rec room," Luke said. "It's empty now 'cause the guys are in class."

"What about those guys smoking?" Aiden asked.

"Probably took a break, but they'll be in class or group counseling until afternoon." He turned to include Garrison and Sam. "The guys hang out here when they have downtime. We're open for visitors on Saturdays and Sundays, and this is one of the few places where they're allowed to come. Follow me." Luke led the way around the corner and into a large dining room. "When the guys first get here, they move into the Phase One housing. Those are like dorms. They have little fridges for water and soda—if they want to bring soda. They can have snacks in their rooms, too, but there are no kitchens. There are two guys to a room, and eight guys share a house and two full baths." He indicated the dining area. "They eat all their meals here." He looked at Aiden. "We have some great cooks. You'll love the food."

"If you say so," Aiden said.

Luke turned to Garrison and Sam. "You two can come on the weekends and join us for lunch anytime you want."

"Sounds great." Garrison glanced at Sam with a smile. She didn't say anything.

Luke led them through another door, where they saw a giant room with another TV and a ping pong table. Luke turned to Aiden. "You play?"

"My dad and I used to."

Before the divorce. Charlene had kept the table because it didn't fit in Garrison's house. He wondered if Aiden ever played anymore.

"You'll have lots of opportunity to play. We have some really good players, too. In the summer, we spend more time on the volleyball court, but once it cools off, the competition moves to this."

"Great," Aiden said with forced enthusiasm.

Garrison couldn't blame him. The thought of sending his son to a place like this made him sick to his stomach.

Luke led them back outside to a little patio area. "Have a seat."

They did. Aiden's arms crossed, then uncrossed. Garrison

was proud of his son for trying to exude confidence when he could have been all mopey and childish. Instead, he'd chosen a mature route. The question was, why?

"How old are you?" Luke asked.

Aiden sat up straighter. "Seventeen."

"Turning eighteen...?"

"January."

"Okay. Good." Luke kept his focus on Aiden, but he was careful to glance at Garrison and Sam as he spoke. "What makes this place perfect for you is that we're for young men ages fourteen to twenty-four. We don't often get them that young. We have two fifteen-year olds right now, the rest are sixteen and up. If you were to go to a facility for teens only, you'd be just about the oldest person there. I don't know if you know this, but younger teen boys can be really annoying."

Aiden laughed.

"But you're not old enough for an adult facility, and those have guys all ages. My second rehab, I roomed with a guy who was seventy-two. He always complained because I needed an alarm to wake up. Apparently he'd trained his"—he made air quotes with his fingers—"internal clock, and I could too if I just tried hard enough."

"No kidding?"

"You meet all kinds in rehab, but mostly nice guys, like you. And that guy was a good roommate. But here, the guys are all around your age, dealing with the same stuff you are. There's something to be said for that."

Aiden shrugged, the first teenager movement he'd shown since they'd arrived.

"It's a ninety-day program?" Garrison asked.

"It's a very intense program, and it begins with ninety days." He focused on Aiden. "After two months, you'll move to one of the Phase Two houses. There are six guys in each, one of whom is the manager—I manage one of the houses here. Each has two full bathrooms, a full kitchen, and a living room. They're small, but there you'll have a little more freedom."

"That's cool," Aiden said.

Garrison tried to imagine his son with his own house to take care of. A kitchen, a bathroom.

"Who cleans the houses?" Garrison asked.

"Chores are assigned every week. All the residents pitch in, clean, work in the kitchen, serve the meals. They're also responsible for keeping their own spaces clean."

That'd be a nice benefit for Aiden—not that he'd appreciate it.

"Sounds like a blast," Aiden said.

Luke chuckled. "It could be worse. Trust me, this place is awesome. It's like camp with the twelve-step program."

"I hated camp."

"Oh." Luke seemed unsure what to say to that. "Any questions I can answer for you?"

"How much does it cost?" Garrison asked.

Luke gave them a number, and Garrison whistled. His savings account had enough, but there'd be no early retirement for him.

"Dad, that's ridiculous. You can't spend that on me."

The number, the money worries crumbled like dust. He reached out, grasped his son's shoulder. "I can't imagine a more important way to spend my money."

Aiden blinked twice, lowered his gaze.

Sam cleared her throat.

Garrison realized she hadn't spoken a word since they'd started the tour. Her color was good, though. She seemed to be managing the anxiety.

"Can you give them any indication what the success rate is?" she asked.

A good question. Garrison turned to see Luke sigh.

"It's not easy to get hard numbers on that. If we quit hearing from a person or about a person, we figure they've relapsed. I'd say about half our guys relapse within a year."

Half? Within a year? What were they doing, wasting their time at this place?

Luke must've read his expression. "The relapse rate for addicts nationwide is really high—much higher than that. Definite numbers are impossible to collect, but experts will tell you that somewhere between fifty and ninety percent of addicts will relapse eventually."

The numbers tore into his chest like bullets. Almost everybody relapsed? What was the point?

"I know how hard that is to hear." The kindness in Luke's eyes said he did. For such a young man, he seemed to overflow with compassion. "I'm a recovering addict. My drug of choice was heroin. How about you?"

"Uh..." Aiden glanced at his father. "Oxy, I guess."

"Yeah, that's bad stuff. It's all bad." Luke turned his attention to include Garrison and Sam. "I've been clean for four years and three months. My parents forced me to go to two rehabs. The first time, I talked them into taking me out after thirty days. I promised them on my grandmother's grave I'd never use again. I was clean for five days after I got home. I thought, I'll just smoke a little pot. I'll never use the hard stuff again." He held Aiden's gaze. "Within two weeks, I was shooting heroin."

Aiden swallowed.

"I hid it, and maybe they didn't want to see it, until I turned eighteen. Then they did this whole intervention thing, and I agreed to go to another place. That's where I roomed with the old guy. I stayed about a month, then took off. Called a friend who picked me up in the middle of the night. I was high before we got out of town.

"I didn't call my parents, not even to check in, for months. I lived on people's couches, sold drugs to feed my addiction. I'd get a job, try to work. But I'm not one of those guys who can be high functioning. I never could hold down a job. I ended up getting arrested for dealing. The judge gave me a choice—rehab or prison. I chose rehab. And that time, I got clean." He turned back to Garrison. "So those statistics I told you—it includes people like me. I went to rehab three times and relapsed twice, so sixty-six percent of the time, but now I'm clean. Will I always be sober? I have no idea. But I'll be sober today."

Had Luke told him that story to give him hope? Because he felt more hopeless than ever.

"People who want to stay sober can. The program works if you work it. The people who relapse don't want to stay clean, not enough." He turned to Aiden. "Do you want to quit using drugs?"

Aiden opened his mouth, then closed it again.

Garrison waited, forced himself not to speak.

Sam slid her hand in his and squeezed. A quick grasp, then she slid it away before Aiden could see. But the slight touch infused him with strength. He could do this. He wasn't alone.

Aiden sighed, swallowed. "I don't want to *want* to use drugs, if that makes sense."

"Perfect sense," Luke said. "We can work with that."

Garrison's eyes prickled. He blinked back the sudden emotion.

"So after the ninety days, we have another phase of rehab, where the over-eighteens move into yet another house on the edge of campus. They're allowed to have cars, and they're expected to hold down jobs. Once they do that for a few weeks, they're released. Even then, we highly recommend sober living."

"What's that, exactly?" Aiden asked.

"It's a place where people who're recovering from addiction live together and learn to live in society again without drugs and alcohol. It's not rehab, but a lot of places—the best ones, anyway —require therapy. The residents have jobs and cars, if they can afford them. They have a level of freedom they haven't had since before rehab, but they also have rules. Curfews, group meetings, drug tests, stuff like that."

Aiden glanced at Garrison before focusing again on Luke. "You think I'd need that?"

"We recommend it for everyone. The recovery rate is so much higher for guys who lived in sober living than it is for people who go straight back to their old environments. You can get clean in rehab, but you can't learn to live a normal life, because life isn't regimented in the world like it is here. It's good to practice, surrounded by people who understand what you're going through, before you go out there on your own."

"Oh," Aiden said. "I guess that makes sense."

"It's not something you have to worry about right now. Just keep it in mind. While you're here, you'll learn more about it." He turned his attention to Garrison. "While Aiden's getting help, you can look into it. Where you guys from?"

"We live on Long Island," Garrison said.

"Oh. What brings you to New Hampshire?"

Aiden looked at Sam, who blushed and looked away.

Garrison spoke. "Sam is letting us stay in her rental property on Clearwater Lake."

"Been there. Beautiful place."

"I like it," Sam said.

Garrison said, "We just thought, as long as we're up here, we'd see what you have to offer. Do you think there's a benefit in him not being near home?"

"Absolutely. Especially for young people, because teens are generally more dependent on friends than adults are. And those friends are often not the best influences." He met Aiden's eyes. "Would you agree?"

Aiden actually chuckled. "Yeah, probably."

"So the farther you are from home, the less likely some yahoo will show up to rescue you."

Aiden didn't say anything.

"The downside, of course," Luke said, turning his attention to Garrison, "is that you don't get to visit as often."

"I could work around that," Garrison said.

Sam leaned forward a little. "What about school? Aiden's a senior this year."

"We allow the students to enroll in online school, and we have counselors on staff to work with them. They need to be self-motivated, though." He turned to Aiden. "You want to graduate with your class?"

"That's the plan."

"Then you need to get your work done. But it's on you."

"I could do that." Aiden's confidence—or bravado—was back. He was being far too cooperative. What was the kid up to? There had to be a catch to all this good attitude. Did it have something to do with Matty, with their call this morning?

But maybe Aiden really did want help. Maybe this wasn't an act, and he would come here and try and actually quit using drugs.

Or maybe Garrison had made a mistake letting Aiden use his phone. He had no idea. He should have consulted his *what to do when your kid's an addict* handbook.

Someone should really write that.

Luke led them back to where they'd parked.

Garrison studied the buildings and tried to hold onto Luke's words. Like camp, he'd said. One of the better ones. And it didn't seem bad, not really. The guys they'd seen earlier had been laughing, seemed well fed and happy enough. Still, was Garrison really considering leaving his son at a place like this? A place with locked gates, a place filled with addicts, most much worse than Aiden? And did every parent think that—that their kid wasn't as bad as the rest? He tried to tell himself they were all the same, that Aiden was just like all the guys here, those guys smoking and laughing. But Aiden wasn't like those kids. Aiden was Garrison's son, his responsibility. There was no comparison. Maybe someday, but right now, he had to believe that a life of addiction was not his son's destiny.

Addiction. Rehab. How had they gotten here?

Maybe this was more than Aiden needed. Maybe Aiden could quit. He'd admitted he wanted to, and wasn't that the most important thing, the desire? They could go to Narcotics Anonymous meetings together. They could do some kind of outpatient thing, couldn't they?

He'd almost convinced himself, and then he remembered the amount of oxycodone they'd found in Aiden's blood, the way he'd gone through withdrawal all weekend. His son was an addict. There was no point trying to pretend otherwise.

He thought of Charlene's words. Rehab facilities were like prisons, she'd said. She'd never send her son to one. Did that mean Charlene loved Aiden more than he did? Was it love to shelter his son from consequences? Or was it love to send him anyway, even when it hurt?

How could those be the only two choices?

"Do you have any more questions?"

He had plenty of questions, but he doubted Luke could comprehend the conflicting thoughts going on in this father's mind. Garrison looked at Aiden, who said nothing. "Not right now."

Luke handed each of them a business card. "Call anytime." He held onto the card when Aiden tried to take his. "When you feel yourself slipping, when you just need to talk, I answer the phone at all hours of the day and night. I mean it, man, call if you need to."

"Yeah, okay." Aiden took the card and shoved it in his back pocket. "I'll do that."

He wouldn't, though. Garrison could tell by the look in his son's eyes, a flash of honesty. Aiden was just going through the motions. Well, who could blame him? Garrison wouldn't want to come here, either.

Sam slid the business card into her purse. "You have openings?"

"Oh, right. I meant to say, we don't have any beds available right now, but we have one person graduating this week for sure —so we should have a bed available late this week or early next. But I'd need to get you on a waiting list."

"So we should decide soon," Garrison said.

"The sooner, the better."

SEVENTEEN

Samantha had done it. She'd gone to Dover, toured the rehab with them, and survived.

They were nearly back to the cabin when she got a text from Rae, her oldest and, finally again, closest friend. Sam read the text, then turned to Garrison. "Rae wants to know if you and Aiden want to come for a cookout tonight."

"That'd be fun." He glanced in the rearview mirror. "What do you think, son? You want to meet some of my friends?"

"Whatever."

"Wow, dude. Dial back the enthusiasm." He softened his words with a smile. Aiden didn't respond. "I guess that's a yes. What can we bring?"

Sam texted Rae and asked the question. "She said for you to bring nothing." Sam smiled to herself at her friend's hinted message—*tell Garrison not to bring anything, unless he knows your caramel brownie recipe*. Sam always kept the ingredients on hand, so she replied that she'd come with dessert.

Another text came in. She read it, then said, "Nate and Marisa will be there with Ana. And a few more people you haven't met. And it looks like Caro and Laurie are coming, too."

Sam turned to face Aiden. "Caro's your age. Laurie's twenty-two, I think. You'll like them."

Aiden's smile was polite. Or maybe tolerant was the right word. "Great. Sounds like fun."

Sam turned back to face the front. She'd offered to sit in the back again, but Aiden had insisted. He seemed to be in the middle of some internal battle. Sam could practically hear the clanking of swords in his mind. She wondered what ideas were vying for power in there.

"Just so you know, nobody knows why you're here. I just told my friends"—she glanced at Aiden—"your dad's friends, too, that you're here for vacation."

"Great." Aiden glanced at the back of his father's head. His expression darkened. Anger? That's what it looked like. "Good to know."

"Not that you can't tell them. It just wasn't my place."

"Yeah, buddy," Garrison said. "That'd be up to you."

"Wouldn't want to embarrass you, though, Dad. Wouldn't want your friends to know your son's such a screw up."

Garrison blew out a long breath, sighed, and pulled the car over on the narrow road leading to the lake.

Sam faced forward, afraid she was about to overhear something they maybe didn't want her to hear. She considered getting out of the car while Garrison shifted into park and turned to face his son.

"You'll never be an embarrassment to me. You've made some bad choices, but you're not defined by your choices. You are more than an addict. I'm proud of you. I've always been proud of you. Nothing's going to change that."

His words filled her eyes with tears, her heart with tenderness for this man who would work so hard to ease his son's fears. Her throat ached with emotion, and it was all she could do to keep her hands in her lap, to not reach out to him, to comfort him the way he was comforting Aiden.

She didn't look to see Aiden's reaction, felt like she didn't belong, but she didn't want to be anywhere else in the world.

Aiden's voice was broken by emotion. "If you say so."

"I say so. If you want to tell people what's going on, then do it. If you don't, then don't. It's entirely up to you, and I'll support you whatever you decide."

"Okay."

Garrison settled back in his seat, looked at Sam out of the corner of his eye, and nearly smiled. He maneuvered back onto the road, and they continued silently until they turned into the driveway.

EIGHTEEN

Garrison stepped into the speedboat. "You sure you don't want to come?"

Sam untied the boat from the pier and tossed the ropes toward him. "I've got some work to do this afternoon. You two have fun, though. Sorry you can't ski."

"Why can't we?" Aiden asked.

"We need a third." Garrison turned to his son. "To be a spotter, in case something goes wrong."

Aiden glanced at Sam with a smirk. "That's stupid."

Garrison turned back to her. "Thanks for letting us use the boat."

Her smile was kind, her eyes, though...what was that look? "See you tonight."

Garrison watched her walk away until his son spoke beside him. "Dude, you're, like, whipped."

"I'm not your dude." Garrison maneuvered away from the pier. "What are you talking about?"

"You should see the look on your face when she's around. Could it be more obvious?"

Garrison kept his gaze forward as the boat motored toward

open water, careful to avoid a couple of buoys. "We're just friends."

"You trying to convince me or yourself?"

Aiden's voice had gone from playful to serious pretty fast.

Garrison longed to hit the throttle, make the engine too loud to talk over, but he was still in the no-wake zone. He wasn't ready to talk to Aiden about this. Wasn't ready to face the truth himself. Coming to Nutfield had been a mistake. He should be focused on Aiden and Aiden alone, but there was Sam, kind and helpful and...what was that look he'd seen in her eyes?

He could feel Aiden's gaze on him.

"Not trying to convince either of us," Garrison said. "It's just true."

"You obviously like her."

Obviously? Was it obvious to Sam, too? Was Sam just helping him because she felt sorry for him?

"Dad?"

Right. His son was waiting for a response. "Okay, if you think I like her, how do you feel about that?"

"How do *you* feel about it?" Aiden asked. "After Mom."

Aiden knew too much about what had gone down between him and his ex. Charlene had done a heckuva job on Garrison's ability to trust. She'd racked up massive debt. She'd lied to him so often he'd quit believing anything she said. And then she'd left him.

In the beginning, Garrison and Charlene had been happy. They'd had a good marriage, a happy home. And then everything changed. The woman he loved had become someone else, someone ugly and selfish.

Garrison puttered past the final buoy and pushed on the throttle. The boat lurched forward, the engine purring too loudly to talk over.

Which left Garrison with nothing to do but think.

His feelings for Sam were obvious to Aiden. Were they obvious to Sam? If so, what would she do with that knowledge?

Sam was nothing like his ex, but that didn't mean she didn't have faults. She wasn't perfect. He'd never met a soul who was. Yet, he'd trusted her with his heart, with everything. For months, he'd been baring his soul to her. Talking into his cell phone, he'd felt safe with her. She knew so much. She knew too much. About his feelings. About his fears and doubts.

Sheesh, how pathetic had he been, whining on the phone like some tween girl? Sam had seemed to like how he'd shared, but now, what did it mean for them?

Garrison couldn't have gotten through the tour of that rehab facility without Samantha.

He couldn't have gotten through any of this without her. Without Sam, he'd still be slogging on the internet, trying to figure out what to do next. She'd helped him with that, helped him with everything.

He'd promised himself after Charlene he would never allow himself to become dependent on a woman again. On anyone. Ever.

Yet here he was, dependent on Sam.

The thought hit him hard as he maneuvered the boat across the smooth water. He turned to his son and saw the wide smile. At least Aiden wasn't thinking about Sam any longer. He'd let the boy drive in a minute. Right now, he had to think.

He remembered the look she'd just given him at the pier. Yes, he could name it, though the thought of it made him ill. Pity.

She'd looked at him with pity.

He recognized it because he'd seen it before. He'd seen it in his ex-wife's eyes after he'd bared his soul to her. What had Charlene done with his honesty?

She'd stockpiled his hurts like weapons.

No chance Garrison would let that happen again. Not with Sam. Not with anybody.

NINETEEN

Samantha had considered joining Garrison and Aiden on the boat that afternoon but decided she'd better not. Poor Garrison had seemed so overwhelmed by it all. Who could blame him? And Aiden had put on a good front, but he had to be reeling from all they'd heard. They needed time alone together.

And she needed to get her head on straight.

Just because she'd been able to go to Dover without incident didn't mean anything. She'd been filled with anxiety every moment of the trip. Only when she'd stepped into the cocoon of her own home had the last of the fear drained away. But she knew it would be back.

She'd done it. For Garrison, she'd done it. After a long shower and a cup of tea, she was able to appreciate the small victory in that. She stepped onto the back porch of her condo and aimed her gaze at the sky. God was with her. He'd helped her get through the trip today.

Thank you.

The birds trilled in the trees and competed with the sounds of the family enjoying the playground across the way. Lots of families lived in this complex, so she had plenty of opportunity to observe, to yearn for what they had. She'd given up on ever having a child of her own. To do that, she'd have to have a husband, and she'd given up on that, too.

She'd cared for Garrison since she met him, had even allowed herself to dream of what it would be like if he lived here, if they could be together. But after witnessing him with Aiden these last few days, after seeing the unconditional love in the man's eyes when he looked at his son, she realized that her feelings went far beyond *care*. Her feelings for him were deeper than she'd felt for any man in a long time. Maybe ever.

She was falling hard.

The thought made her physically ill. She rushed to the bathroom. The tea came up and splashed in the toilet, joined in the bleach-scented water by her tears. She sat back on the cold tile, allowed the chill to seep into her warm skin and bring her back to reality.

What was she doing? Didn't she already know how this would end?

Shame fell on her. She allowed herself a moment to remember. Just a moment to keep her sane, keep her planted firmly on this floor. No dreaming, no hoping, no planning.

She'd made her choice a long time before. There was no going back. And no going forward. There was just this. This condo, this town, this life. And it was enough. She had friends, she owned her own business. When she felt the need to explore, she did it through the portal of the internet, used her fingers instead of her feet, and went anywhere she wanted. She didn't need anything more.

She didn't.

After she brushed her teeth, she met her eyes in the mirror. "There can never be anything with Garrison."

Her eyes seemed to say, "But maybe..."

But maybe there could.

Maybe going to Dover today was the first step to healing.

Maybe she could learn to trust a man again. Maybe she would be stronger this time. Maybe it wouldn't end it heartbreak.

Maybe she shouldn't shut herself off.

Her heart couldn't help but hope. She feared she'd pay for that soon enough.

She baked a pan of caramel brownies, then worked the rest of the afternoon, one eye on the clock. At five-thirty, the anxiety hit. Should she even go? Maybe she should give Garrison and Aiden a break, let them enjoy the rest of their day without her, let Garrison catch up with his friends. Garrison had grown close to Nate and Marisa during their long ordeal last spring, and he and Brady had hit it off as well. They didn't need Sam there. Probably didn't want her.

And there she went again, allowing her fear to dictate her life. These were her closest friends in the world. If she didn't show up, they'd think something terrible had happened. When they learned the truth, that she'd blown them off, they'd be hurt she'd avoided them.

Before she could dwell on it any longer, she grabbed the brownies and pushed out her front door.

Ten minutes later, she pulled into the driveway at Rae's house. Well, Brady's, too, now that they were married, but she had a hard time thinking of this as his place. Rae had grown up in this old farmhouse. She, Sam, and Brady had spent endless summer days of childhood exploring the woods out back, picking wild blueberries, and climbing tall pines. Sam tried not to think of the years she and Rae hadn't been friends. Like most of Sam's traumas in her past, that too was all her fault. But Rae had forgiven her, and they were as close as ever.

Garrison's Camry was parked in the long driveway. Sam parked behind him, grabbed the brownies, and went inside. The house was quiet, but she could hear voices coming through the screen door that led to the backyard. No central air in this place, so all the windows were open to let in what little breeze there was. She set the brownies on the counter and stepped onto the back porch.

She saw Garrison first. His skin was darker after a day on the water, and his smile was wide when he joined her at the door. "So glad you made it."

His nearness was like a salve, soothing her anxious places. She was tempted to step even closer, to lean against him. She stepped away instead. "I'm not late, right?"

"Just a few minutes." Garrison's gaze was magnetic, and she couldn't look away.

There was so much she wanted to say to him, how well she thought he was handling things with Aiden, how strong he was, how kind.

Rae spotted her and stepped in for a hug. "Did you bring the brownies?"

"Would I let you down?"

"You never have," Rae said.

Sam let the generous lie slide.

Eric Nolan called out, "Hey, Sam."

She led Garrison to where Eric, one of the Nutfield police officers, stood beside Brady at the grill. She gave him a quick hug. "It's been a while."

"Since you quit working for the town," Eric said, his Texas accent as thick as ever, "I never see you."

"Like most citizens, I try to avoid the police."

"We only get to spend time with the ones who can't seem to stay out of trouble. Who signed me up for this job?"

"Don't lie," she said, "you love it."

"I do. But I missed you last week. Arrested a guy who had seven cell phones in his car. Stolen. Without you there to break into the phones, it's so much harder to get them back to their owners."

"All you have to do is call. I love doing that stuff."

Brady piped in. "As long as you use your hacking skills for good, not evil."

"No promises." Sam bumped Brady's arm with her shoulder —didn't help that she was a foot shorter than he was—and spoke to Eric. "How've you been?"

"Working like a dog."

Brady smirked as he flipped the burgers. "An old lazy dog, maybe."

Eric punched him, nearly caused one of the burgers to slide off the spatula.

"You drop it," Brady said, "you eat it."

"You'd have to make me, Chief."

Garrison joined her, and the men fell into a conversation about catching bad guys. Eric seemed interested in Garrison's career with the FBI, and within a minute, Garrison was sharing stories about some of his cases. Nobody asked him about his work as a forensic accountant. She wasn't sure Garrison was all that interested in it, either.

When the back door opened, five-year-old Ana burst out at top speed. She spied Sam, raced across the patio, and plowed into her.

Sam crouched down to hug her. "How's my favorite girl?"

"Mama said you brought those brownies I like. Can I have one?"

"If you eat your dinner."

Her little mouth turned down at the corners, and she said something in Spanish that Sam didn't understand.

Marisa stepped behind her. "English, *pajarita*."

Sam sized up the child. "Not sure your mama will be able to call you little bird much longer. You're getting so big."

"Nate says I'll be bigger than Mama soon."

"Are you excited about school?"

"*Sí, no puedo esperar.*"

"She can't wait," Marisa translated.

Sam kept her focus on Ana. "Maybe you can teach me Spanish. I'd love to learn."

"Spanish is easy," the child said. "It's English that's hard."

Considering the girl had spent her first five years in Mexico, her English was pretty perfect. Didn't hurt that her mother was American, and a teacher. Marisa would start her job at Nutfield Middle School in just a few weeks. She'd been hired as an aide to the Spanish teacher, but Sam knew she'd much rather teach art. Maybe when she finished her college degree, she'd be able to slide into that role.

Sam stood to greet Marisa, but the woman was hugging Garrison. They pulled apart and spoke to each other in quiet voices, then Garrison stepped back and focused on Ana.

"I've heard a lot about you, little one."

Ana pressed into her mother's side.

Marisa knelt beside her daughter. "When you were missing, Mr. Kopp helped us find you."

Her beautiful chocolate eyes widened. "You did?"

"I didn't do very much," Garrison said.

"He did," Marisa said.

Ana leaned tentatively away from her mother, stepped toward Garrison, and lifted her arms.

He looked at Marisa for permission. When she nodded, he scooped up the little girl and rested her on his hip.

"*Gracias*," she said.

"*De nada*."

She turned to her mother. "*El habla español.*"

Marisa's eyebrows lifted as she addressed Garrison. "Are you fluent?"

"I can order a beer, inquire about how much something costs, and ask where the bathroom is. Does that count?"

Marisa looked to Ana for the answer. "What do you think?"

The little girl shook her head. "I'll teach you."

"I'd like that."

Nate stepped into their circle of friends, and Ana leaned toward him until he took her from Garrison's arms. He managed to free his right hand to shake Garrison's. "Great to see you. Sam says you're back for a little vacation."

"My son and I needed to get away." He turned, looked over the grass. Sam followed his gaze.

"Where is Aiden?" she asked.

"He and Caro took Johnny for a walk in the woods."

"Caro's a sweet girl," Sam said. "Makes good choices." She tried to convince him with her gaze that Aiden wouldn't get into trouble with Caro. Garrison nodded as if he believed her. Caro wasn't trouble, but her sister could be. She looked around but didn't see her. "Did you meet Laurie?"

"That's the girl's sister, right? Caro said she had to work." Garrison turned back to Nate. "When Aiden gets back, I'll introduce you."

"I'd love to meet him. Are you enjoying the lake?"

"Sam let us use her boat this afternoon," Garrison said. "We're hoping to try water skiing later this week. Maybe you can join us."

"Love to." He cracked his knuckles. "I'll show you two how it's done."

Garrison chuckled. "Actually, we'd appreciate that. I haven't skied since college, and Aiden's never been."

"Then you'll believe me when I tell you how good I am." Nate looked at Ana. "This one thinks I'm amazing."

Little Ana rolled her eyes.

"Let me check my schedule and get back to you," Nate said.

"Sam says you have a new job," Garrison said. "You like it?"

Nate settled Ana on the porch, and she took off into the grass. "It's not the *Times*, but yeah. It's different from what I did in New York."

"You're with the *Union Leader* now, right?"

"Just part time."

Marisa linked her hand in Nate's elbow. "He's ghostwriting for a former Wall Street bigwig."

Garrison's eyebrows lifted. "Anyone I'd know?"

"Yup." He lowered his voice. "If I tell you, then I'd have to kill you."

"I'd like to see you try."

Nate chuckled but didn't disagree.

Marisa pulled her long brown braid off her neck as if she were hot. As if this was anything like the heat she'd endured for years in Mexico. "It's keeping him busy."

"Nice ring," Garrison said.

She dropped the braid over her shoulder and admired the diamond on her left hand. "Nate picked it out all by himself."

"She acts like that was some sort of major accomplishment." Nate slid her hand into his.

"Not that you did it," she clarified, "but that you chose so well."

She leaned toward Nate for a kiss, and Sam turned away, watched Ana attempting cartwheels on the grass. She was happy for her friends. But soon everybody would be married, paired off, having more kids, and she'd still be alone.

That had been the life she'd chosen. Alone and safe. But her heart suddenly seemed to want more.

Maybe there was hope for her relationship with Garrison.

What was she thinking? He lived in New York. She'd hardly made it to Dover, New Hampshire. Had she lost her mind?

She tried to be strong, to resist her heart, but as she listened to Garrison talk with Nate and Marisa, she let his deep voice soothe her frightened places. She was a glutton, but she couldn't seem to help herself. She'd savor the moment, not worry so much about how this would play out, about how she'd feel when he went home.

Their voices faded, then Sam felt a hand slide around her waist. It felt so warm, so natural. Garrison's voice was close to her ear. "You look beautiful tonight." He led her to the railing that overlooked the backyard, a few feet from the others.

She smiled, enjoying the feel of his arm around her. Maybe this could work. Maybe, if she just went with it, allowed herself to trust him, maybe they could have something more than friendship.

She turned to him. "So how was the lake?"

A shadow crossed his features, but he covered it quickly with a forced smile. "It was fun."

"Oh." But that sadness remained in his eyes. "Did something happen?"

He forced a chuckle. "Just life with a teenage drug addict. Hey, that'd be a good name for a book."

She wasn't sure what to say to that. He wasn't usually flippant with her. He'd always been so honest, even with the hard things. "And how are you? How are you handling all of this?"

He shrugged. "I'm fine."

Fine? What kind of answer was that? "But this has to be hard for you, trying to navigate—"

"It's just parenthood. You know."

"I don't, actually."

His forced smile remained. "Right. Lucky you."

Lucky her? Her dismay must've shown on her face because he added quickly, "You know what I mean."

She didn't. "You don't want to talk about it right now."

His arm dropped from her waist. "I don't need to talk about it at all. You hungry?"

Sam blinked at the rebuff. It felt very familiar.

She stepped back. "Not much."

He tilted his head to the side. "You okay?"

"We don't want Aiden to get the wrong idea."

His expression darkened. "Would it be the wrong idea?"

She opened her mouth, closed it again. "You need to focus on him right now."

"That wasn't the question."

Movement in the yard caught her eye, and she turned to see Aiden and Caro emerge from the woods. Aiden was carrying Johnny, who was babbling baby talk in long paragraphs. The boy had learned to walk, just barely. Both teens wore big smiles.

It was good to see Aiden happy. She turned to Garrison. Was

that worry for his son she saw on his face? Or frustration with her?

If it was the latter, she knew exactly how he felt. So fine, if he didn't want to go deep, then neither did she. "Aiden looks like he's having fun."

Garrison nodded once before he walked away.

What had just happened?

TWENTY

Aiden stopped on the grass, put Johnny down, and watched Caro walk with the kid toward the house.

He hadn't expected to have any fun at this stupid cookout, but Caro was cool. She worked at some little pizza place in town, and she'd told him about some hangout for teens where she liked to go. For a few minutes there, he'd almost felt normal.

Then he'd thought about that teen hangout. He could probably find something there, something he could use to take the edge off.

And now, he was thinking about getting high. Getting lost in the high, where all the bad feelings were dulled, all the good feelings better.

What he'd told the dude at rehab earlier that day was totally true. He didn't want to need drugs. But he did need them. Right now, he needed them bad.

He pressed his hands together, then pulled them apart. He wanted to punch something.

Fine. Someday, he'd quit. He wasn't going to lose his future to painkillers. He wanted college, a good job, a family, and he wasn't going to be a screw-up parent like his mother. He would definitely quit. Just not today. Not yet. He was still in high school, still enjoying the best years of his life. No reason why he couldn't party, have a little fun before he had to behave like an adult. And besides, this feeling—being sober? It was awful. Painful. His stomach was all jumbled again. His whole body ached. Before he'd tried drugs, sober was fine. Now... He couldn't do sober now. Not anymore. Not for long.

He and Caro had taken the little kid for a walk. Johnny kept trying to shove sticks and crap in his mouth. Was that normal? Maybe the kid was brain-damaged or something. When he suggested that, though, Caro only laughed.

"That's what babies do."

He thought it was weird. This was all weird. The fact that his dad was friends with all these people in New Hampshire was weird. It was like his dad had this whole other life Aiden knew nothing about. He wasn't sure what he thought about it. But Caro was fun and pretty, so the night wasn't a total bust.

Caro climbed the steps to the porch and handed Johnny to his father. Not his real father, though. The kid was really dark. Aiden would guess black, except his hair was straight. So maybe Indian or Middle Eastern or something. And the mom and dad were both totally white. So at least one of them wasn't the kid's actual parent. And even though the skin color was wrong, Johnny looked like his mother, the lady who lived here. Reagan. It was the bone structure, the shape around the nose and mouth. So obviously the dude the kid called Dada wasn't actually his dad.

At least Aiden knew his real parents. At least he didn't have to learn to live with any step-parents. That was something.

That might change if his father and Sam continued on their path. It was pretty obvious they both wanted to be more than friends. How long until they gave up pretending?

Dad walked away from Sam, probably because he saw Aiden coming. Didn't want him to get the wrong idea, or the right idea. Like Aiden was an idiot and didn't see right through their stupid charade. She should just move in, stop pretending this trip to the backwoods of nowhere had anything to do with Aiden and getting him clean.

Rage poured over him. Hot. Stickier than the humid air. Dad didn't care about him. He just came here to see Sam.

Crap, Aiden needed an oxy. Just one to make all these feelings fade. Better yet, two so he could enjoy himself. And think straight again.

The thought of it started his hands shaking like he was right back where he'd been on Saturday.

His father jogged down the back porch steps and across the yard. "Hey, kiddo. How was your walk?"

He fought the urge to scream at his father, to shove him, to run... But Aiden wasn't mad at his dad. He just needed...something. Maybe somebody'd brought tequila. He wasn't a fan of the swill, but just a sip or two to keep him from wanting to kill everybody in sight.

He forced a smile, knew it must look totally fake. "Fine. The kid likes me."

"Obviously. You get your charm from your old man."

Dad was being nice again. For months, he'd painted his father as this cruel, hateful tyrant. All his rules, all his questions. But these few days with him had reminded him that his dad was actually a pretty cool guy.

Aiden was the screw up. He'd ruined everything.

Maybe just a beer. Somebody must've brought beer. Everybody drank beer at cookouts. Even Dad did that. Aiden scanned the patio for a cooler, for evidence of alcohol. Saw those red plastic cups, which could have had anything in them.

But he could practically smell beer, keg beer dripping over the edges. Reminded him of the party Friday night. Beer everywhere, and he'd had his share, especially after he dropped the acid. He'd done LSD before, but it had never been like that. He'd hated the feeling, like he couldn't figure out what was real, what wasn't. Like his body would never be the same. He'd hoped the alcohol would soften its effects, but no. The beer hadn't helped, and then... Then he'd started laughing. And he didn't remember what happened next. Knew he must have freaked out, based on the texts he'd read on his way to rehab this morning. All his friends had said was that he'd started screaming stupid stuff, got really aggressive.

No. Not thinking about that.

Aiden didn't like beer, but his mouth watered anyway. He'd have to drink a lot to feel better, but it would be worth the hangover.

"You okay?"

He looked at his dad again. "Yeah. Fine."

"The girl's pretty."

"She's cool. Is there food yet? I'm starving."

A lie. He wasn't a bit hungry. He was...he didn't know what he was. If he didn't get something to take the edge off soon, he'd go crazy.

"We're about to eat." Dad looked at the patio, where guests were headed inside. "Too many flies out here so we're eating in."

The flies were nothing compared to the crazy stuff flying around Aiden's brain.

They climbed up to the patio, and Dad stepped aside to let Aiden go first into the house. He'd have preferred to stay outside until this...this urge passed. It usually did. The ache was always there, but sometimes his cravings were so bad, he had to hide. Didn't want Dad to see what a weak little loser he was.

He wanted to run. To escape. But he had to stay, be nice, be cooperative. Had to prove to his father he could be trusted.

He told his dad he had to use the bathroom, and his father pointed him in the right direction. He closed the door behind him and opened the medicine cabinet. Nothing in there.

He looked under the sink. They had to have something. But this was a guest bath. They probably kept the good drugs in the master bathroom, and that'd be upstairs.

He came out of the bathroom and looked at the staircase, then toward the living room. Caro waved from her seat on the couch. Okay, he'd try later. Stupid. He should have thought of that when everybody was outside.

Seriously, what was wrong with him, thinking about stealing drugs from his father's friends? That Brady dude was the police chief. Aiden had to get a grip.

He fixed himself a plate in the kitchen. Cheeseburger, potato chips, and some kind of pasta salad. The adults pushed chairs around a kitchen table, but there was no room for him. Not that he wanted to sit with them anyway. Aiden took his plate to the living room, where Caro was seated on the couch by herself.

Aiden set his plate on the coffee table. "You need anything? I gotta get a drink."

She looked at her plate, then at his. "I'm all set, but you should get yourself a brownie. They're wicked good."

He nodded like he gave a crap about the stupid brownies. Unless they were laced with something. He stared at Caro a little too long. She was young, she was normal. Maybe she could help him out. He smiled like he was about to share a joke. "Where can a guy get a beer around here?"

She sorta smirked. "Haha."

That was helpful. He returned to the kitchen, grabbed a Sprite while he checked out the other drinks. Tea, soda, water. No alcohol.

He was totally screwed.

He chose a brownie, not because he wanted one, but because Caro had said to, and he didn't want to be a jerk.

He sat in the chair beside her and dug into his food. The burger and chips were good, but the pasta salad tasted gross. At least the food took a little of the edge off.

"Tell me about that hangout, the Nuthouse."

Caro swallowed her bite. "Yeah. Stupid name, I know. It's attached to the pizza place. There are arcade games and pool and ping pong and stuff."

"It's just for teens."

"Yeah. The church runs it."

"Oh. So it's all church kids?"

"Everybody goes."

"Not much to do in this little town."

She shrugged. "Probably not compared to New York."

It might be just what he needed. Where there were teenagers, there were drugs. He just had to find the place, to find the right person. But he could. Matty'd supplied most of his drugs, but he could usually tell who used and who didn't. He was pretty sure Caro didn't, but she could still help him. "Where is it?"

"You planning to go?"

He shrugged. "Kinda boring hanging out with Dad all the time. I thought he might take me."

She eyed him like she wasn't sure. "It's downtown. Did you see the old white church with the steeple?"

He'd seen it on their way back from rehab earlier that day. He nodded.

"It's next to that."

"So not far from the lake?" He couldn't remember.

She shrugged. "I don't know. Couple miles, maybe."

"How late's it open?"

"Midnight in the summer."

Could he get there by midnight?

"I'd offer to go with you tonight, but I have to be home early."

"Oh." He took another bite of his burger, tried to ignore the fresh wave of craving. Just thinking about what he might find at the Nuthouse had his hands shaking again. He needed something, anything. "It's weird they're not drinking beer. Nobody drinks in New Hampshire?"

Caro laughed. "Not this crowd. Why, do you?"

"Not much."

She watched him a minute. Her eyes squinted. "You prefer other stuff?"

Now she was talking. "Can you hook me up?"

She set her plate down. "I stay away from that."

Great. Was she the type to go running to her mommy and daddy about the druggie at the party? He hoped not. The way she was looking at him made him think there was more she wanted to say. He didn't want to hear it.

"My dad's in prison for dealing."

Great. Everybody had a story.

"My mom's an addict, and my sister..."

The sister. Caro'd mentioned her. Maybe she could help him out. What had Caro said about her earlier? She lived nearby. If the Nuthouse didn't work out, he could track her down. He just needed to figure out her name, her address...

"My sister's clean now, so stay away from her."

Was his need written so clearly on his face? "I don't even know her."

Caro grabbed her brownie and took a bite.

He bit his, too. Then looked at it. Chocolate and caramel. It was delicious.

"Wicked good, right?" Caro's smile was back.

"Yeah."

"Samantha's specialty."

Sam. Of course. He thought about putting the dessert down in protest, but it really was good.

"So like, just so you know," Caro said, "I'm against drugs. They totally ruined my family. I live with my grandparents because my mom can't take care of me. I think you're a nice guy, but I'm just saying, if you're going to use drugs, I'm not really interested in hanging out."

"It's not like I even live here."

"I know. I'm just saying, while you're here."

Fine. What did he care if the girl wanted to hang out with him? He wasn't going to be here very long anyway.

He thought of Matty. His friend had sounded really scared, like there was something seriously wrong. Of course, Matty was the worst exaggerator in the whole world, telling Aiden how he was going to buy a car with all the money he was making from dealing. Yeah, right. And what would his mother say about that—the kid had no job but could afford a nice car? Whatever.

But this was different. Matty hadn't been bragging. He'd sounded scared. If he wasn't careful, he was going to end up in prison. Like Caro's father.

"It sucks your parents are so messed up," Aiden said.

Her frown softened a little. "Yeah. Your dad seems cool."

"He's okay."

Aiden considered telling her about his mother but decided against it. Mom used drugs sometimes, but she wasn't a druggie. She could still take care of him, hold down a job. She'd totally screwed up their family, but that probably wasn't all the drugs. Mom wasn't a real addict. Aiden was like his mother. He liked the drugs, needed them, but he could manage his life. If he'd stayed off the LSD Friday night, none of this would be happening. He'd tried it before, but he'd never had that kind of reaction. So now he knew—acid wasn't for him. He could just stick to oxy, and everything would go back to normal.

How to convince his father of that, though.

The craving had settled back to a dull ache. Good, because he needed to think straight. He needed to take the edge off these cravings. Then, he had to figure out what was going on with Matty. Aiden had been as cooperative as he could be these last couple of days, even trying to make nice with Sam. He'd agreed to visit the stupid rehab place. He didn't want to go. Couldn't imagine himself there. Wasn't willing to try. He'd back out somehow. But not yet. He had to figure out how to earn back his father's trust and convince him he didn't need rehab.

No idea how he was going to do that. He couldn't even get his father to take him home for a day to get clothes.

When he'd suggested it, Dad had said they weren't going back. Like, at all. Aiden could still feel his father's huge hand on his shoulder, a weight as heavy as his words. They'd been anchored in the middle of the lake, taking turns jumping off and swimming. It was fun, hanging with his dad like that. Maybe if they'd done more of that over the years, Aiden might have made different choices.

Right. Blame Dad. What a freaking cop-out.

After they'd tired of swimming, they'd just floated on the boat, getting sun. Everything had been going well until Aiden had suggested a trip back home.

And Dad had refused.

He shouldn't have gotten mad. He probably shouldn't have called his father those names, but he wanted to go home. Needed to get away from here, back to his friends.

He needed an oxy.

The afternoon had been ruined, and Aiden figured his father would be mad at him the rest of the night. But no. Dad was nice as ever, understanding even. Wouldn't let him use his phone—and no matter how hard Aiden tried, he couldn't figure out where his father had hidden the stupid thing. Wouldn't agree to take him home. But he was nice about the whole thing.

It made Aiden feel so much worse about what he had to do.

TWENTY-ONE

Garrison couldn't get Sam's response—or lack thereof—out of his mind. Maybe he hadn't bared his soul to her. Her response was to cut him out? He'd invited her to give him a hint about what she was feeling, and she'd avoided the question like a criminal in an interrogation room.

He tried to enjoy dinner with this group of friends. Sam was acting like everything was fine. Normal. Well, maybe it was. Maybe all these feelings were only on his side. Maybe he was only seeing what he wanted to see. Maybe he was realizing the truth too late. That's what he got for letting his guard down, believing he could count on her. He didn't have time to figure all that out right now. She was right about that. He did need to focus on Aiden. Didn't mean he couldn't get to know Sam better, as long as he was here. Once Aiden was settled in rehab, they'd have more time together, assuming Garrison actually relocated.

Was he crazy to consider it?

Not that the move would have to be permanent. But if Aiden went to the rehab place in Dover, Garrison could be closer to him, closer to Sam. And he could work from here, head back to Long Island once every couple weeks to check in at the office. The plan was perfect. Assuming Sam wanted him here.

How could he know for sure?

Nate asked a question, and he rejoined the conversation at the dinner table.

After the meal, he stood to help with the dishes, but Rae shooed him back to his seat. He talked with the guys and played with Johnny, who happily bounced on Garrison's lap. He remembered when Aiden was this age, little, giggly, all smiles. Back then, Aiden had thought his dad could do no wrong. Thought him a superhero.

Little Johnny would grow up to idolize Brady. Would he reach his teen years and turn away, realize his dad wasn't the superhero he'd once thought, reject everything Brady had taught him?

How could this innocent little child make those choices? How had Aiden become the angry teen in the other room? And what could Garrison do to fix it?

He watched Sam wipe down the kitchen counters while she chatted with Rae and Marisa. Ana had gone into the living room and turned on the TV.

Garrison peered in there, saw Aiden and Caro talking, one eye on the cartoon on the screen.

Finally, Sam dried her hands and looked around the clean kitchen for something else to do.

Marisa set the pan of brownies in the middle of the table and settled in her chair beside Nate. "In case anybody wants seconds."

Brady and Nate both reached for one. Garrison wanted a second brownie, too, but he wanted to talk to Sam more.

"Thanks for your help," Rae said to her. "You don't have to run off, right? Come back and sit."

Sam smiled at her friend. "I'm just going to the restroom."

After she walked out of the room, Garrison stood, handed Johnny to Brady, and headed toward the living room to check on Aiden. He stopped at the door.

"Dad used to be an FBI agent," Aiden told the girl. "Now he's just an accountant."

Garrison hadn't meant to eavesdrop. He wished he hadn't. Not that Aiden had lied. Garrison was an accountant. A six-foot-four gym rat who used to have a reason beyond vanity to stay in shape. Who used to carry a gun to work, not a calculator. Who used to investigate suspects, not numbers. His world had turned into a long list of used-to's. But he'd given up his dream job to save his marriage and build a better relationship with his son. Fat lot of good that had done. His marriage had crashed like an antique computer. His son had to snort, smoke, or swallow whatever he could find to make life with dear old Dad tolerable.

Crap, he missed his old life. Missed the badge, missed the authority and respect that came with it. Missed the other agents. He even missed the criminals with all their lies and excuses and stories that had made life interesting. Now, the only one who lied to him was Aiden—generously, expertly, shamelessly. And when Garrison wasn't trying to save his son, he got to study numbers until he wanted to light all the spreadsheets on fire and throw himself into the flames.

"Hey, Dad."

Garrison forced himself off that train of thought. "You guys doing okay?"

Aiden looked at the TV. "Fine."

Caro giggled. "We're watching my favorite show."

"Mine, too!" Ana jumped up and sat next to Caro on the sofa. "Can I sit with you?"

"Sure, squirt."

Sam returned from the restroom, and Garrison met her in the kitchen, on the far side, away from the table. Just five minutes alone with her. That was all he needed.

Her smile was natural, her pretty dimples pronounced. She acted like everything was normal between them. As if she hadn't rejected him an hour earlier. "Sounds like you guys enjoyed the lake today."

The lake. Aiden. Of course that's what she wanted to talk about. He'd mentioned it at dinner, but he hadn't told everybody about their conversation, about his son's outburst. And until he talked it out with Sam, he wouldn't know how to process it.

That's what she'd become to him. His sounding board, his wisdom. For months, every difficulty, every funny story, every argument with Aiden had become fodder for their evening phone conversations, as if those things didn't make sense until he'd shared them with Sam.

What had he become to her in those months? Was he just a burden, a guy who needed her help? Maybe she felt like helping Garrison was her Christian duty.

Maybe he was an idiot. He'd thought Charlene cared for him, too. But she'd tossed away their marriage faster than an empty pill bottle. And here he'd confided in Sam, shared more with her on those phone conversations and in the last few days than he had with anyone in a long time. He'd done it again, given away too much information. Too much of himself.

Sam tilted her head to the side. "Did something happen?"

He was being melodramatic. Sam already knew about Aiden and the problems they'd had. He should tell her about their day on the lake. But he didn't need Sam taking what was left of his broken heart and crumbling it to pieces.

Broken heart? Sheesh. Aiden would tell him to grow a pair.

"He wants to go back." Garrison blurted the statement, relieved at having said it. "To pack." He smirked with that last word. Aiden couldn't care less about what clothes he wore, not these days. He used to dress sort of nice, stylish even. Now, his hair was shaggy, his clothes ratty. Seemed all Aiden cared about was drugs.

"What did you tell him?" Sam asked.

"I called the place and talked to Luke before we came over here. He confirmed a bed would be available on Friday, and they'll reserve it for him. It looks like we're staying until he moves into rehab. That is, assuming your cabin is still available. I brought a check to pay—"

"You're welcome to stay as long as you want, and you're not paying for it. The house doesn't have a renter for the rest of the summer."

"I can't stay without paying."

"Tell me about Aiden."

He wasn't going to take advantage of her kindness. He'd fight that battle later. "I suggested we go see another rehab place tomorrow, that one up north. I think he'd like to live in the mountains, but he didn't seem interested. Said the one today was fine, and I agree. I like that they cater to people his age, not younger kids, not old men. Maybe that'll be good for him."

"It has an excellent reputation," Sam said. "Expensive though."

"I talked to that guy you hooked me up with. Reed. He knows a lot of guys who've gone there and gotten sober. And he's going to help me get the best price. I guess you can negotiate with these places."

"Like you're buying a car?"

"Ridiculous, right?"

"Completely. Will insurance help?"

"Probably not, but I'll call tomorrow."

"Good," Sam said. "So that's the plan? Aiden will stay close by?"

Was that hope he saw on her features? Did she want him here? Or was he just reading into this to make himself feel better? "It's my plan."

"What does Aiden think?"

Garrison glanced toward the door that led to the living room, though he couldn't see his son from where he stood. "He says he's considering it. That it might be a good idea. That's what makes me nervous. Why is he being so cooperative?"

"Maybe he really wants to go."

If only Garrison could believe that. "It's possible."

At the table, this group of people who'd invited him into friendship chatted and laughed. Garrison felt more at home with this crowd than he'd felt in a long time, since he'd retired from the FBI. This camaraderie was what his life had been missing. This...and Sam.

The memory of her rejection had him backing up a step.

She tilted her head to the side, her brown eyes wide with concern. "You okay?"

He should return to the table, let their earlier conversation slide. Maybe she had no feelings for him whatsoever, and if that was the case, did he really need to know tonight?

Yes, he did.

"So." That was all he could come up with? Good start.

"I'm sorry," she said.

He kept his mouth shut, hoped she'd go on.

"I haven't been in a...a relationship in a long time, and I have no idea what I'm doing."

"But you... I got the impression that maybe you don't want that. Maybe you're happy with us just being friends. And if that's the case, then whatever." Quoting his teenage son. "It's fine. I just want to know. Because..." What? How was he supposed to finish that statement?

"I don't know what I want," Sam said. "I feel like..." Laughter at the table had her gaze darting to the crowd.

"Like what?"

Her eyes filled with tears, but she blinked them back. "I'm damaged."

Damaged? This beautiful, tenderhearted woman? Was she nuts?

"I can't leave my hometown without medication, Garrison. And that's... I'm not what you think I am. Here, with these people"—she nodded to her friends at the table—"I look so normal. But I'm not."

He took her hand, wanted to pull her close. Would she let him? Would she run? Now, in this setting, wasn't the time to find out. He lifted her hand to his lips, kissed the soft skin. "You are a lot of things, Samantha Messenger, but you are not damaged."

She pulled her hand away. "There are things you don't know." She swallowed, stepped back. "I just don't think...I don't know how to do this."

"I haven't dated in a long time myself. We'll figure it out together."

"It's not just dating. It's..."

"What?"

She looked at the floor. Her hair fell over her shoulder, hung beside her face. He wanted to touch it, to feel if it was as silky as it looked. To push it back so he could see what she was thinking.

"Sam?"

She looked up. Her expression looked frightened, tortured. "I just don't know if I can."

"Are you married? Hiding a husband I don't know about?"

She nearly smiled. "Never married."

"Have you taken some kind of vow? No dating guys from New York?"

Her lips twitched. "I considered it."

"Can't blame you for that. Trouble, that's what I am."

"Right. Trouble." She smiled, and those dimples made an appearance. "We've never even been on a date."

"I look forward to changing that."

"But right now, Aiden's your priority."

Aiden. Right. He wanted to stay in this little fantasy a little longer. But until Aiden was settled, he couldn't focus on Sam. Couldn't consider what might happen between them.

If anything could. Because if Garrison didn't get his son healthy, nothing else would matter.

IT WAS dark by the time Garrison parked in front of the cabin that night. He hadn't left any lights on, so he and Aiden groped to the front door, where Garrison managed to fit the key in the lock. He flipped on a couple of lights inside and sat on the sofa that had been his bed the previous two nights. It would be tonight, too. He needed to be able to hear if Aiden sneaked out.

He set his keys and phone on the coffee table. He would have brushed his teeth and changed his clothes for bed, but Aiden seemed in the mood to talk. He'd told Garrison about Caro, Johnny, and their walk on the way home. Garrison got the feeling the kid was talking just for the sake of it, or to impress him or something. But whatever the reason, at least Aiden was trying.

Aiden headed to the kitchen, and Garrison heard the refrigerator door open.

"You can't be hungry," Garrison called. He didn't mind his son eating. When he'd seen Aiden in his swim trunks today, Garrison had been shocked at how much weight he'd dropped. How had he not noticed? Aiden had lost ten pounds, maybe fifteen, this summer, but he'd kept wearing the same clothes.

Just excuses. A better father would have noticed, would have known long before now how bad the addiction had become.

Aiden came into the living room with a sandwich, a bag of chips, and a Pepsi. He sat on the love seat adjacent to Garrison.

"That drink'll keep you up tonight."

"Trust me, Dad, it won't. Caffeine doesn't affect me at all."

Caffeine was a mild drug compared to what Aiden was used to.

Garrison longed to lay his head down. "You want to watch a movie or something?"

"Maybe. In a minute. But I gotta tell you something first."

"Okay." Garrison went to the kitchen and grabbed himself a Pepsi. He needed to be awake. He sat, leaned forward, and rested his elbows on his knees. "What's up?"

Aiden set his plate on the table. Blew out a long breath. Turned toward his dad. "I just wanted to say that you're right. I do need to quit. I've been fighting this...this craving, since Saturday. I keep thinking it'll go away, but it doesn't." He looked away, looked at the plate, looked at his hands. "I'm sorry. I thought...I thought I could be strong like you, but I guess I'm not."

A wave of annoyance had Garrison's voice rising. "You think I wouldn't get addicted to the drugs you've been using?"

"Probably not."

"That's baloney." Not the first word that popped into his mind. "Anybody abuses drugs like that, they're going to get hooked. You know why I'm not a drug addict? I've never abused them."

"But some people are more prone to it than others. I think I'm one of them."

He stifled the words *cop-out* and *excuses.* "That may be true, but you don't have to be prone to it to get addicted to narcotics. What you've been taking? That's one of the most addictive substances on earth. If I abused it, I'd get addicted too."

Aiden's eyes narrowed. "You really think so?"

"Remember when you were a kid and I injured my knee?"

Aiden leaned forward, nodded. "I always figured you were chasing a bad guy through a dark alley or something."

Garrison's chuckle felt good. "I was jogging and accidentally stepped in a hole."

Aiden laughed out loud. "Wow. Good job, Dad."

"So much for your cool old man."

"Aw, you're still cool. For an old man."

Garrison shot him a *watch-it* look tempered with a smile. "Anyway, they prescribed painkillers for that. I took two, then flushed the rest down the toilet."

"Are you joking? You didn't like them?"

"I liked them too much. I wasn't about to flirt with addiction. I'd seen too many people..." Nope. He wasn't going to let this turn into a lecture. He'd done enough of that in the last few days. "I managed the pain without the pills."

Aiden's smile faded. He grabbed his sandwich, took a huge bite, set it back on the table.

Garrison kept his mouth shut.

Finally, Aiden spoke again. "You're smarter than me, I guess."

"I'm older than you. When I was your age, I did my share of stupid stuff."

"But no drugs."

"No." He hadn't wanted to try drugs. He'd only wanted one thing when he was a kid—to prove to his old man that he could make it. He'd worked his tail off, gotten an academic scholarship, joined the military, gotten hired by the Bureau, and had a family. Dad still wasn't impressed. "I did my share of stupid things. I was lucky."

"How so?"

Details. The kid wanted details. Fine. "I was lucky no girls turned up pregnant. I was lucky I never got in a wreck. I drove like a madman back then." Even Garrison's rebellion had been designed to elicit some sense of pride from his father. *Look at all the girls who like me, Dad. I like cool cars, too, Dad.* Not that he'd realized it at the time. No matter how many times his father let him down, Garrison had never quit hoping.

Lot of good that had done.

"Girls, huh?"

Figured Aiden would latch onto that. "Don't follow in my footsteps." He'd warned Aiden against that when they'd had *the talk*, but who knew what the kid did for fun these days? Obviously, he didn't have a lot of moral qualms about anything. "Girls just mess with your head. Trust me."

Aiden didn't offer any insight into his own choices, and Garrison didn't ask. They had enough to deal with right now.

"I didn't drink when I was a kid," Garrison said, "because my father drank. A lot. And he was a mean drunk."

"Grandpa? I can't picture him drunk. Or mean."

"He had a hair-trigger temper back then, worse when he drank. So my mother tiptoed around him, didn't ask him to do anything when he got home from work, and trained us to not make waves. The only things my dad cared about were his job, his car, and football. He'd throw the ball with me all the time. I wanted to try out for quarterback, but Dad said no. Thought I had good hands and trained me to catch. And if I missed, if he'd been drinking..." Garrison didn't finish, didn't need to tell Aiden all his father's faults. Or his mother's, for that matter.

"I can't picture him like that."

"He quit drinking years ago. I think maybe Mom got fed up. I never knew the whole story, but your aunt Nadine hinted that Mom threatened to leave at one point. I guess they worked it out."

"Lucky them."

Garrison blew out a long breath. "I wish your mom and I could have."

"Do you, really? Because you and Sam..."

He gave his son time to voice his concern, but Aiden clammed up.

"I didn't meet Sam until March. And we're just friends. She had nothing to do with what happened between your mom and me."

"What did happen?"

"Not a chance, son. I know it sucks for you. You were the victim of our stupidity. Still are, I guess. But that doesn't change the fact that our marriage is our business."

"Mom tells me stuff."

The anger flashed like hot oil and a lit match. Charlene would poison his relationship with Aiden for sport, and who cared how it hurt their son as long as it also hurt Garrison. He closed his eyes, imagined the anger burning itself out. Opened his eyes again. "That's her prerogative."

"She makes it sound like everything's your fault."

"I wasn't perfect."

"But you tried, right? You guys went to counseling and stuff. And I remember..."

After a moment, Garrison said, "Remember what?"

"I overheard you guys talking. You were trying to get her to go to counseling one time, and she didn't want to. She was just, like, I don't know. Like she didn't care."

Garrison had enough anger directed at Charlene for both of them. Aiden didn't need to carry any of it. "I think I was too late," he said. "I should have left the Bureau years earlier. I should have been home with you guys."

"At least you tried. I never saw Mom do anything but...but hate you. And take pills." Aiden dropped that bomb, then went back to his food and drink like it was no big deal.

"I don't want you to think of your mother that way. Before she started abusing drugs, she was a great mom. When you were a kid, you remember how she used to be? How she always cooked your favorite meals for supper, how she always had some kind of homemade cookies in the jar?"

"Yeah. And for special occasions, she used to make those muffins that were covered in cinnamon and sugar."

"And butter. Those were delicious."

Aiden nodded, paused, ate a bite of his sandwich. Sipped his Pepsi. "I remember that."

"She was a good wife," Garrison said. "And a good mom."

"Until she discovered painkillers."

Garrison didn't say anything. He didn't need to. The truth was like a monster snarling in the corner.

"Anyway," Aiden said, "I just wanted to tell you I'm, like, sorry for all of this. And I know I need to quit. I just think I can do it, you know, without having to go to rehab. So, like, if we could look at other options...counseling or whatever."

"Your mother tried outpatient therapy, and it didn't help at all."

"But she didn't really want to quit. I think I can do it myself."

"Do you really want to quit?"

"Yeah." Aiden swallowed. Shrugged. "I mean, I want to want to."

"Well, we need to get you to actually want to."

"I can get there. I just need to keep doing what I'm doing. Stay sober. Quit hanging out with certain people. I can do it."

Garrison wasn't falling for that again. Aiden had made promises before—and broken every one. "There's no shame in getting help."

"Really, Dad? Because I never see you asking for help."

"I was on the phone half the weekend—"

"Trying to fix me. Not for you."

"I'm not the one addicted to drugs."

"Right. I know." Aiden heaved a big sigh. "I'm just saying, you're totally independent. You don't need anybody for anything. I thought I was like you."

Garrison opened his mouth to respond, but what could he say? Aiden was right. Garrison was terrible at asking for help. He'd rather go it alone—and do it wrong—then admit he needed anything from anyone. And all that independence had gotten him right here—with a son who needed rehab and refused to go so he could be like his old man. His stupid, independent old man.

He angled toward Aiden. "I have a problem trusting people. You're like me in a lot of ways, but you don't want to be like that."

"You want me to be needy?"

"Nobody's completely independent." How had this conversation gotten so offtrack? "We all need each other. And if I've shown you otherwise, I'm sorry. I need people."

"Who? Who do you need?"

Samantha's image filled his mind. He'd grown to need her. He didn't like the feeling.

"I need you to be healthy and happy."

Aiden leaned back on the sofa. "Whatever."

"I'm sorry," Garrison said. "I don't know what you want from me. I can tell you that when I was your age, I wasn't independent, and you're not either. And if you ever want to hold down a real job, pay your own bills, have a life, you need to quit using drugs. And that's going to take rehab. I don't want you to go, either. But as hard as it'll be on you, it's your best chance. You go, get it over with, graduate with your class, and then live your life with this in the rearview mirror."

Aiden looked at his empty plate, took a deep breath. "Yeah. I guess that makes sense."

"You're saying you'll go willingly?"

Aiden shrugged.

Garrison stood, pulled his son off the couch and into a hug. "You're a smart kid, and you're making a wise choice." He patted him on the back, wanted to hold onto him forever. "I'm so proud of you."

Aiden sat, wiped his eyes quickly, and clicked on the TV. "Wanna watch a movie?"

He wanted to sleep, desperately. But he settled on the couch and said, "Sure. See what you can find."

TWENTY-TWO

Aiden peeked at his father, snoring on the couch beside him. He snatched the blanket from the chair where Dad had laid it that morning and draped it over him.

Then he sat again, kept watching the movie, but his mind was not on the screen.

Dad was serious this time.

He'd half-heartedly suggested rehab in the spring, more as a threat than a real possibility—"You need to quit, or you'll be looking at rehab."

Aiden hadn't taken him seriously then. He should have, though. Should have quit before the need got this big. Before it got so hard.

The visit to rehab, the talk tonight. Dad was serious.

There'd been a moment when he'd considered actually going to that place. When Dad was talking about Mom, when he told Aiden about some of the stupid stuff he did as a kid, when he told him he was proud of him.

But now, in the quiet, he knew he couldn't go to rehab. Couldn't even make it to rehab before he got high again. Because as peaceful as this place was, the truth was screaming in his mind. And he had to shut it up.

Three days sober is nothing.

You know you'll never quit.

Think of all the fun you're missing. Partying, laughing, danc-ing, girls. They're out there, having a blast, and you're here, doing nothing.

The voices were getting louder, more insistent, and he knew he'd listen. He'd known all along there was no chance this would work. He didn't even want to get sober. Not now, not yet. There was too much fun to be had out there. When he was an adult, then he'd get sober, get a job, be responsible. This time of life was made for fun.

He'd go home, settle into his old life. His old man would give up and go home, and either he'd let Aiden move back in on Aiden's terms, or he wouldn't. That would be fine. He'd just live with his mother. She'd let him do whatever he wanted.

Assuming she'd have him. But when Dad had filed for full custody, Mom hadn't even contested it. Just told him he'd better do what his dad said. She'd keep a bedroom for him for week-ends. Except, half the time, she cancelled their weekends together.

No. She'd want him. Of course she would. He was her son.

How would she react when he showed up on her doorstep? He forced an image of her happy face, but it didn't stick. Maybe she'd send him back to his dad.

So maybe going back to New York wasn't the answer.

He didn't know, couldn't think straight, couldn't make any decisions feeling like this. The need was too big to fight.

He glanced at the clock. Eleven-thirty. That place Caro told him about closed at midnight.

Dad was still snoring quietly. Aiden lifted Dad's cell phone off the coffee table, clicked it to silent, and turned it on. He'd watched Dad put in his passcode a few times that day. He pressed the numbers, and the screen came to life.

He peeked at Dad again, stepped into the kitchen, and found

the address to the Nuthouse. A long walk, but just a ten-minute drive.

Did he dare?

He looked into the living room where the images on the TV cast a bluish glow over everything. The keys were resting beside where Dad's phone had been.

Aiden pulled his wallet out of his back pocket. He hadn't opened it since before the party Friday night. Did he have any money left? He checked, saw a couple of bills and his bank card. Worst case, he'd hit an ATM machine for some cash.

Would this work?

Aiden could go, get what he needed, and be back before Dad ever woke up. And if he did wake up, Aiden would just tell him he went for a drive. Dad wouldn't believe him, but whatever. Dad didn't believe anything Aiden said anymore.

He just had to get a few pills, maybe some pot. Anything to take the edge off. Then he'd figure out his next step.

Just thinking about it had his hands trembling.

He gently lifted the keys and pocketed them. Then he waited, watched his father as the seconds ticked away.

He slipped his father's phone in his pocket—that's what he got for taking Aiden's—and walked to the front door. Froze. Nope. A window would be better.

In his bedroom, he messed up his bed as if he'd been sleeping. Then he opened the window and climbed out.

TWENTY-THREE

Garrison rolled over, tried to get comfortable, but his too-tall frame didn't fit on the too-short sofa. And the lumpy furniture had not been designed for sleeping.

The TV was still on, but Aiden wasn't in the chair. Must have gone to sleep.

Garrison couldn't handle another night on the sofa. He'd sleep in the master tonight. After the talk they'd had earlier, Garrison believed Aiden was willing to get clean. He allowed the thought to settle as he stood and flicked off the TV, leaving the room in darkness. He headed down the hall toward his bedroom, stopping at Aiden's closed door. He twisted the knob, peeked inside. The bed was empty.

He checked the bathroom. Empty. "Aiden?" His shout reverberated off the walls.

No answer.

Garrison's whole body trembled as he checked his room. Then he pushed out the back door and called again. "Aiden?" His voice carried across the still lake and echoed back to him, mocking.

He jogged toward the shore and called again. Maybe Aiden would answer. Maybe he'd just gone for a walk.

Maybe Garrison was an idiot.

Garrison had the sudden urge to bang his head against a tree. How could he have been so stupid? He'd told himself for days to hold onto his suspicion. Told himself to not believe a word the kid said. Then he'd let himself get sucked in. Why? Because he'd wanted to believe. He'd always wanted to believe the best about his son, so unlike the way his father had always treated him.

You think you're so smart, kid. His father's voice boomed in his head. *Like those stupid grades make you smart. You don't know anything.*

Dad had been right. Garrison didn't have any idea what he was doing. He had no idea how to parent his son, this boy bent on destroying his life.

Garrison lumbered back to the cabin. Part of him longed to climb into bed, pull the covers over his head, pretend none of it was happening. If he didn't try to rescue his son, then he couldn't fail. And fail he would, Garrison had no doubt. He would try, he would pour his heart, his life, into rescuing Aiden, and Aiden would reject him, reject sobriety, reject freedom. And end up...

How to describe the unthinkable?

He reached the bottom of the porch steps, paused, and gripped the railing. Took a deep breath. Blew it out.

He just needed to know what to do right now. Then he'd figure out what to do next.

Right now, he'd look for his son.

He stepped back in the cabin and flipped on the light. Where had he left his keys? He glanced at the kitchen counter, but no. He'd come straight in and sat on the sofa. Exhausted. Which meant the keys and phone should be on the coffee table.

They were both gone.

Garrison yanked open the front door and peered at the empty driveway.

The kid had taken his car. He had half a mind to report it stolen.

Not a bad idea. Except to do that, he'd have to call the police, which meant Brady and Eric, the guys from the cookout that night. Did he really want their help? Things hadn't gotten that bad yet. Garrison could be overreacting. It was possible Aiden had taken a drive. Took Garrison's phone so he wouldn't get lost.

Yeah, right.

He returned to the coffee table, sat on the floor, and reached under it. Aiden's phone was still taped to the underside where Garrison had left it. He'd known the kid would dig through every drawer and cabinet looking for it, but he didn't figure he'd think to check here. At least about one thing, Garrison had been right.

The phone was nearly dead. He plugged it into his charger in the kitchen and dialed his own phone. It went straight to voicemail.

He flipped open his computer, navigated to the right website, and searched for his phone's location. He'd used this app enough to track his son's phone. Just lucky he could also find his own.

Except the phone was offline. Either Aiden had shut it off or he'd turned off the location tracker.

He dialed Sam's number from memory. A moment later, she answered, her voice scratchy from sleep.

"I'm sorry to wake you," he said.

She cleared her throat. "What happened?"

"Aiden took off. I wouldn't bother you, but he has my car and my phone. I thought I'd get an Uber to your house and borrow your car."

"I'll be there in twenty minutes."

Sam was coming. The thought made him feel better. Then it made him feel worse. What kind of man needs to call a woman in the middle of the night to rescue him?

For the second time that night, his father's words echoed in his brain. *Too scared. Too weak.*

Weak. He'd never wanted to believe it, but he felt it right now. Weak and afraid, relying on others for help. He'd been there enough to know where that would get him.

Problem was, he had no idea what else to do.

TWENTY-FOUR

Sam dressed quickly and yanked her hair into a ponytail. It was not quite two a.m. How long had Aiden been gone?

The despair in Garrison's voice had broken her heart. She knew how it felt to fail the one you loved, and she knew that was exactly how Garrison saw this. Never mind that he'd brought Aiden hundreds of miles away from his friends and the drugs. Never mind that he planned to send him to rehab, at a cost that had taken her breath away. Never mind that he'd done all he could to connect with Aiden, to make this trip not just helpful but enjoyable for both of them. Aiden had rejected his father and snubbed his nose at all his efforts.

The boy was practically an adult, and, whether Garrison wanted to face it or not, Aiden was the one making these choices.

But Garrison couldn't see that. And Sam understood how he felt.

She closed her eyes, prayed for guidance, prayed for Aiden, and prayed they'd find him.

Her heart broke for that boy. She was angry at him, but how lost and troubled must he have felt? And how did he feel now that he was gone? Did he feel free? Because running back to drugs was going to bring a lot of things, but it wouldn't bring freedom.

She slipped on her shoes, grabbed her stuff, and bounded out the door.

When she reached the cabin, Garrison was in the driveway, pacing. He yanked open her passenger door and folded his frame inside.

"Any idea where he would go?" she asked.

He shook his head. "I hoped you might have one."

She pulled out of the driveway and headed toward town because she didn't know what else to do. "Maybe you should call Brady. Or Eric. Didn't he say he had to work after the cookout?"

Garrison kept his gaze on the ditch beside the narrow road. "I considered reporting the car stolen, but I'd rather look around for him first."

"Okay. But you don't have to report it stolen to ask for Eric's help. He could just—"

"I don't want to call yet. If we don't find him, then I'll think about it."

"You mind if I ask why?"

"God forbid he's gotten high. If I have the cops looking for him and he gets pulled over, they could arrest him. That would just complicate things."

"Might. Might be the wakeup call he needs, though."

Garrison didn't respond.

"And you might be able to get them to drop the charges. I can't imagine Eric or Brady forcing the issue."

A beat of silence passed before Garrison said, "You want me to take you home so you can go back to sleep?"

Apparently he didn't want to discuss that any longer. "I know the town. I'll stay with you."

Silence filled the car like an enemy force. They reached downtown Nutfield and snaked along a few roads past houses and businesses, the park and the school. A mile or so past Rae's house, Sam turned around and headed back.

"Where we going?"

"I don't know. Just driving."

"Why'd you turn?"

"That road leads nowhere."

"But maybe he's on it, just a little country road, driving around."

"Maybe." She wanted to add that country roads led into and out of town from every direction. If Aiden was driving aimlessly, they'd need a miracle to find him. She prayed for a miracle and said nothing.

They returned downtown. Sam passed the bank, McNeal's, and the church.

"What's that?" He pointed at the Nuthouse.

The lights had been left on, like they were every night, to keep prowlers away. Through the storefront window, arcade games flashed. No cars were lined along the road, though. "It's a hangout for teenagers. But it's closed."

"I can see that."

"What time did you fall asleep?"

In the dim light cast by the streetlamp, she saw Garrison shrug, his face tortured. "I don't know exactly. Maybe eleven. I was so tired."

"There's no sin in sleeping."

"But Aiden..." His words trailed off.

"You can't control his every move."

He didn't respond.

She kept driving, followed every road surrounding the main drag, then wandered through neighborhoods and along more country roads. Time ticked by. Garrison remained silent.

This was fruitless. Surely by now he realized that. "Have you tried calling him?"

"Obviously." He dialed his phone anyway. Then hung up. He sat quietly for a few minutes, sighed, and dialed again. She only heard his end of the conversation.

"Nice language, Matty. It's his dad. Have you heard

from him?"

Ah, Matty. The best friend.

Garrison said, "He took off tonight. Thought he might've contacted you."

He stared out the window as he listened. "No. We're still in Nutfield." A beat, then, "It doesn't matter where. Listen, he's in trouble. You know he's been using drugs?" Matty's answer was short. "It's bad, and he needs rehab. I'm afraid he's going to hurt himself or somebody else. If you're really a friend, you'll encourage him to get help." He paused to listen, then, "Thank you. And you'll call me if you hear from him. Okay?"

Garrison ended the call and tossed the phone in her center console. "He hasn't heard from him."

"That was a good idea. I'm surprised Aiden didn't call him."

"I wonder if he knows the number. He's so dependent on his contact list he's lost without his phone. I'm not even sure he remembers my number. I've given him a hard time about it..." His words trailed off to nothing, and she kept driving.

They'd only seen a few cars, none that looked like Garrison's.

She circled toward the lake and turned onto the side street where his cabin was located.

"Where are we going?"

"Maybe he went back. Maybe he didn't go that far, and he's around here somewhere."

Garrison didn't say a word, but his stony silence told her what he thought of that idea.

They passed the cabin. No Camry.

She took a deep breath and considered pulling into the driveway. She peered at the little beach down the street, thinking maybe he'd pulled in there, then continued around the lake until the road dead-ended. She turned around and headed back to the main road, where she headed toward another of the little roads around the lake. The chances of them finding him were getting slimmer every minute. Aiden could be halfway to New York by now.

Sam took Garrison's hand. "I think it's time to call the police."

"It hasn't been that long. We just need to keep looking."

She looked at the dashboard clock. They'd been driving for an hour. "We need help."

"I don't need help." He pulled his hand away. "I can do this myself. In fact, why don't you let me take you home? I'll just borrow your car. That way you don't have to waste your night."

Irritation rolled over her. "You don't want my help?"

"I can find him myself."

"Really? How exactly can you do that?"

"I'm just saying..." Garrison blew out a loud breath. "You don't seem to have any insight into where he'd be. There's no need for you to lose sleep."

"You think I'd sleep if I went home?"

"He's not your problem."

Not her problem. Like she was just some bystander. Like she had no stake in this. And she didn't, did she? She was just the landlady. Never mind that she'd given them a cabin for the week, gone to tour the rehab facility with them, gone grocery shopping for them. Never mind that she'd prayed for them constantly since the call Saturday morning. Apparently none of that mattered because it wasn't her problem. She pulled over, put the car in park. "Fine. Do it yourself."

He turned toward her, blinked.

"You don't need my help, so get out."

"I didn't mean anything by that. I was just trying to let you get some rest."

"I get it."

He reached for her hand, but she pulled it away.

"Samantha—"

"It's fine." She spat the word like a curse, then took a deep breath. "What I don't get is why you don't call the police. I don't have any special insight, as you pointed out, but they actually do. If Aiden hasn't headed back to New York—"

"He wouldn't dare, not in my car."

"Then he's likely in Nutfield, and the police could probably find him in minutes. Which means you lied to him."

He crossed his arms. "I don't know what you're talking about."

"You told him you weren't ashamed of him or embarrassed about what he's going through. But you obviously are. Otherwise, why not ask for help?"

He turned, looked out at the black of forest. His voice was quiet when he answered. "I'm not embarrassed. This has nothing to do with that." A beat passed, and he turned back to her. "I just don't want to waste their time—"

"Because the police are so busy on a Tuesday morning at"— she glanced at the clock—"three-thirty a.m. This is their job, Garrison."

"Aiden is my job." His tone was cold. "My responsibility. Not yours, not theirs. And I can find him."

"Great." She nodded to the far door. "Good luck with that."

"You won't let me borrow your car?"

"You don't need my help."

His shoulders hunched forward like a weight had fallen on them. "What do you want from me?"

What did she want? She had no idea, and she was definitely going to regret this little outburst later. The last thing Garrison needed was her giving him a hard time. She should just back off, drive around, keep her mouth shut. And she would, except she was right.

"I want you to stop pretending you don't need help."

He turned toward the window. "I don't. I can handle this. I only called you because he took my car."

"Great. Thanks for that."

He turned to her. "I didn't mean it that way."

"This isn't about me, okay? I'm fine. I just want you to quit wasting time. Either call the police or get out."

TWENTY-FIVE

Matty sat up straight in Aiden's bed and opened the web browser on his phone. He'd used the code on the garage door opener to get into the Kopps' house the night before. He'd had it since Mr. Kopp and Aiden moved in, had used it a couple times when he'd gotten here before Aiden after school. Matty figured Mr. Kopp would be ticked if he knew Aiden had given him the code. Like that mattered now.

Matty hadn't known where else to go. He'd texted that Robert guy, told him he was going to get the package and would be back soon. The guy had texted back with, "I'll keep an eye on your house while you're gone."

A threat. A definite threat directed at Mom and Jimmy. A threat that kept him from going home. When he'd fallen asleep in Aiden's bed the night before, he'd been filled with fear, but now he had a plan.

Mr. Kopp hadn't meant to, but he'd given away the name of the town where they were staying. It wasn't an exact address, but the town name was a good start.

Matty typed *Nutfield* into the browser. Only one town option came up, and it was in New Hampshire. Not close, but totally drivable.

Now...how to get there?

Matty'd told his mother he was going camping with Aiden and his dad. Mom had agreed immediately—she'd always liked Mr. Kopp. Matty did, too. He hated to think about what Aiden's father would say if he knew Matty had been the one to introduce Aiden to drugs. The thought settled in his stomach like lead.

He had bigger worries right now.

His car was still parked where it had broken down. Even if he could get it running, he doubted the clunker would make it all the way to New Hampshire. Which left just one choice.

He'd have to take his mother's car. And he'd have to leave her a note telling her he took it so she wouldn't report it stolen. He hated to do it, but what choice did he have? He had to get the package, and he needed a car to do it, or else she and Jimmy would be in danger.

If Matty ever got his hands on his father, he'd punch him in the face.

He imagined confronting his father while he threw on his jeans, turned off all the lights, and stepped into the darkness. He grabbed his bike and rode to his neighborhood, then hid the bike in a huge bush in front of Mrs. Caldwell's house around the corner from his. She wouldn't see it from her windows—she was probably half blind, and anyway, who cared if he lost his bike?

All of this was Dad's fault. Rage he could barely contain had his heart pounding, his breath short. He clenched his fists and wished he could punch him right now. Would he have the courage? Would his dad hate him for it, or respect him more?

Matty didn't want to admit it, but he hoped for the second.

He had to quit caring. Obviously his old man didn't give a crap about him.

Focus. How could he get the car away from the house without Robert and his driver seeing? Matty could easily climb over the fences behind the houses, but there was no way to pull out of the driveway without being seen. Maybe they weren't there. Would they be watching in the middle of the night?

He crept to the end of his street. A few cars lined the road, as usual, but none that looked out of place. None that looked like the SUV Robert had forced Matty into the other day. Would they be driving the same car? Why not, when Robert had told him they'd be watching?

He had no idea. He bent to a crouch and looked through the windows of the truck that belonged to the house down the street. He studied the rest of the cars on the street, the ones he could see from there, anyway. They were all familiar, the same cars that were parked on his street every single night.

Maybe Robert and his buddy had decided to get some sleep.

He crept closer to the house, peered through his neighbor's car windows. No silver SUV.

Still he waited, watched, as minutes ticked by. No movement. No glow of a cell phone or flash of a lighter. The street was completely still.

Matty took a deep breath and jogged toward his house. He was passing the bushes that marked the border between his house and the one next door when he felt movement. He twisted his gaze to the right. Something grabbed his left hand.

He started to call out, but another hand covered his mouth.

"Shh. Stop."

The whispered voice seemed to scream in his ear. He yanked, tried to get away, but the arms were too strong.

"Shh. Matty, it's me."

The voice sounded familiar. He quit fighting.

"You going to scream?"

He shook his head.

The arm pulled him toward the bushes. Finally, the hand lifted from his face

Matty whirled around, fists up ready to strike.

The man backed up a step. "Hey, it's okay." The voice, which he'd kept just above a whisper, sounded like his father, but this man looked nothing like the person Matty'd seen at the airport Friday night. He hadn't shaved in days. He'd lost the high-priced suit and loafers and now wore shorts, a Hawaiian shirt, and flip-flops. A pair of sunglasses were perched on his head.

Matty looked closer. The face looked so different from the Frank O'Brien he knew, but those hazel eyes hadn't changed. "Dad?"

"I didn't mean to scare you. I just didn't want you to wake the whole neighborhood."

He stepped closer to his father, seething. "Where have you been?"

"Keep it down." He looked over his shoulder, then over the other. "What are you doing?"

"Trying to fix this mess you got me into."

"Me? You had one job, kid. Take the package and drop it off. Seems you're the one who got us in this mess." Matty's father pulled on his arm, practically dragging him between Matty's house and the neighbor's.

When they were hidden from the street, his dad whirled to face him. "Where have you been? I've been waiting for you for hours."

"Why didn't you call?"

"Had to lose the phone. Somehow they figured out where I was."

"You mean the Bahamas?"

Matty's father's eyes widened, then narrowed. "How did you know that?"

He wanted to whack himself upside the head. He shouldn't have said that. Could he trust his father with the truth? Or should he just get away, follow his original plan—get the package, contact Robert, be done with it? If he told his father what was going on, what would happen? Could his father help him?

Not that it mattered now, the way his dad was looking at him. He'd let the truth slip, and there was no going back.

He was terrible at all this cloak-and-dagger crap.

"Some dude named Robert—"

His words were cut off by his father's whispered curse. "When?"

"Sunday. He told me you stole whatever's in that package and that it's his job to get it back. Told me he works for the government."

"Not our government," his father said. "He works for the DRC."

"It's true? You did steal...whatever that was?"

"I was asked to get it out of the country and to a buyer."

"But if their government is after you, then it was illegal, right?"

"The Congo isn't like America. Their government isn't perfect. The people I'm working with are trying to fight them."

"What does that mean? They're like freedom fighters or something?"

"Something like that."

He knew it. His father was a good guy. "You're trying to help fund a revolution?"

Dad opened his mouth, then closed it again. "It's not that clear cut. This side needs money, and I'm helping them get it."

Matty nodded, happy to finally have his theories confirmed. "Right. So they can overthrow an evil..."

"Life isn't a Marvel comic, kid." Dad ran his hands through his hair. They snagged on the sunglasses, and he grabbed them and shoved them in his pocket. "There's no good versus evil. Just one side versus the other."

In other words, Dad didn't care what side he was on, as long as he got paid.

Matty stared at his father, at the beach-bum clothes. Apparently he was good at disguises. Good at stealing, good at breaking the law. He just sucked at being a dad.

"This is about money," Matty said.

Dad's expression shifted fast from arrogant to excited to pleading. "A lot of money, which I'm planning to share with you, as soon as we get that package delivered. Whatever Robert offered you, I'll double it."

Of course Dad assumed Robert had tried to buy him. And of course he figured Matty would betray him for a few bucks. Like father, like son. Because, of course, his dad wouldn't hesitate.

Anyway, if this was the kind of stuff his father was into, Matty had been way underpaid. His dad was just a greedy jerk. And no matter how much money was involved, it wasn't enough to make Matty put his family in danger.

Maybe the apple had fallen a little further from the tree than Dad realized.

Dad's eyes narrowed. "How much did Robert offer you?"

He had to think. Dad was greedy, yeah, but he wouldn't want his family harmed. Would he work with Matty to protect them all? Matty tried to imagine that, but another image took its place. His father, the suits, the way he'd yanked Matty into all this crap.

He couldn't trust his father.

The words formed on his mouth and felt like sawdust. "Ten thousand. But I only agreed because I didn't know what else to do. I wasn't going to betray you."

"Good. Good. Okay, twenty grand. I can handle that."

Unbelievable that his old man believed him. Now what? Escape his dad? Or use him. He was finally close to finding the package and ending this thing.

"Do you have a car?"

"Yeah, yeah," Dad said. "Rental. I parked on the next block."

"Is it safe? Do you think they know about it?"

He affected a Southern accent. "This ain't my first rodeo, kid."

Like it was a big joke.

"My car broke down," Matty said. "I was about to take Mom's. I know where the package is."

"Great! Let's go!"

As he followed his dad to the car, Matty tried to figure out how he was going to find the Kopps, get the package, and hand it over to Robert without his father knowing. He had no clue. He'd have to solve that problem when they reached Nutfield.

TWENTY-SIX

Aiden could hardly think straight. He should have settled for an oxy, but he'd wanted to save those for later. Instead, he'd smoked pot. And then somebody'd offered him another pill—something he'd never tried before. He couldn't remember who gave it to him, couldn't remember the name of it, and had no idea what it was. All he knew was, he was wasted.

He liked it. Liked it a lot, but he had to do something. Something was wrong.

He had to think.

He forced his gaze up from the chair. Saw the TV on. *Call of Duty*. Two guys were seated on the couch with headsets, talking and playing the video game. One was the guy he'd met at the Nuthouse—Bill. Or maybe Bob. He thought the other was the owner of this house. He could hardly remember now.

The place was a dump and stank like stale smoke and cold pizza. Oh, right. There was a pizza box on the floor. Aiden had bought it when the munchies hit. A few pieces, one with a bite taken out of it, were left lying there, but Aiden couldn't imagine eating now. His stomach was twisted in a knot. Like something was wrong. But he couldn't remember what.

Curled up on the chair across from him, a girl was sound

asleep, her arm hanging off the edge. He didn't think he'd ever caught her name. She wasn't cute or anything. Her hair was stringy and gross, and her face had some sort of rash on it. He thought she went with the guy who lived there.

Seeing her reminded him of something. Someone asleep.

Crap. That was it. Aiden had left his father sound asleep at the house. He'd planned to go straight home. Then planned to get high and go straight home. Then there'd been the pill, the pizza, the sofa.

He had to get back before Dad woke up.

He sat up, stretched. Checked his pockets. The other pills he'd bought were still there. They should be enough to get him through the week. He stood, and the room spun. He waited for the feeling to pass, figured he'd be better when he hit the fresh air. "I'm outta here."

The Nuthouse guy—Bill/Bob—barely glanced away from the screen. "You need anything else, you know where to find me. I can hook you up."

Aiden would need to make what he'd already bought last the week. He'd found an ATM and taken out what little cash was in his account. After the pizza, there was none left.

The air outside was warm and thick with humidity—not the refreshing blast he'd hoped for. He unlocked Dad's Camry and slipped inside, blinking to wake himself up. He was usually fine after an oxy, but whatever he'd taken was making him so tired. He had to get back to the cabin and crash before Dad woke up and saw how wasted he was.

He backed out of the drive, then slammed on the brakes when he saw a car in the rearview mirror. It was parked on the street across from the driveway. Thank God he hadn't hit it. No way to explain away a dent.

He turned carefully onto the little suburban street. Was this the right way? He couldn't remember, and he didn't want to power on Dad's phone just yet. If Dad was awake, and if he was trying to find him, then turning on the map program might enable his locator. Last thing he wanted to do was have the cops show up here, raid Bill/Bob's stash. He'd just drive, put some distance between himself and the house. Maybe he could find his way back to the cabin without the map.

He looked for anything that seemed familiar. Nothing did, but he kept on. Random lefts and rights until finally he reached the road they'd come in on—he hoped. No traffic, hardly wide enough for two cars. This little hick town didn't even know how to do roads right. Still, it was kind of cool with the lake and all the trees, and apparently they weren't very far from the ocean. Like twenty minutes, Bill/Bob said. They'd talked about going to the beach. Aiden had been all for it, but then they turned on *Call of Duty*, and that was that. Boring.

Boring, but still better than sober.

The car drifted off the pavement into the dirt on the right, and Aiden jerked the wheel to the left, then had to fight to straighten the car. Where were the curbs? And the sidewalks. Sheesh. A guy could kill himself out here.

He cranked up the music and the A/C. Had to stay awake until he got back to the cabin. This wasn't like driving wasted back on Long Island. He knew every road and alley in Hempstead. This was all different. And dark. Where were the streetlights, anyway? How did people drive like this?

A car came toward him, and Aiden concentrated on staying in his lane and driving straight. He focused on the road, kept his hands at ten and two like Dad had taught him. The car passed. Was that a cop? He thought he'd seen lights on the top, but he was scared to even check the rearview to find out. Dad would kill him if he got arrested.

He drove another ten minutes before he pulled over. He was never going to find his way back without the map. He powered up the phone, saw missed calls and messages from his own phone.

Crap. Dad was looking for him.

Hands shaking, he navigated to the map program. At least

he'd had the brains to drop a pin at the cabin so he could find his way back. Following Siri's directions, Aiden swung the car around and headed in the opposite direction. He wasn't going to call his father back. He'd just get to the cabin and act like everything was fine. He just had to do it fast.

Thirty seconds later, a car came toward him again. He clenched his hands on the wheel, stayed in his lane, and watched as the car passed. Definitely a cop.

In the rearview, he saw brake lights. That cop was going to swing around and stop him.

If he got pulled over, he'd fail a sobriety test for sure. Aiden floored it. No way was he getting arrested tonight. No freakin' way.

TWENTY-SEVEN

Eric had been very understanding.

It really ticked Garrison off.

He didn't want the cop's help. He didn't need his help. Aiden would have gone back to the cabin on his own whenever he was finished...whatever he'd been doing. And now he'd probably get picked up for DUI, all because Garrison had called the cops.

Because of Sam.

She was staring straight ahead, hands on the wheel, unmoving. She'd been like that since he'd made the call, like she was waiting for him to say something. Probably to admit she was right.

And maybe she was. He wasn't convinced, but she hadn't left him any choice.

He should say something. She'd been nothing but nice to him, nothing but helpful. And if anybody else were in this situation, Garrison would recommend they call the police. It was the right move, if he wanted to find his son. If he'd wanted to do nothing, he could have done that from the cabin. Just waited, hoped the boy would come back.

He probably should have done that. Not called anyone.

Because then Sam wouldn't be sitting beside him, looking anywhere but at him. And Eric wouldn't have been understanding and patronizing on the phone, all eager to help. And Garrison wouldn't feel utterly impotent.

In the end, he knew how this would play out. The cops wouldn't be helpful. Sam wouldn't, either. Garrison had to figure this out on his own. That was the only way.

Unfortunately, it was too late to undo his choices now.

They'd been stopped on the side of the road for fifteen minutes.

"Do you want to take me back to the cabin?" he asked.

"Do you want to go back to the cabin?"

He tried to imagine what it would feel like to sit there, to pace and worry, all alone. If he asked her to, Sam would stay with him. For support. But he didn't need her support. He didn't want to need it. He couldn't be alone, and he didn't want to need. He hated to need.

"Let's keep driving," he said. "Maybe we'll see him."

She drove down each little road that led to the lake, and they looked for some sign of Aiden. No deal. Then she headed back toward town. He was getting a feel for the layout now that he'd driven every street of this tiny hamlet. Under different circumstances, he'd be charmed.

But there were drugs here, too. Drugs everywhere.

When Garrison called the police, he'd been happy to hear a woman's voice. He hadn't wanted to talk to Eric or Brady. Better to make this impersonal. But, apparently, when the dispatcher passed the information along to the guys on patrol, Eric recognized the name. Because *Aiden Kopp* wasn't *John Smith*, was it? Of course Eric had called.

"I got a few ideas where he could be," Eric had said. His Southern accent wasn't as pronounced now as it had been earlier, but it was still unmistakable. "If he hooked up with one of the dealers in town, I might be able to locate him."

"Great. Thanks."

"You bet. Sorry to hear this. He seemed like a nice kid."

Seemed. As if Aiden couldn't be an addict and a nice kid at the same time. Was Aiden a nice kid now? An addict, a liar, a thief? A single guy with no kids like Eric could never understand. Garrison wasn't even sure he did.

Garrison heard himself say, "He used to be."

"I don't know what this is going to look like, especially if someone else finds him first. But if I do, I'll go easy on him."

Go easy. As Sam maneuvered the car along the streets of downtown Nutfield, Garrison wondered if he should have told Eric not to go easy. What Aiden needed was the fear of God put into him, and maybe that meant getting arrested and thrown in jail. Maybe it meant being knocked around a little bit. But of course Eric and the other cops in town wouldn't do that unless Aiden resisted arrest.

He'd been taught better than that.

Course, he'd been taught not to use drugs. He'd been taught not to sneak out of the house and steal his father's car.

They reached the police station and inched by. Would Garrison see the inside of that building tonight?

His phone rang. A local number. "Kopp here."

"There was an accident." Eric's voice was all business now. "Aiden ran off the road and hit a tree."

Oh, God. "He okay?"

"Just shaken up, I think. Paramedics are on the way." He rattled off directions, which Garrison repeated.

Sam swung the car around and picked up speed. "Tell him we're ten minutes out."

Garrison spoke into the phone. "You know what happened?"

"I think he saw me and was trying to lose me."

Garrison's anger rose suddenly. "You were chasing him?"

"No," Eric said, irritatingly calm. "He saw me behind him and panicked, I think. The ambulance just got here. I'll explain more when you arrive."

Garrison hung up the phone.

"An accident?" Sam asked.

"Yeah. He said he thinks Aiden saw him following and tried to get away."

"Oh, no."

Sam might have said more, but he couldn't listen to her. He felt like he was in a trance. What if Aiden had died? What if it was worse than Eric had said? He tried to imagine what that would feel like to lose his son, but he couldn't do it. He only felt numb.

Maybe Aiden wasn't dead, but maybe he was badly injured. Paralyzed. Or brain damaged. He wouldn't be using drugs anymore, in that case.

The thought, so casual, like it didn't matter. Like his whole life didn't hinge on this.

Maybe Aiden would get arrested, thrown in jail, charged with DUI and possession. Assuming he was possessing—which Garrison did. Maybe he'd be facing jail time in New Hampshire. Would Garrison relocate here to be close to him?

Would they have mercy?

Would they throw the book at him?

Garrison experienced all these thoughts as if he were watching a movie. Look at how despondent he felt. Look at how helpless. Look at how useless and impotent. He could name the emotions, but he didn't really experience them.

But then the anger came, and that one felt real. Angry at Aiden for sneaking out. For putting him through all this. For getting addicted in the first place.

Angry at the police for screwing this up. Angry at himself, for trusting the kid, for letting himself hope.

Of all the emotions, the anger won. He glanced at Sam through a haze of it, thought of a thousand things he could say. What came out of his mouth was,

"I never should have listened to you."

TWENTY-EIGHT

Sam had tried. She'd done everything she could think to do to help Garrison and Aiden, and it wasn't enough.

Why was she surprised?

The wheels rumbled along the gravelly road, and the sound scraped against her fear. Foolish woman. Foolish, useless woman.

She shook her head clear of the selfish thoughts. This was about Aiden. *Please, let him be okay.* If he was okay, then maybe Garrison would forgive her for meddling. If he was okay, then maybe things could go back to the way they had been. But she knew no matter what, there was no going back.

No. Focus on Aiden. Pray for Aiden. She had to stop thinking about herself. No wonder nobody loved her.

She forced her focus to Aiden and Garrison, forced herself to pray.

Finally, they reached the site of the accident. Two police cars, a fire truck, and an ambulance were parked along the road, lights flashing. All those emergency vehicles—was it that bad? In the darkness, she saw men walking around in their dark uniforms, talking to each other. Nobody running. No signs of panic. But where was Aiden?

She stopped behind one of the cruisers. Garrison was out of

the car and jogging toward the cluster of men before she'd shifted into park.

Maybe she should just leave. One of them would give Garrison a ride back to the cabin. Nobody needed her there.

She glanced across the street and saw Garrison's car, smashed and mangled against an unyielding tree. Her stomach roiled at the sight.

She had to know if Aiden was all right. She stepped out and followed Garrison around the ambulance.

She stopped when she saw Aiden sitting on a gurney, head in his hands. His father was seated beside him, trying to hug him, though the boy seemed to want nothing to do with it. But he was alive. Sitting up. Seemed all right.

Thank God.

She didn't get closer. She stood beside the ambulance and prayed for him, for them.

Garrison looked up and met her eyes.

She turned and headed for her SUV. She wasn't needed here.

The wind rustled the leaves, and she peered into the deep woods. They called to her.

No. She wouldn't think about that. Tonight wasn't about her. She'd already been selfish enough, and nobody had time to manage her anxiety. She could do this. Hadn't she gone to Dover? If she could drive to Dover, she could get home from here. She was only a few minutes from town.

The trees along the side of the road snickered in the breeze.

The spinning red and blue lights flickered against the trunks and played havoc with her vision.

She heard footsteps behind her and froze. Planted her feet. Braced herself. As if she could stop it from happening again.

Someone grabbed her arm.

She wheeled around and yanked away.

Garrison let her go and lifted both hands in surrender. "I didn't mean to scare you."

She took a deep breath and tried to force her heartbeat back to a normal rhythm.

"I'm sorry," he said. "I called out. Didn't you hear me?"

She hadn't. Hadn't heard anything but the echoes of the forest. She couldn't speak.

"Are you all right?"

A deep breath. "I'm fine." She swallowed a bubble of fear and forced herself to sound normal. "Is Aiden okay? I didn't see him up close, but from where I was standing... Is he hurt badly?"

"Just shaken up. The airbag deployed. He's probably good and bruised. He'll be sore tomorrow. I think he's too high right now to feel much of anything."

"Oh. Sorry."

He rubbed his hand over his short hair. "It's not your fault, Sam. None of this is your fault. I'm sorry I was such a jerk."

"It's fine."

"No, it's not."

But she didn't belong with Garrison and Aiden. Didn't belong anywhere, except maybe with the trees that drew her in, their limbs like skeletal arms longing to hold her again, their twigs like witches' fingers beckoning her toward them. She wanted to go, to let the darkness and shadows embrace her, to hide her in their crooks until nothingness descended.

The wind whispered its lies, and she leaned into the sound like a lullaby.

She stepped toward the edge of the forest, toward darkness and death and oblivion. Toward freedom.

A hand on her arm. Not twigs and leaves, but human fingers.

"What's wrong?" Garrison asked.

She stared into the woods that still called to her, longing to give in to the temptation, to disappear into forest and forgetfulness.

She shuddered and shook out of Garrison's grip. "I have to go." She slid inside her SUV and slammed the door.

No. She'd fought it for so long. But now, the world was closing in on her. Darkness, silence, the call of death.

The car door opened. She gasped, frozen in fear. She'd almost done it. Almost gone willingly into the abyss.

Not a heart attack. Not a heart attack.

Fear of nothing. She was crazy.

Something touched her, and she jumped.

"Hey." Garrison's voice, tender beside her. "Hey, look at me."

She couldn't open her eyes, couldn't think.

Her heart would explode any minute. The pain was unbearable. Her fingers cramped. She couldn't move them. Couldn't get enough air.

Garrison crouched beside her. His voice sounded as if it were coming from the far end of a long tunnel.

"You need to slow down your breathing, Sam. Can you look at me, please?"

She forced her eyes open, saw him beside her.

"There you go. Good girl."

He breathed slowly, steadily. She tried to mimic it.

"That's it."

"My heart." It felt like it might explode.

He kept breathing steadily. "You have a beautiful, healthy heart, Samantha." Another slow deep breath. She focused on matching it. "That's it."

She had no idea how much time passed before she felt better. Minutes. Hours. But the pain subsided. Oxygen filled her lungs. Her heartbeat slowed. She felt almost normal. As if.

"You all right?" Garrison asked.

She nodded, looked at her knees.

"Wow, you weren't kidding about those anxiety attacks." She glanced at his face. His warm brown eyes crinkled at the corners. "I like the way you throw yourself into whatever you're doing. Shows great dedication."

He was joking. Probably a good way to deal with a crazy person.

"And heck," he said, "if you have to have a medical emergency, where better than here? Paramedics everywhere."

She looked down, wanted to melt into the seat. How could he still be there, still be kind, after everything?

"You take my car," she said. "I'll get one of these guys to drive me home."

He closed his mouth, tilted his head to the side. "You're not going to forgive me?"

"Nothing to forgive. You need to take care of Aiden."

His voice hardened. "He's fine."

"So am I. I'll get a ride home. I don't think I can drive."

"But I can—"

"You need to take care of your son. I'm fine." She met his eyes, motioned with her hands for him to get out of her way, and he stepped back.

She walked toward Eric. "Can somebody drive me home?"

Eric's eyes flicked to Garrison. He said nothing.

"Sure," Eric said. "I'll get Donny to drive you." He pointed to a cruiser. "That's his. Climb in the front and don't play with the buttons."

She attempted a smile but couldn't pull it off. She walked toward the cruiser.

Garrison was still beside her.

"Your son needs you."

"What about you?"

"I'm fine. I'll be fine at home. It's just..." She glanced at the forest, shook her head. "I'll be fine." But she didn't get in the cruiser. Couldn't sit in there by herself. "Go."

Garrison stood with her until Donny ran up. He introduced himself to Garrison and said, "I understand the plan is to get him into rehab."

"How did you know that?"

"He told me."

Garrison looked surprised. "Oh. Yeah, that's the plan. If we survive until then."

"You will. It's a good idea." Donny looked at her. "Ready, Sam?"

Garrison turned to her. "Get some rest. I'll drop your car off tonight, if I can get one of these guys to drive me home. Okay if I leave the keys on the floorboard?"

"It's fine."

"Okay. I'll call you tomorrow."

"You don't have to."

He started to say something, then stopped and kissed her on the cheek. "Tomorrow."

TWENTY-NINE

Garrison watched until Sam and the police officer disappeared down the twisting road. He'd really botched that up. What had he been thinking, getting a woman with an anxiety disorder to drive him all over town in the middle of the night—and giving her a hard time about it, too? He hadn't been thinking, not about her.

He'd be lucky if she ever forgave him.

He had half a mind to tell the cops to haul Aiden to jail and follow her.

Instead, he turned toward Eric, who was standing by Aiden. But his gaze caught on the Camry.

The thick oak tree that had taken the brunt of the crash stood straight. But the car... The hood was mangled, the front passenger side mashed in. If somebody'd been in the passenger seat, he'd be seriously injured. Or dead.

He looked away before he threw up. He'd seen his share of tragedy in his life, but this was different. This was his tragedy, his son.

Aiden could have died tonight.

Garrison forced his gaze up, saw Aiden watching him. He approached Eric. "What happened?"

Eric led Garrison to the far side of the ambulance and out of Aiden's earshot. "There's a fellow who hangs out at the Nuthouse. We suspect he's dealing, but we haven't nailed him yet. I was heading to his house to see if your car was there. On the way, I saw the Camry coming toward me. I let him pass, then turned around, thinking I'd follow at a distance. But then your son did a U-turn and passed me a second time. I tried to play it cool, but I guess when he saw the cruiser in his rearview, he panicked. Floored it. I stayed pretty far back so Aiden would relax." Eric pointed to a street sign and a narrow country road Garrison hadn't noticed before. "I'm guessing he saw that road and thought he'd turn, try to lose me, but he was going too fast and lost control."

Garrison pictured the scene.

Eric lowered his arm. "Your boy's lucky this is such a winding road. If he'd hit a straightaway and been going much faster, this could have been a lot worse."

Garrison swallowed and turned to gaze at Aiden, who was still seated on the gurney, hunched over, head in his hands. A paramedic stood beside him, asking questions.

"This is awkward, you being a friend of the chief's."

Garrison returned his focus to the officer. "Worked with him on a case last spring."

"I was there when they found Ana, heard you were involved. If you need some recommendations for facilities, call the station tomorrow. We got a guy in town with a lot of experience."

"It's not Reed, is it?"

"Good. Sam already hooked y'all up. Take his advice. He knows what he's doing."

"I plan to." He gazed at his son, watched as the paramedic looked into his eyes with a small flashlight, then shut it off and slipped it into a pocket. He stepped away.

Garrison turned back to Eric. "What are you going to do here?"

Eric shook his head. "I'm still thinking about it." He

approached Aiden, stopped a few feet away, and crossed his arms across his thick chest. Though Eric was a few inches shorter than Garrison and Aiden, the man was all muscle. Intimidation personified.

Garrison followed and stood beside him.

"Look at me, boy," Eric said.

Aiden looked up, saw his dad, then focused on the police officer.

"I got you for possession, reckless driving, DUI, disobeying a police officer..." Eric paused. "I'm sure I could come up with a few more."

Aiden's eyes filled with tears. "Yes, sir."

"You could have killed yourself. You could have killed somebody else. You understand that?"

"Yes, sir."

He pointed to the mangled car. "You could have been pulled out of that and shoved straight into a body bag. Can you picture that?"

Tears streamed down Aiden's face. He looked down, nodded his head.

"Imagine your dad standing beside your body. Imagine him having to plan your funeral."

Garrison's eyes stung. That picture came too easily.

Eric's voice was harsh. "Look at me."

Aiden did. His lower lip trembled, and Garrison wanted nothing more than to wrap his child in his arms.

Maybe...maybe this would be the wake-up call.

Eric gazed at his cruiser for a long moment, looked back at Aiden. "You want to go to jail tonight?"

"No, sir."

"Do you deserve to go to jail tonight?"

Aiden's gaze flicked to Garrison. He nodded.

"Didn't hear you," Eric said.

Aiden looked up. "Yes, sir."

"In my job," the cop said, "I often have to choose between justice and mercy. You know what those words mean?"

Aiden nodded.

"Okay?" Eric waited, eyebrows lifted.

Aiden looked at Garrison, who nodded at the cop.

"Don't look at him, boy," Eric said. "This is on you."

Aiden met Eric's eyes. "So, like, justice is when you get what's coming to you, I guess."

"I like that," Eric said. "And mercy?"

Aiden shrugged. "I guess it's when you don't."

Eric nodded slowly, as if he were digesting the words. "Good. That's a good way to put it. If you get what you deserve tonight, it means jail, right?"

Aiden nodded.

Eric looked at Garrison, looked at his police cruiser, looked at Aiden. "I'm going with mercy tonight. Don't make me regret it."

Aiden dropped his shoulders, which shook with sobs.

Garrison could hardly hold in his own tears as he turned to the man and shook his hand again. "Thank you."

"Get him in a facility right away. Let us know if you need anything."

"Will do."

Eric stepped forward and clasped the boy on the shoulder. "Let this be rock bottom. Then the only way to go is up."

THIRTY

"Why don't you look up the address on your phone so we know where we're going when we get to Nutfield?"

Matty had been dreading this moment for four hours while his father drove. "I don't know exactly where they are."

His father's quiet exhale spoke volumes. "What do you know?"

"Mr. Kopp let the name of the town slip when I talked to him."

"That's it—the name of the town? What if there's another Nutfield in another state somewhere."

"I'm not an idiot. I checked that."

"And what are we supposed to do when we get there, just walk around calling their names until we find them? Look for their... Aw, crap. You're sure they have their car, right? You did at least ask that."

Matty's heart pounded. The thought had never occurred to him. He considered it, considered the distance to New Hampshire. "It's not at their house, so..."

"Airports have parking lots, you know."

No. No way they flew. "I guarantee Mr. Kopp didn't get

Aiden out of the hospital and then book flights. They're not the kind of people who fly to the Bahamas at the first sign of trouble."

He shouldn't have said that. He snuck a peek at his father but saw no reaction. Frank didn't say anything, and the quiet was worse than his father's quick anger.

"Sorry. I didn't mean that."

"I was trying to stay alive and out of jail. Maybe your hero Garrison Kopp would have made a different choice."

His hero? Matty wanted to disagree, but his father was right. Mr. Kopp had always been a hero. He'd never have been in a situation where he needed to flee the country. He was a stand-up guy who valued the law. A good guy. Not like Frank O'Brien, who was only a father by DNA. Matty couldn't say any of that, though.

His father thumped the steering wheel. "You're telling me that all you know is the name of the town?"

"That's all he said."

"Nothing about landmarks? Nothing about where they're staying?"

Matty thought back, thought of the conversation with Mr. Kopp, and the one with Aiden. "They're staying on a lake. Aiden's dad was mad he told me that."

"Good, good. Check it out."

Matty opened a browser on his phone and searched. "Clear-water Lake. That must be where they are."

"Unless it's a really small lake, that probably doesn't narrow it enough. You got pictures of your friends?"

Matty opened his photos. There were a bunch of Aiden, none of Mr. Kopp. "Some."

Dad nodded slowly, stayed quiet a minute. "Look and see how many roads go in and out from the lake."

Matty studied the map. "Looks like one main road from town. It keeps going past the lake, but there doesn't seem to be much beyond it for miles."

"Either we ask around or we just park and watch for them."

"We could do that. They have to get out sometime."

"If we don't see them in a couple hours, you'll call."

"And say what?"

"That you're in town and need help. He'd come, right, the big FBI hero? He wouldn't just ignore you."

Acid soured his stomach. "I was sort of hoping we could just find the Camry, get the stuff, and leave without him knowing anything."

"Right. Wouldn't want to disappoint your hero."

His father's voice was thick with sarcasm. Was he jealous? Couldn't be, because that would mean he cared, and Matty had quit believing that. No father who cared would put his kid in this situation. Not without good reason.

But maybe his dad had good reason. Maybe all this was worse, more dangerous than Matty even realized. "What's in the package, anyway?" Matty waited through a long silence before he added, "I think at this point, I have a right to know."

"A right? Like there's some consti-flippin-tution? You got no rights here, kid."

"Seriously? You drag me into this, but you won't even tell me what it's about? Yeah, that feels about like what you'd do."

"What's that supposed to mean?"

"Look at me, Dad!" Rage filled every pore of his being. "Look at this situation we're in. You don't think after all I've done, all I'm trying to do to get that stupid little box back, I don't have any right to know what's inside?"

"Calm down."

"Don't tell me to calm down. You want my help, you'll tell me what's in the"—he barely held back a curse—"package."

Dad exhaled a long breath. "You got quite a temper on you, boy."

"Don't call me boy."

"What's your problem? I call you kid all the time."

"I don't like that, either. I have a name, in case you forgot."

"How could I? I was there when we gave it to you."

"Congratulations. At least you can say you showed up once."

Dad lifted one hand in surrender and glanced his way. "Dial the anger back, would ya?"

Dial it back? He had to clench his hands together to keep from striking out.

"I'll tell you if you calm down."

Matty spoke through gritted teeth. "I'm calm."

There was a long pause while the landscape passed outside. The sun was close enough to rising that Matty could make out the shapes of the trees in the forest that lined the road, but everything looked black and gray, like an old movie. He felt like he'd been caught up in some crazy black-and-white flick like his mom always watched.

"You have to understand." Dad said. "The people who gave the stuff to me, they didn't steal them. They found them."

"Found what?"

A long exhale. "They're uncut diamonds."

Diamonds? Holy cow. A thousand questions popped in his head, but he landed on, "What do you mean, they found them? Like, on the sidewalk?"

"The Congo is filled with diamond mines. These were mined, but they weren't turned over to the owners. The miners who mined them smuggled them out and got them to a guy who's trying to start a revolution. He passed them to me to convert to cash for him. I deliver the diamonds, the buyers wire the money to my contact in Africa."

This was utterly insane. He knew his father was into some strange stuff, but this went far beyond what Matty had imagined. "You're helping start a war? Why? What's in it for you?"

"I get a cut of the price. It's a lot of money. I've already got half. I get the other half when it's done."

"These guys you're working for, are you in favor of their cause? Do you think they'd be better at running their country than the people Robert works for?"

"I don't do politics. This is strictly business."

Business. For a minute, he'd thought his father might have a conscience.

"What happens if we don't get the package, the...diamonds"— he could hardly say the word, it felt so weird on his lips—"to these people? Are they gonna, like, kill you?"

"We're going to get it, so it doesn't matter."

"I'm serious. Like, is your life in danger?" He wanted to add, *is mine*? But he was afraid of the answer. Because...diamonds, revolution. This sounded far too serious for Matty.

Dad scoffed. "Don't be stupid. Nobody's going to die. I made a promise to these people, and real men keep their promises. That's a good lesson for you, kid. Keep your promises."

Right. His father had never kept the promises he made to Matty and Jimmy and their mother. Dad had broken every one of those. But of course there was never money to be made with those promises, only money to be spent. Wasted, Dad probably thought, on stupid things like clothes and food and rent. Well, they weren't Dad's clothes, Dad's food, or Dad's rent, were they? What did his family matter when there was money to be made?

He glanced at his dad. With the sun rising, he could see him better now, the puffiness under his eyes, the dark circles. What kind of life was that, always looking over your shoulder? All in search of what?

Why had Matty ever wanted to follow in his father's footsteps? But if he didn't, what would he be? What could he be, if this was all his father was?

Assuming they survived, what choices would Matty have in his future?

"I know what you're thinking," Dad said. "And I haven't been the best about promises, but I'm going to fix that."

Another empty promise. Just what he needed. "Whatever. What if, this time, you can't keep your promise? What if you can't deliver the package? Then what?"

Dad shrugged as if it was no big deal. "That's really not an option."

"Just pay the money back. Then this will all be over."

"You think they'll just forget that I was carrying a million bucks' worth of diamonds?"

A million dollars. A million dollars.

Matty had had a million dollars' worth of diamonds in his pocket. He'd stuck a million dollars' worth of diamonds into the trunk of Mr. Kopp's car.

All because of his father's crazy schemes. For what? Another trip to Atlantic City so he could blow it at the blackjack tables? It hadn't been the lawbreaking or the lies or the broken promises that led Matty's mother to boot Dad out. It had been the gambling. Matty could still remember the fights, the way his mother cried when he came home penniless. Again. Risked his life for nothing. Again. Left her to fend for herself and her children. Again.

His father was a fool. Of course these people would demand their diamonds. What would they do if the diamonds were lost? Or turned over to the police?

"But what about the African dude, Robert? He's who you're running from, right? Is he going to kill you if he doesn't get his stuff back?"

"What's with you and the killing? Nobody's going to kill anybody."

Matty remembered the threats Robert made against his family. He didn't believe his father's words and doubted Dad believed them either. "Then why are you running if you're not scared?"

"I'm not running. I'm trying to get the merchandise so I can deliver it."

"The Bahamas—"

"Okay, fine. That might have been considered running, but sometimes that's the best move—get away, regroup. I'm trying to stay out of jail."

"You ever been to jail?"

"Nope. Not once. Not even arrested. Been questioned a few times, but they couldn't prove anything. I'm too good."

"Maybe a little lucky."

"Aye, the luck o' the Irish."

The affected brogue didn't bring a smile to Matty's face because even Irish luck ran out eventually. And whether Dad wanted to admit it or not, Matty was pretty convinced this Robert dude would hurt his family if he didn't get the diamonds, and the guys who'd given Dad the diamonds wouldn't be too thrilled if he didn't get them delivered. It sucked to have to betray his father, but in the end, if he had to choose... Dad had always chosen himself. Matty? He'd choose Mom every time.

THIRTY-ONE

It was after ten by the time Garrison and Aiden sat down to breakfast. Aiden would still be sound asleep if not for him, but no way was the kid sleeping all day. As soon as Garrison had opened his eyes, he'd dragged Aiden out of bed and tossed him in the shower.

Aiden's plate of eggs and bacon had hardly been touched.

"No appetite?"

"No."

Garrison finished his own meal, pulled Aiden's plate across the table, and ate the bacon. "You're missing out."

"I know."

Aiden had hardly spoken all morning, and Garrison didn't have much to say, either. What was he supposed to do here? How were they supposed to get back to where they'd been the day before?

No. The day before, Aiden had snuck out, stolen his car, gotten high, and nearly killed himself. Garrison needed to get back to the year before. Maybe the year before that. Maybe all the way back to his son's childhood, so Garrison could figure out where he'd gone wrong.

He pushed back his chair, cleared the plates, and set them in the dishwasher.

"Want me to do the dishes?"

Garrison turned at his son's offer. That was a first. "Sure."

He sat and watched as his son scrubbed the pans and put away the food, then wiped down the counters. When he was finished, he returned to the table and sat.

The silence was as thick as the newly scarred oak tree. Garrison didn't know how to get around it and wasn't sure he wanted to. Why fight for this kid who was determined to kill himself? If only Garrison didn't care.

Aiden's voice was weak when he said, "I'm sorry about your car."

"You think I care about the car?"

Aiden shrugged.

Garrison wanted to shake him. He leaned back, crossed his arms.

Aiden said, "I'm sorry I left last night."

"Okay."

"I'm sorry about—"

"When we were sitting in there"—Garrison pointed toward the living room—"talking, were you planning to leave?"

Another shrug.

"Your ability to deceive me, to manipulate me—"

"I wasn't trying—"

"Don't interrupt me." The words came out harsher than he'd intended. Maybe he shouldn't yell at the kid. Maybe he should. He'd tried reasoning with him. Tried calm and collected. Tried loving. Maybe Aiden needed a little fear. Maybe he needed to feel Garrison's wrath. Maybe that would straighten him up.

Maybe it would send him away for good.

And then Garrison would have his life back.

And what kind of father let that thought seep in? But he couldn't do this anymore. He couldn't be the kid's warden and guard and savior.

Unfortunately, the only other option was unthinkable.

"I'm tired of being lied to," he said. "I'm tired of being played. What you did last night...luring me into trusting you. That was... impressive. Diabolical."

Aiden looked at the table, then back up. He met Garrison's eyes, though it seemed an effort. "When we were talking, I wasn't sure what I was going to do. I wanted to go, but I wanted to stay, too. I wasn't trying to manipulate you, Dad. I was just...I was trying to not want to get high. I just...I'm not strong enough. I can't do it."

"You could have asked for help. You could have been honest."

Aiden focused on his lap, said nothing.

"But you chose to deceive me. Again."

Garrison remembered Reed's words from Sunday. *Addicts' very survival depends on their ability to deceive. That's not your son. That's the addiction.*

Well, it looked a heckuva lot like his son right this minute.

"I'm sorry." The words were a whisper from across the table.

Garrison had never felt so helpless. He'd thought they were on the right track, but now, now his son's recovery seemed as distant as the moon. "What do you want to do?"

Aiden looked up, tried to hold eye contact, failed, and focused somewhere around Garrison's chin. "Is that rehab place still an option?"

"They're holding the bed for you," Garrison said. "I told you that yesterday."

"But, I mean, will you still, like, let me go? Will you still pay for it, even though I stole your phone and wrecked your car?"

The uncertainty in his son's voice had Garrison shifting his chair to face him. "Of course." He leaned forward, wanted to reach out, but didn't. He'd done enough of the reaching. "Of course. What did you think, that I would just write you off because of one relapse?"

Aiden shrugged, and his eyes filled with tears. He tipped forward just enough, and Garrison pulled him into a hug. "All I want is for you to get better." He held his son a moment before he angled back, studied Aiden's face. "You understand that, right? You know how much I love you?"

Aiden nodded and buried his face in his dad's shoulder. "I'm sorry, Dad."

"I know. It's going to be okay." He rubbed his back, tried to infuse Aiden, and maybe himself, with courage. "We're going to fix this." He leaned back, met Aiden's eyes. "You have to believe that, believe it's possible. Do you believe it?"

"I don't know."

Garrison nodded slowly. "Okay. Right now, I'll have to believe enough for both of us."

THIRTY-TWO

Sam checked the caller ID on her phone. It was Garrison. She sat at the desk in her office, steeled herself, and answered.

"I didn't wake you, did I?" His voice was tender. He would be kind. Of course he would, because he was a kind man, a gentle man. His rude remark the night before was the result of stress and fear. This Garrison would never have said it—*I never should have listened to you*—even if it was true.

"I've been up for a while," she said.

"Did you get some sleep?"

She hadn't, not much. The images from the night had plagued her whenever she'd closed her eyes. The crushed car, the red and blue lights, the menacing forest. She'd dozed a little, but even now that she'd been out of bed an hour her eyelids felt like sandpaper. "Yeah. How about you?"

"A little. Listen—"

"How's Aiden?"

"He's okay. He's watching TV. I've been on the phone all morning trying to figure out the car situation. But I wanted to—"

"How is the car?"

"It's... I don't know yet. It doesn't matter. I don't want to talk about that. I'm trying to—"

"Do you need help with anything?"

"Would you please let me talk?"

She stared out the window and across the landscaped grounds of her condominium complex. She could guess what he was going to say, and she wasn't ready to hear it. Either he would dump her for what she'd done the night before, or he'd feel so guilty about her stupid panic attack he'd apologize, as if it had been his fault. But it had had nothing to do with him and everything to do with her and her irrational mind.

She knew where this train was going, and she needed to get off now, before it pulled her into an abyss she wouldn't survive again.

She could still picture Garrison jumping out of the car, running to his son's side. Of course it had been the right response, the only response of a great father. Aiden was his priority, Aiden needed to be his priority.

Garrison's life was all about Aiden, his school, on Long Island. His job, on Long Island. His life, on Long Island.

Sam was just the woman with the cabin. Even if Garrison wanted her to be more, even if on some level, he did care for her, his life was on Long Island. It wasn't and would never be in New Hampshire. Deep down, he knew that. Maybe she had to help him realize it.

"Sam, are you still there?"

Whatever he planned to say, she couldn't listen. It would be easier for both of them if she just ended this now.

Except...not now. Not after last night. After they'd both rested. After Aiden was squared away, then she'd end it. "I should probably let you go."

"Your anxiety attack last night...I'm sorry I left you the way I did. It was selfish. I just forgot."

"You were worried about Aiden."

"That's no excuse, and I'm sorry."

It wasn't his fault. It was her fault. She was the one who was damaged. "It's fine. I have to go."

"What is wrong with you?"

The anger in his tone flicked a long-buried memory. *What's wrong with you? I told you to get rid of it. Did you think I'd change my mind?*

Yes, Garrison knew it too. Knew they weren't supposed to be together.

"Sam, I'm sorry. I didn't mean to yell at you."

"I have to go."

"I need your help."

Her finger hovered over the red button on her screen, but she couldn't bring herself to disconnect. She returned the phone to her ear. "What can I do?"

"First, you can let me say what I want to say."

"There's nothing to say."

"But—"

"No." Why was she torturing herself? She didn't owe Garrison anything. She'd done all she could for him. "If you need help, you should probably call Nate or Marisa, and if they can't help you, try Brady or Rae. They'll be happy to do whatever you need."

There was a long silence. For a minute, she feared he'd hung up. Feared it? If she was afraid of that, then what was she doing, pushing him away?

Protecting herself, that's what. She'd barely be able to handle the broken heart now. Any deeper and she'd be destroyed for good.

She heard his breathing, could feel his questions. "I'm sorry."

"I don't want their help." His voice sounded weak, quiet. "I need you."

"I'm sorry," she said again.

"I'm in love with you, Samantha."

His words ricocheted like a gunshot through her memories. *I'm in love with you, Sammy. Just you. I'll always want you.*

Just not like this.

She ended the call.

THIRTY-THREE

"Are you still there?"

Like an idiot, Garrison waited, held his breath, hoped. And then he looked at his phone's screen.

She'd hung up.

He'd told her he loved her, and she'd hung up.

He collapsed into the chair on the back deck and ran his hand over his hair. What just happened?

He snapped his laptop closed. All the details about the rental, the garage where they'd towed the car, the deductible didn't matter right now as he played back the conversation. Had he said something stupid, something inconsiderate or insensitive? He'd hardly said anything, and what he had said, she hadn't wanted to hear. Hadn't wanted to talk to him, that was for sure. Perfect time to tell her he loved her.

Talk about a bonehead move.

He looked at the phone again. Even if she hated him, loathed him, he couldn't imagine her hanging up on anybody, ever. She was too kind.

He was missing something.

He'd caught her off guard, and she'd...what? Panicked?

The thought had him flashing back to her anxiety attack. Surely telling her he loved her wouldn't bring that on, would it?

What would happen if she had a panic attack at home? If she couldn't breathe. He imagined her all alone, frightened, unable to get oxygen. He stood, started for the door. To go where, without a car? And obviously, she didn't want to see him right now.

He sat and texted. *Just tell me you're okay, and I won't bother you again.*

I'm fine.

You want me to call somebody for you?

No.

A moment passed, and then she added, *Thank you.*

She was fine. Able to text, and, presumably, able to breathe.

So much for that theory.

Which meant she'd hung up on him on purpose.

Great. Nearly lost his son, did lose his...well, girlfriend wasn't the word, though he'd hoped it might be, someday. What a stellar week he was having.

And what kind of crazy relationship-sabotaging demon had possessed him to tell her he he'd fallen in love with her? He hadn't even allowed himself to think that, much less say it aloud, not even to himself. But he'd felt her pulling away, and, in that moment, he'd known. Known he was in love with her. Known that he wanted her. Known, God help him, that he needed her.

He'd taken a leap of faith and landed in a pile of fresh manure.

"You okay?"

Garrison looked up to see his son in the doorway.

"Uh, did something happen?" Aiden asked.

"Everything's fine. Why?"

"I don't know. You look funny."

He forced a smile. "Funny peculiar or funny ha-ha?"

Aiden shook his head, tried to quell the amusement that flitted across his face. "Did you get a rental?"

"Yeah. I'm trying to find us a ride."

"What about Sam?"

Excellent question. "Sam's busy."

"Oh. Are you gonna get an Uber?"

Uber. That was an idea. "Yeah. I'll try that. Thanks."

Aiden went back inside, and Garrison opened the app. As it loaded, his phone rang.

"Are you up for water skiing today?" Nate sounded far too chipper. Obviously word of his son's wreck hadn't spread. Garrison was thankful for that. Nate continued, "I've got the afternoon off, and there's a chance of rain tomorrow and Thursday. It looks like this'll be the best day this week."

"I'm not sure we can make it work today."

"Uh-oh. What happened?"

Was his voice that much of a giveaway? "Aiden had an accident last night, so I'm trying to figure out the rental situation."

"Is he okay?"

"A little sore. It could have been much worse."

"Were you guys on your way home from Brady's?"

"Not exactly." Garrison wasn't about to tell him the whole story, but he figured in a town like this, news would get out eventually. "The kid decided to take a little joyride after I fell asleep. He drove into a tree."

"Oh, no. Thank God he's okay. I did that once when I was about his age. Took my father's car. I managed not to dent it, but when Dad realized what I'd done... Well, let's just say I never pulled that stunt again."

"What'd your dad do?"

"He grounded me forever. I'm lucky I'm allowed to drive now." A slight chuckle. "But it wasn't the punishment. It was the lecture. Before that, he'd trusted me. Man, when I saw the disappointment on his face, I swore I'd never do anything that stupid again. It took me a long time to earn his trust back."

"My dad was always disappointed in me, so it didn't matter much what I did."

A beat of silence, then, "That sucks."

Garrison blew out a long breath. "I don't know why I said that. It was a long night."

"What can I do?"

"Nothing. We're good."

"You said you got a rental. I guess Sam'll give you a ride?"

Yeah, Aiden had guessed that, too. "I'm getting an Uber."

"Nah. I got nothing else to do. Then we can take the boat out this afternoon. What do you think?"

"Not sure I should take my kid waterskiing after he wrecked my car."

"Huh." Garrison waited through a long pause, figured Nate was building up to something. "I don't pretend to know how to parent a teenager, but I can tell you, no matter how mad my father was, he always got over it fast, especially if there was something fun for us to do together." He said the words with a hint of laughter, then added more seriously, "Honestly, those times with my dad are some of my best memories. Maybe you two need to keep making good memories."

Good memories. Could there be any from this terrible week?

Did it hurt to try?

"Yeah. Okay. After I get the rental, there's something I have to do. And then, boating sounds great."

THIRTY-FOUR

Sam wiped her teary eyes, yelled, "Coming," and headed for the front door. She'd been wallowing in confusion and sadness long enough. As she went down the stairs from her office, she straightened her shoulders. This was her life, and she loved it. She wouldn't long for another.

She figured she'd find the postman on her stoop with a package. Nobody else dropped by in the middle of the day. Good thing, too. She was in no shape for company.

She peeked through the peephole and stepped back as if she'd seen a dragon.

Garrison.

She considered ignoring him, and maybe he read her mind, because he said, "I know you're there, Sam. You just said you were coming."

She went into the small guest bath, checked her face in the mirror. Eyes, red-rimmed. Cheeks, blotchy. Hair, ridiculous. She yanked out the scrunchy that was holding her messy bun in place and finger-combed her long hair. It wasn't better.

The doorbell rang again.

She checked her clothes—black pajama pants and a red T-shirt with the Patriots logo across her chest. Could she look worse? She stepped back to the door. "I'm not dressed."

"You were dressed enough for whoever you thought I'd be."

"Well, I'm not dressed enough for you."

"Hubba hubba."

Fine. He asked for it. She swung the door open. "What do you want?"

He regarded the outfit. "Love the pants, but you have to lose that terrible shirt. I'll get you a Jets one."

"I'll burn it in effigy."

"Giants?"

"I'll douse it with lighter fluid and then burn it in effigy."

"Wow, I'll keep that in mind when Christmas rolls around."

Christmas. Like they'd still be in contact. Which they wouldn't. She leaned against the doorframe and crossed her arms. "What do you want?"

He cleared his throat and pulled a piece of paper and a pen from the back pocket of his shorts. "Right. Well, I'd just like a few moments of your time, ma'am." He consulted the paper, or at least pretended to. "You just escaped a short relationship with Garrison Kopp. He likes to conduct a survey after he gets dumped—an exit interview, if you will—so he can avoid making the same mistakes again. You can imagine how often I have to do these things." He rolled his eyes, and she had to fight a smile. "Do you have time to answer some questions?"

"You haven't been dumped, Garrison—"

"Me?" His hand flew to his chest. "No, not me. You're confused, obviously. I'm his dashingly handsome twin. My brother's the bonehead. Gets dumped all the time. Like daily. Hourly, in fact." He shook his head. "He's quite a disappointment, that one."

"You can tell him he didn't do anything wrong."

Garrison lowered the paper as the amusement slid off his face like a mask. "That can't be true. Can we please talk?"

The part of her that wanted to send him away, to never see

him again...that part lost the battle as she left the door open and walked to her living room.

She sat on her favorite chair while he closed the door behind him.

"Have a seat."

Garrison paused and gazed at the room, taking in the kitchen, dining area, and living area that made up most of her downstairs. "It's gorgeous."

She followed his gaze and had to agree. She'd spent a lot of money remodeling. Top of the line appliances, granite counter-top. The tile floors that looked like wood were her most recent upgrade, and she loved them. Durable and beautiful. She figured, if she had to spend the rest of her life trapped, she might as well be comfortable in her prison.

He sat across from her on the sofa. "I'm sorry about what I said earlier."

She'd known he would be. Too tired, not thinking straight, worried about his kid. Desperate for help. None of that meant he truly loved her. "It doesn't matter."

"My timing was terrible. And I didn't know I felt it until I said it. But when I said it, I knew it was true."

She let the words process. "You mean when you said you shouldn't have listened to me?"

"What? No. Are you still mad at me for that?"

"I'm not mad. Your son wouldn't have gotten in that accident if you hadn't called the police. That was my fault."

"He ran into a tree because he lied to me, stole my car, got high, and then decided to drive home. That had nothing to do with you."

"But if he hadn't seen the cops—"

"Eric didn't even turn on his lights. He was following at a distance, just wanted to make sure Aiden got home. Aiden was so high I'm amazed he could drive at all."

"Oh."

Garrison heaved out a breath. "My timing...I mean telling

you I love you. Today, on the phone. That was stupid, and I'm sorry. And..." He searched her face, met her eyes. What did he see there? What did he see in her that made him believe she was worth his time?

"Obviously, you don't feel the same way about me."

She looked away. "I can't do this."

"Why not?"

She shrugged, looked around her perfectly decorated condo, usually her escape, her solace. But was that really what she wanted? Safety? Silence? Or did she want more?

"Is there someone else?" he asked.

"No. Just you. I mean, not that there's you."

"Okay." The word hung there, inviting her to explain.

She had no idea what to say.

"Okay." This time, the word held resignation. "You're making yourself clear, and I need to take the hint." He stood, headed for the door. "You want us to get out of your cabin?"

She stood and followed but stopped a safe distance away. Too far to reach out, too far to touch. "The cabin is yours for as long as you need it."

"You'll have to let me pay for it, considering..."

She sighed. As if she cared about the money. "Whatever makes you feel comfortable."

He set his hand on her doorknob, and tears prickled behind her eyes.

He turned to face her, studied her. As much as she wanted to, she couldn't seem to force her gaze away. His hand dropped from the doorknob, and he stepped nearer. He seemed to wait for her to react, but she was frozen. Fear? Hope? She didn't know.

He took another step toward her, then another until he was close enough that she could feel the heat radiating from his skin. He reached out, rested his hands on her hips.

She told herself to back away.

He leaned down, and she looked up. His gaze flicked to her

lips, back to her eyes, and he waited. Now was her chance to stop this. To protect herself. To stay safe.

He closed the inches between them and kissed her. Gently, once. Twice. Then longer.

She melted into it, felt warm and safe and protected. Her heart stirred, longed for more of this, more of him.

She stepped away.

"I'm sorry." He took a step back. "No, that's a lie. I'm not even a little sorry." His arms hung at his sides, his eyes narrowed as he studied her face. "I'm not great at this, but you don't seem like the type of girl who kisses every guy who knocks on her door with a fake survey. I think maybe you have some feelings for me, too."

"It doesn't matter."

"It does matter to me, Sam, considering I'm in love with you. Seems the least you could do is explain."

What could she tell him? That among her many fears was falling for someone again? That she was too damaged to ever be worthy of his time or attention?

But the broken look on his face melted her resolve. This man deserved better. He needed to know it. Then he could move on.

"Fine." She resumed her seat and nodded to the sofa across from her. "I'm not sure what you want me to say."

He leaned forward. "Why don't you tell me what you're afraid of?"

That was one of the things she was afraid of—telling him. Telling anybody. "You have more important things to do than listen to my issues."

"I really don't."

"Don't you have a son who needs you?"

"Aiden's with Nate, and I'm sure he's enjoying the break from me as much as I'm enjoying the break from him. They took me to pick up the rental, and then they headed to the lake to get your boat ready. Nate said he checked with you."

"Right." Nate had texted that morning, before her conversation with Garrison.

"I told them if I wasn't there when they got the boat in the water, to take it out, and I'd call when I got there."

"But still, your focus—"

"Sam, I get to have a life, too, you know. My focus has been on Aiden, and it will be again, but right now, I want to focus on you. There's plenty of time for waterskiing."

"I still don't know what you want from me."

"Tell me what you're afraid of."

"Fine. I'm afraid everything. Maybe you should get out your piece of paper, and you can keep a list. I'm afraid of the woods. I'm afraid of the dark. I'm especially afraid of the woods in the dark. I'm afraid of—"

"Let me rephrase." He held up his hand. "Can you tell me what caused all these fears?"

Just the thought of sharing that story had her cheeks filling with fire, her heart filling with shame. She looked at her hands, folded on her lap, wished Garrison would just go away.

But oh, she could still taste that kiss.

"There is a story, then." His voice was gentle.

Oh, yes, there was a story.

"Have you ever told anybody?"

She looked up. "My counselor."

"Pretend I'm him."

"Her."

He spoke in a falsetto. "I could be her."

She smiled, and a tiny portion of the tension fell away.

"Maybe you should take the couch," he said, "and I'll sit in the chair. I'll do my best Freud." Now he did a terrible Austrian accent. "Ven did you first realize you vere in love wit your chihuahua?"

"You're insane."

"*Nine, fraulein.* You are ze crazy one."

That was too true. "Obviously you've never been in counseling."

His smile faded. "For a little while, with Charlene. Maybe it would have worked if we'd had Freud, but..."

"I'm sorry."

"Nothing to be sorry for." He smiled tenderly, earnestly. "I really would love to hear the story, but if you don't want to tell me, I understand."

She didn't want to tell him.

She did want to tell him. Because then he'd understand why this could never happen between them.

Right. That was a colossal lie if she'd ever heard one. She wanted to tell him, and she wanted him to say it was all okay, that he understood, that he could still care for her despite it.

But would he, or would he walk away? And even if he didn't, could she ever fully give her heart to him after what had happened?

She had no idea, but she did know one thing. Keeping it to herself hadn't done her any good. If she was going to lose him, she might as well lose him for the right reasons. She didn't want to let her fears rule her life anymore. As cozy as this condo was, it would never warm her the way Garrison's kiss had.

THIRTY-FIVE

"You're never going to find them with your face in that screen."

Matty slid his phone in his pocket. "I can hear when a car is coming. It just takes a second to look up."

"You need to keep your eyes on the road, kid. The phone is a distraction." Frank sipped his coffee and stared out the window.

Frank, Matty thought. At one time, Matty had wanted this man to be a dad to him, a real dad like Mr. Kopp was to Aiden. What a joke. After spending the last few hours with him, after seeing his father's shortcomings and selfishness, Matty no longer believed this man could ever be a dad.

From now on, he'd just be Frank.

The realization was a few days too late.

A car passed. A red pickup truck.

"Was that them?"

"Like I said, he drives a black—"

"I know what you told me," Frank said. "But what if they're not in the Camry, huh?"

Matty didn't see the point in arguing. He and Frank had done enough of that in the previous nine hours. "Looked like a black woman, so no, it wasn't them."

"Could be a friend."

"It wasn't them."

Matty took a long sip of his Dr. Pepper to cool his frustration. He grabbed a snack from the bag on the floor, a little package of powdered donuts. They'd bought a good selection of food at a truck stop in Connecticut, but there were just a few items left. Matty longed for a real meal, a burger and fries, a pizza. But Frank didn't want to be seen in town, wanted to stay off the radar.

Matty didn't know why and didn't want to think about it. Surely they weren't going to be committing a crime. No matter what Dad—Frank—planned, Matty wouldn't be doing anything illegal. He just wanted to get the package, call Robert, and deliver it. And whatever happened to Frank after that wouldn't be Matty's problem.

Still, the thought had him swallowing hard. He couldn't think about betraying his father. Couldn't think about his mother and brother being in danger. He focused on the dry donut and decided not to think at all.

Another car passed, an SUV. The driver was a woman. No passenger. "Obviously not them."

"We'll give it another hour. If we don't see them, you can call."

"I'd really rather—"

"I don't care what you'd rather. I gotta get those diamonds. If Kopp doesn't like you because of this, that's the price you gotta pay for shoving the package in his car."

"I told you a thousand times—"

"I know the story. You should have gone back for it sooner."

Matty wasn't about to have this argument again.

Another car approached, this one a silver sedan. Not the black Camry, but Matty looked closely. The driver was a dude, curly hair. The passenger...

His heart rate kicked up a notch. "That's him."

"Kopp? You sure? He looked—"

"No. Aiden was in the passenger seat. I don't know who the driver was."

Frank swung the car around and followed. He closed the distance too fast and followed too closely, but Matty didn't say anything. He had no influence on his father's actions.

Less than a mile later, the car turned left, and Frank followed. He kept his distance this time, going slowly along the rough road. The sedan turned down a driveway, and Frank passed the house, went past another driveway and turned around in the third one. He crept back toward where Aiden had gone, and Matty peered through the woods.

"I see the house," Matty said.

Frank stopped. "Did they go inside?" He looked, too. "I don't see a Camry."

"Me, either. Looks like just Aiden went in."

They waited in the silent car, watched the front of the rundown cabin.

"Why don't I just run up there and ask him?" Matty said. "Mr. K's not here, but Aiden can tell me where the car is without getting his dad involved."

Frank seemed to consider that possibility, then shook his head. "The other guy's a wildcard, though. Now that we know where they are, we should wait until Kopp comes back. I can break in the trunk, get the package, and get out of here without anyone knowing we were in town. I'd rather not get the fed involved if we can help it."

"Former fed."

"Once a cop, always a cop."

Again, Matty had the impression his father had more planned than he was letting on. Or maybe he was just planning for every contingency. Considering he'd been a criminal all his life and had never been charged with a crime, Matty figured he should trust his father's instincts. Unfortunately, trusting his father felt as natural as the powdered donuts that were sitting in his stomach like concrete.

After about five minutes, Aiden came outside carrying a couple of towels and wearing swim shorts and flip-flops. He slammed the door behind him.

"Hmm," Frank said. "Looks like they'll be gone a while. We'll follow, see if they meet up with the Camry, go from there."

Matty couldn't come up with any reason why that wasn't a good idea. None of this felt right, spying on his best friend and his dad, but he was out of options.

"He told me to get rid of it." A short pause. Then, "*It.*"

"What a..." She was a Christian. She probably wouldn't appreciate any of the words that were on his tongue. He settled on "...turd."

Nearly a smile. "I just knew he'd come around. I stayed with him. I waited, thinking when I started to show that he'd fall in love with the baby, too. When he could feel the baby moving, when he really understood there was a child, his child. I could imagine him, the baby. Pink cheeks, soft skin..." Her words trailed off a moment. Then she said, "I kept going to classes. The baby was due in the summer. I figured I'd find childcare—my parents would help me. By summer, he'd have graduated and gotten a job. I could finish college. We'd get married. It would be perfect."

He hated to think where the story was going, almost didn't want to hear it.

"We went to a party one night. Everybody was drinking, except me, of course. I wasn't going to risk my baby. But Chandler was drinking. I thought he was having fun. And he was—for a while. Then, when it was time to go..."

Garrison resisted the urge to cross the room and sit with her, to hold her hand and offer his support.

"I wanted to drive. He wouldn't let me. I thought he'd had too much to drink, but we were way out in the country, and I could tell he was getting agitated. He kept yelling at me to get in the car. He was so loud, and there were a lot of people outside, and they were looking at us. So I just...I got in." She paused, added, "It's not what you think. We weren't in an accident. He just started driving in the wrong direction, away from campus. I asked him where he was going. He ignored me. Told me to shut the...whatever up. I started to get nervous. Not scared, though. Not like...I didn't think he'd hurt me."

Her voice returned to the monotone she'd started with. "We went to school at Plymouth State. It's up north. In the mountains. I loved it up there. It was so pretty, and we used to go

THIRTY-SIX

"It happened in college."

Garrison had to keep his head together and not s
away. Then, maybe she'd get through the whole st
wanted to get nearer to her, but perhaps she needed the

"There was this guy. Chandler."

He refrained from commenting on the name, just ba

"We met in one of my business courses. He was sv
charming."

Charming Chandler. Garrison hated him already.

"I was a freshman." Her voice was flat, like she wa
numbers out of the phone book. "He was a sophomore.
together for a long time. My junior year, I moved in v
My parents didn't approve, but I thought we were in lo
anyway."

She stared out the window for a long time.

"I got pregnant. It's such a stupid story. Such a fami
Mundane, even."

"It wasn't stupid or familiar or mundane to you."

Her gaze met his. "It wasn't. You're right. I was thi
idiot, apparently, because Chandler..."

Obviously wasn't thrilled.

hiking and biking. Skiing in the winter. I had friends who had four-wheelers, and we'd take them out.

"Chandler kept driving north, away from campus. Away from any place I'd ever been before. Away from the main roads and highways. He was so angry, the way he was gripping the steering wheel. He wouldn't talk to me. Wouldn't answer me when I talked to him. And then he made a few turns, which felt random, but I don't know. Maybe he knew exactly where he was going. Maybe he'd planned the whole thing.

"He stopped on this narrow single-lane dirt road in the middle of nowhere. Nothing but a drainage ditch, and behind that, thick forest on both sides of the road. He came around the car, opened my door, and yanked me out."

The image was so clear in Garrison's head.

"I had my phone in my hand. I'd been thinking about calling someone or texting or something. I didn't, though. I believed...I never thought. Even that far north. Away from everything. I was so stupid."

"You trusted him." Garrison spit the words out, then immediately wanted them back. He had to shut up and let her talk.

A moment passed. Then another. Then, "I did. I trusted him. I felt safe with him. He took my phone, shoved it in his pocket, and got in my face. 'This is your fault. If you'd ended it like I said, everything could have gone back to normal.'

"I didn't know what to say, and I was afraid I'd make it worse. I thought maybe he was going to hurt me. Maybe try to...to end my pregnancy himself. But he didn't. He yanked me to the edge of the gravel road and shoved me. I stumbled. Fell into the ditch. There was a little stream there. The top of it was covered with a thin layer of ice, and I remember the tinny sound it made when I cracked it, the way the icy water seeped into my clothes.

"I had to protect the baby. I lay there, my arms wrapped around my middle, waiting for him to hurt me. To kick me or something. And then I heard the car start. He drove away."

"He left you there?"

She nodded.

"What did you do?"

"I thought he'd come back. Even then, I was still so stupid. I thought he loved me. I thought he'd come to his senses and come back for me. And then I was so sad. I lay there in the icy stream. I had on a jacket, but..."

Garrison couldn't stand it any longer. He crossed the room, stood in front of her, and offered his hands.

She stood, and he folded her into his arms. He held her against him, felt her shivering despite the heat, and wanted nothing more than to go back in time and rescue her from that monster. He didn't ask her for more of the story. She'd tell him when she was ready. Right now, he wanted to hold her, protect her forever.

They stood there like that for a long time.

Finally, her shivering stopped, and she leaned back. He looked into her eyes. They were red-rimmed, moist.

"Thank you," she said.

"For what?"

"For this." She leaned against his chest, and he held her close, ran his hand over her silky hair, enjoyed how perfectly her tiny frame fit against his oversize one.

"I need to get through it." She sat, and he took the chair beside her.

"I was so cold, shivering uncontrollably, and then I wasn't. I felt fine. Perfectly comfortable. I sat up, saw the forest, and wanted to walk into it. I'd always loved the woods. The trees seemed to call me."

Hypothermia. The thought had him swallowing hard. He could have lost her before he'd even met her. "Did someone find you?"

"No. Not...really. But yeah, someone did."

That was clear as string theory.

"There was this voice. Like...maybe I was crazy. But a voice told me to stand up."

"But nobody was there?"

She blew out a long breath. "I know you're not a Christian, but I am. This is why I am. This voice told me that he loved me. That I was worthy. That I was not meant to die there. He told me to get up and start walking. I stood and stared into the trees. I can't tell you how strong the pull was to walk deep into those woods and disappear. It was so irrational, so bizarre, but I wanted to be surrounded by that forest more than I'd ever wanted anything. I walked a few yards in, would have kept going that direction. But the voice told me to turn around. Go the other way."

She'd been hallucinating, obviously. Another symptom of hypothermia.

"The voice was commanding, filled with love. I staggered back to the road and started walking, not the direction I'd come from, but further down the road." She was quiet for a minute or two, which gave him time to picture the scene, her stumbling, hallucinating, all alone in the dark mountains. Had there been a moon? Had Sam been dressed for a hike in the woods? No. She'd been a college student. She'd probably have worn something pretty and totally impractical. Probably high heels—she wore those a lot. What had the temperature been? Cold enough that there was ice.

His heart hurt thinking about it.

"I know what you're thinking," she said. "You think I was hallucinating. That the voice was nothing. My subconscious or something. But I don't think so. Because it wasn't just a voice. It was a presence. He was with me. He was warm and comfortable. I could feel his love. Does that make sense?"

"Not really."

"Okay." She nodded slowly, deliberately. "The fact that it doesn't make sense to you—does that mean it's not true? Or is it possible that maybe I had an experience you've never had?"

"Obviously it's possible."

"But you don't believe it?"

He shrugged. Wished she'd get back to her story. "It's not that I don't believe there's a God. I mean, the world is pretty well designed, and I'm not somebody who believes it all just happened. But who is that God? What's it like? I don't know."

"Maybe I do."

Maybe she did know something he didn't. Because here was a woman he knew to be intelligent and wise. There was obviously a whole bunch of stuff Garrison didn't understand in the world. Like how a man could do something as terrible as what Charming Chandler had done to Sam.

"I walked for a while," Sam said. "Maybe thirty minutes. Maybe an hour or more. I have no idea. But then I smelled smoke from a fireplace. And as I walked, I felt better. Cold again, and shivering, but that was good. I'm not sure I knew it at the time, or maybe I did. But anyway, it was good that I felt cold. It meant my body temperature was going back up. And then I saw a light."

Garrison's hands ached from clenching them, as if he were there, watching the scene unfold. As if her life were in danger at that very moment.

"It was a house, and I knocked on the door, and they took me to the emergency room and called my parents."

"Thank God."

"Exactly. He saved me. I just…I don't know why."

He grabbed her hand. "How can you say that?"

"I thought God wanted to save my baby. I was so sure of it. And then, a few days later, I miscarried."

"Oh, honey, I'm sorry."

"It was probably the hypothermia. No doctor has confirmed that, but that's my theory. So Chandler did manage to kill our child. Almost killed me."

"I hope you had his butt thrown in jail."

She didn't say anything.

"You did, right?"

"I quit school. Went home. My dad and my brother got all my things when I knew Chandler would be at class. I never saw him again. For all he knows, he has a child. Not that he ever cared enough to check."

Chandler. Garrison needed the guy's last name.

"I was wrong about everything."

"You trusted the wrong guy, Sam. All that says about you is that you're trustworthy, kind, gentle. Maybe a little naive, but this was a guy you'd been with for years. His cruelty was his fault."

"I know."

Her words were flat again.

"You don't really know, though, do you?"

"When I first moved back to Nutfield, I stayed in town to recuperate. Then, I don't know. I finished college online. I got a job with the town, moved into an apartment, and sort of avoided leaving. I didn't admit I was doing it at the time. I told myself I preferred the local market to the big grocery stores. I bought my clothes online or at the shops downtown. I'd always dreamed of owning my own business, so I bought the first little cabin on the lake. That's when I went to the mall. I was looking for curtains and stuff to decorate the new cabin. I could feel the anxiety rising even as I drove myself to Manchester, but I forced myself to go. And then I had the anxiety attack. And then, for a while, it was easier to stay home than fight it."

"But last night..."

"It was the darkness, and I was feeling...I don't know." Her gaze met his, flicked way. But he knew. He'd made her feel like a failure with his cruel remark, feel insignificant when he'd run off without her.

"I'm sorry."

"It wasn't you, Garrison. You acted like a father. I just...sometimes I don't think straight. And the woods. They still call to me like they did that night. It's crazy. I know it's crazy."

"It's different. But you're not crazy, Samantha. You're struggling. You're trying to work through it."

Silence filled the space. He waited for her to continue. When she didn't speak, he asked, "It's better than it was, right?"

"A few years ago, I found a good counselor and started seeing a shrink, who prescribes the medications."

He slid off his chair and knelt in front of her. "You've built this amazing life for yourself, Sam. And you're overcoming your fears."

A sob seemed to bubble up in her heart.

He wrapped her in his arms. "I think you're brave."

"I'm not. I'm afraid of everything."

"Bravery isn't not being afraid, Samantha." He leaned back so he could see her face. "Bravery is facing your fears. That's what you've been doing all these years, what you did with me when you went with us yesterday. And again last night, out in the woods. And I left you by yourself after all you'd done for me."

"It's fine. You were worried about your son."

"I was, but it's not fine. That anxiety attack last night was my fault. I'm sorry."

She rested against his chest again. He wanted to keep her there forever.

THIRTY-SEVEN

Sam's day had certainly taken a turn.

After she'd finished her story, Garrison had held her for a long time. Then he'd met her eyes and spoken words she'd never forget.

"You are a treasure, Samantha, and Charming Chandler, aside from being a jackass and possibly a felon, is a total moron."

She'd giggled, her relief bubbling up from a long-locked box deep in her soul. She'd told him everything, even the crazy God-talked-to-me stuff, and he was still with her.

She'd tried to send him off to the lake alone to spend the day with his son, but he was having none of it. She certainly wouldn't complain if he wanted her by his side. She'd slipped on her bathing suit—a royal blue one-piece—and surveyed her reflection. She let the first word that came to her mind—fat—fall away. Not fat. Curvy. And—she smiled at her reflection—maybe even attractive. Well, now she was just being silly. She pulled her white cover-up over her head and returned to the living room.

Garrison's whistle had her cheeks burning. She waved him off. "You're crazy."

"You're hot."

She ducked away so he wouldn't see her smile and found

her beach bag. They were just about to leave when she got a call from her management company. Apparently, one of her cabins had lost power. The company couldn't send anybody until that evening and hoped she could stop by sooner than that.

She disconnected the call and slid her phone in the bag. "I'm going to take my own car. I have an errand to run."

Garrison agreed, and she followed him to the lake. She drove past his rental to the one with the faulty wiring not too far away. She knocked, waited, then let herself in. The place was empty of tourists. She wasn't sorry. No need to waste a minute being friendly to strangers, not when the lake and waterskiing and Garrison beckoned. She found the circuit breaker panel, flipped the switch, watched the lights flick on, and headed back to Garrison's cabin.

She knocked on the screen door. "Mind if I come in?"

"Come on."

She stepped inside to find Garrison in swim trunks and a T-shirt, standing in the middle of the living room. His eyes were closed.

"What's wrong?"

He turned, shook his head, then went into the kitchen. "Something's not right."

She followed. "What is it?"

He shook his head, sniffed. "Did you have anybody coming over today? A contractor or...?"

"No." She followed his gaze, tried to see what he was seeing.

"Maybe I'm just being paranoid. Does it smell like cologne to you?"

She sniffed. "I guess, a little."

"Not Aiden's."

"Could be Nate's." But the scent wasn't familiar to her, and Nate wasn't the kind of guy to load up on cologne.

"Before the lake, though. Why would Nate...?" His voice trailed off.

Garrison didn't seem the paranoid type, but all this fuss over a faint smell was a bit over the top.

He shook his head and dialed Nate's number. "It's Garrison. We're at the cabin. What do you guys want?"

Garrison waited while Nate responded.

"Pepsi and sandwiches," he said. "And you have a cooler, right?" Another pause, then, "Okay, we'll be at the boat ramp in a few minutes." He disconnected the call.

She grabbed the bread and started on the sandwiches. "You think we have enough food to fill Aiden?"

"I'm just glad he's hungry. I didn't know, after last night..."

Right. She'd been so focused on herself, she'd forgotten about Garrison's bigger issue. "I'm sorry I dumped all that—"

"Don't even start, Sam. I practically forced it out of you." He took her hand. "I wanted to know. I'm glad I know."

"But Aiden."

"I can handle it. I've almost perfected the walking and chewing gum thing, too."

"That I have to see."

"It's quite a sight." Garrison slid a few cans of soda into a paper sack. "Aiden was going to grab food when he came over earlier, but I guess he forgot."

Sam arranged the sandwiches on top of the sodas, then added a bag of chips. "Do we need to get water?"

"Nate's got that covered." He grabbed the bag. "Ready?"

She stepped outside before him, then waited while he took one last look around before he locked the door behind him.

"Are you always this paranoid?"

He shook his head, no smile. "It's been a weird week."

She couldn't argue with that.

She started to open her car door, but he cleared his throat behind her and said in his deep cop-voice, "Step out of the way, ma'am."

She let him open her door for her. "I'm not used to such chivalry."

His set the paper bag on the ground. "What about the idiot from college?"

"Uh, no. Not his style."

"Seems like Chandler wasn't charming after all."

"Very true."

Garrison's eyes narrowed. "Has there been anyone since Charming Chandler?"

"Nope."

He kissed her temple and waited while she sat in the passenger seat. "Sort of selfish of me, but I'm glad."

He stowed the bag in the backseat and sat beside her. "Can I ask you a question?"

"Sure."

"What was it about last night that brought on your anxiety attack? Do you know? I'd like to know your triggers so I can avoid them. Not lead you into them like—"

"That wasn't your fault." She squeezed his hand. "It was just being outside in the dark, by myself. And the woods."

"I'll be more careful, but you need to tell me if I'm asking too much. I'm sure the rest of your friends are sensitive about those things."

She glanced across the car where he waited for a response and decided to go with the truth. "My friends don't know."

"What? How can that be?"

She shrugged. "Brady was off at college when it all happened, and we'd lost touch. Rae was...well, we'd had a falling out. It's a long story."

"And Nate?"

"I didn't know Nate then. And of course none of us had met Marisa. Most of my other friends from high school had gone on to college, and, anyway, I wasn't really close with anyone but Brady and Rae."

"But how could you not have told them since?"

"It's not the kind of thing that comes up in normal conversation. Rae asked me to go dress shopping with her when she and

Brady married. I was going to do it—to try, anyway. But she didn't want to wear a bridal gown, and she ended up finding something in a boutique downtown. It was a small wedding, family and a few friends. They had the reception at the Lion's Club in town."

"That sounds fancy."

Sam thought back to the intimate reception, the way Rae's young friend Caro and her classmates had decked out the old building. And she remembered how Brady and Rae had looked at each other on that dance floor, how guilty she'd felt for almost destroying their lives.

No, she wouldn't go there again. Brady and Rae had forgiven her. She had to let it go.

"Rae's first husband"—not that he was really her husband, but that was too long a story for today—"was very wealthy. Her first wedding was on a yacht in the Mediterranean. I think she wanted this wedding to be nothing like that one."

"Sounds like there's a story there," Garrison said.

"There is, a long one. But it's not my story to tell. And if you ask, they probably won't tell it. It's all very hush-hush."

"Now I really want to know."

Sam thought back to the events that had brought Rae home—and nearly gotten her killed. Then she considered what Nate and Marisa had been through just a few months before—the kidnapping, the murder. And here she was, over thirty and still scared of the dark

Good thing she didn't have any danger in her life. She'd probably die of fright.

THIRTY-EIGHT

Matty stared at the launch ramp where Aiden and the other guy had backed a boat into the water and sped off. There weren't a lot of vehicles in this lot, and Frank had found a spot in the back corner where they could watch cars coming and going. Not that there was much of that going on today.

"What if Mr. Kopp doesn't show up?" Matty asked.

"If he does, we'll have all the time in the world to get into the car, get the package, and get away."

"But what if he doesn't?"

Frank blew out a long breath. "Then we'll deal with it. There's no guarantees in life, kid." He opened his car door. "I gotta take a leak."

Matty twisted to watch as his father headed not toward the restrooms in the little hut attached to the dock but to the woods behind them. He'd almost disappeared behind a tree when Matty saw him pull out his phone.

Who was Frank calling? He'd told Matty his plan was to recover the package and take it to Long Island to deliver it to the buyers. Maybe he was just updating them. But if that were the case, then why lie about it?

Frank was planning something.

Did he have any idea Matty was planning something, too? And how would Matty get his hands on the diamonds? Maybe he should call Robert, get the guy here to fight for the diamonds himself. Because Matty had no idea how he was going to get the package from his father and get away. He was so far out of his league, like a little leaguer pitching for the Mets.

But he couldn't call Robert, not yet. What if Robert hurt Frank? The guy might be a jerk, but he was still Matty's dad. His other option was no better, though. Try to get the diamonds away from Dad, and then what? Take a bus back to New York?

No, then he'd call Robert. When he had the package, he'd run, hide somewhere, and call Robert. He'd make sure he put a lot of distance between himself and Frank, try to protect his old man.

How could he protect them all? And himself?

Crap, how did he get himself into this mess? More importantly, how could he get himself out?

Mr. Kopp... Aiden's father would help him. He'd know what to do. Maybe Matty should confess the whole thing. Mr. Kopp wouldn't want Frank to get hurt, and he'd protect Matty and his family, too. Matty should have fessed up from the very beginning. Was it too late now?

No. Mr. Kopp would help him. He'd know what to do.

He pulled out his phone and searched for Mr. Kopp's number in his contacts. Now that he had a plan, his hands were shaking. He finally got the number and started the call.

The car door opened, and Matty disconnected. He'd lost his opportunity.

"Put that thing away," Frank said. "You gotta stay alert."

"Whatever." Matty slipped his phone into his pocket. He'd find a way to make the call. He couldn't use his father's excuse and go into the woods, because he'd done that when they first got there. Fine. He'd wait.

He took a long sip of his warm soda.

Fifteen minutes passed in almost complete silence. And

then, a red sedan pulled in. Matty'd already discounted it when he saw the driver step out of the car.

From twenty-five yards away, it was easy to tell who the man was. Really tall frame, really short hair, really broad shoulders. "That's him."

Frank swore under his breath. "That's not a black Camry."

"I noticed."

Frank swore again while they watched Mr. Kopp and a short brunette walk to the end of the dock. He carried a paper bag. She carried some sort of tote. They talked a minute, then the speedboat pulled up. Mr. Kopp and the chick climbed on board, and they all drove away.

His father's voice dripped with sarcasm. "Now what, genius?"

Matty stepped out of the car and slammed the door while a rage he'd never known poured over him.

He heard the other door open and slam. "We don't have time for a hissy fit."

Matty balled his fists, told himself not to speak.

Frank rounded the car, stopped right in front of Matty. "You got a problem, kid?"

It was that word. Kid. Like his father didn't know his name. Couldn't care less about him. About the fact that he'd put Matty and Jimmy and their mother in danger. Matty's arm was moving before he could stop it. He landed a blow on his father's temple, and Frank staggered back.

He bent at the waist, grabbed his head in both hands, and didn't move.

The rage fizzled out, and shame replaced it. "Dad, I'm sorry."

Frank stood up straight, and Matty resisted the urge to step back. But his father rounded the car and slid into the driver's seat.

Matty waited for something, he wasn't sure what. But, despite what he'd just done, the world hadn't changed a bit. The sun's rays glared off the tops of the cars in the parking lot and forced beads of sweat down his back. The air was so still it seemed to be holding its breath.

Matty opened the passenger door and sat.

"We'll go back to the house," Frank said. "Maybe the Camry is there."

"Why don't I just call Mr. Kopp, tell him I left something in his car, and ask where it is?"

"We won't have to do that if the car is at his house. Maybe the red car belongs to the lady he was with. Was that Aiden's mom?"

"They're divorced. I've never seen that lady before. Or the car."

His father's logic was sound, but Matty desperately wanted to call Mr. Kopp. He needed the man's help, needed to know he wasn't in this alone. He needed a father, and he couldn't count on his own.

THIRTY-NINE

Apparently, Garrison could no longer water ski. It really ticked him off.

He hadn't tried since college. He'd been able to do it back then. As he wiped out the fourth time—just seconds after being pulled to his feet—Garrison decided water skiing was stupid.

Nate swung the boat around and idled beside him. "Had enough, old man?"

Garrison hoisted himself onto the boat. "Anytime, anyplace, Boyle."

"Except on water skis, I guess." Nate's smug look had Garrison wishing he'd arrested the guy when he'd had the chance.

Sam held out a towel. "It was a good effort."

He snatched the towel and looked at Aiden, who was fixated on the phone in his hand. Must have been Nate's because Garrison had buried his own at the bottom of Sam's bag with hers. Well, at least one person hadn't witnessed his humiliation. Then Aiden cracked up, stood, and angled the phone toward Nate. "Dude, you gotta see. I put it in slow-mo."

Nate watched, roared with laughter. "That was the best wipe-out yet."

Great. Just great.

Sam bumped his shoulder. "Don't listen to them. You looked good."

Garrison lifted his eyebrows. "Isn't it a sin to lie?"

She giggled and snatched a life preserver. "It's my turn."

Five minutes later, watching Sam cut through the smooth water, Garrison nearly forgot his humiliation. The lake was surrounded by cabins nestled among pine trees. The sun shone and glistened off the surface. With Sam smiling at him, the sight was breathtaking.

Aiden handed him a bottle of water, sat beside him on the back of the boat, his eyes on Sam. "She's good."

"Yup."

"Looks hot in that bathing suit, too."

Garrison kept his focus on Sam in case she got into trouble but leaned toward Aiden. "That's not creepy at all."

Aiden laughed. "I'm just saying, she's really pretty." A short pause, then, "There's still nothing going on between you two?"

Garrison couldn't help it. He flashed back to their kiss, those moments when he'd held her in his arms. He'd hoped to put this conversation off. "We were just friends, but things have...progressed."

He glanced at Aiden. His son was staring back at Sam and nodding slowly.

"Is that a problem?"

"Sam's okay. I like her."

He met his son's eyes. "Yeah?"

He shrugged. "I guess."

Garrison turned to watch her again. She jumped the wake and swung out beside the boat, sending a perfect spray onto the glassy water. She was more than hot. She was beautiful. And kind. And for some reason Garrison couldn't comprehend, she liked him.

And Aiden didn't hate her.

Maybe at least one part of this story could have a happy ending.

Aiden was quiet so long, Garrison figured the conversation was over. Then, "She didn't tell you, did she?"

"Tell me what? She didn't tell me anything."

"Oh. Okay."

Sam slid effortlessly back across the first bump of the wake, then the second, and swung out toward the other side of the boat.

"She caught me in your bedroom," Aiden said, "on Sunday. I was looking for my phone."

"Ah. She didn't tell me. Not that I'd have been shocked."

"You hid it well."

"I'm a pro."

"Where was it?"

Garrison had already duct-taped the cell back to the under-side of the coffee table. "Good effort, son. I'll tell you when you have a teenager of your own."

Aiden laughed. "Can't blame a guy for trying."

A few minutes passed while Sam showed off her skills.

Other families were out today, some skiing, some tubing, some anchored in coves and swimming off the side of their boats. With the hum of the motor and the waves and smiles from fellow boaters, Garrison felt at peace.

Aiden took the seat beside Nate, and the two of them had a conversation Garrison couldn't hear. He'd need to ask Aiden later what they'd talked about while Garrison had been with Sam. Whatever it was, the two seemed to have bonded in the hour or so they'd been together. That was a good thing. Garrison could use all the help he could get.

After they'd skied, Nate maneuvered the boat to a quiet cove, and the group jumped off the side and swam until they were exhausted. Then they climbed on board, reclined in the seats, and snacked on the food Garrison had grabbed from the cabin. The sun dipped low, and shadows crept across the water.

"It's been a good day," Nate said, "but Ana's expecting me to come over and tuck her into bed."

"You two don't live together?" Aiden asked. "I figured, since you're engaged and all."

"That's not really any of your business," Garrison said.

"Don't worry about it," Nate turned to Aiden. "We decided to do things the right way. First the wedding, then the living together. Now, if I had my druthers, we'd already be married. But she wants the whole shebang—fluffy dress, bridesmaids, fancy wedding."

Aiden looked at Sam. "Why are chicks so weird about that stuff?"

Her blush was slight as she glanced at Garrison. He winked, and she looked at Aiden. "Most girls dream about their weddings their whole lives."

Aiden smirked. "That's a stupid thing to fantasize about, a poofy dress and some dude in a tux."

"Maybe," Sam said. "Maybe it's like how guys dream about hitting a walk-off home run."

"Or the big catch for a touchdown," Garrison added.

"Sure," Aiden said. "But sports are cool."

Nate chuckled. "I guess weddings are cool for girls. Whatever Marisa wants, I'm fine with it."

Garrison said. "She agreed to marry you. You better not give her any reason to wise up and back out."

Nate snapped a towel at Garrison, who barely angled out of the way. "You wanna go back in the water, Boyle?"

"Right. Like you could put me there."

Aiden laughed, and Sam said, "Now boys, let's try to be a good example for the youngster," which only made Aiden laugh harder.

Nate pushed the throttle forward, and Garrison wondered if the afternoon could have been better. Three more days, and Aiden would go into rehab. Three more days for Garrison to figure out how to make this work.

FORTY

Matty stared at the white SUV in the driveway in front of Aiden's cabin. Frank had parked on the narrow road in front. No point in trying to hide when the only people who would recognize them were on a boat.

"I guess I need to call Mr. Kopp now," Matty said.

Frank grunted. "Doesn't make any sense. Do you think they flew?"

"No way. Even when they go to Pittsburg to see Aiden's aunts, they always drive. That's a lot farther than this."

His dad didn't respond, just stared at the house.

Matty did, too. It was small but right on the water. A fun place to spend a week, especially considering what Aiden had put his father through on Friday. Maybe he just wanted him away from bad influences. Like Matty.

"Here's what you say."

When Frank shifted toward him, Matty could see the welt where his fist had made contact, right above the eye. It would bruise later. A tangible reminder of what he'd done. "I'm sorry about—"

"Don't." He looked out the window like he couldn't meet Matty's eyes. "You tell Mr. Kopp you think you left something in his car and ask if he'll check for you. Something small, like a book or—"

"My phone charger."

"Yeah. That'll work. He'll tell you he didn't see it, but you have to say you think you stowed it somewhere—but not in the trunk."

"Obviously." He imagined the car. Where would Mr. K not have looked? Not the glove box—he might've had to get in there for something. "The pocket on the back of the seat. When we're all three together, I sit back there, and Mr. K took us to dinner a couple of weeks ago."

"Okay. Then why didn't you need your charger before now?"

"I had a spare, but now it's not working. If it's there, then I'll keep borrowing Mom's charger until they get back. If not, I'm out of ideas, and I'll have to go buy another one."

"Good. That's good."

Matty felt a bizarre surge of pride. Yup, he could spin a lie just as well as his old man. Like father, like son. He dialed Mr. K's number. It rang four times before voicemail picked up. He ended the call. "No answer."

Frank swore under his breath.

"I should have left a message," Matty said.

"We'll wait a few minutes, then try again."

Matty snatched the bag of powdered donuts. Almost empty. "We gotta get food. I'm starving."

"You'll survive."

His stomach growled, and he shoved a donut in his mouth. What he wouldn't give for a steak right now. And a huge baked potato. And to be anywhere but here.

A knock on the window had Matty jerking the bag of donuts. Powdered sugar spilled on his pants. He turned toward the sound, saw a man bent over, looking in his father's window. Little guy. Dark hair, dark glasses, suit and tie. Probably a neighbor wondering what they were doing there.

"Crap." His father rolled down the window. "I told you I have it under control."

Wait. His father knew this guy?

The man pushed up his glasses on his too-big nose. "Prat and I thought you could use some help."

"You thought wrong. We'll have your merchandise by the end of the day."

"You've been saying that since Saturday." The man looked across the car, saw Matty. "That your son?"

"Matty, meet Lionel."

Lionel reached across the car, and Matty shook his hand. It was hot and damp. "Nice to meet you."

The man kept Matty's hand and squeezed. "You should have delivered the package on Sunday."

"He ran into a snag," Frank said.

Matty wasn't sure what to say. He kept his mouth shut.

Finally, the man released his grip.

"I'll have the package soon," Frank said. "Maybe you can find a place—"

"We're working together now." He looked up, nodded at the cabin. "Let's go inside."

"They're not there."

"But maybe the package is."

"No." Matty's father shook his head like he was all confidence, but his fingers were shaking. If Dad was that nervous, then this was trouble. "The guy who has them doesn't know he has them. They're hidden in his car."

A shadow had Matty turning toward his window. A man was standing there. All Matty could see was a belt over jeans and a torso covered with a black shirt. The man didn't bother to look in the window.

Frank grabbed Matty's wrist, and Matty just about lost the donut. His father never touched him. This was bad. Very bad.

"Let's just theorize," Lionel said. "What if the man found the package and opened it up? What would he do with it?"

Mr. Kopp would turn the diamonds over to the authorities, of course, because he used to be an FBI agent. But Matty wasn't dumb enough to say that.

Frank let go of his wrist and settled his hand on the gearshift. *Yes, just take off.* That was their only choice. They'd go to Mr. Kopp, tell him everything, get his help.

"He didn't find it," Frank said. "If he had, he wouldn't be waterskiing right now, that's for sure."

"You're awfully confident for a man who's had zero luck getting his hands on the package."

"We're so close, we can smell it," Frank said.

"Well, then, you have nothing to worry about."

Frank pushed the button on the gearshift. Matty willed him to put the car in drive.

A tap on his right. He turned toward it. Saw a handgun. Nearly crapped his pants.

"You don't want to do that." Lionel nodded toward the gearshift. "You might get away, but your son would end up with a bullet in his head."

Frank lifted his hand, fingers splayed. "Now, let's not make threats. You and I have done a lot of business. I told you where we were, kept you updated on our progress all along. You can trust me, you know that. Tell Prat to put that thing away before somebody gets hurt."

"Why don't you shut the car off and give me the keys."

The engine, and Matty's hope for escape, died. Frank handed the car keys to Lionel.

"Thank you. Let's all go inside, shall we?" Lionel pulled the door open.

Frank turned to Matty. "Just do what they say."

Matty managed to nod.

The man beside his door pulled it open, and Matty stepped out. His legs jiggled like rubber, and he held onto the car door to keep from falling over.

The man—Prat, Lionel had said—was tall and had dark skin

and straight black hair that reached his shoulders. His T-shirt was tight enough that Matty could see the definition beneath it. Matty figured this guy could finish him off in about thirty seconds, even without the gun.

The man was expressionless as he stepped out of the way and gestured with the pistol toward the cabin.

Frank came around the car and grabbed Matty's wrist. "Let's go, son."

Son.

Not kid. Not boy. Son.

Crap. They were gonna die.

They reached the cabin door, and Lionel pushed it open and stepped inside.

Matty followed his dad and froze.

The place was a wreck. Tables overturned. Drawers empty, their contents strewn across the hardwood floors. Obviously, Lionel and Prat had already been inside.

A man was standing on the far side of the room, in front of the TV. Bald, as tall as Mr. Kopp, body of a guy who spent his life in the gym. He looked like the dark-side version of Mr. Clean. He remained expressionless but slid a gun from the pocket of his gym shorts and aimed it at Matty's dad.

Prat pushed Matty from behind, and he stepped farther into the space.

"I take it you didn't find the package," Frank said casually.

Lionel said, "If your man sold them—"

"I'm telling you, he doesn't even know they exist. They're hidden in his car."

"Which is where?"

Frank shrugged. "We haven't figured that out yet, but it has to be close. We had a plan, but now... The guy's going to freak out, Lionel. This was a bad play on your part."

Matty cringed at his father's words. Didn't figure it was a great idea to antagonize the guy holding all the power. Prat was right behind him. He could feel the man watching. That gun poised.

Lionel stepped closer, pushed his glasses up on his nose. There was nothing scary about this guy. He looked like a bank teller or something. Slight, unattractive, nerdy. Nothing intimidating about him—except the look in his eyes. "I think my bad play was trusting you. Sit down."

Frank pulled Matty across the debris. He picked up cushions from the floor and set them on the couch. Much of the stuffing had been pulled out, and what was left poked from rips in the fabric. He and his father sat facing Lionel, their backs to the door. To Prat. Mr. Clean didn't move, stood against the wall on the right.

"Now what?" Frank said.

"Now we wait." He looked over their heads. "Tie them up."

"This is ridiculous." Frank pushed to his feet, but Prat's dark hand gripped his shoulder, shoved him down.

Lionel reached inside his suit jacket and pulled out a handgun. "Go ahead."

This wasn't happening. It couldn't be happening. But five minutes later, Matty and his father had zip ties binding their hands behind their backs.

Lionel pulled Frank's keys out of his pocket and tossed them over Matty's head. "Move the car."

The front door opened, then closed.

Lionel dragged a chair through the debris and sat across from them. "Here's the problem." He set the handgun on his lap and pulled out a cell phone.

Matty recognized the case. Black with a white lightning bolt across the back. It was Aiden's.

"If this guy's on the up-and-up," Lionel said, "then why did I find a phone duct-taped to the bottom of that table?"

"Uh..." Matty cleared his throat of the fear that had lodged there. "That's my friend's phone. He's in trouble. His father probably hid it—"

"Right. Because the average Joe thinks to duct-tape contra-band under tables. Most people would hide the kid's phone in an underwear drawer."

"You obviously don't have teenagers," Frank said. "They're smart enough to look in an underwear drawer."

Lionel tapped the phone against his open palm. "No teenagers. No kids. No wife. I never had the urge to saddle myself to some whiny, demanding woman or a bunch of needy brats."

"There you go," Frank said. "Parents share tricks like that. Seems perfectly reasonable."

"I have a couple of theories," Lionel said. "One, your man found the diamonds. He's trying to find a buyer, make a little money, and figured we wouldn't find him up here in the boonies."

"No." Frank shook his head furiously. "No. This guy didn't find them. And if he did, he wouldn't sell them."

"How can you be so sure?"

Frank gulped, glanced at Matty. "He's a buttoned-up kind of guy. Wouldn't do that."

Lionel straightened his tie. "I'm a buttoned-up kind of guy, Frank. People aren't always what they seem."

"But not this guy."

"What's he do for a living?"

"I don't know."

"Maybe you do know, and you don't want to tell me. Maybe he's more like me than you want to admit. Maybe he's not on the up-and-up. Which brings me to my second theory. You and this guy are in on it together. You got him the diamonds, and when he fences them, he's going to share the money with you. How much did he offer you, Frank?"

"No, no, no. I would never screw you, Lionel. You and I have been doing business for years. Why would I burn my best source of income? And if that were my plan, why would I tell you the truth about where I was? Why would I send the location to this cabin?"

"And told me repeatedly you could handle it. Even when I offered to help."

"I knew I could retrieve the diamonds myself, and I didn't want you screwing it up and then blaming me. Which is exactly what you're doing."

Lionel's voice remained calm when he said, "I'm screwing it up? I think you screwed it up." He turned his attention to Matty. "Or maybe you're behind this debacle. Your dear old daddy told me you put the package in the man's car. Why would you do that?"

"Uh, so like, my car broke down, and I was walking home, and I walked by a house where there was a party going on, and—"

"I don't need to hear the story you've concocted. I don't have teenagers, but I've known a few in my time. If they're talking, they're lying." Lionel looked around the cabin, focused on Frank. "Why this guy? Why would you choose—?"

"It was me," Matty blurted. "His son is my best friend. I thought I could get the package back before he ever knew anything."

Lionel turned back to Matty. "What's this man's name?"

Frank hadn't told him, which meant he didn't want him to know. But Matty glanced at the gun, at Mr. Clean's weapon. He didn't want to give anyone a reason to aim his way. "Garrison."

Lionel lifted the gun, crossed the room, pressed it against Frank's heart, and leaned in close. "And what does Mr. Garrison do for a living?"

Frank said nothing.

"He's a forensic accountant." The words popped out of Matty's mouth. Lionel lowered the gun, turned to Matty, and lifted his eyebrows.

"A very specific answer, young man. Leads me to believe there's truth in it."

"There is. That's what he does. He's a total numbers guy."

"That begs the question, why did you choose him?"

"The cops were coming, and I didn't want the package to get confiscated. Aiden's car was unlocked. I mean, Mr., uh, Mr. Garrison's car, so I hid them in there. I swear, nobody's trying to screw you."

Lionel sat back, looked back and forth between Frank and Matty.

"Which one of you really knows what's going on?" The question sounded rhetorical, and neither of them answered.

The silence in the room was broken when the door opened and closed. Lionel focused above their heads, presumably at Prat. "It's hidden?"

Silence again. That Prat dude was terrifying.

Lionel talked to Prat as if they weren't there. "If Frank knows more than Matty, then I need him alive. If Matty's story is true, then I suspect he's told Frank everything. Which means, of the two, Matty's irrelevant."

He felt a jab on his temple, cold steel.

Tears filled his eyes. He squeezed them closed, waited for the bullet.

"No!" Frank's voice was frantic. "You can't kill him. Garrison and his kid, they don't know me from Adam. They won't do crap for me, but they consider Matty part of the family. Isn't that right, son?"

Matty couldn't open his eyes, couldn't move.

"If you kill him, they won't cooperate with you at all. If you have to take out one of us..." His voice trailed. A second passed, another one. Matty heard his father draw a deep breath. When he continued, his voice was strong. "If you have to kill one of us, then you should kill me. I'm the one who screwed this up."

The pressure on Matty's temple decreased, and then the gun was removed all together.

His father had saved him. Protected him.

He opened his eyes, saw the gun pressed against Dad's temple. He looked at Lionel. "Please, don't. Please... We're telling you the truth. Everything. I swear it. Dad's only been trying to get the diamonds to you. We both have. Please."

Lionel looked over their heads, nodded.

Matty squeezed his eyes closed, begged for relief, begged for rescue while a thousand years passed.

"It's okay, son."

Matty opened his eyes and saw his father looking at him. "We're okay." He turned to Lionel. "Now what?"

"Now, we wait."

FORTY-ONE

It was nearly dark by the time they returned the boat to her storage unit. After they'd gotten it backed in, Garrison's phone rang. He opened the passenger door for Samantha and answered it.

The call was quick. A moment later, Garrison climbed into the driver's seat. "That was the rehab center. I had a few details to work out."

Aiden had settled himself in the back. "What kind of details?"

Garrison twisted to see his son. "You know, payment plan, stuff like that."

"It's too expensive. We should—"

"Uh-uh. We're not going back to that." Garrison turned and shifted into drive. "I have the money, and there's no better way to spend it than to get you healthy."

When Aiden didn't respond, he continued. "Anyway, it looks like they'll have a spot for you on Thursday."

That news was greeted with silence. Garrison steeled himself for the argument he feared was coming. He should have waited until Sam wasn't with them to have this conversation.

He pulled out of the storage facility and waited.

Finally, Aiden said, "That's like...the day after tomorrow."

Garrison glanced at Sam, whose focus was straight ahead.

"You don't have to go on Thursday if you don't want to," Garrison said. "But since you're struggling, maybe it would be a good idea."

"Yeah, like, I don't want to go at all. But I know I have to. I mean, I get that. Just...I don't know. What do you think, Sam?"

She looked up, eyes wide. Garrison didn't blame her—the question surprised him, too. She smiled and turned to face him. "My mother always said, sooner begun, sooner done. Probably anticipating it will be worse than actually doing it."

"Is that what it's like with you when you're scared to do something?"

Garrison said, "Son, maybe—"

"No, it's a good question." Sam smiled at Garrison, then back at Aiden. "Going with you guys on Monday was really hard, but when I was thinking about it, I imagined all these terrible scenarios, and none of them happened. I didn't have an anxiety attack and embarrass you two. We didn't go over a bridge into icy water and drown or die of hypothermia."

"Yeah," Aiden said, "it's like summer, so probably we wouldn't freeze."

Garrison reached across the front seat and squeezed her hand. He knew the story. He understood.

"I know, of course," she said. "And my biggest fear didn't happen, either. The people in white coats didn't realize I was crazy and send me to a mental institution." She laughed. "It sounds pretty stupid when I say it out loud, doesn't it?"

"Kinda, yeah," Aiden said.

Sam continued. "Maybe part of the reason you don't want to go is because in your head, you're imagining scenarios—maybe not totally crazy ones like mine, but still... Maybe when you get there, it'll be fine."

"It'll still be rehab," Aiden said.

"There is that." Sam said.

Garrison glanced at her, this amazing woman beside him. The way she interacted with Aiden, the way Aiden seemed to be taking her opinion seriously... If they were alone, he'd take her into his arms and kiss her soundly.

Aiden's voice interrupted that thought. "But like, I'm sorta having fun today with you guys. I don't want it to end."

"Well, we don't have to decide tonight," Garrison said. "By tomorrow, you'll probably be so sick of me, you'll be begging me to take you."

"Yeah, probably," Aiden deadpanned.

They drove in silence for a few minutes. Sam yawned beside him, and Aiden mimicked her in the backseat. Garrison stifled his own yawn and squeezed Sam's hand again.

"Why don't I just drive you home? We'll get your car to you tomorrow."

She sighed. "That would be lovely, but I have an early appointment. It'd be easier just to get my car tonight."

A few minutes later, Garrison parked in the cabin's driveway beside Sam's Isuzu. He'd barely gotten the door open before Aiden hopped out and trudged up the front steps. Garrison walked around the car, opened Sam's door, and helped her out.

She stood and gazed up at him, radiant in the glow from the moon. Her eyes sparkled, and he wanted nothing more than to kiss those beautiful lips.

"Uh, Dad? You think you could let me in so I don't have to, like, witness this?"

Sam giggled, and he pressed a kiss on her forehead. "Don't leave," he whispered. "I want to say good-night properly."

He bounded up the porch steps, slid the key in the lock, and turned it. "I'll be just a sec."

Aiden pushed the door open and froze.

The place had been tossed.

Garrison grabbed his son's arm to pull him back out, but it was too late.

A pistol pressed against Aiden's temple. A dark hand, an

arm. A man came from behind the door and lifted his finger to his lips.

Garrison wanted to shout, to warn Sam. But he didn't dare.

The man yanked Aiden, who stumbled into the room and nearly tripped over a lamp lying broken on the hardwood. The man gestured for Garrison to follow.

He took in the space. A huge bald man stood beside the television set, a pistol aimed at Garrison.

There were two figures on the couch, their backs to him so he only saw the tops of their heads. By the way they were sitting, still and facing forward, Garrison assumed they, too, were captives.

Captives. Garrison and Aiden had, somehow, in the time it takes to unlock the door and step inside, become captives.

A third man stood on the far side of the room, a third pistol, this one aimed at Aiden.

One gun, he could take out. Maybe. But three? It wasn't worth the risk.

He thought of Sam. He willed her to go. Just get in her car and leave. Garrison shouldn't have left her standing out there, alone, all because he wanted a good-night kiss. If only, if only, if only he'd taken her home.

Maybe the men didn't know she was out there.

Garrison glanced behind him at the door. The man who'd been there was gone.

No. Please...

Garrison couldn't move. He stared at the door, willed the dark-skinned man to return alone. A moment later, Sam stepped into the room. Her eyes were wide, her mouth open in shock.

"I'm sorry," Garrison said.

She didn't respond as the man—he looked Indian or Pakistani, maybe—pushed her until she stood beside Garrison.

The man in the suit said, "Come in, come in."

What was this? These people didn't look familiar, but maybe they were friends of somebody he'd put away in his days at the

Bureau. Through his work, had he put the two people he cared for most in danger? If they got hurt, he'd never forgive himself.

Garrison picked up on the scent of cologne he'd registered when he'd come home to change. So these people had been here then. Had they been hiding in the house, or just outside the door? He stepped deeper into the room and forced his gaze to the figures on the couch. Matty? Garrison had seen a missed call from him after they'd stowed the boat in Sam's storage unit. He'd tried to call back, but Matty hadn't answered. Maybe the boy had been trying to warn him.

Maybe this didn't have anything to do with Garrison's work.

Now Matty was looking at Garrison, tears streaming down his face.

The man sitting beside him wasn't familiar, but he looked enough like Matty that Garrison guessed this was the absent father. He had a round face, reddish-brown hair, and hazel eyes, one of which was puffy and red, as if he'd been punched. Was he behind all this? Garrison knew enough from Allison, Matty's mom, to know the boy's father was a lowlife. What had he dragged them all into?

The smallest man said, "Tie them up."

The Indian man started with Garrison, slipping a zip tie around his wrists and binding them behind his back. Now would have been a good time to subdue the guy if not for the other two pistols.

When the Indian moved on to Aiden, Garrison focused on the man who'd given the order. He looked like a mid-management insurance guy, certainly not the type to wield a weapon. As Garrison's years at the Bureau had taught him, people were rarely what they seemed. In fact, the guys like this one, guys who behaved normally, relaxed, were often the most dangerous.

The weapon looked like a Smith and Wesson—like the one the other man had pointed at Aiden's head. Hard to tell the caliber, not that it mattered. Baldie's weapon was different. He'd guess it was a Glock. They were reliable weapons, and in this small a space, could kill any one of them in an instant.

When they were all three tied, the suit-and-tie said, "Let's have a seat, shall we?"

"Where would you like us to sit?" Garrison looked around at the destroyed room. "Seems most of the furniture is unsuitable."

The man pointed with the gun to the floor in front of the stone fireplace, directly across from Matty and his father. "How about there?"

Garrison urged Sam forward first, then followed her, searching the debris-strewn space for something, anything, he could use as a weapon, or even to cut through the tie binding his wrists. All he saw were books, papers, and scattered stuffing. Garrison settled between Samantha and his son on the hardwood floor and stared at the man on the sofa across from him.

"I assume no introductions are necessary." Suit-and-tie moved to where he could see both clusters of prisoners.

"We know Matty, of course." Garrison looked at the teen, whose tears were still falling. "You okay, son?"

"I'm sorry. I never meant—"

"That's enough," suit-and-tie said.

"I know," Garrison held the boy's gaze. Matty was a good kid. Seemed to have kept out of the trouble Aiden had fallen into lately. Matty would never have hurt Aiden or Garrison, not intentionally.

Garrison looked at the man beside Matty, who met his eyes for a moment before he looked away. Garrison moved on to the Indian, then across to Baldie, then to suit-and-tie. "I'm afraid I haven't had the pleasure of meeting the rest of you."

"You expect me to believe you have no idea who that is?" Suit-and-tie pointed at the man beside Matty.

Garrison shrugged. "It's true."

"Your sons are best friends, but you've never met."

"I wasn't around much," Matty's father said.

The man dropped his arm. "Hmm." He looked toward the sofa. "Maybe you were telling the truth, Frank."

Frank nodded. "Just like I told you, he has no idea."

"We'll see." Suit-and-tie dragged a kitchen chair to the spot where, at one point, the club chair had been. From there, he could keep an eye on all the prisoners.

The Indian guy stayed on the perimeter of the room, nearer the front door. Baldie hadn't moved.

"Mr. Garrison," suit-and-tie started.

Good. They didn't know his real name.

"What do you do for a living?"

"I'm a forensic accountant."

The man glanced at Matty and Frank. "So far, so good." He looked back at Garrison. "Have you been a forensic accountant for long?"

Surely if Matty hadn't given them his last name, he wouldn't have told him he was former FBI. "Most of my adult life."

"Seems your young friend has been honest."

"I think your guns would be good at discouraging lies," Garrison said.

Suit-and-tie nodded. "True, but one must be sure."

"One must," Garrison agreed.

"You're not built like the typical accountant," suit said.

"They're not allowed to discriminate based on height."

The man nearly smiled.

Garrison said, "You're not exactly the prototype of a gangster."

This time, the man did smile. "I'm not a gangster. Just a businessman."

"I see. The guns threw me off. My mistake."

Suit looked at the Indian. "The problem I'm having is, I think an accountant would be more nervous, don't you?"

The Indian remained expressionless. If he'd been the other kind of Indian, Garrison might think he belonged in a cigar store.

He kept that thought to himself.

The suit looked at Baldie, who also didn't respond.

"I talk when I'm nervous," Garrison said. "Maybe if you'll just tell me what you want, I can help you get it. Then we can all go on our merry ways."

Suit shrugged. "Can't hurt. We're looking for a package. Unfortunately, I've never seen it." He turned toward the sofa. "Why don't you describe it, Frank?"

Frank looked at Garrison. "Just a small box, about the size of a pack of cigarettes. It's wrapped in brown paper."

"Okay." Garrison turned back to the suit. "And why do you think I have it?"

"Our young friend here"—suit pointed to Matty—"claims he stowed it in your car."

The pieces started to click into place. Matty had his gaze focused down. Smart. Crazy killers needed to be treated like aggressive dogs—never look them in the eyes.

Garrison would, though. He needed to keep the suit's attention on himself and off Aiden, Sam, and Matty. Frank? Garrison would bet his life savings Frank had started this whole thing. Frank was on his own. "Matty, can you tell me the story?"

Matty could barely look at him as he relayed the information. Garrison had been right—the package had come from Frank. Matty's own father had pulled his son into this. What kind of a man would willingly, purposefully, put his kid in danger? If he got the opportunity, Garrison would throttle the guy. Matty continued his story until he talked about the party—the party that had landed Aiden in the ER. Apparently, it had also been the impetus for this.

When Matty finished, Garrison said, "The package is in the Camry?"

Matty glanced at Lionel and nodded. "I stuck it in the compartment where the jack goes."

"Okay." He looked at the suit. "I assume you're wondering where the car is."

"Naturally." The man pulled something from the inside pocket of his suit jacket. "And I'm wondering whose this is."

From the corner of his eye, he could see Aiden was also focused on the floor. Garrison resisted the urge to look at Sam, who sat on his other side. Surely, she too was focused downward. Only Frank was watching the scene, sitting up straight, as if he weren't terrified. The guy was a good actor.

Garrison turned back to the man. "That's my son's."

Aiden looked up, looked at the phone, then looked back down.

"He's grounded, so I hid it."

"Unique hiding space."

"Got the idea from a novel. You read James Patterson?"

The man slid the phone back into his jacket. "The car?"

"My son was in an accident." Had it just been the night before? It seemed like an eternity ago. Garrison thought of the day he'd had with his son, the conversation with Samantha. It had been a good day. A great day. Would it be their last day?

No. Garrison had saved lives before, and he would save these. If he died trying, he would save Sam and Aiden. Matty and his father, too, if he could. He just had to figure out how.

"An accident?" the suit prompted.

"Last night. The car was towed to a garage."

"Where is it?"

"I have no idea. I had them tow it to the place my insurance company recommended. But I could find out, assuming you didn't demolish my laptop."

The suit looked at the Indian. "Get it."

The man went into the kitchen.

Garrison met Frank's eyes and held them, hoping to see something there. Fight. Anger. Because if they were going to get out of this, they were going to have to take some risks. They were going to have to attack and pray they could keep the armed men busy while the other three escaped. If he could get one of the guns, he could probably subdue a second. But Frank would have to handle the third. All they needed was an opportunity—and a lot of luck. But all Garrison saw in Matty's father's eyes was resignation before the man looked away.

Great. Garrison was on his own.

The Indian returned a moment later with Garrison's computer. He set it on the floor in front of the suit, then took out his gun, stepped close, and pressed it against Aiden's head.

Rage rose at the sight of the weapon pointed at his child. Rage at the men who dared to threaten people he cared about for the sake of a package. Rage that these men didn't care a whit for the lives they threatened, the families they could destroy. It didn't matter what was in the package, it wasn't worth more than the people in this room.

Garrison wanted nothing more than to rise, to attack, to fight. But with the gun at Aiden's temple, he would sit still, obedient. Impotent.

Beyond the Indian and Aiden, the suit set his gun on the floor, grabbed the laptop, and opened it. "Password?"

Garrison considered keeping the information to himself, but only for a moment. He had no cards, no leverage as long as these guys had prisoners. He told him the password, and the suit typed it in.

Garrison could tell by the glow from the computer that the password had worked. The man looked up. "And where would I find the information?"

"In the notes. Should be on the bottom. Looks like a notepad."

"Ah. There it is." He read the information, then looked up. "Excellent. The only question that remains is who's going to get it?"

The suit stared at Frank. Frank stared back but said nothing.

The suit shifted to Matty, who had no idea he was being studied as he kept his gaze on his knees. The teen had not stopped crying. A normal reaction, especially for a kid, especially if the kid thought this was his fault. But all Matty had done was trust his father.

The suit shifted his gaze to Aiden.

Garrison looked, too. His son's too-long hair was hanging like a curtain beside his cheeks as he stared at the floor. But Garrison saw no signs of tears, no sobbing, no trembling. His son was handling this well. Hiding his fear. But not showing bravado. Smart kid. He had more in common with his old man than he knew.

The suit turned to Garrison, who stared into the man's hazel eyes and wondered what lay behind them. Was there compassion there? Was there kindness? Most bad guys Garrison had put away had been decent people at one point, decent people who'd made poor choices. They weren't cold-blooded killers. They weren't pure evil. Surely, in this man's soul, Garrison would be able to find some humanity. But he didn't see a trace of sympathy or decency or mercy.

Garrison remained silent. Eventually, the suit moved on to Sam.

Her head was down, her long hair sheltering her face. Her breathing was steady. He'd been listening all along for signs of anxiety. In the back of his mind, even as he'd tried to process everything else, he'd known it was possible. And maybe that would be a good way to distract the suit. But the Indian guy and Baldie—they didn't seem easily distracted. And, somehow, Sam seemed to be doing all right. Made no sense to Garrison how being surrounded by cops on a quiet street could possibly have been scarier than this, but Sam seemed to be holding it together.

The sound of footsteps had Garrison turning. The Indian crossed the room and stood behind the sofa, his gun trained on Matty's head.

The suit stood, walked inches from Garrison's knees, and stopped in front of Sam.

Whenever the suit moved, the Indian pointed his gun at one

of the boys' heads. How could Garrison possibly fight them without losing one of the boys?

There had to be a way.

The suit crouched down and lifted Sam's chin with his hand.

Garrison studied her face. Her eyes were red, her skin pale, but otherwise, she looked like she was managing the fear.

"What's your name?"

"Samantha."

"What do you do, Samantha?"

She swallowed, held his gaze. "I'm a real estate investor."

"Interesting. What kind of real estate?"

"Places like this."

He looked around. "You own this cabin?"

"I do."

He nodded like he was impressed. "You're awfully young to be a real estate mogul."

Sam's gaze darted to Garrison, who said, "She's a regular Donald Trump. You in the market?"

The suit ignored Garrison, kept staring at Sam. He still held her chin, kept her from looking away.

A fresh wave of rage filled Garrison. He could take the man down right now, tackle him...and then what?

Get shot in the head.

He clenched his hands behind his back and willed himself to be still and silent.

The man looked at him, smiled. "I don't see a ring on her finger, but you seem bothered. Are you and Samantha dating?"

"We're friends," Garrison said. "And you're making her nervous. Why don't you back off?"

Garrison had hoped antagonizing the suit would get him to let go of her chin and focus on Garrison again. But the suit wasn't easily distracted. He turned back to Sam, leaned forward, and kissed her temple.

Sam closed her eyes but didn't move.

Rage filled Garrison's mouth with bile. He struggled against the restraints, tried to free his hands.

His son's quiet, "Don't" had Garrison freezing. He looked at Aiden. Of course he was right. Garrison took a deep breath and focused on the floor.

The suit chuckled, but Garrison kept his eyes on his crossed legs. He had to stay alert, and anger would only keep him from thinking straight.

"You're as cool as they come, aren't you, honey?"

The suit's words had Garrison looking up.

Sam actually smiled. "Not even close."

The man let go of her chin and stood. He turned to the Indian. "Samantha will go with you. She'll be perfect."

FORTY-TWO

Sam processed the words one at a time. *Samantha...will...go.*

"No!"

Garrison's shout came before she could formulate a reply. "She can't."

The man in the suit stared at Garrison, a quizzical look on his face. "What do you mean, she can't?"

"She has agoraphobia."

He looked back at Sam, smiled. "Is that true?"

Garrison said, "It is, she can't—"

His words were cut off when the man pointed his gun at Garrison's head. "Stop talking."

Garrison glanced at her, and she willed him to be quiet. She would have to answer for herself, have to do whatever they asked of her. She didn't know how to do it, didn't know what he'd require, but she would have to find a way.

"I thought agoraphobics couldn't leave their houses," the man said. "But I didn't see anything that led me to believe a woman lived here." He looked at the scary guy. "Did you?"

The guy didn't respond, which apparently the suit took as a no.

The suit turned back to her, pushing his glasses up on his

nose. "If you don't live here, but you *are* here, then you can't be agoraphobic."

Garrison inhaled like he was about to speak.

"I think I told you to be quiet." The man didn't break Sam's eye contact when he spoke to Garrison.

Garrison remained silent.

"I used to be like that." Just answer honestly. It was all she could do right now. She probably should have shown more fear by this point, but she'd been all right. It didn't make sense, really, but somehow, she'd managed the fear. She even felt calm. Sort of crazy calm. Crazy, obviously. Because for some reason, even in this, she had to have an element of the insane. "I used to stay mostly at home. There were a few places I'd go, but just a few, and none very far from my condo. But then, I got a little better. Now, I can go all over Nutfield."

"And these cabins you own?" he asked.

"They're all around the lake."

"I see. The car is in Manchester. That's not far. You can make it to Manchester."

She hadn't been in years. Not since her panic attack at the mall. And the thought of that had her inhaling deeply, then blowing out the breath. Garrison scooted closer and rested his shoulder against hers, his arm against hers. His strength, his warmth, his comfort. She took another deep breath, blew it out.

"It's been a long time since I've been to Manchester. Years."

"I see." The suit backed up, looked around the room, and sighed. He addressed the dark-skinned guy. "We can't send Frank. Knowing him, he'll bolt at the first sign of trouble, leave everybody else to fend for themselves."

"I would never do that!" Frank's voice was vehement as he looked at the suit, then at his son. "This is my son. I would never... I can go, do whatever you want me to do, and come back. I would never abandon my son." He looked across the room, seemed to remember there were others there, and added, "Or any of these people."

The suit shrugged. "That may be true. But I think you'd say whatever you have to say to get out of here." He looked at Matty. "Young Matthew is a wildcard. His explanation for all of this might be true. It might not. I'm not convinced he isn't talking out of both sides of his mouth. And teenagers these days...one can never be sure." The suit shifted, tapped Aiden's knee with his toe.

No. She didn't want Aiden to do it. He needed to stay with his father. She tried to speak, but all that came out was a pathetic squeak.

Garrison pressed into her shoulder.

"What's your name?" the man asked.

Garrison shifted to watch the scene while his son looked up and shook his hair out of his face. "Aiden."

"You look like your father."

Aiden glanced at Garrison, then back at the man. "I'll do it. I won't cause any trouble. All I want is for my father and my friends to be safe. I'll do exactly as I'm told."

"Perhaps. How old are you?"

"Seventeen."

"I see." The man looked at the Indian guy, who shook his head slightly. "I tend to agree." He let his gaze roam the room. "The problem is that we need somebody who looks innocent, somebody who, if a guard or a cop approaches as we're retrieving the package, can seem legitimate. No offense, but it's the teenager thing again. What cop will believe a long-haired greasy teenager isn't up to no good? And then, my friend over there would have to kill the cop. And we'd prefer not to go that route."

Kill the cop. The man's words ricocheted like bullets in Sam's mind. She gasped, tried to blow the breath out, but it felt stuck there. She gasped again.

"It's okay," Garrison said. He inhaled slowly, then exhaled. She had to relax, had to get her breathing under control. She listened to Garrison breathing, matched his breaths again and again until she felt normal.

She leaned toward him, pressed against him. "Thank you."

"You're okay." He kept his shoulder pressed against hers. The feel of his breath in her hair calmed her.

She looked up, saw the suit watching them. "Are you two done?"

"She has an anxiety disorder," Garrison said. "I'm guessing your talk of killing people frightened her."

The man studied her, and she tried to hold his gaze. Maybe ten seconds passed before she looked at the floor again.

Amazing, really, that she was doing this. Some part of her wanted to stop, to analyze it. What was different now from the night before? She was very aware of the danger of a panic attack, had nearly had one. But she hadn't. With Garrison's help, she'd controlled it.

She sent up a quick prayer, just one more among the constant stream she'd prayed since she'd seen the scary guy and his big black gun approach from the house. That moment, the world had seemed to stop. She'd thought at first she was hallucinating, thought it until the man had grabbed her arm, propelled her forward. She'd stumbled, fallen on the gravel driveway. The man had just stood there with his scary gun and waited.

She'd stood, gone inside, and seen Garrison and Aiden. She'd seen the other two prisoners, a man and a teenager. She'd known then that a panic attack would make everything worse. All she could do was pray.

She still prayed. Surely, this wasn't how God intended for any of them to die.

And if he did, she wasn't going to go like this, cowering on the floor. She gazed up, saw the man studying Garrison.

"No, you won't do," he said. "You may be a forensic accountant, but you carry yourself like a cowboy. Or a soldier. Or a cop. Spend some time in the service, did you?"

She felt his shoulders rise and fall. "A few years. Mostly clerical work."

"Right. You look like the typical secretary."

"You should see my shorthand."

How could Garrison make jokes? The man was nuts.

The suit smiled and shook his head. "Sorry, but I'm not buying it. You're staying right there where we can keep our eyes on you. Where we can keep our guns aimed at your son, keep you in line." He shifted to look again at Sam. "And I'm back to you, sweetheart."

She held his gaze.

"She can't," Garrison said.

"Let me do it," Aiden said. "I can be convincing. Ask my dad —I'm a great liar."

Matty said, "No. I'll go. I swear I'm not up to anything. I just want to make all this right."

Frank said, "Send me. You know I won't double-cross you, man. We've worked together enough. You should trust me."

Garrison repeated, "She can't. Any of the rest of us can do it."

Through it all, the suit stared at her. And she at him.

"I can do it," she said.

The suit nodded. "If you care about these people, you'll have to." He returned to his seat, pulled a small notebook and pen from an inside pocket, and peered at the computer screen. He wrote something down, tore the sheet off, and handed it to the scary guy. Then he picked up his gun and aimed it at Aiden again.

Garrison tensed.

Aiden looked down.

Sam prayed and watched the scary guy type on a cell phone, then slip the phone into his jeans' pocket and pull his gun out again.

The suit aimed at Matty. "Stand up and sit in front of your friend over there."

Matty pushed himself up, crossed the debris, and settled beside Aiden.

"Do you not comprehend the words, 'in front'?"

Matty shifted until he was directly in front of Aiden, facing the sofa where his father still sat.

"Your turn, Frank. Right in front of the accountant-slash-secretary."

Frank obeyed, settling in front of Garrison. Probably a human shield to keep Garrison from moving.

"There we go. Isn't that cozy?" The suit disappeared into the kitchen. He returned with a knife and motioned for Sam to turn around. She slid so her back was facing him, and a moment later, the plastic tie fell away.

She shifted her hands, turned, and met Garrison's eyes. "I'll be okay."

He held her gaze. "I'm so sorry."

"It's not your fault." She kissed him, a quick peck that had the suit sighing.

"You can do this." Garrison stared into her eyes like he was trying to impart a message. "Just another day at the office."

The office?

"Whenever you're ready," the man in the suit said.

She squeezed Garrison's forearm. "I'll be okay." Then she stood and approached the door.

"The white SUV," the suit asked, "is it yours?"

"Yes."

"And the keys are where?"

She had to think. "They're in my purse, in Garrison's rental."

"Okay." The suit turned to Garrison. "Is it unlocked?"

He shrugged. "I think so. We hadn't finished unloading it."

"And the keys to the Camry?"

"They're with it," Garrison said. "I don't have another set with me."

The man smirked. "Does it have an alarm?"

"Yeah."

"Of course it does." The suit looked back at her. "You know what the car looks like?"

"Black Camry, New York plates. There probably won't be more than one."

The suit nodded, his face solemn. He looked at the other prisoners, then approached her. Just a foot away, he stopped, looked into her eyes. "Listen closely."

She swallowed. Didn't speak.

"If you don't come back, they die. If my friend doesn't come back, they die. If the package doesn't come back, they die. You understand me?"

"Yes."

"If you try anything funny, you die. Any questions?"

"No."

He stepped back and smiled like he was sending them off for a holiday. "Hurry back."

The scary guy motioned toward the door with his gun.

She turned, met Aiden's eyes, then met Garrison's. With a deep breath, she stepped into the warm night air.

A breeze rustled the treetops and carried with it the scent of rain. Ever since little Ana had been rescued a few months before, she'd associated the scent of rain with the presence of God.

Maybe the scent was a gift.

Maybe it was a coincidence, and she was grasping for any reason to hope.

"Get your purse."

She jumped at the words. It was the first time the scary guy had spoken. She'd imagined him with an Indian accent, so the Brooklyn accent threw her.

She opened the passenger door of Garrison's rental and lifted her pocketbook. She started to reach inside it, but the scary guy yanked it out of her hand. He tipped it over and shook the contents onto the gravel at her feet. He toed the things there. In the dim light coming from inside the car, she saw her wallet, the little bag with her lipsticks in it, her cell phone, her checkbook, a couple of pens. And of course, her keys.

He stepped back. "Get the keys. Put everything else back in the purse, then put the purse in the car."

She did as she was told, then at his prompting, climbed into the driver's seat of her SUV. This was one of her safe places, but it felt anything but safe right now.

He climbed in beside her, rested the gun, his hand still ready to aim and fire, on his lap. "Turn left."

Though the highway was in the other direction, she turned left. They drove past a few cabins. When she reached the little parking lot beside the beach, he said, "Stop behind the BMW."

The luxury car was parked on the beach out of sight of the road unless you were looking for it. There was a dark sedan beside it. Like the BMW, it had New York plates. She did as she was told. The man took keys from his pocket and pressed a button. The trunk popped open. He stepped out of the car and pointed the gun at her head. She looked away, stared straight ahead at the gaping hole of the other car's trunk. Swallowed. Prayed.

"Don't move. I'll be right back."

This could be a moment of escape. If she could move fast enough. If he aimed and missed. She could imagine the gunshot reverberating across the lake. The man in the suit would hear it. Garrison would hear it. They would all hear it, and they would know something had happened. And then...what? The man would wait for his friend. His friend would return. They would start killing people.

Sam closed her eyes, gripped the steering wheel, and breathed deeply. In and out, in and out.

She heard the trunk slam. A moment later, her back door opened. Something metal clanked behind her before the door closed again.

And then he slipped in beside her.

"Good choice." He fiddled with his phone, and a woman's monotone voice prompted her to head east.

She backed out of the driveway and turned toward the highway.

They passed the cabin where Garrison waited for her to return. His words came back to her.

Another day at the office. That remark had made no sense, because she only had her office at home, and he'd never seen that. So maybe he'd just been trying to encourage her, but his words seemed so specific. A secret message she was meant to figure out?

She hadn't worked in an office since she'd quit her job with the town. They'd been talking about that on Monday night—which was only last night, which hardly seemed possible. They'd been talking about her job with Eric and Brady. She'd joked about how she never saw them anymore, since her office wasn't attached to the police station.

And that was it, of course. Garrison was telling her to try to get the police involved. Try to escape. Try to alert Brady or Eric or any of them to the trouble at the lake. But even if she had the opportunity to get away, would she dare? Could she risk all of their lives on that gamble?

Not a chance. She'd do what she was told. She wouldn't take any risks with Garrison's life. With Aiden's or the others' lives. Even if she had the opportunity, she knew she'd do everything in her power to return to the cabin with the package. It was her only chance to save the people she loved.

FORTY-THREE

Aiden glared at the dude in the chair, who smiled at him like they were friends or something.

"Isn't this nice," the guy said, "fathers and sons together."

Dad scooted a little closer to Aiden. "This isn't exactly what I had in mind when I brought us up here for vacation."

"A nice place for a week away," the dude said. "You guys do anything fun?"

"We went water skiing today." Dad was talking like he and this guy were old friends. "Aiden got right up, and Sam...she's really good."

"How about you?" the man said.

"Oh, I stink. Wiped out like the buffoon I am."

The dude seemed to think that was funny, but his smile faded fast. "You know where my name comes from?"

"Don't." Frank cleared his throat, said a little louder, "They don't know your name. No need to tell them."

"But you know it, Frank. And young Matthew knows it. Why not let them in on it?"

"We're not gonna tell anybody."

The man chuckled. "Right." He focused on Aiden's dad

again. "My name is Lionel. Not a lot of Lionels in the world. You know where I got it?"

"Family name?" Garrison asked.

Lionel's chuckle turned to a sneer. "Far from it." He pushed his glasses up on his nose. "Seems my mother or father or, perhaps, both decided I wasn't worth keeping. The way I picture it, my mother gets onto the subway, pushing me in a stroller. Then she gets off and leaves me there."

"Sad story," Dad said. "Some women aren't cut out to be mothers."

"True, true," Lionel said. "Have you guessed?"

Aiden didn't have a clue.

His father paused, then said, "Ah. After the model train sets."

Lionel smiled, but there was no happiness in it. "Some boys are named after their fathers. I'm named after the place where my mother abandoned me."

"That's a real tear-jerker, Lionel." Dad sat up straighter and lifted his chin. "But I've heard a lot worse from men who grew up to be heroes, not villains."

What was his father doing, trying to goad this man?

"Is that so?"

Garrison shrugged. "You hear a lot in the forensic accounting game."

The man didn't respond. Seconds ticked by, dragging minutes with them like dead bodies.

Dead bodies. Not an image that would help him relax.

The silence in the room ticked away. It grew and expanded until it felt like an entity that might explode at any moment.

Aiden couldn't stand it.

His hands twitched. He could feel the trembling starting. The need.

If he could just focus on the situation, on the moment. But all he could think about were the feelings he craved. The emptiness, the high. Because being here, facing those guns, was bringing far too much to the surface. They said when you thought you were going to die your life flashed before your eyes. His past wasn't flashing so much as being projected like a slideshow.

His fifth birthday—a photo of him with his mother on one side, his father on the other, all smiling.

The Christmas Eve they'd driven to his aunt's house in Pennsylvania in the snow, singing carols all the way.

His father taking him and Matty for ice cream after they lost the championship, cracking stupid jokes to cheer them up.

Another image came. His mother, passed out on the sofa, an empty bottle of Kentucky bourbon on the coffee table. Aiden bent beside her, put his palm in front of her face to feel her breath. Because he'd thought painkillers and alcohol didn't mix. Since then, he'd learned they mixed really well.

His need settled inside him, expanded. He was sure it would swallow him whole.

Why didn't somebody say something? It was better when they were talking. At least then there was something to focus on. But now, whenever he looked up, all he saw were Lionel and his gun.

Obviously, this guy was going to kill them all as soon as Sam and the other dude got back. Especially now that they knew his name. Were they just going to sit here, wait for their deaths? Surely that wasn't Dad's plan.

He looked at his father out of the corner of his eye.

"It's going to be okay, son," Dad said.

Aiden looked down again.

It wasn't going to be okay. They all knew it. But what were they going to do about it?

Aiden would do something. He'd rush the guy in the suit. Then, maybe Dad could charge the creepy bald guy. With Frank and Matty sitting in front of them, it would be hard. If they could all, like, coordinate or something so everybody moved at once. Confuse the dudes. Maybe get them to fire wild. Maybe it would be okay.

He shifted from his cross-legged position to his knees.

"Don't." His father's voice was commanding.

"Just getting more comfortable," Aiden said.

In front of him, Matty twisted his shoulders to look. Frank kept his eyes forward, on the suit. See, they were already working together. Aiden would just stand up, see what happened.

He turned his toes under, preparing to stand.

His father shoved him with his shoulder, and Aiden tumbled onto his side. "What the—?"

"Don't do it, son."

The bald guy aimed his pistol at Aiden.

Lionel said, "Sit down."

Aiden's stomach filled with rage. What was his father doing? They had to do something. They had to try, didn't they?

He pushed himself back to his knees and glared at his father. Then he looked at Lionel. "Sorry. I was just trying to get comfortable."

"Not on your knees," Lionel said. "On your butt."

Aiden didn't want to go back to that position. He waited to see what would happen.

The man stood, aimed his pistol at Dad's head. "Your daddy pissed me off, anyway. Give me an excuse to shoot him."

Dad stared at the man, practically willing him to shoot.

Aiden shifted to his backside and crossed his legs. "Sorry. Sorry."

The man kept his arm outstretched, kept the gun pointed, kept staring at his father.

Seconds ticked past.

Dad shifted his gaze to the floor.

The man lowered the gun. "Well, that was fun."

Aiden's heart pounded like it was trying to escape. Crap, he'd almost gotten his father killed.

But somebody had to do something. How could they communicate? How could they get out of this? Aiden looked around, searched for something, anything he could use as a weapon.

His father turned his back to him, reached with his bound hand, and grabbed his arm. "Don't, son."

Aiden met Lionel's eyes. "I'm not doing anything."

Dad spoke again. "I can feel it. But it won't work, whatever you're thinking. So don't."

Fresh rage washed over him like lava.

"You think you can try something, maybe rescue us all." His father's voice was tender, his hand still gripping Aiden's arm. "You know what'll really happen? You'll get yourself killed, and that'll destroy me. Or you'll get someone else killed, and that'll destroy you. It's not worth it."

"Listen to the accountant, kid. He's a smart man."

"But he's not going to let us live, right?" Aiden voiced the question that had been fighting its way to the surface from the instant he'd felt the pistol against his head. They were going to die. There was no way out of this, because they'd seen these guys' faces. Knew this guy's name. As soon as Lionel got his package, they'd be dead.

His father slid his hand down Aiden's arm and took his hand.

Tears filled his eyes. This was not how he wanted to die. He couldn't die here, not now, not like this. Not after all the stupid stuff he'd done. All the time he'd thought he'd have. Time to get clean. Time to make things right with Dad. Time to have a good life, have a family, have a job, make his dad proud.

All that was gone now.

Dad squeezed his hand. "Let's just get through this minute. We'll face whatever happens together."

Aiden held onto his father and tried to believe things would be okay. He'd trust his dad.

"You're not going to kill us, right?" It was Frank who asked the question. "He's not going to kill us, because he's not a killer. A smuggler, yeah. A businessman who dabbles in the black market. But he's not a killer."

Lionel watched Frank, a slight smile on his lips. "I hope not to kill anybody today." He looked at Aiden. "I'm glad you decided to follow directions."

Aiden looked at the floor, tried not to think about what he could have done.

"But when you get your package," Frank said, "you're going to let us go, right? We don't need to tell anybody about what happened here. Everybody will be fine. No harm, no foul. You get away, maybe leave us tied up so we can't contact anybody until you're far from here. It'll be fine."

The man nodded slowly. "A good suggestion, Frank. I'll consider it."

Consider it. But it was a lie. If they didn't do something, eventually, this guy was going to kill them all.

FORTY-FOUR

Samantha drove silently, slowly, through Nutfield. They passed a police car right after the only stoplight in town. In the glow from the streetlights, it looked like Donny in the driver's seat. He waved, and she waved back, as if her driving with an armed Indian-slash-New Yorker in the middle of the night were the most normal thing in the world.

"The cops wave to everybody in town," the man asked, "or do they know you?"

"I've lived here all my life. I know a lot of them."

Sam stopped at the only light in Nutfield and glanced at the man to find him looking at her, studying her. She turned toward the highway.

"Are you a cop?"

A chuckle powered by fear and nerves bubbled up. "A cop? Please."

"Answer the question."

She realized he was serious. "I used to be a glorified secretary. Now I'm a real estate investor."

As if she could have signaled Donny with a wave. Even if she could have, would she dare? Would she risk the lives of the people back at the cabin? No chance. Which meant she had to get to Manchester, help this guy get the package, and get back. And then trust that these men would let them go.

She wouldn't think about that right now. One step at a time.

But the town line came up too fast. The invisible line she never crossed. She'd gone to Dover with Garrison the day before, but that was in the other direction. And she'd been with him. And it had been daytime.

But she could see it in her headlights, the sign marking the Nutfield border.

And the bridge just past it. She'd forgotten the bridge. It was just a normal bridge—nothing special about it. Not particularly high. Not particularly narrow. But it was a bridge, and a creek ran below it. Right now, in midsummer, the creek wouldn't be high. But she imagined running water. Icy water. Frigid temperatures.

Without her permission, her foot shifted to the brake. The SUV slowed to a stop.

"What are you doing?"

She opened her mouth, closed it, swallowed. Took a deep breath. But she couldn't get enough air. She took another one, then another.

The man beside her swore softly.

She tried to speak, couldn't make the words come. The world of night darkened further, the darkness so thick, she couldn't think through it.

The man beside her pulled in a deep breath. Then blew it out.

She couldn't do it.

The man did it again. "Inhale, exhale. Now."

He inhaled, she inhaled. He exhaled, she exhaled. Again, again, again.

Minutes ticked away while she fought for air, fought to stay conscious. She fought, and finally, she won. She breathed a silent prayer of thanks.

She wasn't sure what to say. She focused on her breathing and said nothing.

"Drive."

Could she? Did she have another choice? It wasn't like this guy would just let her go. And he wasn't going to go back to the cabin and switch prisoners. Her choices were to risk all their lives or drive to Manchester.

She would drive.

She took another deep breath and forced her foot off the brake and onto the accelerator.

They inched over the bridge. And just like that, they were on the other side. She managed to get through another few miles of country driving. Hers was the only car, though she had seen headlights behind her a time or two on the winding road. Odd, considering how slowly she was driving, but whoever was behind her clearly wasn't in much of a hurry. Finally, they merged onto the highway toward Manchester.

"You're not much of a talker, are you?" she asked.

"I talk."

"Back at the cabin, you didn't say a word."

He said nothing.

She focused on her breathing while she followed the instructions of the mechanical voice of the phone.

Twenty minutes later, she exited toward Manchester. It was after eleven, and with no restaurants or clubs nearby, this part of town was nearly deserted. There was one car behind her a half mile or so back, a few coming toward her, but little else. As she turned onto a road she hadn't been on in a decade, the man spoke.

"We get out and get to your boyfriend's car, okay? I break in, you look around, let me know if anybody's coming. If someone does, then you act like it's your boyfriend's car. Tell them you have to get something out of it. Tell 'em they can call your boyfriend, call the cops in your town, whatever. Keep him talking. I need you to keep his attention focused on you. Then I'm gonna take him out."

"How exactly—?"

"I'll knock him in the head."

Samantha could hardly believe she was agreeing to this.

And if she did all he said, then what? He needed her alive right now, but what about after he got the package? What was to keep him from killing her?

No, she had to have hope.

And then the images from September 11, 2001, filled her mind's eye. Three planes turned into weapons while the passengers did nothing. And what had kept them from acting? It wasn't the terrorists' threats. It was the hope. *Do as we say*, the terrorists had said, *and we'll let you live*. The passengers on the fourth plane believed it, too, until their phones started ringing. Then they knew they had to act, or they would die—and take a lot of other people with them.

Hope had killed thousands of lives that day.

Was hope about to kill her and her friends, too?

She sucked in a breath, blew it out, felt the hope seep out of her with it.

No.

She wouldn't give up. She wouldn't give up. Because she'd been in an impossible situation before, and she'd given up hope, and if not for a voice, she'd have died that night on the side of the road. That night, she'd encountered the voice of hope, and he was still with her now. And if that made her insane...well, she'd known she was on the wrong side of the crazy line for a long time.

She would continue to hope until her last breath, and after that she'd fall into the arms of hope for eternity.

Until then, she'd do what the man said.

They reached the body shop.

"Pass it slowly," he said. "Don't turn in."

She studied it as she passed. It was a large white building

with empty spaces in front for parking and a chain link fence that extended from each side of the building and wrapped around a large parking lot in back. Floodlights shone from the building. The lot in back was filled with cars.

She looked in her rearview mirror. In the streetlights above, she saw a silver SUV behind her. He was probably annoyed she was creeping all of a sudden.

The man pointed at a narrow road right before a gas station a hundred yards ahead on the corner. "Take a left."

"Why not turn around in the gas station?"

"There might be cameras."

Oh. Smart. The kind of thing law-abiding citizens didn't consider.

"And we're not turning around."

She turned left. The car that had been following passed and disappeared. They were alone on this dark road. She took a deep breath and crept past a few rundown houses. At the first left twenty-five yards up the road, he said, "Turn here," and she did. When it curved back to the right, he said, "Pull over."

She parked, and he stepped outside to look around. She knew what he was doing—looking for a back way into the body shop. Its lights were showing between the trees and houses. Though it might be possible to get there, they'd have to cut through a yard and then through dense forest first. And maybe he could do that without freaking out. She couldn't.

He sat back in the car and swore. "It'd be hard to make a quick getaway through those woods."

She agreed, especially if she had a panic attack, which she was bound to do. She couldn't walk through woods. She was amazed she was able to sit here.

But she was sitting here. She was doing this. She'd marvel at the miracle later.

"The thing is," Sam said, "if we say we're there to get something out of my car or even my boyfriend's, then why would we sneak in? That would make our story seem implausible."

"Yeah, but if there's no car, prob'ly nobody will even stop, see? We don't want to attract attention."

That made sense. "How do you plan to get past the fence?"

"Climb over it."

He said it like the answer was obvious.

"It's, what, ten feet tall? You think I can climb it?"

He looked at her, sighed. "I got bolt cutters. We can walk through the fence."

That must have been what he'd grabbed from the BMW back at the lake.

"I don't do woods," she said.

He glared at her. "You'll do what I say."

"Woods cause panic attacks." She forced a deep breath. Blew it out. "I have no control over them."

He continued to glare, and she feared he'd decide there and then she wasn't worth the trouble. He wouldn't be the first man to reach that conclusion.

"Fine," he said. "I'll cut the chain, and we'll drive around back. We'll close the gate behind us. Nobody will be the wiser."

She pulled to the main road and looked both ways. No headlights or taillights in either direction. She maneuvered onto the road, then into the driveway of the body shop.

The man jumped out, cut the chain, and opened the gate in less than thirty seconds. She drove through, and he closed the gate behind him. In the rearview, she saw him toss the chain between two parked cars.

And there it was, in a long line of smashed and dented vehicles, Garrison's black Camry.

She parked her SUV nearby and stepped out.

He tossed the bolt cutters back into her SUV, spotted the Camry, and jogged to it. She followed, keeping her gaze on the road. A car drove by, and she peered closely to make sure it wasn't a cop. No blue lights.

The man studied the Camry. "You stay here, keep watch. Anybody comes, you warn me."

She nodded, tried to look more confident than she felt, and he disappeared to the front of the car.

She heard the sound of metal against metal, then a clank.

Then a muffled snick, like the breaking of a twig. She looked beyond the chain link fence to the forest behind the car, but she didn't see anything there. Her imagination running wild? Maybe.

Another snick.

She swallowed. "Did you hear that?"

"What?" He came around the car. "Somebody coming?"

She stared into the woods. "I thought I heard something."

"There's no cops in the woods. Prob'ly an animal or something."

Why didn't that make her feel better?

She kept her focus on the gate where they'd come in, but her attention kept shifting to the woods beside them. She couldn't help thinking there was somebody there. Crazy. She was crazy, and she knew it.

And what was she worried about? They were going to get the package and get back to Garrison and Aiden. Who knew what would happen then, but she had to believe they'd find a way out of this. Maybe the man and his friend would leave them there.

Maybe not. Garrison would have a plan. He had to have a plan, because she had no idea what to do next.

"Got it." He appeared beside her and lifted a small brown package.

A loud boom, and she jumped out of her skin. She turned to the man, but he'd disappeared.

Fallen.

On the ground.

She knelt beside him. In the dim light, she saw blood seeping from a circle on his forehead. His eyes were open.

She gasped, gasped again. Turned and vomited on the pavement.

She heard a metallic rattle, the thump of footsteps. Then

voices. She should run, but she couldn't make her legs work. She crawled away from Prat's body, from her vomit. Tried to crawl toward her SUV.

Black, shiny shoes stopped by her head, and she froze.

A man crouched down beside her. He was hardly visible in the darkness, his skin as black as the night sky overhead. His eyes were huge, a bright contrast to the body that surrounded them. "What is your name?"

He had an accent, maybe French.

"Samantha."

"What is your last name, Samantha?"

"Messenger."

"Ah. An interesting name. And you are a smuggler? A thief?"

She shook her head. "No. No. No. I... They're holding my friends prisoner. I don't know anything about it. I did what they said."

"I see. Is one of your friends a man named Frank?"

"Yes. I mean, no, I don't know Frank. He's not my friend. But he is one of the captives."

The man looked up, past her. "This is very confusing."

Another voice said, "We must go."

"Indeed. But what do we do about her?"

"She is not our problem," the man behind her said. She didn't look, didn't turn. Couldn't take her eyes off the man in front of her.

"True." The man in front of her grabbed the package out of the dead man's hand. "Today, you will live, Samantha."

"No! You can't take that. He'll kill them. He'll kill us all if we don't get him that package."

The man stood and brushed off his pants. "That is also not our problem." He slid the package into his pocket. "Since you are a messenger, you can tell Frank and his buyers that Congolese diamonds belong to the Congolese people."

With that, the man and his partner strode across the lot, jumped the fence, and disappeared in the woods.

FORTY-FIVE

Garrison hadn't felt the cut on his hand. He'd been too worried about Aiden doing something stupid when he'd slid closer to the boy and grabbed him. He'd scraped the fireplace in the process.

Now, he could feel a tiny drop of blood sliding off his fingertip. He shifted so it would land on the floor, not on Aiden. His son was too keyed up. Garrison feared he'd jump, maybe alert Lionel that something was wrong. And they couldn't have that. Not when they'd finally gotten a smidgen of good luck.

He looked up to see the bald man staring at him. The man had been motionless all this time. Pretty impressive. Garrison focused on the floor, watched the man's feet, which shifted often. He was getting tired. Odd that he didn't sit or at least move.

Garrison squeezed Aiden's hand, spoke softly but loudly enough for everyone to hear. "Promise me you won't do something stupid."

Aiden sighed. Garrison couldn't see him, of course. In order to hold onto him, Garrison had had to turn his back to him. But he could hear the agitation in the breath.

"I'm going to let you go now," Garrison said. "Promise me."

"Fine."

There was that teenage attitude he was accustomed to. It made him feel better.

Garrison shifted, acted like he was trying to move away. Aiden turned, and Garrison mouthed, *I have a plan.*

Aiden's eyebrows lifted, and he lowered his gaze to the floor so Lionel and Baldie wouldn't see the reaction.

Maybe it wasn't a full-fledged plan. It was a start, though.

Garrison scooted back and leaned against the stacked stone fireplace. If he could find the place where he'd cut his hand—or any spot sharp enough—he could try to cut through the tie. How to do it without Lionel noticing?

"This is your fault." Aiden leaned forward, pushed his shoulder into Matty's.

Was Aiden trying to distract Lionel? Smart kid. A distraction would be good. But they probably didn't need to argue.

Matty's shoulder's slumped. "I didn't know any of this would happen."

Lionel was focused on the teens. "Let's not fight, boys."

Baldie shifted on his feet, watched the scene silently.

Garrison ran his hand along the fireplace. That sharp spot had to be here somewhere.

"I'm not fighting," Aiden said. "I'm stating the obvious. If not for Matty, none of this would have happened."

Lionel looked at Garrison. "What are you doing?"

"I have an itch." He scraped his back along the rough stones.

Lionel shook his head.

Frank turned and glared at Aiden. "Ain't his fault, kid. He did what I told him."

Garrison shifted closer to his son. Maybe the sharp spot...

"You're right." Aiden glared at Frank. "This is what he gets for trusting you. What kind of father are you, anyway? It's one thing to abandon your son, but then you come back to use him? Get your kid to do your dirty work?"

Garrison resisted the urge to silence his son. The noise was good. Kept the gunmen's focus off of him.

"I didn't know anybody was gonna get hurt," Frank said. "And anyway, if you weren't such a friggin' loser drug addict—"

"Hey!" Garrison said. "Watch your mouth about my son."

"Your son is my son's biggest customer." Frank tossed the remark at him like a grenade. "Did you know that?"

Garrison looked at Matty's back. The boy slumped until his face nearly touched his knees. So Matty was the dealer who'd been supplying Aiden all this time?

Aiden turned to look at Garrison, eyes wide.

Garrison blew out a long breath. "I did not."

Lionel chuckled and gazed at Baldie. "Looks like there's trouble in this little father-son paradise."

Baldie's expression didn't change. Where did these expressionless goons come from? Lionel had probably coached them in the fine art of intimidation.

Frank turned to Matty. "Sorry, kid. I figured he knew."

"Don't call me kid."

Frank didn't say a word, and the room remained silent. But Garrison needed the fight to continue. Or at least the conversation.

"You know, Frank," Garrison said. "Despite his recent choices, your son's a great guy. You might try getting to know him."

Frank glanced at Matty, who kept his gaze on the floor. "Yeah. You are a great kid...young man. And you have a heckuva right hook."

"You did that?" Lionel laughed. "You punched your own father? I'd love to hear that story."

Frank turned to the man on the sofa. "I'm trying to have a moment here."

"Oh, right. Sorry." The man's smile and rapt attention showed he wasn't a bit sorry.

Garrison continued his search for the sharp rock in the fireplace. There! It was higher than he'd thought, and closer to Aiden. This would be awkward, but he'd have to sell it, make it look natural. He adjusted his legs, kicked Frank. "Sorry. Trying to get comfortable."

Frank said, "I hear you. I'm too old for this."

Garrison shifted like he was miserable. He looked at Lionel. "My butt is killing me."

"Seems an accountant's butt would be used to it."

"I have one of those standing desks. Extra-tall, of course. Haven't you heard? Sitting is the new smoking."

Lionel shook his head. "I hate health nuts."

"I'm a big cashew fan, myself." Garrison pushed up against the fireplace, his palm pressed to the sharp spot. He shifted until one of the plastic zip ties was against it, then stopped.

"You good now?" Lionel asked.

"Yes, thank you. Seriously, they don't call it hardwood for nothing."

Aiden shook his head. "Sheesh, Dad. You're not funny."

"I'm a little funny." He chuckled, scraped the plastic against the rock, and heard a click. They'd need to keep talking.

"Matty, have you told your father about when you used to play baseball?"

The boy shrugged. Very helpful.

"Frank, Matty was a catcher. Best catcher in the league one year."

"Just little league, though," Aiden added.

"Same league you were in," Garrison said, "and you weren't the best catcher."

"That's 'cause I played shortstop."

Garrison tapped Frank with his foot, scraped the plastic against the stone again. "You ever play baseball, Frank?" *Click.*

"I played catcher." Frank looked at his son. "I didn't know you played the same position as me."

Matty shrugged. "Mom told me. I was good at it."

"Good hitter, too," Garrison added. "Like Aiden." He turned to his son, scraped the plastic again. *Click.* "Remember that home run you hit over the fence against...who was it?"

"Chargers," Aiden said. "Won the game."

"Walk-off homer," Garrison said. "I was all puffed up with pride. All the other ten-year olds' dads were jealous."

"Big moment for you, I guess," Frank said.

Garrison chuckled, scraped the plastic again. *Snap.*

He coughed to cover the sound, felt the plastic fall away. Thank God.

"Why are we talking about baseball?" Lionel asked.

"You're right," Garrison said. "Baseball's not worth talking about, not right now." He gripped his hands together to keep himself from letting on that he was free. He met Lionel's eyes. "I can't speak for your mother, but I'm betting your father didn't know you existed. Because what father could do that? Could leave his kid behind?"

"Let's leave my nonexistent parents out of this," Lionel said.

Garrison shifted his gaze. "And you, Frank. I bet even you, when you left your family, had their best interests at heart."

"I did." Frank nodded, looked at Matty. "Your mother kicked me out. I swore I was gonna make good, get her to take me back. But...I don't know. I could never do it. She said I was no good for you boys." He looked at Lionel, shrugged. "Guess she was right."

Lionel blew out a long breath. "Let's go back to baseball."

"No, no." Garrison shook his head. He was tempted to bump his son on the shoulder, but he didn't dare move, didn't dare risk Lionel or Baldie seeing the sliced zip tie behind him, or the drops of blood. He'd have to figure a way to hide those. "I want to use these minutes well. Because, you know, we might not get any more."

Garrison wouldn't think about what would come next. He concentrated on Samantha, on how brave she'd been as she'd walked out the door with the other man. How determined, despite her anxiety disorder, despite the gun pointed at her back. Remarkable, that's what she was. Brave and beautiful and stronger than she knew.

He squeezed his eyes closed. Samantha needed to be

rescued. *Please...* He didn't even know who he was begging, God or that voice she'd told him about. He just knew they needed help. *Please let her be safe. Please let her escape. Please let her be rescued.* Garrison didn't care as long as she stayed far, far away from Lionel and his goons.

Sam needed to live through this. Then it would only be Aiden who Garrison needed to save. Aiden, his only son, who'd made a few bad choices but was still a wonderful, kind, generous, talented young man. He deserved to find out what the world had in store for him. Garrison loved his son more than his own life.

He blinked back the affection—the fear—that tried to leak from his eyes.

"You boys need to know," Garrison said, "that though most of us fathers try our best, we don't always know what we're doing."

"Ain't that the truth," Frank said.

"But we want what's best for you. Always." He lowered his voice, said it again. "Always."

Aiden glanced his way, and Garrison met his eyes. "I love you, Aiden."

"I love you, too."

Garrison took a deep breath, shook off the emotion. He needed to be strong now, to be alert when the opportunity arose. "The thing is, it's hard for teenage boys to understand that no matter how much they think they know, they don't know as much as we do."

Aiden lifted his eyebrows, and Garrison continued. "It's hard for you to trust us. But you need to trust us because even when we do it wrong, and even when we do it badly, and even when somebody gets hurt, we do what we do because we love you."

Garrison held his son's gaze, willed him to understand. When the time came, Garrison was going to throw himself at one of these gunmen, and he'd probably get shot in the process. But if it gave Aiden time to escape, or time to fight back, then Garrison's sacrifice would be worth it. If he didn't survive, he wanted

Aiden to know he'd sacrificed himself on purpose, and for a purpose. For him.

Lionel groaned. "Either go back to sports or shut up. I can't stand this anymore."

Aiden faced forward. A minute passed, then another.

And then Frank said, "How 'bout them Yankees?"

FORTY-SIX

Samantha stared as the man and his partner jogged away. They crossed the street to a parking lot in front of a dark building, climbed into a small silver SUV, and took off.

That was the car that had been behind them earlier. How long had they been following? Who were they?

The sound of sirens had her standing too fast. Her legs still felt like jelly, but she managed to keep her feet.

She couldn't get caught up in this. She had to get out of here, to figure out what to do next. She wouldn't look at the dead man. She jogged to her car, climbed in, and crept out of the lot.

Less than a quarter mile away, a police car passed her going the opposite direction, its lights spinning. She continued straight, prayed she wouldn't get pulled over.

She stopped at a red light and caught sight of the man's phone. He'd left it on her console.

She pressed the button, swiped to open it. There was a passcode. She'd broken into enough iPhones to know how to get past that. It was a skill that had come in handy when she'd worked for the town. The cops had come to her often enough for help, usually trying to return a stolen or lost phone to its owner.

She held down the home button, waited for the beep, and said, "What time is it?"

The clock came up.

A few more steps, and...

Bingo.

She was in.

She dialed Brady's number and pressed the gas.

He picked up on the second ring.

"Brady Thomas." He sounded like he'd been asleep. Made sense. It was nearly midnight.

"It's Sam."

He cleared his throat. "What happened? Whose phone is this?"

"Long story. Garrison and...I..." The words halted. A sob bubbled up, and she started to tremble. She pulled over, took a deep breath.

Through the phone, she heard Brady speaking to Rae. "I don't know yet. Something's wrong." Then he spoke to her again. "Sam, what happened?"

She took another breath, swallowed the rising nausea. How could she even explain it? What would she say? Where should she start?

"I just witnessed a murder."

"What? Where are you?"

"You have to be quiet and let me talk. I was with a man, and he was shot. The killers were..." She started to say African American, but stopped herself. They'd both had accents, so they weren't American at all. "They were black. I only saw one from the front. He had darker skin than any man I've ever seen. And a scar on his neck. I don't know how old he was, or how tall." She explained where the auto body shop was and the type of car they were driving.

"You need to call the Manchester PD."

"Garrison and Aiden are being held captive."

Brady had on his detective voice when he spoke next. "Start at the beginning."

"First, call the police in Manchester so those guys don't get away."

A short pause. Then, "Fine. Hold on a sec."

She heard him speaking on another phone, Rae's, no doubt. He relayed the information she'd given him, claiming he'd received an anonymous tip. He came back on the line.

"You'll tell them the truth tomorrow. Now, tell me what's going on."

She pulled back onto the nearly deserted street. For the next ten minutes, she relayed all that had happened—leaving out the place where Garrison and the rest were being held—and ended with the murder.

"Tell me where they are."

"We have to figure out how to rescue them."

"That's my job, Sam."

"No. No. Look, I need your help, but if I don't go back there, he'll kill them. He was very explicit."

"He had to say that so you wouldn't try to escape."

She turned onto Route 101. "That doesn't mean he won't do it. I'm not going to risk anybody's life to protect my own."

There was a long pause. His voice was quieter, the voice of a friend, when he spoke next. "Sam, Garrison won't want you to risk your life to save him."

"Not him, no." She knew that. But Aiden. Garrison would do anything for his son.

"Not any of them," Brady said. "And you're too important to me, to Rae, to all your friends. I can't let you step into harm's way."

"You can't stop me. Either help me figure out how to do this, or I'm going to hang up."

"You have to trust me. This is what I do."

"I know. That's why I'm calling. But you can't guarantee anything."

"Neither can you."

"I can do something, though. I can get in the door, or maybe..."

Yes, that was it. She had to make the man believe she had the package. It was her only leverage.

"Samantha, tell me where you are, and we'll figure this out together."

She couldn't do it alone. She'd need Brady's help.

"Here's the deal, Brady. I'll meet you, and you can help me formulate a plan. But you have to promise me you're not going to charge in there, and you're not going to try to negotiate for their release. This guy...I don't think he'll hesitate to start killing people. And he's already pegged Garrison as his biggest threat. The first bullet will be for Garrison."

SAM SPIED Brady in front of McNeal's, leaning against his pickup truck and tapping his foot. She parked behind him and shoved the man's phone in her pocket. By the time she stepped out of the car, Brady was there.

He pulled her into a bear hug and held her tight. When he finally let her go, he shook her shoulders. "I can't decide if I'm happy to see you or ticked you're being so stubborn about this."

"Let's go with happy to see me."

"How are you holding up? You went to Manchester alone...at night."

She opened her mouth, then snapped it shut. "Wait. You know?"

"That you never leave Nutfield?"

"How long have you known?"

Brady shook his head. "Sheesh, Sam. We've been friends forever. You think I didn't notice? I am a detective, you know."

"But...you never said anything."

He shrugged. "Figured if you wanted to talk about it—"

"Does Rae know?"

"Why do you think we had our reception at the Lion's Hall?"

Sam had believed Rae's reasoning. "I...but... She should've..."

"She wanted you to be there. And she didn't want you to be afraid. And it didn't matter to us, as long as we were married. We love you, Sam. Which is why I can't let you do this."

She'd told him her idea while she'd driven here, and he'd spent as much time arguing about why it wouldn't work as she'd spent explaining it.

"This is the best way to assure that at least the teens survive. And if I can get his focus on the front of the cabin—"

"They're at a cabin? The one where Garrison's been staying?"

She hadn't meant to say that.

"Which one is it?" When she didn't respond, he said, "I'll call Rae. She probably knows."

"No, it's okay. I'll tell you, if you hear me out."

"I'm not letting you put yourself in danger."

"There are kids in there, Brady. Two teenage boys."

"I understand that."

"What if it were Johnny?"

"It was Johnny!" His words reverberated off the downtown buildings. He took a breath. "Johnny and Rae were in danger, and I had about twenty guys with me."

True. And Sam had thought Rae was crazy to put herself in danger like she had. Now, Sam understood. "You had a plan."

"And Rae didn't trust me and could have gotten herself killed."

"I trust you, Brady. You tell me how we can do this, and I'll do everything you say. I promise."

Brady crossed his arms, stepped back. "Okay." He stared at the police station across the street. "Okay. I'll call the guys."

"Not the whole town. It's quiet out there."

"Which cabin?"

She waffled, but in the end, she had to tell him. Had to trust him. Because there was no way Sam could do this alone.

The man's phone dinged.

A text message from a man named Lionel.

You got the package?

She scrolled up to read the other messages. Nothing too telling. She paused on one from the other man, sent just forty-five minutes before, and sucked in a breath.

Take care of her as soon as you get the package.

"What?" Brady said. "Let me see."

She showed the screen to Brady.

"Seems this Lionel guy doesn't plan to leave anyone alive."

"He looked like a Lionel. Didn't look dangerous. Which was maybe the scariest thing about him." She scrolled back to the latest message. "Should I respond?"

"Yeah." He took the phone, paused, and then typed into it. He showed her the screen. *Just now. On my way.*

"Sounds right." He hit send. "Maybe we can use this."

Brady looked at the phone, at her. "Eventually, he's going to know his man is down. The question is, how is he going to take it?"

FORTY-SEVEN

Garrison had been free an hour or more, and he still hadn't had any opportunity to act.

He'd driven through Manchester on his way here. It wasn't that far. Samantha and the other man should be close.

Lionel had sent a couple of texts. Both times, it was over so fast Garrison hadn't been able to move. And how could he possibly take out one gunman and keep the other one from shooting everybody?

Garrison had been working on a plan all this time. So far, all he had was jump up, hurdle Matty, lunge at Lionel, and scream "Run!" If Frank would barrel toward Baldie, and if Garrison could get the gun from Lionel, then they'd have a chance.

Too many ifs. He had to figure a way to tell Frank. But how?

A distraction. Then he'd do it.

Lionel's phone dinged. He lifted his gun and aimed it at Aiden's head. Then he read the message. Smiled. "Won't be long now."

Garrison had to act before Sam got back. Because when Lionel had his package they would all die.

But the guns remained pointed. Garrison was willing to risk his own life. Willing to risk Frank's. But not Aiden's.

They'd run out of things to talk about. Garrison would start a conversation, but he couldn't take his mind off what he was planning. Because though he was willing to die, he didn't want to.

He felt like he was finally rebuilding the relationship with Aiden that had been stripped away by divorce and drugs and lies. Garrison wanted desperately to see what kind of man his son would turn out to be. He wanted to see him healthy again. He wanted to see him graduate from high school, go on to college, meet a girl and marry her, become a father. Even the hard moments of parenting—and the previous months had been the hardest of his life—were worth it when he thought about the man his son could become. Garrison had earned the right to see it, hadn't he? Earned it with the late nights pacing the floor, the worrying. Earned it with all times he'd said *I love you* and received only a grunt in reply. And all of that—the good, the bad, the hard, the torturous—he'd do it all again and more if it would save Aiden.

At least he'd told Sam he loved her. Stupid as it had been to blurt those words out, he was glad he had. He wanted to kiss her again. Wanted to marry her. Wanted to be by her side forever.

He thought of his mother, always loyal to his father. And then he thought of his father. Garrison had been a disappointment to the man for forty-three years. No matter what Garrison had accomplished, Dad had never been impressed. Would Dad cry at his funeral?

He would.

Dad would be sorry he'd never spoken his true feelings. Somehow, though Dad had never said it, Garrison knew his father loved him. Knew beneath all that bluster and hate was a proud man who had no idea how to show his feelings. Was Garrison like his father? He'd always hoped not to be. But hadn't he spent all his life trying to prove himself? Prove he was strong, capable, independent? Like Dad. Dad, who never needed anybody. Dad, who'd never been happy.

That wasn't the life Garrison wanted. To pretend he didn't

need others when he obviously, desperately did. He needed Aiden. He needed Sam. He needed help, right now, so he could spend his life with those he loved.

A quote by Kierkegaard popped in his head. *The most painful state of being is remembering the future, particularly the one you'll never have.*

FORTY-EIGHT

Six police officers surrounded the cabin. Two were hidden in the woods across the street. One was beneath Aiden's window. One was on the other side of the house, under the kitchen window. And two had crept up from neighboring cabins and were hidden on the lake side just beyond the back patio.

They were all prepared to take the gunmen out if they showed themselves.

Even with all those guns, Samantha feared this would go badly.

She parked her SUV on the street in front of the house, where Lionel could see it if he looked, but far enough away that he probably wouldn't risk shooting at it—at her. She stepped out and stared at the cabin while Brady, who'd parked at the staging area about a quarter mile down the quiet road, crept up the narrow road to meet her. She was surrounded by familiar trees, secure trees, her trees. This was one of Sam's safe places, and Lionel was not going to ruin that.

Brady yanked on her hand, and they both crouched beside her rear wheel. He handed her the gunman's phone. "You remember what we talked about?"

She nodded, took a breath, and dialed. Brady leaned close to listen.

Lionel's phone rang once. "Why are you calling me?"

"It's Samantha. Plans have changed."

"Put Prat on the phone right now."

"Your man is incapacitated."

A long silence. "Interesting. How did that happen?"

"I saw your text, Lionel. The one where you told him to take care of me. I'd like to think you meant no harm, but your actions say differently."

"Shall I kill Garrison first?"

Her heart dropped, her stomach followed right behind. Brady mouthed *stick to the plan.*

"Not if you want your package," she said.

Lionel blew out a long breath. "I'm curious. How did you *incapacitate* my man?"

"I guess...Prat, did you say? Prat figured I'd go along with whatever he said. He figured wrong."

"Keep going," Lionel said.

She took a deep breath and relayed the story she and Brady had concocted. "He had to cut a chain to get into the lot. He left the bolt cutters on the ground behind him. So I whacked him in the head with them."

Silence met her words.

Brady nodded for her to continue.

"He's not dead. I'm no murderer. I wrapped his hands and feet with duct tape."

"You just happened to have that in your car?"

"I keep a toolbox in the back of my SUV. When you own sixteen cabins, stuff breaks."

"Where is he now?"

"He and the package are close. When my friends are safe, you can have them."

"You have the package?" Lionel sounded skeptical.

"Of course."

"What's inside it?"

"How would I know?" Samantha said. "I'm not stupid enough to open it."

"How much does it weigh?"

"I don't know." She didn't—she'd never handled it.

"Ballpark it."

"Couple of ounces, maybe? I'm not good at guessing those kinds of things."

A pause. Then, "So you expect me to believe that you came back here to make this trade all by yourself."

"I thought about calling the cops. But I can't see any way all my friends would survive if you thought there were cops. You don't seem to be a hands-up-don't-shoot kind of guy."

There was long pause. He didn't deny it, and even if he had, she wouldn't have believed it.

Finally, he spoke. "Samantha, since you seem to think you're calling the shots, what now?"

"You let Aiden and Matty go."

"I don't think I will." His voice sounded calm, too calm. "I think instead of letting them go, I'll just start shooting them until I get my package."

She looked at Brady, who nodded for her to continue. They'd considered this possibility. She took a deep breath and spoke. "You start shooting, and every cop in the county will be here in minutes. Then you'll have no opportunity for escape."

"Ah. But therein lies the rub," Lionel said. "Because I think, perhaps, you've already called the police." There was a pause, a deep breath. "Here's what we're going to do. You're going to get the package and bring it to me. You're going to walk right up to the front door, package in hand, and you and I are going to leave together."

Brady met her eyes. Shook his head.

She looked into the woods. Blew out a long breath. "Okay. First, you send out the teens."

"Where are you?"

"If you look out the front window, you'll see my car. I'm near it."

The phone went dead.

FORTY-NINE

Samantha got away?

Thank God.

When the phone rang, Garrison had known they must be close, that his time was almost up.

Based on Lionel's questions, not only was Samantha free, she'd done something to the other man. Good for her.

Garrison listened to Lionel's end of the conversation, watched the man's facial expressions. The rage only lasted a moment. It was too soon replaced with resolve.

Not the reaction Garrison would have hoped for. Obviously Lionel was quite intelligent, but it was clear from the way he'd behaved so far, from the way he was reacting to the news of his partner's capture, perhaps death, that he lacked something even the worst criminals shared. He lacked a conscience. He lacked the ability to empathize. Which meant Lionel could kill without a twinge of guilt.

Garrison heard his demand that Samantha return to the cabin, package in hand. Surely Sam had called the police. And Brady would never let that happen.

Then Lionel ended the call and stood.

"Which one of you dies first?"

He looked at Matty, then at Aiden.

"Nope. You two are my best collateral."

He met Garrison's eyes, smiled. "Your brains splattered everywhere would convince her I mean business. On the other hand, maybe your girlfriend would lose it then. I need her rational."

He yanked Frank up by the arm. "Nobody will miss you."

Frank stood, stumbled, but Lionel kept him on his feet.

Baldie aimed his gun at Aiden.

Garrison had to think. Cops were out there. They had to be. He imagined the outside of the cabin. If he were in charge, there'd be cops guarding every exit and aiming through every window.

The windows. That was a thought.

Garrison looked at Baldie. Where he was standing, it would be nearly impossible to shoot him through the windows on either side of the fireplace. Maybe that was why he'd chosen that spot. If Garrison was right, then maybe if he could get Baldie to move forward...

Frank stumbled toward the front, Lionel's gun pressing into his temple.

"Listen," Frank said, "don't do this. This was all one big misunderstanding."

Lionel pushed him to the window. "Pull the curtains back."

Frank turned like he was going to try to grab them with his bound hands, but Lionel whipped him back to face the window.

"Use your teeth."

Frank bit the fabric and managed to slide it to the side.

Lionel stayed hidden behind the wall. Lionel knew he was surrounded. Garrison would have had snipers, but he doubted there were any on call in this little town on a Tuesday night.

"What do you see?" Lionel asked.

Frank faced Lionel. "Listen, man. You know I'm on your side. You and me, we're alike, right? If this goes south, I have as much to lose as you do. More, considering my kid's here. Let me—"

Lionel's gun pressed against Frank's forehead shut him up. "What do you see?"

Frank blinked, backed away from the gun, and turned to look outside. "It's dark. But...through the trees, there's that SUV that was here earlier."

"You see any people?"

"No. No people." There were tears in Frank's voice now.

Garrison wanted to draw the gunfire away, but Lionel was too far to reach. He'd be able to shoot Frank, and Baldie could easily take care of Garrison before he made it halfway across the room. Which meant he was helpless.

Lionel backed up a step, kept the gun pointed, yanked the phone out of his pocket, and pressed a button. Garrison heard the phone ringing. Lionel must've put it on speaker.

"Hello?"

Samantha's voice, so calm and sweet. He wanted to scream at her to run, to get away as fast as she could.

"You hear me, Samantha?" Lionel asked.

"Yes."

"You're on speaker so everybody in the room gets to hear what you have to say. Can you see Frank?"

"Nobody has to get hurt," Sam said. "I'll give you the package if you'll just free the boys."

The boys. Sam was trying to save Aiden and Matty. She was fighting for the boys, for his son.

He loved her. How he loved her. *Please, don't let anything happen to her. To any of us.*

Lionel scoffed. "You think I'm stupid enough to believe that if I let the kids go, we can make a trade, and I'll walk away?"

"I don't care about this package," Sam said. "You can have it. All I want is the people in there to be free. Don't hurt them."

Garrison stared at Frank's back.

Frank seemed to be staring out the window, probably desperate to be on the other side of that thin pane of glass. "Please." Frank's voice was high, laced with tears. "Please don't."

"This is your fault, Samantha." Lionel's voice was loud. Calm. "Next time, it'll be Aiden."

He pulled the trigger.

Sam's scream carried through the phone.

Garrison nearly showed his freed hands, his desire to reach out to Aiden and Matty was so strong. He clamped them together behind his back, angled so his hands were hidden from Baldie, and scooted forward. He pressed his shoulder against Matty's. At least the body had fallen on the other side of the sofa, so the boys didn't have to see it. "Matty, I'm sorry."

Matty turned and wept onto his shoulder.

Garrison twisted and glared beyond Matty to the man standing beside the window. His gun was trained on Aiden's head.

He wanted to look at his son, to say something, to comfort him. Instead, he kept eye contact with Lionel. *Pick me, you coward. Pick me. I dare you.*

No chance. Lionel was afraid of Garrison. If he shot Garrison, it would be from the other side of the room. No way he'd let Garrison get that close.

Garrison turned to Baldie. He had to get the man to move. There was no time left. "What's your name?"

The man didn't even flinch.

"Come on, man. We're all going to die. You know that, right? You're going to die, too."

That had the man's eyes narrowing, his gaze flicking to Lionel.

"You heard him," Garrison said. "He knows there's no way out of this. I mean, if you walked out with your hands up, I assume they wouldn't shoot you. And of course, we'd tell them the truth. You haven't killed anyone. Yet."

Lionel lifted the phone, ended the call, and looked at Garrison. "Shut up."

"Why should I?" Garrison said. "When we both know, we all know, that nobody's leaving this cabin alive. You're going to die tonight, and you're going to take the rest of us with you. Isn't that right, Lionel?"

Baldie eyed Lionel. "You have a plan."

It was the first time he'd spoken, a deep voice that resonated through the room. Both Matty and Aiden looked up.

"Of course I have a plan." He looked at Garrison. "You're next."

"Right," Garrison said. "Then the boys. And Sam, if you can get to her. And then, what? You think she didn't bring cops? You know she did—there are cops all around this place. Your only hope is to surrender." Then Garrison opened his eyes wide, as if something had just occurred to him. "I know what you're going to do. You're going to shoot us all, then shoot your man here, and then tell everybody he went crazy and did it. I bet that's it."

Lionel looked at Baldie. "Shoot him. I don't have time for this."

Aiden gasped. "No!"

But the man didn't move. "What is your plan, Lionel?"

Lionel lifted his gun, aimed it at Garrison.

Baldie aimed at Lionel. "It's not a hard question."

Lionel's face flushed red. "My plan is to get the package and use the woman as a shield to get us out of here."

Garrison laughed. "Right. That five-foot-tall woman is going to be a human shield for both of you?" He nodded toward Lionel. "You, maybe. Scrawny guy like you. But him?"

Baldie didn't lower his weapon.

Lionel sighed. "You know me. After all these years, don't you trust me? Are you really going to listen to this...this accountant?"

Garrison stared at Baldie, willed him to fire his weapon.

Save them all.

But Baldie shifted his aim to Garrison.

Crap.

Lionel lowered his weapon, lifted his phone, and dialed. The ring was loud—speaker again.

Garrison looked at Baldie and whispered, really low. "Except he doesn't seem to care that your other partner is probably dead."

Baldie's gaze darted to Lionel, who'd seen their exchange even if he hadn't heard it. The phone stopped ringing, but nobody said hello. All they heard was a sniff on the other end.

"Well, Samantha. How'd you like my show?"

Silence.

His voice was sing-songy when he said, "Sa-maaaan-tha?"

"You shot him."

Her voice was trembling.

"You need to show yourself, or Aiden dies."

Garrison shifted to look at his son. Tears streamed down the boy's face. Fear, horror. Garrison met his eyes. Kept his whisper nearly silent. "If he takes you, when you get to the window, fall."

Aiden's eyes narrowed.

"Fall."

Maybe, maybe Lionel would shift in front of the window, and the cops would take him out.

Aiden nodded, and Garrison turned back to face Baldie. Baldie was his best chance.

Lionel was focused on the phone, on the window. "Are you in sight, Samantha?"

Silence.

"Aiden, come here."

Garrison scooted fast, grabbed his son's arm. "No."

Lionel turned, eyebrows lifted. "No?"

"You want someone, take me."

Lionel looked at Baldie. "I told you to shoot him."

"No, no!" Aiden wrenched out of his father's grip. "I'll go. I'll go."

God, please. Please not Aiden.

Through the phone, Samantha cried, "No! I'm coming. I'm coming."

They heard a scuffle through the phone, then, "I'm out. You should see me now."

Lionel looked. "Walk all the way to the front door and let yourself in."

Garrison screamed, "Samantha, don't!"

Lionel aimed his pistol at Aiden's head. "One more word—"

Garrison had to stop. Had to breathe. He closed his eyes. *Think. Think.*

He looked at Baldie, whispered very quietly. "Your last chance."

The man's eyes narrowed. He glanced at Lionel, who was facing the front door.

Garrison lowered his voice more. "The other man trusted him, and now he's dead."

The man leaned forward a twinge. It was human nature, wasn't it, to lean in when you couldn't hear someone? Garrison resisted the urge to look at the window. He knew where it was. Knew where Baldie was. The question remained—was there a shooter out there?

Another inch. Just one more inch.

"If you want to survive..." Garrison's words were barely a whisper now.

A knock sounded on the door.

The man leaned forward another inch.

The front door opened. Lionel pulled Sam into the room.

The window exploded, and Baldie collapsed.

Garrison dove, grabbed the gun from the dead man's hands, and aimed at Lionel.

Lionel was turning, aiming not at Garrison, but at Sam.

No time left.

The gun went off.

FIFTY

These things were supposed to happen in slow motion.

That's how it worked on the big screen.

But in real life, it happened so fast.

One minute, Samantha had stood on the stoop, trembling, still reeling from the whispered fight she'd gotten into with Brady. Brady, who'd said that Samantha was absolutely not, under any circumstances, going to show herself. Brady, who'd actually grabbed her arm to keep her from running into the yard when Frank had stood at the window. Brady, who'd been as surprised as she when the gun had gone off. When Frank had fallen.

Somehow going back into the cabin had started to feel inevitable after Frank was murdered. She was drawn to it like she was drawn to the trees. But it wasn't the same. Because the trees called to her like the voice of death. The cabin didn't represent death to her. With Garrison and Aiden inside, the cabin represented hope. Terrified as she was to die, she would go back if Lionel insisted.

And she knew he'd insist.

When Lionel threatened to shoot Aiden, Brady muted the phone. "You promised."

"I can't let him shoot Garrison's son."

"You think Garrison wants you both to die?"

"I have to try. I have to."

"I will handcuff you to this car, Samantha."

"But—"

"You said you trusted me."

She did trust Brady. She did. But she wasn't going to hang Aiden's life on it. "You're right. I trust you."

Brady let her go, spoke into his walkie-talkie. "Keep your eyes open. Any shot. There's no more time."

She paused, nodded like she agreed with this plan. Then she ran.

He'd almost managed to grab her. She felt the whoosh of air behind her elbow. She feared he'd run into the yard and tackle her, but the cops were worried if they showed themselves there'd be a shooting match, and nobody inside would survive that. The best option was to keep up the lie that she hadn't brought cops.

"Get down," Brady whispered. "Get back here."

So she made it to the stoop.

And knocked.

There was a cop in a tree in the yard, aiming at the door. If Lionel showed himself, she'd drop on the ground, give the man a good shot.

Only Lionel's hand came out. He grabbed her arm, yanked her inside.

And then, a bang. The sound of breaking glass, all while she was stepping inside.

Garrison flew across the room.

Lionel's eyes went wide, and he jerked the gun toward Garrison. She knew Lionel would shoot him, kill him, and then kill the rest of them. She wrenched away from his grip, felt a scream climb up her throat.

A gunshot. And another.

And then Lionel collapsed.

Screaming, lots of screaming. Maybe it was her.

Garrison crossed the room, nudged her aside. He kicked Lionel's weapon away, then felt at the man's neck.

"Dead."

Garrison jogged to the bald man and checked his neck. Then he looked at her, looked at the boys.

"It's over."

Just like that. Ten seconds. Probably less.

He stood, crossed to the boys, and wrapped them both in his arms.

She stood there, staring, as police streamed inside. Shouted questions. Lowered their guns and surveyed the scene.

Brady stepped in front of her. "You lied to me."

She couldn't respond.

He stared, waited for a response, and then stepped in and hugged her. "You okay?"

"I don't know." She wanted Garrison. Brady was one of her best friends, but she needed Garrison.

A moment later, Brady stepped back, and he was there. Garrison wrapped her in his arms, kissed her hair, her forehead, her lips, and held her close.

He didn't speak. He didn't have to. She knew. She knew.

FIFTY-ONE

It was all a blur.

Aiden sat on the floor beside Matty, close enough their shoulders could touch. He didn't know what to say to his best friend. All he could do was be there.

Matty stared into space.

Dad had tried to get them to go into Aiden's room, but neither of them wanted to move. Neither of them could.

His dad had been calm after it happened. Right up until he'd stepped away from Sam. Then he'd rounded on the police chief, the dude from the party the other night, and started yelling at him.

The dude's hands went up, and he stepped back. Aiden wasn't sure what the guy said. Whatever it was, it didn't help. Dad still looked like he wanted to kill somebody.

Somebody else. He wouldn't think about that right now.

Then Sam had nudged him, and he turned and hugged her again.

Now he was telling the chief what happened. Brady. That was his name.

A couple of guys came inside—paramedics. One stopped

and spoke with Dad, who pointed to Sam, then to Aiden and Matty.

One paramedic laid a blanket across Sam's shoulders. He tried to get her to sit, but she shrugged him off.

The others came over and threw blankets over Aiden and Matty. Nuts to need thick blankets. It was August. But despite the heat, Aiden shivered. He had to work to keep his teeth from chattering.

The dudes started asking questions. Were they hurt? How did they feel?

Stupid questions with no answers. They responded as best they could.

Cops were everywhere. Some in uniform, some not. Some snapping pictures. Some making notes. Some standing around. All muttering in a language Aiden couldn't seem to make out.

Lionel and Matty's father were on the far side of the room, hidden beyond the sofa and the many people. And there were a lot of cops standing between Aiden and Matty and the bald guy, too, so they could hardly see that body, either.

Then white fabric was snapped. It fluttered slowly over Baldie. Two more snaps, two more sheets, and all three of the bodies were covered.

Other guys with stretchers took the bodies away.

Dad left the cluster of cops, came over, and sat on the floor in front of them. "How you guys doing?"

Aiden shrugged.

Matty looked like he wanted to say something. Nothing came out.

"Yeah." Dad rested his big hand on Matty's shoulder. "It'll take some time to process." He looked at Aiden. "How are you, son?"

"I don't know." He did know, though, and he felt terrible about it. Because while he knew it really sucked that Matty's father had died, he was happy to be alive. His father and Sam and Matty were alive, and it was all over. They were safe. He kept telling himself that, trying to get the truth to sink in.

Poor Matty, though. Would he ever get over it? Matty'd been wanting a relationship with his father for so long, and now it could never happen.

Dad rubbed Matty's shoulder. "I talked to your mother. She's on her way."

Matty looked up at that. "Mom knows?"

"She knows you're here and that you need her."

Matty's eyes filled with tears, and Dad scooted closer and pulled him into a hug. Matty cried, like really cried, on Dad's shoulder. Aiden thought maybe he should look away or something, but he didn't. He couldn't seem to make himself. And his own vision blurred, and he ended up wrapping his arm around his best friend and his dad and crying with them. The blanket the paramedics gave him fell away. He didn't need it now. He was warm enough.

They stayed like that for a long time. When Aiden finally looked up, he saw Sam watching from the other side of the room. He waved her over. She came, but she didn't say anything or ask how he was. She just took his hand in hers and sat beside him.

He liked having Sam there. She was good for his dad. And she was good for him, too. She was kind and funny and sweet. And she'd risked her life to save his.

The memory came back, Lionel threatening to kill Aiden, Sam putting herself in danger for him.

He turned, dropped her hand, wrapped her in his arms, and held on tight. She held him right back. He needed to say thank you. He couldn't seem to make his mouth work. Maybe she knew already. Maybe some things didn't have to be said out loud.

He imagined what they must look like, this cluster of people, crying and hugging on the floor. Ridiculous. But what else could they do? They were the only people alive who knew what had happened that night. They were the only ones who'd ever understand.

Eventually, somebody came over and needed Dad, and he stood. "Son, why don't you go pack your things? And mine, too, if you don't mind. We'll leave soon."

"Where are we going?"

Dad shrugged. "Not sure yet."

Brady came over. "We have a spare room you can sleep in. The boys can take the couches downstairs."

"No." Sam stood and spoke to Dad. "I'd like it if you'd stay with me. I have a spare room and a sofa bed in my office."

"You sure you don't mind? Teenage boys aren't the tidiest people in the world. And—"

"I want you there. All of you. And..." She shrugged, looked at Aiden, and smiled before she turned back to Dad. "I think I'll sleep better if I'm not alone."

Dad turned to Brady. "We'll go to Sam's. Thanks for the offer, though."

Brady turned to Sam. "Do you need anything, then? Blankets? Pillows?"

She focused on Aiden. "Grab the pillows off the beds back there. And maybe an extra blanket or two."

"You don't think the owners will mind?"

She smiled. "I'm the owner."

"Oh, yeah." He'd forgotten. And probably she wished she weren't, now that three men had died in this place. He wondered what she'd do with the cabin. Would she fix it up like she'd planned, or would she sell it? He didn't know. He'd find out eventually, though. Because if his guess was right, Sam was going to be in their lives for a long time.

Aiden stood and offered a hand to Matty, who stared at it.

"I could use your help."

Matty shrugged.

Aiden kept his hand there. He figured letting Matty sit here by himself wasn't going to help anything. "Let's go."

Finally, Matty grabbed his hand and stood. Away from the

living room, the world seemed suddenly normal again. Until they got to Aiden's room.

Of course, it had been searched, too. The mattress was off the bed, the blankets piled on the floor. His stuff was everywhere. He swore and stepped inside. "Guess we'd better get to work."

Aiden hoisted the mattress back onto the box spring, turned to grab the blankets to get them out of the way, and saw Matty standing silently in the doorway. "You could help."

"I just...I wanted to say, like..."

Aiden stood straight. "What?" And then he knew what. "Listen, what I said earlier, about this being your fault, or your dad's fault—"

"It was, though. I never should have stowed that stuff in your car."

"There's no way you could have known. I wasn't really mad at you, or at your dad. I was ticked off, and craving. And anyway, it seems to me the only guy we should be mad at is that Lionel dude, and maybe his two goon friends. This wasn't your fault."

Matty's eyes filled with tears, and Aiden looked away. "So don't just stand there, dude. Help me find all my crap."

"Yeah. Okay."

From the corner of his eye, Aiden watched Matty start picking stuff up. They were friends. Maybe things would never be the same, but they could still be friends.

FIFTY-TWO

Garrison needed to sleep.

It was an hour or more before they were able to leave the cabin. They dragged themselves inside Sam's condo. She'd left a few minutes earlier than he had, so the beds were made and ready for them. He shooed Matty and Aiden to bed, then checked on them a few minutes later.

And there they were, two man-sized boys, sharing a queen-sized bed in her spare room. If they weren't so tired, they might've made a fuss about it. As it was, with the A/C pumping, the room was chilly, and the boys were curled up under a thick blanket. Garrison settled himself beside Matty, who was on the nearer side of the bed.

"When will my mom be here?" Matty's voice was small, and Garrison was reminded of the many times he'd tucked this boy in when he'd slept over at their house.

He patted his shoulder. "Another couple of hours. You may as well sleep."

"Are we going straight home?"

"I wish you could. I bet you're ready for your own bed. But the police want to talk to you tomorrow."

Aiden yawned hugely, and both Garrison and Matty did,

too. Garrison chuckled and addressed Matty. "Did you sleep last night?"

"Some. In the car with—" His words cut off.

Garrison squeezed his shoulder again. He wished he was better at this comfort thing. "Right. We were up most of the night, too. Let's try to sleep."

"But when Mom gets here—"

"I'll take care of it, Matty. Trust me, okay?"

He nodded, yawned again.

"Right now, you're safe, and you're warm, and you're in a comfortable bed surrounded by people who love you."

Matty's eyes filled.

Aiden said, "Sheesh, Dad. Be a little more sappy, would you?"

Garrison leaned across the bed and punched his son lightly in the arm. "You know you love it. You need a big wet sloppy kiss?"

"Go away." But Aiden was smiling. "We'll never get any sleep with you here."

"I'll be downstairs if you need me." He stood, but Matty grabbed his arm.

"I wanted to say...I mean, I know it won't ever make up for what I did, but, about the drugs..."

Garrison was tempted to cut the boy off. Instead, he kept his mouth shut. Matty needed to say it.

"I'm sorry," He turned to Aiden. "I shouldn't have...I knew you were using too much."

"You told me to quit, like, a thousand times."

"When you wanted them, I sold them to you." He turned back to Garrison and dropped his grip. "Saying I'm sorry is sort of useless. I don't know what else to do."

Garrison nodded, glanced at Aiden, whose smile had disappeared entirely. He reached across the bed to pat his son on the shoulder, then patted Matty's. "Are you going to quit dealing?"

"Definitely. I'm done breaking the law. I saw where that leads tonight."

"Good. That's not who you are," Garrison said.

"I know. I mean, I think. The thing is, it *is* who my dad was. I guess I don't know who I am."

"You're a good kid. You're a smart kid. After today, you're a wiser kid. You'll figure out the rest as you go along. And you'll always have a place in our family."

The boy's eyes filled again. Garrison squeezed his shoulder. "Thanks for the apology. We're good."

Matty turned to Aiden, who said, "It's not your fault I'm an addict."

Garrison stepped to the door and grabbed the handle. "Good night." He closed it behind him and went back downstairs.

Sam was curled up on the end of the sofa. "Your bed is all ready for you."

"If it's okay with you, I'll sleep on the couch. Then if Matty's mother wants to stay, she can take the sofa bed."

"I thought you got her a hotel room."

"I did, but I'd rather she stay here. Matty needs to sleep."

"So do you," Sam said.

"I'll sleep." He nodded to the sofa and the pile of blankets and pillows the boys had carried inside. "I'll sleep fine right there. You, young lady, need to go collapse in your bed." He held out his hand, and she stood. He pulled her into a hug and whispered in her ear. "You were a rock star tonight. If you ever put yourself in danger like that again... I'm still mad at you."

"I was trying—"

"I know. I know. And we're all safe." He choked up thinking of what could have happened if Sam hadn't done what she did. Would Aiden be safe upstairs? Or in a body bag. "I can never thank you—"

"You don't have to."

He hugged her tight. "You were so brave."

"I was terrified."

"We were all terrified."

He broke the embrace, resisted the urge to kiss her lips. Instead, he gave her a safe peck on the forehead. "Go to bed, my brave, beautiful woman."

"If Matty's mother wants to stay—"

"I'm perfectly capable of showing her to the office. I've known Allison for years. We're not friends, exactly, but we're close enough. I can handle it."

She seemed to vacillate, and then she yawned. "Okay." She stepped out of his embrace and reached for the blankets Aiden and Matty had dumped on the end of the sofa.

"I can handle it, Sam. Go to bed."

She walked out, came back thirty seconds later with a sheet. "At least let me..."

Five minutes later, Garrison collapsed onto the couch, thankful for the cool sheet beneath him. He pushed away all the images from the day and fell asleep.

It seemed no time had passed when he heard a faint knock on the door.

He opened it to see the sun was already turning the dark skies gray. Allison O'Brien was standing on the doorstep in jeans, a gray sweatshirt, and sneakers. Her brown hair was pulled into a ponytail, and she had no makeup on. He'd known Allison for years, and he'd never seen her without makeup. Her lower lip trembled like she might cry.

"Everything's okay." Garrison stepped out of the way so she could come inside.

"Want to tell me what's going on? I thought you guys were camping."

Camping? He hadn't heard that part of the story. "I promise to tell you everything. Right now, you just need to know that Matty is safe, and he's not in any trouble."

"You said that on the phone."

Right. "Well, it's still true." He led her to a chair at the kitchen table beyond the sofa, where he longed to return to sleep.

"Matty's asleep. I would recommend you not wake him right now. He had a rough night."

She sighed. "I had to drop Jimmy off at my mom's and rush up here in the middle of the night, and now I'm supposed to do what? Take a nap?"

"He needs you here, Allison."

"Tell me what happened."

Garrison wasn't going to be able to put this off. As quietly and quickly as possible, he filled Allison in on all that had happened in the past twelve hours.

By the time he'd finished, the woman was weeping and angry. "If Frank wasn't already dead, I'll kill him myself."

"Yeah. In the end, he tried to protect Matty. Maybe knowing that will help your son deal with this."

Through tears she said, "I really want to put my arms around my son."

"I'm sure you do. Thing is, he's exhausted. We're all exhausted. And you must be, too. You drove all night. Why don't you go upstairs and fall asleep?"

"Oh, I couldn't. I don't even know whose house this is."

Sam stepped around the corner from the stairs. "Sorry. I didn't want to interrupt." She approached, introduced herself to Allison, and pulled her into a hug. Allison fell into her arms and wept. "I could have lost him."

How did Sam do that? How could she connect so quickly with someone she'd never met?

"I know," Sam said. "You didn't, though. He's safe. He'll recover."

They held each other while Garrison stood there awkwardly. Finally, Sam stepped back. "Let me show you to the room. You'll be comfortable up there. If you're still asleep when Matty wakes up, we'll send him in."

Allison nodded, and five minutes later, Sam had settled her on the sofa bed in her office. She came halfway down the stairs. "You need anything?"

Garrison shook his head. "Thanks for"—he waved toward the second floor—"that. For being here."

"Least I could do." She smiled, stepped back. "Help yourself to anything you need. I'm going back to bed."

Garrison collapsed on the sofa again, the memory of Sam's smile keeping him company.

FIFTY-THREE

It was after eleven the next morning when Sam tiptoed out of her bedroom and made her way down the stairs. The scent of coffee warned her she wasn't the first one awake. She peeked at the sofa where Garrison had slept only to find the blankets neatly folded. She turned toward the kitchen table and saw him sipping coffee and reading her newspaper.

He looked up and folded the paper. "I hope you don't mind. I helped myself."

"Of course not."

"The pot's still half-full."

She filled her cup and joined him at the table. "Anything interesting in the news today?"

"Honestly, I was reading the movie and book reviews. I wasn't up for hard news."

"I can't blame you for that."

They sipped their coffee and chatted about nothing until Matty staggered down the stairs. "Where's my mom?"

Garrison stood. "She's in the office. We promised to send you in there when you woke up."

"Okay." He climbed the stairs again.

A moment later, Aiden came down. "What's for breakfast?"

Garrison shook his head. "Son, we're guests—"

Sam stood, tried to hold back her chuckle. "I was about to see what I have."

"What's the big deal, Dad? She knows we eat like pigs. She's been feeding us all week."

Garrison looked at her and shook his head. "That's true."

"Not pigs," she said. "Boys. The problem is, I don't eat like a boy."

"We're going to starve to death," Aiden said. "We shoulda grabbed the food from the fridge last night."

"Believe it or not," Garrison said, "your wise and brilliant father has managed breakfast. It should be arriving any minute."

Sure enough, not three minutes later—an eternity according to Aiden's growling stomach—the doorbell rang. Brady stepped inside with two huge sacks of food dangling from one wrist, a tablet in the other hand. "You guys hungry?"

"Famished," Aiden said. "Whatcha got?"

Sam took the food from Brady. "You rescued me. I had no idea what I was going to feed these guys."

"All I did was pick it up. Garrison ordered it."

She turned to Garrison and winked. "You're always one step ahead." After Sam spread the options across her kitchen counter, she pulled out dishes and silverware. Aiden and Garrison filled their plates with eggs, pancakes, bacon, and sausage. The scent must've carried up the stairs because Matty and Allison came down a few minutes later.

Matty filled a plate while Allison watched nervously.

Sam caught her eyes and gestured to the array of food. "There's plenty. Help yourself."

Allison did, and then Garrison introduced her and Matty to Brady, who was leaning against the far wall, watching the scene.

When everyone had filled their plates, Sam chose a half a bagel and spread some strawberry cream cheese on top. She sat at the bar and waved Brady over. He snatched a piece of bacon and sat beside her.

"You still mad at me?" she asked.

"I thought Garrison was going to take my head off last night."

She winced at the memory, could still hear Garrison's shouted accusation. "What were you thinking, letting her put herself in danger like that?" There'd been more, words she wasn't comfortable thinking, much less repeating, as Garrison's fury had erupted.

All Brady had said was, "I trusted her."

Brady had glared at her then. But Garrison had wrapped her in his arms.

Sam sipped her coffee and gazed at Garrison, who was seated between his son and Matty, eating like he hadn't had food in years, cracking jokes between bites. "He doesn't seem mad now."

"If anything had happened to you..."

"It's over now. Let's not."

Brady shook his head and bit his bacon. Yup, he was still mad. What had he expected her to do? Let that crazy man put a bullet in Aiden's head?

The thought had her setting her bagel down.

"When Rae hears what happened last night," Brady said, "she's going to kill me."

"She'll understand," Sam said. "She's been there."

Brady's look said he wasn't happy for the reminder.

"You forgave her," Sam said. "You'll forgive me."

"Maybe." He grabbed her bagel and took a bite. When he'd swallowed, he said, "Eventually."

Yup. He'd forgive her. Probably sooner than he wanted to.

When everyone had finished eating, Brady stood and cleared his throat. "I got some news. Not much..." He looked at Allison. "Have you been briefed?"

She shrugged and looked at Garrison, who said, "I told her most of it. I don't know that the boys know how Sam got away last night."

"Okay." Brady looked at Sam, shook his head again, and told

the boys what Sam had witnessed in the parking lot of the body shop the night before. It was odd how the events he recounted seemed like they must've happened to someone else. Had she really witnessed a man's murder? Had she really left the scene, called Brady? Had she really done all that?

She must've, because the images were there.

She didn't know how she'd done it, but she had. Later she'd weep at the horror. And marvel at the miracle.

Aiden said, "Dude, that's like, nuts. I'm impressed."

Sam wasn't used to being called dude. She met his eyes and shrugged. "I was running on instinct."

"Anyway," Brady said, "the state police stopped the SUV last night and apprehended one of the men." He grabbed his tablet off the kitchen counter and turned it so Sam could see it. "Do you recognize him?"

The very black man with very black eyes and a scar on his neck was smiling in the photograph. He wore a suit and tie and stood beside a blue, red, and yellow flag. "That's him."

"Thought so. The guy's a foreign diplomat. He admitted to murdering your captor." Brady looked at the tablet. "By the way, your captor's name was Pratap Tambe. He was a U.S. citizen, lived in New York."

And now he was dead.

Garrison stood, took her hand, and leaned against the bar beside her. "You're saying all you have is a diplomat."

"Unfortunately," Brady said. "He's in custody for now. They'll have to let him go."

Wait, what? "They're going to let him go? How can—?"

"I know," Brady said. "It stinks. He has diplomatic immunity."

Garrison sighed. "Any luck finding his partner?"

"No sign of him."

Garrison said, "I guess the package wasn't found, either."

"We're assuming the second man took it and is trying to get it back to the DRC. The problem is, without a physical description of him, he'll be hard to find. All we know is he's black and has a French accent."

That was all she knew. She'd seen the man run away, thought maybe he was the same height as the diplomat. She should have turned, should have looked at him. She'd apologized for that. All Brady had said was, "And maybe then they'd have shot you."

She decided not to think about that.

"The guy's in the wind," Brady said. "But this diplomat"—he consulted his notes again—"this Robert Mutombo—"

"Wait!" It was the first time Matty had spoken. Everybody looked at him. He cleared his throat. "His name was Robert?"

"Yeah." Brady said. "Why?"

"Can I see the photo?"

"Sure." Brady handed the tablet to Matty. He stared at it, shook his head. "I met him. He threatened..." Matty looked at his mother, and his eyes filled. "He threatened to hurt you and Jimmy. I was going to call him as soon as we got the diamonds. I was going to betray Dad to save you guys. I never got the chance."

Allison scooted her chair closer and wrapped her son in a hug. "It's a choice you never should have had to make."

"I couldn't let him hurt you."

"Of course not."

Garrison cleared his throat. "How did he find Sam last night?"

Brady looked away from Allison and Matty and at him. "We'd thought maybe a tracker on Frank O'Brien's car, but forensics didn't find one. Maybe..." He crossed to Matty. "Do you have a cell phone?"

Matty nodded, pulled it out of his pocket, unlocked it, and handed it to Brady. "He took it. Programmed his number into it."

"Ah," Garrison said.

Sam looked at Garrison, but he was watching Brady. "What?"

Brady did a cursory check, then handed the phone to Sam. "I bet you can find it."

"Find...? Oh. Tracking software?"

"Yup."

Sam pressed the settings icon, searched. "I found it. A tracking program."

Brady held out his hand, and she put the phone in it. "That explains how they found you."

"You're saying I'm the reason they found us?" Matty's eyes were wide as they darted between Garrison and Brady.

"Matty," Sam said, "who knows what would have happened if Prat and I had returned last night. It might be that this tracking software saved all our lives."

"Probably," Garrison said. "I can't imagine they would have let us go."

"Great. I accidentally helped." Matty's words were thick with sarcasm. "Except the whole thing was my fault to begin with."

The room silenced. Then Aiden punched his friend's shoulder gently. "Don't be an idiot. This isn't your fault. That dude Lionel and his goons, and that Robert guy, and...and—"

"My father."

Allison turned to face her son. "Your dad didn't do any of this on purpose. He was into all sorts of shady stuff, but he would never have hurt you. He loved you. He must have gotten himself in too deep."

"You think so?" Matty asked.

"I know so. He loved you."

Matty's eyes filled with tears again. Sam figured these boys hadn't cried this much since they were in diapers. But she knew how they felt. The relief, the horror, the images—she'd be fighting tears for weeks.

She looked up at her ceiling but whispered beyond it. "Thank you."

FIFTY-FOUR

Two weeks passed. Two weeks while Garrison and Aiden existed in a sort of crazy stasis. Like they were holding their breaths before a long exhale.

Garrison had called the rehab facility the day after the incident and explained why Aiden would need more time. They'd given away Aiden's bed but had put him on the list for the next one.

Aiden hadn't mentioned rehab, and Garrison hadn't pushed it. Yet.

Samantha insisted they move into another of her cabins on the lake. The problem was, it was rented every weekend. That first Friday, they'd moved back to stay with her, where he and Aiden shared the queen-sized bed so they wouldn't invade her office space.

"Dude," Aiden had said the first night. "Why don't you, like, go be with Sam. I won't care. I get that you two are totally into each other."

Garrison kept his voice low in the darkness. "We're not sleeping together."

"I mean, you love her, right? And she loves you, so like, why not?"

"I do love her. Not to be cliché, but she's not that kind of girl. And do you want that kind of girl, really? The kind who tries out every guy who comes along?"

Aiden chuckled. "Well, maybe not to marry."

Garrison stifled his sigh. "You don't. Not even to mess around with. Sam's a treasure." He tried to figure out how to say what he was trying to say. "She's worth waiting for. She's valuable."

"But, I mean, aren't they all valuable?"

Garrison turned toward Aiden to see his son watching him. Taking this conversation very seriously. "Of course. But they don't all know it. You want to find someone who values herself. And maybe, if you meet someone, and if you value her, she'll learn to value herself better. If that makes sense."

"I guess. But like, if you love each other, and you know you're going to get married eventually, then why wait?"

"I'm not sure that we know anything yet. It's a little soon to be planning a wedding. And anyway, there's a certain order to these things. First you marry. Then you sleep together."

That remark was met with silence. Aiden was quiet so long that Garrison drifted toward sleep.

Aiden's voice jarred him awake. "That's what Nate said about him and Marisa. Is it that big a deal?"

He blinked his eyes open, tried to catch up with his son's thoughts. "Sex, you mean? Yeah, it's that big a deal."

"Oh." Silence. Then, "Did you and Mom wait?"

Crap. Not a conversation he wanted to have with his son right now. Or ever. He could lie. He could tell the boy it was none of his business—which would answer the question for Aiden, anyway. He was left with only one option. "Your mother and I made a lot of mistakes. I loved her. I was head-over-heels for her. If I could go back, do things differently, and save our marriage, I'd do it."

"I know. You tried."

"Maybe not enough."

"Maybe if she'd tried, too."

Garrison sighed. "I wish I could have shielded you from what happened between us."

"I know. We're good."

A moment later, Aiden's breathing evened out as the boy fell asleep.

It wasn't so easy for Garrison after that conversation. Too many regrets when he thought about Charlene. So he turned his thoughts to Sam. Bad idea. As Aiden had very helpfully pointed out, her bedroom was right across the hall. That fact definitely didn't bring thoughts of slumber.

The following weekend, he insisted they rent a hotel room. Sam seemed hurt, but he couldn't stand sleeping under the same roof as she did and not being with her. It was that big a deal, and he wouldn't push it. He wasn't going to torture himself, either.

When he explained that, her cheeks turned a very pretty shade of pink.

Maybe it wasn't too soon to start planning a wedding.

They were back in a cabin. This was the cabin Nate and Marisa had stayed in when Ana had been kidnapped. If not for that terrible situation, Garrison would never have met Sam. Not that Garrison was convinced or anything, but it sure seemed there was some big power whose hand was on all of this. Because somehow he'd met the love of his life during a kidnapping, and he'd grown closer to his son than he'd ever thought possible thanks to a homicidal diamond smuggler.

The world was a crazy place. The idea that there might be something, someone bigger than they were, someone who cared enough to listen when they called out, to intervene when they were helpless—he liked that idea. He could see why Sam was convinced. He thought maybe he'd be convinced one of these days, too.

Garrison had worked from home during the long, lazy days, trying to get caught up on his job. Aiden had been sleeping a lot. Swimming a lot, too. They'd gone boating a few times. Spent a lot of time with Sam.

Samantha... She'd done something amazing a few days before. She'd gone to Manchester, alone. To a fabric store, where she'd picked out material for curtains for one of her cabins. She'd stayed there nearly thirty minutes before she'd headed back. It wasn't everything yet, but it was something.

He couldn't be prouder of her.

The routine they'd settled into was good. If it were up to him, they'd have kept right on with it. All seemed well.

But Luke, the guy from the rehab facility, had called that morning to tell Garrison they had a bed for Aiden, a bed they could only hold for a few days.

Garrison finished making the pancakes and called Aiden to breakfast. The boy sat across from him and scarfed down a stack. Garrison was still eating when Aiden had done the dishes and headed back to his bedroom. He'd been different since that terrible night. He hadn't mentioned drugs, and he hadn't seemed to crave them. But Garrison knew those cravings wouldn't go away that easily.

Which meant he'd have to wreck this comfortable routine and have a conversation about it. Now would be a great time for that big power in the sky to help him out. He looked at the ceiling and thought...prayed, he figured, *this is going to be hard. Not as hard as being held prisoner by a sociopath, but hard. If you could help, I'd really appreciate it.*

The voice Sam had told him about was silent, but that didn't mean he wasn't listening.

After he finished the dishes, he swigged the last of the coffee and headed for Aiden's room.

Before he knocked, he reminded himself of all he needed to say. That he loved him, that he was proud of him, and that he had every confidence in him. That this rehab thing—it was the logical next step, and the sooner Aiden went, the sooner he'd be done. And after rehab maybe sober living, which everyone said was really important to the process. Mostly, he needed to remind Aiden that he would be there through it all.

"Come on in."

Garrison pushed the door open and saw Aiden sprawled on his bed, drawing in a notebook Sam had given him. The colored pencils—also a gift from her—were scattered all over the messy blankets. He sat up and brushed his too-long hair out of his eyes. "What's up?"

"What are you working on?"

He shrugged and turned the notebook so Garrison could see. Garrison lifted it, studied the image there. It was a pencil sketch of their previous cabin, except it was different. The windows were bigger. The floors were tile, not hardwood. The wall between the kitchen and the living room was gone, replaced with a long bar.

"It's a lot like this place. Did you know Sam designed this? She said it was old, like our last cabin, and she fixed it up. I thought it might look nice..."

Garrison couldn't stop staring.

"Forget it. It's stupid." Aiden started to grab the sketchbook, but Garrison pulled it out of his reach.

"You're really talented."

Aiden fought a smile and lost. "Not really, just—"

"Seriously. You should show this to Sam. She's coming over in a few minutes. She'll be impressed."

"You think?"

"Are you kidding? It's great."

He shrugged. "I'm never going to get to see it done, though. She said she's putting that place on the market."

"She'll buy others. And anyway, you can design your own stuff someday."

Aiden's smile held. "That's what I want to do. I want to go to design school, maybe even study architecture."

Garrison couldn't fathom studying something like that. The math aspect of it—sure. Aiden had probably gotten that from him. And Charlene was crafty. Perhaps Aiden had gotten that from her. Together, they'd created this amazing, talented person.

"You could do it. Me? No way."

"I know. Mom couldn't either." He shrugged. "I think I can."

"You can. I have no doubt." He took a deep breath. Now was the time to bring up rehab. Never mind that it would ruin their nice conversation. "I wanted to—"

"I have a plan." Aiden stopped. "I'm sorry. Go ahead."

A plan? "You first."

"Uh, okay." He sat on the side of the bed. "Like, I'm glad we had this time to recuperate or whatever since that night. It's been nice hanging out with you and everything, but I think it's time."

The kid was going to ask if they could go home, and Garrison was going to have to break his heart. "Time for what?"

"For rehab. I mean, if you're still willing to pay for it."

Garrison started to speak, but Aiden rushed ahead.

"I figure, I need to go. The cravings were, like, nothing those first few days, even that first week, but now, they're getting bad again."

"They were gone, though? Why do you think that is?"

Aiden looked away for a moment. When he looked back, his eyes were filled with tears. "You, like, risked your life to save mine. They were going to kill you. Then, that guy was going to kill Sam, and she put herself in danger to save me."

Aiden had never spoken about those last few moments.

"And you..." Aiden continued, "you just, you managed it. You fixed it. You saved us. And, like, how could I betray you after what you did for me? And..." He sniffed, swiped his eyes real fast. "You said something the other night, about how some girls don't know they're valuable? That night, at the cabin, you and Sam showed me that, like, I'm valuable, too. You guys thought I was worth dying for."

Garrison sat beside him and wrapped his arm around his back. "Of course. Of course you are."

"I don't think I knew that before. I mean, I always knew you loved me. I don't know how to explain it." He shrugged, swiped away a tear. "Anyway, I don't want to hurt you again. And whenever I think about that, I don't want to use drugs. I want to make you proud. The thing is, that's not going to be enough. It's going to fade, and the cravings are going to get bad again. Eventually, I'll give in. I know I will. I think I need to hurry up and go. Because I have to want to quit for me, too. Not just for you. Does that make sense?"

It did, but Garrison wasn't sure he could speak. So he nodded.

"And then, I mean, if it's okay with you, I probably need to go to one of those sober living places the guy was telling us about. And maybe it needs to be here somewhere. Because I can't imagine that I can go back to Hempstead and hang with all my old friends and not get sucked in again. And Mom..."

Aiden had called Charlene the day before, but he hadn't told his dad what they'd talked about.

"Mom was all...irritated that I want to go to rehab. Like, I guess she thought I'd fight it like she did. It was almost like she was disappointed in me. I felt bad about leaving her there by herself. But now...I don't think she's very good for me, either. Which sounds terrible to say. But...it's true. Don't you think?"

"Um..." Garrison was trying to catch up. "Maybe you're right."

"If you go back, that's fine. I get it, because your work is there and everything. Still, though...I'd love it if you stayed close so maybe I can see you on weekends or whatever. I don't know anything about the lease on our house there, but maybe you can get out of it. You could rent something here. Sam's here, and she can't move. I mean, maybe she could eventually. She seems better with the anxiety stuff. But that's between you two."

"Right. Okay."

He heard a knock at the front door. He went to the door of Aiden's room and called, "Come in!"

Sam did. She must've seen something on his face because she waved at him and walked through the house to the back deck, where she slipped outside. Garrison turned back to Aiden. "Sorry. She went outside."

"It's fine. I'm almost done. Anyway, after I get out of rehab, I can get a job, help pay for the rent in sober living. And then I'll finish school. The thing is, I want to go to college, but I'm going to have to be careful, 'cause college campuses have lots of drugs. Maybe I'll do online school for a while, work full-time. Maybe Sam can hook me up with someone who does remodeling. And then, when I have a couple years off the drugs, then I can go to college. But I know you'll be spending my college money on rehab, so I'll earn my own way. You don't have to pay for any of it. I just...I want to know if you think it's a good plan."

It took a minute before Garrison could answer. Because, except for the college thing—of course he'd pay for it—everything he'd been going to tell Aiden, Aiden had just told him. How had that happened?

He nodded, cleared his throat. "I think that's a perfect plan."

"Great. Should I call the rehab place?"

"They have a bed for you now. Luke called this morning."

"Good. Not that I'm in any hurry, but I better go before I change my mind. The sooner, the better."

"Yeah." He pulled Aiden into a hug and held him tight. Then, he backed away, clasped him on the shoulder, and squeezed. "I'm so proud of you."

Aiden shrugged like it was no big deal.

Garrison stepped out, reeling, and closed the door.

It was more than he could have dreamed. Aiden was eager to get clean and restart his life. Garrison should be thrilled.

He was. Of course he was. And also, oddly, unsettled.

He sat at the kitchen table. The dishes were done. Only the syrup remained. Garrison stared at it, thought of the thousand and more breakfasts he'd shared with his son in the past seventeen years. The mushy bananas and rice cereal, the Lucky Charms Aiden had loved when he was six. He was the only boy in the world who picked out the marshmallows and ate the rest.

Then there were stacks of pancakes and waffles and French toast. He thought of how young Aiden would turn up his nose at bacon, and how teenage Aiden could eat an entire pound.

How could Aiden be leaving?

Garrison had given up everything to rebuild his relationship with his son, and now... Rehab for three months. Sober living for much longer. By the time he moved home, he'd be a high school graduate, an adult.

Listening to him just now, Garrison realized his son was nearly an adult already. Mature. Wise. Not the teenager he'd been just a few weeks earlier. He had a plan for the next few years, maybe a plan for his life. And the talent—he couldn't believe the immense talent his son had been given. Where had it come from? Garrison had always known he could draw, but the design he'd conjured for that old cabin. Amazing.

Aiden was well on his way to becoming a man.

And what part would Garrison play in his future?

This was what he'd been working toward, what he wanted, for Aiden to grow up, to take responsibility for himself. But Garrison couldn't help missing that little boy sitting in front of a bowl of floating marshmallows, a dribble of milk on his chin.

"You okay?"

Samantha leaned against the doorframe and crossed her arms. He hadn't even heard the door open.

"Yeah. Why?"

"You're meditating on syrup."

"Fascinating stuff."

She crossed the room, kissed his temple, and whisked the syrup away.

Garrison watched her wipe down the counters and rinse the sponge. When she was finished, she turned and smiled at him.

Without Aiden to care for, Garrison's life would be different. But different didn't have to mean worse. With Samantha, different could be good. It could be very good.

AN EXCERPT FROM INNOCENT LIES

HIDDEN TRUTH BOOK 4

A little boy alone in the wintery woods. A detective determined to find the child's mother. A woman who'll sacrifice everything to protect the ones she loves.

The sound of a car door outside slamming woke Kelsey from her nap.

She hobbled to the window, saw the police car in the driveway, another car behind it.

No, no, no!

She dropped to the floor, crawled to the sofa, and pulled the blankets off. She hooked her arm through the backpack straps and backed herself and all the stuff against the wall, out of view of the front windows and the back door.

With her eyes squeezed shut, she prayed to the God who'd only ever let her down that this time, this time he would help her.

The banging on the front door sent jolts of fear down her spine.

Anything but this. *Please.*

A moment later, she heard more banging, this time from the back. Not that she could have made a run for it, but the cops had cut off the possibility.

The question was, would they enter? Would they give up and leave? Surely, they didn't have keys to the cabin.

Her gun! She yanked it out of her bag, scooted to the sofa, and shoved it beneath the cushions. As she scooted back to the corner, she cursed her stupidity.

A muffled voice, a shout, and the pounding of footsteps on the porch.

Then, the unmistakable jingle of keys. The sound had her blood running cold.

The lock turned.

The door opened.

And her last chance for escape melted like snow.

Order Innocent Lies today.

DEAR READER

Thank you for spending your limited money and time on GENEROUS LIES. If you enjoyed it, would you leave me a review on Amazon, Goodreads, and your favorite retailer? And then tell a friend about my books. You'll be doing me a big favor.

Like Garrison, I have a loved one who struggled with addiction. While all his friends were enjoying their senior years of high school, he was in rehab, then in a sober living house. Now, he's sober, and he shares the love of God and the freedom that can be found in Christ alone with whomever will listen. His is a success story, but there are so many people who haven't been so fortunate. If you have a loved one you fear might be addicted to alcohol or drugs, seek help. There are many resources for those willing to search for them and many recovering addicts and their loved ones who will gladly give you advice. If you don't know where to start, visit Al-Anon or Celebrate Recovery. If not for the people willing to share their expertise with us, I don't know where our loved one would be today.

If you haven't yet, check out the first book in this series, CONVENIENT LIES (sign up for my newsletter, and I'll send you a free copy). It tells the story of Rae, Brady, and their adorable little Johnny. Then move on to TWISTED LIES, which tells Nate and Marisa's story. I think you'll enjoy them both.

If you'd like more information about either of those books or any of my releases, you can sign up for my newsletter, where I announce contests and giveaways and sometimes, offer free books. And of course I'll let you know when I have a new release. I promise not to sell or share your email with anybody, and I promise not to send you stuff every day.

If you're not interested in getting my emails but you would

like to know about my latest releases, follow me on BookBub. They'll alert you when I have a new book coming out.

I'd love to hear from you. Keep in touch on Facebook to hear what's going on with me and to share what's going on with you. And check out RobinPatchen.com to find out about my other books and follow my progress as I write.

Thank you for reading! Nothing makes this author happier than to share her stories.

In Christ,
    Robin Patchen

ALSO BY BY ROBIN PATCHEN

Chasing Amanda

Finding Amanda

A Package Deal (part of the Matched Online anthology)

Hidden Truth series

Convenient Lies

Twisted Lies

Generous Lies

Innocent Lies